War came swiftly to the McIvers. The family plantation, overrun by Yankee soldiers, was stripped of its beauty, left barren and silent. And gone was the glittering, gracious way of life the McIvers had dreamed could last forever.

SOUTHERN BLOOD

Their beloved South was dying. But the McIvers would rise again. There were new worlds to conquer, new dreams to live.

Southern Blood

by
Justin Channing

SOUTHERN BLOOD
A Bantam Book / September 1980

ISBN 0-553-13132-X

Published simultaneously in the United States and Canada

Bantam Books are published by Bantam Books, Inc. Its trade-mark, consisting of the words "Bantam Books" and the por-trayal of a bantam, is Registered in U.S. Patent and Trademark Office and in other countries. Marca Registrada. Bantam Books, Inc., 666 Fifth Avenue, New York, New York 10103.

PRINTED IN THE UNITED STATES OF AMERICA

0 9 8 7 6 5 4 3 2 1

For Helen Barrett and Karen Hitzig
without whom this novel would
not have been written.

My soul is sailing through the sea
But the past is heavy and
Hindereth me.
Sidney Lanier.

1

London - 1869

As twilight approached, a heavy fog was settling on London. Rising from the ground in great greenish-gray billows, the murky haze curled up and around the lampposts slowly dimming the needed beacons of gaslight. The traffic was snarled hopelessly, and people's tempers were short as they struggled to get out of the damp "pea-souper" to their homes and a good cup of hot tea.

Outside the concert hall an elegant carriage waited. Inside, Vanessa stood alone on stage and stared at the empty theater. It was always such an eerie feeling to see row upon row of empty seats. Tomorrow they would be filled with the people who would judge her, an American, in her London debut. Now her only audience was the stage doorman standing in the wings watching her intently. She walked around the platform, her young body tense, sat at the piano, then came back again to center stage satisfied that she had some command of the hall. Impulsively she returned to the enormous piano and again ran through some scales. Then, slowly, and almost reluctantly, she brought down the lid to cover the keys, rushed up the center aisle, through the outer lobby and pushed open the wood and glass door to the street.

The footman, muffled in a heavy cloak, jumped from his perch and opened the door to the carriage. Dimly she could see the outline of the figure hunched in the corner of the seat. She gathered her cloak around herself and prepared to step up into the carriage, pausing for one more look at the theater. Only then did she notice the man engrossed in the poster announcing her recital. Her pulse quickened, and she suddenly became apprehensive.

The voice from the carriage was impatient. "Hurry, Vanessa, I'm chilled to the bone in this foul weather."

But she could not stop gazing at that profile, so familiar, fearing if she broke the gaze, she would lose the memory of him. It was strange she wanted to hold onto his memory at all, for although there had been joys, what she remembered most was the pain.

She couldn't help herself—she moved toward the figure, edging around the side of him, hoping for a better look at his face. Her reflection appeared on the glass.

He spun around. "Vanessa!"

Startled at the unexpected meeting, she blurted, "It *is* you. You are like a ghost from the past."

"Not a ghost. I'm real flesh and blood."

"Of course, I can see that. I only meant . . ." Suddenly she was shy in front of him, remembering—

There was a tiredness in his handsome face, a gauntness that had not been there when last she saw him, and too, the beginning signs of furrows between his penetrating eyes. She had not allowed herself to think of him, trying desperately not to think of the past at all.

He took her hands and squeezed them. "So these are the fingers of the lady who is to make her London debut tomorrow night." He brushed her gloved hands with his lips.

The longing in her body became intense. At that moment, a head appeared out the carriage. Fortunately, in the heavy atmosphere, only Vanessa's back was evident.

"Come along, darling. I must insist."

"I have to go—I wish I could stay a bit longer."

"It's all right, I, too, must hurry along." But he did not move. There was an urgency as he said, "I had no idea you were in London until I read the announcement about your performance in the newspapers."

"I have lived here ever since the end of the war—except when traveling, giving recitals. And you?"

"I also live here—for the time being."

"If only I had known." Suddenly she wanted to be in his arms, being hugged and kissed by him—loved.

"If only we had both known."

There was an intimate pause between them—a silence that said so much.

"Are you happy with your new life, Vanessa?"

Oh no, she wanted to cry out—not happy at all.

The carriage horses snorted, straining at their bridles as the voice from the conveyance called in growing annoyance, "Vanessa. The fog is getting heavier and heavier. What is keeping you?"

He made motions as if to leave.

"Are you coming to the recital?" she asked quickly.

"I doubt it; I don't have a ticket."

"You must come." She didn't want to lose him again. Suddenly she was terribly frightened.

"Vanessa, I'm not sure. I don't know if I will be free, my life is not really my own these days. But I will be thinking of you."

"There will be a ticket for you at the box office. And try to come to the reception afterward."

The voice from the carriage became querulous and loud, "Vanessa, come this instant. We have to be off!"

"Promise you'll do your best to come," Vanessa pleaded.

"I'll try, but if I can't make it, good luck." He turned away and was quickly swallowed by the fog.

The servants listened with half an ear to the practicing as they scurried about trying to get everything ready for the reception to follow the young lady's debut. The house on Belgrave Square had been in turmoil all day—caterers coming and going, flowers being delivered, messages arriving and it was getting late, with so much more for them to do.

Lord Hatfield, the Eighth Earl of Raleigh, one of the richest men in England, had not entertained on such a grand scale since the sudden death of his wife almost a year before. The staff was excited, the state of mourning had been getting on their nerves. They were glad it was over, except for Miss Shields, the grim housekeeper, who was referred to (behind her back) as the Hatfield terror. She called the evening's coming affair sacrilegious, and the servants suspected she would carry her obessive mourning of the late Lady Hatfield into her own grave.

They whispered above and below stairs about the beautiful American lady who had been locked in the music room most of the day with her black servant, opening the door only once when a footman brought tea. Other members of the McIver family, also houseguests for the past week, had been in and out all day, ringing and demanding attention. Except the father, Kenneth McIver, recently arrived from America, who kept to himself, wearing a deep look of disappointment on his face, saying very little.

To the servants, the McIvers were a strange lot—foreigners—and although they recognized them as upper class, they knew they were not of the rich. The shabby luggage, the scuffed shoes they had to polish, the worn underwear they had unpacked, told them so much.

The downstairs maids were stunned and shocked when the door to the music room suddenly flew open and Vanessa McIver, with her sleeves pushed up to her elbows, hair tumbling all about her face, ran out of the room as if being chased by the furies and made a wild dash for the front door. She threw it open without regard for decorum and started to take deep gulps of air. JoJo, the black servant, came out of the room in the next instant, looking just as astounded as they, and moved quickly to her mistress.

"What is it, Nessa? Are you all right?"

"Oh, this air feels good. It was so warm in there, I thought I'd suffocate."

"Please, come away from the door, it's damp and cold."

The gaslight in the hall sputtered and was threatening to go out as the cold November air rushed in, but Vanessa stayed in the doorway, oblivious to the servants shivering in the cold draft behind her.

"Nessa," the black girl begged, "let me shut the door."

"Just a minute more—one more minute and then we'll go back." She fanned her flushed face with the palms of her hands.

"But, Nessa, you have to keep warm before the recital. You don't want your muscles to stiffen—all that practicing will have been for nothin'."

Georgina McIver, her mother, hurried down the marble staircase, "Vanessa, whatever are you doing standing in the doorway?" She glanced at JoJo with an accusing eye, blaming her for allowing her mistress to behave so badly. She wrapped her arm around Vanessa's waist. "Come, my darling, we'll go back to the music room." And then louder for the benefit of the servants, "Mustn't be so worried about this evening's performance—you are going to be just marvelous. The Duke of Wales will be there to applaud you—and other royalty . . ." Under her breath, she whispered, "You are making a fool of yourself."

Reluctantly, the disheveled young woman gave in and slowly walked back into the music room. Georgina closed the door, shutting out JoJo.

A pompous footman appeared and discreetly shut the front door; his face all disapproval at the undignified behavior of a member of the upper class in front of the servants. He snapped his fingers loudly a number of times at the downstairs maids whose eyes were glued to the music room. He had no authority over them, but they resumed their cleaning and polishing in a fluster. There was an expectant air as they worked, waiting for something further to happen.

"Vanessa, whatever can you be thinking of—you must remember where you are. This isn't our tiny house in Chelsea where you can do whatever you want without spying eyes. This is the home of an important man."

Vanessa sat down on the velvet settee and watched her mother sweep around the room as she continued to chide her on her behavior, which was just as upsetting to her and had been ever since the chance meeting yesterday. She had not been in control of her emotions since then.

"The help must never see you in such a state. Never. It's not like back home where the servants used to be loyal. These creatures gossip among themselves and carry tales to the other great houses in London. We must watch ourselves at all times—nothing must go wrong. Oh, Vanessa. I wouldn't be able to stand it. We have been so poor—almost penniless—living on the edge of society like distant, unwanted cousins begging for crumbs—and jammed, all of us, except your father, in that ugly house in Chelsea—just existing. It has been awful! But with this marriage, all our lives will come right again. You'll see. Oh, Vanessa, look at you!" She shook her head as she pulled her eldest child to her feet and dragged her to the mirror over the mantel.

Vanessa stared at herself in the looking glass. She saw her untidy appearance, her hair tumbling about her face and was surprised at the dark circles under her eyes. Her mother started to pace again, talking on and on, but in Vanessa's preoccupation, she heard only bits and pieces as she repinned the tousled curls atop her head and pulled down her sleeves trying to make herself look presentable.,

"Those damn Yankees took everything from us—our plantation, the townhouse in Charleston. Do you know who is living in the townhouse now? Carpetbaggers! Can you imagine! Your father just told me."

Reflected in the mirror, Vanessa saw such beauty and elegance behind her: the massive low hanging crystal chandelier, the fine oil paintings on the walls—scenes by Canaletto, a new Manet, various Hatfields painted by Zoffany, famous for his portraits of the royal family, a priceless oriental screen. So much security represented in the room. She could understand why her mother was so desperate for this marriage to take place. But couldn't all this be taken away so quickly, just like theirs—obliterated by war, fire, or both? So many things. But in this case, not the power behind it, for Lord Hatfield's money was old money, centuries of landed gentry with political force behind it. Not like the McIvers of South Carolina who had only one generation of wealth behind them which crumbled during the Civil War, leaving some of them displaced here in England where they had been struggling to make some kind of life among strangers; and the rest of the family, straining to make a go of it back home, strangers on their own land amidst the spoilers.

"Your sister and I watched Lord Hatfield in Parliament the other day. You should have been there. He speaks so eloquently, and to think he will soon be my son-in-law." She came to her daughter and turned her around to face her. "Oh, Vanessa, good fortune is smiling on the McIvers again."

"I know, Momma."

Her mother's youthful face aged in a split second.

"But deep down I have this nagging fear that something might go wrong. Nothing could go wrong, do you think, my darling?"

Vanessa closed her eyes and leaned back stiffly, trying to rest her tense back on the cold marble mantel. "No, Momma, nothing will go wrong."

"My sweet darling, about your behavior, I'm sorry to be so hard on you, but we must try harder. I know you've had a difficult time. How often I thought, poor Vanessa, obsessively studying her music to try and forget what had happened to her back home—first here in London at the conservatory and then all alone in Rome on that meager scholarship."

"I wasn't alone, Momma, I had JoJo with me."

"But she is just a servant girl—you were away from your family. And that awful traveling from one small city to another under the poorest conditions to gain experience. You weren't brought up to do anything like that. Well, it is over now, and London is going to be our place. Imagine, one of my daughters as mistress of a stunning townhouse on Belgrave Square and chatelaine of a vast country estate, and it all happened so quickly." She dramatized it grandly. "The social but somewhat impoverished McIvers went to a charity tea. Lord Hatfield became smitten instantly and tonight after the reception—an announcement will be made to London society—an engagement announcement. No. Nothing is going to happen to spoil our good luck. My beloved daddy used to say, 'Fortune goes round and round, my baby. Just be patient and shuffle the cards.' Well, I'm shuffling my cards and if I have to, I'll stack the deck."

Vanessa moved toward the piano, quietly struck a note, then several more at random as she thought of him again—a strange reunion—a ghost from the past appearing from out of the fog. What if he didn't come to the recital, would she have the courage to seek him out?

"I'll let you get on with your practicing but please remember what your Momma told you about appearances."

JoJo looked up at the sound of the door opening and waited until Georgina disappeared from sight before she entered the music room to be with her mistress.

The piano playing started again. This time it was more fitful, with ragged starts, stops, and repeats. It put the servants on edge. Moments later there was a slamming of hands on the keys and then fists banging at the board. Maudie, a plump cockney with protruding teeth, pushed her feather duster harder as she exclaimed, "My Gawd, sounds as if her ladyship is trying to kill the piana 'sted of plying it." The others working near her, shook their heads in agreement as they listened somewhat disturbed by the cacophony.

"Wonder what his lordship would say if he heard her music now?" breathed old Sarah. They thought about that for a moment or so and when the sound righted, their bodies relaxed until Daisy, an upstairs maid, came hurrying down in a dither. She told them in a hushed whisper that the other McIver daughter, Miss Amanda, was standing naked as the day she was born in front of a mirror, staring at herself from every which way.

"What," screeched Maudie in dismay. "Staring at everything! Naked? Why would she do that? It ain't decent."

Daisy was breathless. "That's right, and she's singing a song, something about 'I wish I was in the land of cotton,' and when she got to the part 'look away, look away,' she swished her behind like she was waving a flag."

"Imagine," said Maudie as she rolled her eyes, "a young lady like that prancing around with no clothes."

"These McIvers don't seem right to me," confided Daisy very seriously.

"Americans, that's what," informed Sarah as she tucked her chin into her neck. "You never know what they're about."

The playing stopped, and they looked toward the music room only to see the stern housekeeper, Miss Shields, standing in their midst and they sprang back to work like dolls on a tight coil suddenly sprung loose. Caught in a huddle gossiping by the formidable Miss Shields would keep them on the run for the rest of the working day and worry them through their sleep that night.

Vanessa stared at her hands—then flexed them several times before she let them rest on the keys. She had thought for once she had her life all worked out in an unemotional way—all her fervor to be reserved for her music, vowing so often not to let feelings take hold of her again. In the past, love had crushed and almost destroyed her, forcing her to build a shell around herself for protection and survival.

At twenty-five she sometimes felt as though she had lived forever, being tossed like a ship in turbulent waters and caught in ensnaring webs of circumstances—most beyond her control. Of course, some of the events she did feel responsible for with deep guilt.

Her mind spun back to another foggy day like yesterday's, and she allowed herself to pull aside the veil of the past, surprised how brilliant the events of that day and night were printed on her mind. She was in her teens—on the McIver cotton plantation on St. Helena Island off the coast of South Carolina.

2

_____

McIver Hall faded quickly into the distance as she reck-
lessly urged her high-spirited horse into a hard gallop
down the long oak-lined avenue. She was heading for
the swamps and the cotton fields at the end of the
plantation, As she raced up a slight rise at the turn in
the road, scattered a group of mockingbirds, their frenzied
dislocation adding to her upset, and galloping along the
creek that wound through the McIver land into the broad
waters, she fought for composure. Since early morning
all sense of security had been falling from her in a way
she couldn't define. It had started when she heard her
father talking hurriedly, furtively, to the new overseer,
warning him that on that very day Lincoln probably would
be elected president and they had better be on the alert
for runaways or rebellion among the field hands. By early
evening, just before sunset, in a manic way, she had the
urge to get out and away.

Thursday, a little stableboy whose job it was to accompany her whenever she rode off alone, beat his old
horse with a long thin reed trying to keep up. He was
riding bareback, not having had time to put a saddle on
his mount. Vanessa had just run out of the house, saddled
her own horse, used a crate in the stable to mount
and was off before Thursday knew what was happening.
Now he was after her, his frail body bouncing up and
down as it smacked the swayback of the spindly nag.

"Miz Nessa," she heard him shout, "you is goin' too
fas', Lordy, Lordy." His little legs beat harder against the
horse's ribs as he tried to catch up.

After a quick turn in the road, Vanessa could see

the ridges of the cotton fields and slowed her mount. Some of the hands were busy with the plows, throwing up new ridges for next spring's planting, since this was one of the last pickings of the season. But most of the darkies were still hard at work plucking the newly opened pods of the long, silky cotton grown on St. Helena Island.

Vanessa was surprised to see her father in the fields. Something he rarely did, leaving the supervision to the overseer and slave drivers. She watched him for a short while and could tell he was forcing a nonchalance as he looked over his crop and the hands. One of the darkies started to sing, and it was picked up by others one at a time until the sound of the song was rich and full. The slow rhythm reflecting their movements at the end of an arduous day picking cotton in the sun. Vanessa recognized the strains of, "I've Been Down To The Sea, Lord . . ." and she followed the words . . . "I do love to dearly tell—Christ my Lord, does all things well, been down in to the sea . . ."

She prodded her horse into a slow trot, recalling the songs her beloved mammy used to sing to her as she sat on her soft lap—her head resting securely on those pendulous breasts as she was lulled to sleep by lullabies. She had to smile remembering the times Mammy Claire sang so loud that she would have to put her hands over her ears, mammy telling her she was singing thus to be sure the good Lord heard her.

Vanessa could not allow herself to think that any of the slaves on the McIver plantation would suddenly become people to fear. Her father had also told the new overseer to make certain all firearms were cleaned, oiled, and ready. She wished she had not wanted to surprise her father that morning and then she wouldn't have overheard all the talk that had become more and more distressing as the day wore on. On her way home today she would stop in at Mammy Claire's, now called Granny due to her advanced age, and tell her about her qualms, have her comfort her with her sweet talk. How good it would be to lay her head on those great breasts once more and hear her sing one of her soft hymns. But she had been rather distressed when she last visited Granny Claire in her cabin behind the big house after her recent

return from Charleston. Granny had acted so strangely—
her eyes not completely focused. She had brought her
special things for tea and found her seated in her rocker
with the good book in her hand. Granny said she was
reading from Samuel—although her seeing was so bad,
she reckoned, she was really reading from memory.

Vanessa had taken the gnarled hands in hers and
rubbed her cheek with them.

"Granny Claire, you should have come to Charleston
with us for the season."

The old woman looked at her and seemingly recognized her, but her rémark was strange, "My place is
here, chile. Dis is where iz needed. I'z a McIver."

"Of course you are. You're my mammy."

The old woman went on to say, "We buried five.
The malaria was bad this year. Poor old Jeb, fell down
in de fields and never got up. You whites go way in
de summer when the malaria comes. Us blacks, we right
here so it can strike us down."

There was a silence between them, and Granny Claire
slowly pulled her hands away from Vanessa.

"My hands hurt. Dey hurt somethin' bad. You got
somethin' to stop the pain in my hands?"

Vanessa rubbed the enlarged fingers slowly, vowing to
speak to her father about getting the doctor to do something for Granny Claire.

"I'm to play at a big concert at the Dock Street
Theater next spring. Just like you always wanted me to
do. Play for the people. All those hours you made me
practice when I was little are not going to waste. The
money will go to charity."

"Will der be black people in de theater? Dez people."

The glazed eyes took Vanessa in, and suddenly the
old woman fully recognized her and embraced her to her
great breasts. tightly, frantically.

"Dere will be war, chile. The niggers are not the
same. Dey wants to be free. Dey have no rights, chile.
Dey done got nothin'. When you plays, my baby, plays
so loud the Sweet Lord Jesus hears you and helps us
old niggers get free."

A fly buzzed around a crust of bread on the broken
table.

"What I'm gonna do iffen I free? Where will I go?" she wailed.

"Here, Granny Claire. Here. You are a McIver. Your home is here forever." There was another long silence between them. "I brought you a sugar cookie, Granny."

Granny Claire looked at her sadly, absently, as she said, "How you spec me to eat a sugar cookie, chile? I ain't got a tooth in my head."

She rode along in a cadence, keeping a tight rein on the horse, taking in all the sights she had taken somewhat for granted—the scarlet cassena berries gleaming on the roadside hedges and the white tufts of the mockingbird flowers blooming everywhere in the late fall. The smell of the fresh salt air from the sea just beyond so pleased her now, almost washing away some of the troublesome thoughts. The tides had just come in, and she could imagine the waters full of fish and oysters. Large gray white gulls were circling the island, filling the air with sounds of broad flapping wings and then moments of silence as they sailed gracefully on currents of air. Her moment of serenity was short-lived, however, for the gulls suddenly started screeching wildly as they dove savagely into the shallow waters for food. The sight of wiggling fish in their sharp beaks before being devoured, made her shudder. Why was everything so temporary, she thought, as if at any moment something secure could be brutally snatched away.

There was a movement in the bushes up ahead.

"Who's there? Who is it?" she yelled.

Thursday drew his horse closer to her. A ground fog had started to roll in, lifting in swirls around the horses' flanks, and the hazy twilight suddenly turned into murky uncertainty.

"Lordy, Miz Nessa. Let's get out of here. It's getting dark so fas'."

"I said, who's in there? You come on out."

She tried to show no fear, but gripped her crop tightly.

"Come on, Miz Nessa. It might be the ole hag witch. She like it when it gets misty."

A tall, lean man stepped out in the road. He was pulling a shirt over his damp chest. His wet curly blond hair clung snugly to his head, drops of water ran down his face. There was a wide grin on his face as he moved toward her. She recognized him immediately as the new overseer.

"Mr. Yoors."

"That's right, Miss McIver. I hope I didn't startle you."

She spoke tightly, her lips barely parted, "Of course not. I just thought it might be . . ."

"A runaway?"

She tried to make light of her concern, as she looked at Kirk Yoors. Her father had said his background was somewhat of a mystery, but added he was a "hell of an overseer."

"Or the hag," she responded, "Thursday is just dying to meet up with the old witch to see if it really can doff its skin."

Thursday's eyes went round as he fished in his breast pocket bringing out some tiny seeds. "Iffen I see that hag, I'll throw these mustard seeds on that thing and make it go up in smoke."

Kirk smiled, the corner of his mouth curling slightly. "Boy, if you meet up with a witch on these sea islands, it will take more than mustard seeds to make the wicked old woman go away."

Suddenly ruffled at his remark, Vanessa retorted sharply, "What makes you think the hag is a woman, Mr. Yoors? Why can't the old thing be a man like yourself for instance?"

"Doesn't hag mean 'woman,' Miss McIver?" He was all business now. "I would suggest you head home. Not only is there a dense fog rolling in, but times make it a little dangerous to be out without proper protection."

Her answer was quick. How dare he tell her what to do. "Thank you for your concern, Mr. Yoors, but I was raised on this island, and I think I know what is right and wrong better than you."

With that she took her crop and hit her horse hard across the flank and galloped away. Little Thursday looked at her for a second and then dug his heels into his old nag, trying to get the beast moving to keep up.

Vanessa knew she was foolish riding out toward the bluff. He was right, the fog was getting heavier, rising faster from the ground, and also rolling in overhead in big billows. She could hear the renewed screeching of the gulls overhead as they frantically circled and circled. In a few moments she was up against a liquid adhesiveness. Her horse, sensing the danger, slowed to a measured walk. Vanessa could hear the breathing of Thursday's horse coming up slowly from behind.

"Miz Nessa. Where is you? I'z scared."

Trying to still her own fears and give Thursday courage, she slowly mouthed, "Keep coming, Thursday. Keep talking and we surely will find each other."

She heard nothing in reply.

"Thursday, keep talking, you big brave quarter hand."

In the background she heard, "Oh, Miz Nessa. Where is you?"

The voice got louder, and she felt his horse brush up against her leg. She grabbed for the mane or anything to keep them together. Thursday let out a scream which startled both horses, and they veered away from each other. She heard Thursday's frantic cry, "The hag. She's got me. Oh, Miz Nessa. She done got me."

"Keep talking, Thursday. That was no hag, that was me. Try to keep your horse from going toward the marshes. If it feels boggy, head her away. You hear?"

The two horses bumped, and she grabbed the mane of Thursday's old nag again and held on until she got him to hand her the reins. They rode on for a while, together, silently.

Vanessa was feeling very chilled. She didn't know if it were mostly her fear or the heavy mist that was now falling, thoroughly soaking her through and through. She was wise enough to let her horse have its head, and was sure they were heading toward the ocean as she could faintly hear the sound of waves crashing on the shore. She didn't want to risk turning the horses around for fear they would go into the marshes along the river's edge. If they could get to the point, she reasoned, they could stay near the dock or go into the boat house on the wharf until the fog lifted and then head back home. She knew her mother and father would be frantic, but there was nothing she could do. It seemed that they were veering a bit to the right. However, they were still on rather firm ground. Then she felt and heard the crunch of oyster shells beneath the horse's hooves and realized they were now on a well-kept avenue. It had to be the road to the Bonneau place, which sat on a bluff overlooking the ocean. The road leading to the manor house, she knew, was always deeply bedded with oyster shells. Her heart lifted, and she urged the horses into a quicker pace. After about a quarter of a mile she felt she could see the outline of the big house up ahead.

Vanessa knocked at the huge oak door and waited. Thursday was at the hitching post with the horses. She had never been inside the Bonneau mansion. She had been on the grounds for various community affairs along with other neighbors, but never had been invited into the house. One of the first families of South Carolina on both sides, with ambassadors, senators, and governors and other public figures in their lineage, the present Bonneaus did not socialize, and consequently there were many stories and rumors about them. The only heir to the family fortune was Pierre Bonneau, a young man who was a complete enigma to the people of the island. He spent most of his time off in Europe and had been educated abroad from childhood. There was a new rumor that he had recently returned to St. Helena because of the troubled times ahead for the South, but as yet no one had seen Pierre Bonneau. The famous plantation was run by his strong-willed mother Harriet, who had been a Sims before her marriage to Bonneau, and her name was synonymous with the very special sea island cotton she grew, a silky, long staple cotton that was in demand by all the fabric mills throughout the world. Harriet, somewhat antisocial since the death of her husband a number of years back, spent all her time running the cotton plantation on St. Helena and her family's rice fields a few miles away up the Combahee River.

The old servant told her to come in as he went to find Mistress Harriet to tell her of Vanessa's plight. Thursday was sent around to the kitchen. While she was in the hall, she saw a fireplace in the library and went to it immediately and started to warm herself. With chilled, trembling fingers, she unbuttoned her shirt and moved her chest closer to the fire. After a few seconds, on an impulse, she took all her hair and flung it over her face and fanned it toward the heat of the flames, trying to dry it. Then flinging it back, she quickly removed her riding jacket and tossed it, without turning, at the wing chair behind her. She heard the clatter of shattered glass on the polished floor. Turning abruptly she saw a very handsome young man bent over trying to pick up the pieces. She was stunned for a moment and then terribly embarrassed.

"I'm sorry. I didn't know anyone was here."

Then she realized that he had been watching her all along and became incensed.

"Why didn't you let me know of your presence? You didn't say a word."

When he stood, he towered over her tall frame and smiled down at her, his dark eyes sparkled in an arched manner.

"It was more fun watching you trying to dry yourself in front of the fire."

She looked down and saw the buttons she had opened slightly, bared her chest. With awkward fingers, she quickly buttoned up, and her deep blush further amused him.

"What were you doing out in the fog? Wasn't that a bit silly?"

"Not silly at all. I was out riding and the fog just happened."

"You are from a nearby plantation?"

For some reason, his tone was making her feel like an errant child, and she wondered if he were Pierre Bonneau, but could not bring herself to ask. His sophistication was intimidating and at the same time his handsomeness and perfect manner of dress and diction made her shy, and for the moment, speechless. They looked at each other intently for a long moment in the candlelit room, and then he smiled almost seductively, "Cat got your tongue, or are you hiding some deep secret about your identity? A mystery woman?"

Now Vanessa had to smile and at that moment, Harriet Bonneau entered the room.

The pale pink bedroom was high ceilinged and spacious. A large walnut four-poster bed with pink damask side drapes and tented canopy, stood grandly between tall French windows. Vanessa lay on the bed, sunken in soft, feathery down, looking at the windows gracefully swagged in the same pink damask. Fine white lace curtains underneath the draperies billowed in the gentle evening breeze.

Mrs. Bonneau had told her to rest the hour before supper. Her clothes had been taken by a pickaninny to be dried and pressed and her boots to be cleaned and polished. But she couldn't rest, she was too excited. She got down from the bed and stepped onto the flowered Brussels tapestry rug which felt like spring grass under her bare feet. Wearing a green velvet robe, Mrs. Bonneau said Pierre had brought her from Paris, she moved to the window and drew back the lace curtain. Just below the window she saw a lovely formal garden designed in maze fashion and beyond, a large strip of private beach. The fog had lifted some, and Vanessa could also make out the tall, white lighthouse in the distance.

She moved to the small serpentined fireplace and gently stroked the cool pink and white marble. It was topped by a graceful mirror edged in bright gold leaf. All the woodwork around the room was delicately carved with the refinement of Adam's decoration, and now smelled deliciously from the mass of flowers sent up from the Bonneau hothouse, making an already cheerful room even brighter.

She sat by the fire in a small needlepoint chair and stared at the flames, hugging her knees, and thinking of the very handsome Pierre Bonneau.

What a strange young man, she thought, and what a ninny she had made of herself. She had never met anyone like him before, and she now had mixed emotions of excitement and anxiety when she thought of taking supper with the family. Mrs. Bonneau had also mentioned a guest, an English portrait painter, Sir Robert Ashcroft. Vanessa had also never met a portrait painter before— at least not a real one, one sent for all the way from London to paint someone in New Orleans.

She tried to think of interesting things to say at dinner. What do you talk about with someone like Pierre Bonneau? Would you say things like, "I graduated last June from Miss Agnes' Seminary in Charleston and play the piano? Or, I am really too tall, my hands are too large because I practice on the piano for several hours daily and have been doing it for years. Why? Because I love to play the piano. I also love horses, and everyone says I am too quick and therefore make unnecessary mistakes." She wrapped Mrs. Bonneau's robe closer to her. The robe was short on her, but more than ample in size, it was like being enveloped in soft, silky down.

There were several short knocks at the door and two house blacks entered bringing in hot water and towels, another followed with her freshly pressed clothes and polished boots. They bowed out without a word after Vanessa thanked them. Vanessa couldn't help wondering what kind of mistress Harriet Bonneau was to her slaves.

She quickly disrobed and sponged her whole body. Then she rubbed herself dry with a large towel and went to the dressing table to scent her body with some fragrant oils she had found there, wondering if they were also brought from Europe by Pierre.

She rubbed an essence smelling like a potpourri of flowers into her skin, neck and shoulders first and then her long, slender legs. She was sorry she didn't have one of her pretty dresses to put on instead of having to get back into her riding habit. She would have loved to have had her shoulders exposed, shining slightly from the fragrant oil.

She wondered again what Pierre was really like as she sat at the dressing table and started to brush her hair. Was he someone she should be afraid of? Suppose she made some horrible faux pas at supper? She would be mortified. His dark eyes were so devilish and mischievous. She giggled as she remembered what he said, "Are you a mystery woman?" Is he in love with someone, she wondered apprehensively. Some fine lady in Rome or Paris? She stared into the mirror, then started to dress her hair. She wanted so to look elegant and desirable and decided to wear her hair on top of her head with love curls and wisps of hair about her cheeks and forehead, but she had no scissors to cut the wisps and no curling iron to make the love curls. Finally she settled for a loose topknot and puffed her hair slightly about her ears. Some wisps did fall down the sides of her face and neck giving her the appearance of a little girl trying to look grown up.

The riding skirt was tight due to being wet and

pressed dry with hot irons, making it cling to her small hips and showing off her gently curving thighs. The white cotton shirt looked soft and feminine because most of the starch had been wilted out of it. She decided to tie the ascot in a bow, and the effect was attractive, framing her pale oval face and highlighting her gray-blue, almond-shaped eyes. She took one last look at herself in the mirror over the vanity and smiled. She was glad she was not encumbered with crinolines and stays. She was pleased with the soft clinging look. Her mother would be shocked by her sitting down to supper with people such as the Bonneaus in a tight riding skirt with no petticoats. But it somehow suited Vanessa. She pouted at her image. What could she talk about at supper that would make her interesting and intriguing?

"Cat got your tongue," he had also said. If he only knew she rarely stopped talking most of the time. "Too quick, you talk too quick," her mother was always telling her, making her slow down and have periods of silence, forcing her to listen more intently. She will never forget her first encounter with Pierre she thought, then wondered if she would ever get to know him well.

Quickly she pinched her cheeks several times, something she had never done before and rather objected to. She left the room feeling happy but anxious. Just outside the drawing room she heard them talking and hesitated before going in. Again there was talk of Lincoln and the election. She heard a very cultured English voice. That must be Sir Robert, she thought.

"What a shame it would be for the South to have its very way of life destroyed."

Harriet Bonneau answered soberly, "All things come to pass, Sir Robert. We will just have to adjust if it does happen."

Pierre was cynical as he parried with, "You delude yourself, my dear mother, if you think things will just right themselves. Why don't we just sell out and move lock, stock, and barrel to Europe? Enjoy life without the worry of slaves, factors, impending war . . ."

"Your heritage is here, Pierre, and running away will not solve the problems. Sooner or later you would have to come home."

"Why?" was his quick retort.

Vanessa was standing there in a kind of daze, half hearing what they were saying, and not aware that after a moment's silence, both men were standing looking at her. One powerfully built, a hawklike man with deepset eyes under bushy brows, almost ugly but fascinating to look at, and Pierre, tall, slim, dressed all in pale gray with highly polished maroon boots. Harriet Bonneau sat stiffly, her large bulk and her many petticoats, taking up all the space on the green satin settee near the large fireplace.

She smiled at Vanessa and just as quickly she withdrew it. That to her was enough indication of welcome. Harriet Bonneau, called Lady Harriet by her slaves, was known for her imperious nature, and Vanessa had heard rumors that when she walked near the fields, work increased twofold.

Pierre came to her, took her arm and brought her into the room. She was not prepared for the grandeur of the drawing room. Vanessa felt she had been transported to a salon in Paris. She tried to take in as many details as possible as they chatted over an aperitif.

At the far end of the room, looking out on the formal gardens, were two tall, slender columns that sectioned off a portion of the room, forming an alcove. In the center of the alcove stood a magnificent, black lacquered piano. She longed to run over to the piano and plump on the seat and start to play. But she restrained herself and just stood in the center of the room facing Mrs. Bonneau, listening to what she was saying and trying to give the correct answers, becoming completely distracted when she spotted a large oil painting on the wall of a small boy romping with spaniel puppies. She knew it must be Pierre.

She turned full attention to him and Sir Robert when she heard them talking of far off England and London society. She loved the story of Queen Victoria and Prince Albert taking off on a merry expedition through the countryside, staying at common inns disguised as Lord and Lady Churchill. Then Sir Robert told of the notorious quadroon that he was commissioned to paint in New Orleans. A famous earl had fallen in love with her during a visit to that city and had to have a portrait of her for his castle in Devonshire. On and on he went about scandals, the lords and ladies he painted, and of his

many visits to Buckingham Palace and Windsor Castle
to have tea or supper with the queen before the death
of her prince. It was a world Vanessa couldn't fathom,
and she had pangs of jealousy when Pierre talked about
a certain lady he said he knew quite well, and that he
had spent the last year with her and her brother in their
villa in Rome. What did he mean by that, she thought.

Supper was different from the table set at the McIvers,
Vanessa reflected. It didn't groan from the amount of
food. Instead, old Henry quietly served each course from
a large silver tray.

Harriet presided sternly, her dark eyes lingering for
long moments on her son, flickering nervously when he
talked, hanging on his every word. Vanessa was getting
a little heady from the wine. Usually her father
watered the wine the McIver children were allowed on
special occasions. Suddenly she began to get talkative,
interjecting wherever she could no matter what the
others were talking about, stories of her Scottish grandfather, and his beautiful furniture designs executed in the
family factory in Charleston. The factory, she added, was
now mainly run by her Uncle Thomas. Then she regaled
them with the antics of her brother Josiah and how he
wanted to go to school in England, adding she wanted
to travel, too, go all over the world and especially see
London. Sir Robert smiled at her and said expansively,
"Come visit me when you get there. I'll show you
around."

"I will," she answered quickly.

Henry served her a small pinkish mound in a jelly.
"Whatever is that?" she spurted.

Pierre smiled benevolently at her.

"Whatever is what, Vanessa?"

She lowered her eyes and then gave him a coy side-
ward glance. "The concoction on my plate."

"Salmon mousse. Try it. I'm sure you'll enjoy it."

Sir Robert, eating heartily, said, "It's delicious, the best
I've ever eaten," and motioned for a second helping.

Harriet smiled as she looked at her son.

"Pierre is teaching Dinah how to cook French-style.
There was quite a resistance at first, but she is really
learning and it is much better for the figure in the long
run—better than Southern cooking."

"Not teaching, Mother, Dinah is a superb cook in her own right—merely reading her the recipes I brought back from Paris."

Vanessa had to agree, it was delicious and so light. Then she couldn't stop herself from asking, "How long will you be staying on St. Helena this time, Pierre?"

Looking at his mother with heavily lidded eyes, he answered slowly and evenly.

"That depends on the slavery question, Vanessa. We are all slaves in one way or another, going through life shackled either by circumstances or ourselves or possibly both." After a pause he added more casually, "I suppose here on the island or in the immediate area, longer than usual."

Harriet looked somewhat relieved, but that was lost on Vanessa who also missed the double entendre, continuing with, "Well, I'm an absolute slave to the piano. Look at my hands from all the practicing. Someday I hope to be a great pianist."

She spread out both her hands, holding them high for all to see.

Sir Robert admired the large span of her hands and the long, squarish fingers.

"By George, that's quite a spread you've got. Most important for a pianist."

Pierre also admired her hands. The attention she was getting from these people was as heady as the wine, and why, she thought, did she say she wanted to be a great pianist. How vain.

Harriet told her she must play for them after supper, and she surprised herself by saying she would be more than delighted. She knew she was on safe ground there, but she had hiccuped when she said it, and bowed her head in embarrassment.

During dessert Harriet told Sir Robert and Pierre that as a precaution she was slowly going to move some of her field hands off the islands to the Sims-Bonneau rice plantation up the Combahee River. She felt if the Southern hotheads did get them into a confrontation with the North, the islands just off the coast of South Carolina would be a natural sitting duck.

Sir Robert, forking the whipped cream on the strawberry tart, asked with concern, "Do you think it will come to war, madam? What about compromise, and full understanding of the problems on both sides to settle your disagreements? You are after all a Union."

Harriet sadly told him it was too late for all of that. That should have happened a long time ago. At this point she feared it would just be empty gestures.

"My dear mother, I have been away a long time and am not as in touch therefore as you, but you sound positive that Lincoln will win."

"Oh no," said Vanessa softly as she put down her silver spoon and could eat no more.

Pierre looked at her intently as did Sir Robert.

Later in the evening Vanessa felt inspired as her fingers flew over the keyboard. She was exhilarated by the presence of Pierre but soon she forgot she was in the Bonneau drawing room as her music possessed her completely. The pressure on the pedal went from quick to heavy to light once again as she went into a difficult crescendo, peaking very loudly at the climax, filling the room with an unpolished magic and power, astounding those listening. When she finished, she didn't move, she sat there drained, her hands motionless on the still-vibrating keys. Oddly, there was no sound behind her and she slowly turned to her audience. Old Henry and Dinah, the cook, were standing in the hall just outside the drawing room, mesmerized. Old Henry bobbed from side to side muttering softly, "Oh my, oh my, dat was sumthin', Miz Vanessa, that was sumthin'." Dinah had a grin from ear to ear. Vanessa smiled coyly at them and just as demurely, she sought Pierre's eyes. He was staring at her intently, one eyebrow arched cryptically. She locked eyes with him and instantly felt nervous and fluttery. His handsome face revealed no emotion.

Sir Robert was the first to make a move, he sprang up and started to clap ebulliently as he moved to her quickly.

"Jolly good. Jolly good, my dear girl. You play gloriously for such a young person. You really moved me."

Dinah could contain herself no longer as she stepped boldly into the drawing room. "Miss Vanessa, you plays like an angel." She caught Mrs. Bonneau's eyes reproaching her for stepping out of bounds and dropped her head and smiled as she backed out of the room to stand at the entranceway again.

"I don't know. You are so kind. I made mistakes, and I'm still heavy-handed."

Sir Robert took her hands in his and kissed them both. "Possibly, but over all, Vanessa McIver, you gave a grand performance. You captivated your audience brilliantly. What a gift you have."

"Most of the time my mother says my playing gives her a headache."

There was polite laughter and Harriet Bonneau complimented her on her playing, but Pierre still sat staring at her in that enigmatic way.

Dinah cleared her throat for attention and announced in a respectful tone, "Beggin' your pardon, Miz Vanessa, your daddy's overseer, Mr. Yoors, is in the kitchen wanting to talk to you. He said he was part of a search party sent to look for you when the fog got bad and you didn't come home."

"Oh," she said to the others. "I'll go talk to him and be right back."

Sir Robert escorted her to the hall. "Don't be long, my dear, you'll have to play an encore for us."

When Vanessa entered the large kitchen, Kirk Yoors was sitting at the table in the center of the room drumming his fingers loudly on the scrubbed surface, his long, lanky legs spread casually under the table. On seeing her, he quickly scrambled to his feet and smiled.

What was it about this man that set her on edge? She had the feeling that he had set himself up as her keeper as if she were ten years old. A few days ago he had seen her trying to mount her father's new horse, and he quickly pulled her off telling her she'd break her neck as the beast wasn't for the likes of her. She considered herself an excellent horsewoman and was furious. Then earlier this evening his warning her about the fog. Now he was here.

"Good evening, Miss McIver. I'm glad to see you are safe."

"Of course I'm safe. What is this all about? What are you doing here?"

His jaw tightened perceptibly. "I'm beginning to wonder myself."

"Well, that's no explanation, Mr. Yoors. The Bonneaus sent word of my safety as soon as I arrived. The fog had somewhat lifted by then."

"Maybe here it had. And I guess I was already on my way. I came by boat in case your horse got caught in the marshes. Your father set out by horseback. He was probably met by the people the Bonneaus sent."

"Don't you think I'm expert enough to keep my horse on the road, out of the marshes, Mr. Yoors?"

"The fog does strange things to one's sense of direction, Miss McIver."

"There are ways of finding one's way if you are familiar with the land. It's a shame you made the trip for nothing."

"Yes, ma'am, I agree."

Why did she feel he was mocking her? She didn't know what to say, and he seemed to be standing there expectantly.

"Well, I guess you can stay the night or go right back. It doesn't matter to me. Dinah will feed you I'm sure if you're hungry."

Dinah was right behind her and went immediately to the now cooling stove, with the remains of dinner on top. "I'll take care of your overseer, Miz Vanessa. The boy, Thursday, is already bedded down with a full stomach from Dinah's kitchen. And I won't give Mr. Yoors none of the Frenchy stuff—some good corn pone and fried chicken I still got warming in the oven."

"What's your wish, Mr. Yoors?" Vanessa asked in a haughty tone.

"I'll give you a fast and easy answer, Miss McIver. I'm hungry, so I'll eat what promises to be a good meal from Dinah's kitchen." Dinah giggled, her jellylike fat shaking as she watched the two of them. "Then, when my belly is full, if I'm tired, I'll find a bed for myself. On the other hand, if Dinah's vittles fill me full of energy, I'll make it back to my own bed at the McIver plantation. Unless that doesn't suit you, ma'am."

"I'm sure I couldn't care less, Mr. Yoors. You just do what you want."

"I will."

"Vanessa."

She whirled at the sound of Pierre's commanding voice. He was suddenly in the kitchen and was dressed in a long heavy great coat and cap. He held another bulky garment in his arms. He moved toward her, his dark eyes focused on her. Vanessa felt compelled to explain what she was doing.

"I was talking to our overseer . . ."

He cut her off quickly, "I heard. Come, we will take a walk along the beach before you retire."

He unfolded the long cape he held in his arms and put it around her shoulders as he possessively steered her toward the rear door of the kitchen. She was too surprised to say anything. As they started out the door, Kirk Yoors called to her with a contained anger, "Miss McIver. I heard you play as I came round the house. You play real good."

She looked at him for a long moment.

"Thank you, Mr. Yoors. I'm glad you enjoyed it."

"Oh I did, ma'am. I really did."

"Didn't you ever hear me play before at home?"

"Yes, I heard you through the windows, but you never played like you did tonight."

Pierre pulled her out the door. The fog had lifted, and they walked past the kitchen garden and down the grassy slope to the wide strip of sandy beach. They didn't speak.

The night had turned clear and cold. The first killing frost had arrived. Above, the stars sparkled brightly in the midnight blue sky. After walking quite a ways with the wind whipping sharply against them, lifting their cloaks, Pierre stopped and looked down at her. He pulled the hood of her cape tighter around her head, then taking his scarf, he tied it firmly around the hood and under her chin. She looked into his eyes, and he returned her look steadfastly. They didn't move. It was as though they were fixed in time. Then suddenly he pulled her along as he started to walk again. Finally they came to the end of the island and stood on a dune overlooking the vast Atlantic gleaming in the silvery light.

Pierre held her hand tightly as he stared out over the ocean. His chiseled features silhouetted sharply in the bright moonlight.

What a strange man, she thought, and she knew that she was in love with him. His polish, his sophisticated manner and behavior were all so foreign and so intriguing. They stood silently looking out over the shimmering water as if waiting for a decision to be made. The hard wind tried to beat them down. He moved her closer to the ocean's edge. The water lapped at their feet, and they could see groups of gulls bobbing on the water. Finally, Pierre turned to her and looked down into her puzzled, expectant face. Slowly he cupped her chin in his long, slender fingers and raised her pale oval face to his. She trustingly looked into his dark eyes and waited for him to speak. When he did, his voice was deep and hollow.

"Tell me, sweet child. Are you old enough to be courted?"

Vanessa slowly lowered her head until it rested on top of the piano. She stayed there until a warm, tender hand touched her shoulder. "Nessa, it's getting late. Why don't you come away from the piano and take a hot bath?"

She raised her head, the soft blue eyes crinkling at the corner. "JoJo, whatever would I do without you?"

Later, in the hush of eventide, as if in prelude, there was a churchlike silence in the Hatfield house as the tired members of the household staff quietly finished setting up the last of the gilt chairs in the dining room and adjoining conservatory. For the time being all was done for the affair. The rooms had been thoroughly gone over and aired, the heavy silver, and deeply etched glassware sparkled on the polished tables; fragrant flowers had been placed throughout the downstairs rooms and all the fireplaces had been prepared, just waiting in gleaming brass grates for a match to set the logs ablaze.

Lord Hatfield stood motionless after his sitz bath as his valet, Martin, rubbed the lower portion of his body dry with a thick, coarse towel. He was a well-built man of medium height, with large muscular legs and arms from the long hikes he liked to take in the country and from the frequent pitching of hay with his tenant farmers on his vast land holdings in Norfolk. Sometimes short tempered and fierce where his opinions of law and justice were concerned, he was also an extremely passionate man, gentle and loving at given times. With a strong eye for the ladies, paradoxically, he never played the field, preferring to have one woman at his side and in his bed. He had been desperately lonely since his wife's death ten months ago. His wife had been a proper and prim lady, a distant cousin of the queen's. A woman who turned into a demonic spitfire when the door to their bedroom had closed. He hoped his bride to be would possess the same tendencies.

However, at this moment his mind was on something else. He was acutely depressed and for the first time in many months, afraid. He looked to Martin for a clue and searching his valet's face, who was unnaturally intent on the job at hand, suspected it was true. The tall bottle of red medicine on the dresser was also very telling. He felt slightly confused and a bit disoriented. He had to know for sure and knew the only way was to ask Martin who had been with him the entire day.

But a knock on the door prevented his pursuing the question. Martin placed a screen around him and went to answer the door. The hip tub had been placed in front of the fire where it was warm, too warm. The flames were high and beads of water glistened on his squarish face. He grabbed a small hand towel to wipe the perspiration from his face and the hairline of his thick, curly brown hair. His hands were shaky, more from fear, he knew, than anything else, and trying to ignore the unsteadiness, he used the towel briskly and donned his robe. He heard low voices and then the closing of the door.

Papers had been delivered by his secretary, and a footman had brought them to his room as directed.

"Put them by my bed, Martin. I'll look them over before retiring."

"Yes, m'lord. There was also word left by your secretary that the debating on compulsory education for all, was hostile through the day at the Lord's."

"I don't doubt it. Sorry to have missed it. I'll have a lot to add when I take up my own debate on Monday."

"Yes, m'lord," said Martin very proudly.

Lord Hatfield, who had just passed his forty-third birthday, was a prominent statesman, coming from a long line of Whigs that boasted members from the oldest and richest families of English nobility. It was from these Whigs that leading political figures and cabinet ministers had been drawn. His father had been an important member of Earl Grey's government in the thirties, formed mainly from the aristocracy, fighting as Jamie was now doing for social reforms. Oddly, it was the new peers who voted so hotly against reforms and who debated vehemently against Jamie and his group.

Martin approached him with the spoon and red medicine bottle. He started to question him, as he watched him turning the cap, but suddenly decided he would rather not know at this time.

A tall grandfather clock outside the drawing room struck the hour, seven o'clock. The downstairs rooms were still quiet, waiting, and the fog outside had luckily started to lift, the thick vapors turning to a hazy drizzle.

Vanessa moved down the curved staircase on cat's feet. She was dressed for the street in a protective rain cape and carried a large umbrella. When she reached the vestibule, she eased toward the outside door and prayed the butler wouldn't appear as he was likely to do—also on cat's feet—and greet her in his somewhat shrill voice. She was concerned her mother might be in the drawing room and on hearing her leaving would surely stop her from going alone, and Vanessa had to be by herself to collect her thoughts and feelings.

She opened the door furtively, ran down the steps into the bad weather that continued to plague London. Vanessa pulled the collar of her cape closer to her neck as she passed the garden and grounds of Buckingham Palace. The fog was moving in wet sheets. She lifted her head skyward to let the wetness fall on her face, the visibility was only a few yards in front of her, the street lights doing little good in the thick atmosphere. There wasn't a soul about, and she instinctively quickened her pace when she thought she heard footsteps behind her. She crossed the street hoping to find a residential or business area. The fog was moving in wet sheets. She lifted her head herself over these past four years to be strong, but tonight she was all fears again.

The cobblestones were wet and slippery under her high button boots as she started to run—almost falling, her sensitivities acute. Gratefully she heard the clop-clop of horse's hooves and moved quickly in that direction, trying not to slip again. She was in luck, it was a hansom carriage.

"Cabby," she yelled. "Cabby, over here."

A grumbling driver pulled over and bent down to open the cab door for her.

Once inside she felt safe from the outside environs; the smell of old leather and the scent of the horse was comforting—a remembrance. She snuggled into the corner and tried to calm herself, letting her mind flow freely. Her past upon her once again.

"Vanessa, slow down—I can hardly make out what you are saying. You always talk so fast."

"Can you believe, Momma, I hardly spoke at all at the Bonneaus, except of course when my head started to swim from the wine. But at one time, Pierre asked me if the cat had got my tongue."

Her sister, Amanda, hung on her every word. "Oh what's he like, Vanessa? Is he handsome like they say? You have all the luck—meeting a rich young man like that."

"He's the most handsome man I ever saw. And so sophisticated. You wouldn't believe he was an American. He seems more European."

"What would you expect? He lives over there all the time."

"Well, I hope you did yourself proud and acted the proper lady. Did he say he was going to stay here?"

"Longer than usual he said." She was bursting to tell them what she had locked inside her—his last words as they looked out at the sea—and in her impulsiveness, she burst forth with the news. "Momma, he said to me," and she slowed down on purpose so her sister, Amanda, and her mother would get the full impact. "He said, tell me, sweet child, are you old enough to be courted?"

Her mother stared at her in amazement. The very social and aloof Bonneaus—a family she had always held in awe. She looked at her rather overly tall, ungainly daughter and was puzzled. "Tell me again, but slowly, tell me what he said, Vanessa."

She swung around the room, picked up a pillow and tossed it in the air as she retold it all.

Amanda squealed joyously, knocking over the bolts of fabric they had been cutting into lots as Christmas gifts for the slaves. At fourteen, petite and starting to develop, she had many more young beaus calling on her than her older sister, but no one of the stature of Pierre Bonneau.

"Can you imagine, Momma! Vanessa with Pierre Bonneau?"

"When will this young man come calling? Did he say?"

"I don't know. Oh, Momma, suppose he doesn't come calling at all—supposin' he was only teasing me."

"Did he look serious when he said it? Or was he talking in jest?"

"I think it was serious, but I don't know—I was in such a confusion. Oh, Momma, how do I know about such things?"

"You should listen to me when I continuously talk about the proper way to behave when in the presence of a prospective suitor. Then you would know how to answer such questions. Now what did you say when he asked the question—are you old enough to be courted?"

"Nothing."

"Nothing?"

"For the first time in my life I was practically silent —almost the entire evening."

"You, Vanessa, why you never stop talking!" Amanda said, digging at her sister and smarting with jealousy.

"Hush, let me hear this. Amanda, not the better cotton for the hands—that goes to the house slaves. Mind what you're doing." She studied her oldest child. "Vanessa, you must have said something."

"Well, I did say my hands are too big from playing the piano and I'm too tall . . ."

"You're impossible, child. What things to say. Never draw attention to your defects. Dear, dear Vanessa, surely I've taught you better."

"Oh, I hope he liked me." In her heart she knew

she was in love—at least what she thought was love, but the sensation made her behave so differently than she normally did—not like her at all. It was all so confusing and delightfully frightening. "Last night was the most wonderful night of my life, but Harriet Bonneau scares me—she is so stern—doesn't appear to like anybody much excepting her son. Her eyes follow him everywhere."

"Oh, she bullies everybody. Don't let that worry you, but I wonder if she would approve of us?"

"Why not?" pouted Amanda, "we are rich, too."

"It's a different kind of rich, honey. We'll see. It may have all just been said in jest. Time will tell."

Amanda's eyes sparkled as she cut then tore a large piece of dull, heavy cotton from the bolt. "Isn't it strange to have a neighbor like Pierre Bonneau for all these years and never to have laid eyes on him before?"

"You haven't seen him as yet, you ninny, and when he comes to visit, don't you start with your flirting eyes."

Amanda started to chase Vanessa around the room putting Georgina into a nervous fluster.

"Stop it girls—you have got to start behaving like ladies all the time as you should. I just don't know what gets into the two of you."

They stood around her and both started to give her hard squeezes as they kissed her. "Stop, I can't breathe."

Vanessa's tall figure encompassed the tiny woman. "One more big hug, Momma, and then I'll act like a real proper Southern lady, I promise." But she immediately went back to her anxiety. "I hope he does come to call. Do you think he will?"

"I don't know, darling. We'll have to say our little prayers if that is what you want. My, I wish you would fill out a little—we'll have to work on it."

Their father, Kenneth McIver, came into the room with a copy of that day's Charleston *Mercury* and read them the editorial heading. "The tea has been thrown overboard, the revolution of 1860 has been initiated."

"Is it terrible in Charleston, Daddy?"

"On the contrary, Vanessa, our solicitor, who just left, reported that the city is in a holiday spirit—some businesses are closed and great crowds are milling about cheering the election of Lincoln."

"I don't understand," said Amanda as she ran to her father. "In school they told us Mr. Lincoln would destroy the South if elected and that his name wasn't even put on the ballot. Why is everyone so happy?"

"Because the decision has been clearly made for all. Compromise is no longer possible—the South will split from the North and become a nation on its own."

Georgina was becoming clearly annoyed by the discussion. "Well, I don't care about all these politics— it gives me a headache and anyway will it affect us?"

"Of course, it will affect us," Kenneth McIver said angrily. "Believe me, life will change a great deal."

"Your own brother, Thomas, says life will only be better. I tend to believe him, after all he is right there in the center of it all."

"He is in the center all right. I'm told he held court on election night at the bar of the Planters Hotel, chiding the Northerners, quoting Yancey about slavery. '. . . It's an institution that doesn't harm you people— we don't let our niggers run about to injure anybody— we keep them—take damn good care of them . . .' The man's a fool, even if he is my brother. He has already donned his old Virginia Military uniform and has openly sought support for a post with the future government."

A long silence filled the room—only the ticking of the grandfather clock in the hall and the sound of scissors cutting the fabric were heard.

Vanessa suddenly got up and crossed to the door. "I have to leave, Momma. I want to bring Granny Claire some pills the doctor gave me for her. I'll help you and Amanda later."

"It's all right, Vanessa—my back is tired. We'll finish tomorrow."

She watched her father for a moment from the door. He stood contemplatively in the center of the room and when he spoke so quietly, there was a great sadness in his voice.

"I left our new overseer settling up the end of the harvest count. I'll be home for an early supper."

She was out of the room before he finished, grabbing a shawl from the back hallway hook, eager to escape the gloom that had suddenly descended on them with the discussion of politics and possible civil war.

She ran along the path of crushed oyster shells leading to the slave quarters, her heels sending bits of shell flying at the turkeys in their cage at the corner of the vegetable garden, causing them to fly into balls of squabbling feathers.

The orange trees lining the quarters were bare now, and the houses were silent except for an occasional sound of an unseen broom fighting the endless battle with dust. She went to Granny Claire's house and saw her dozing in a rocker near a dying fire. The woman was hardly aware as Vanessa woke her gently to give her a pill and directions.

"Bless you, chile," she mumbled and fell back into a deep sleep, an easier look on her withered face. Vanessa left the bottle on the three-legged table next to the chair, hoping Granny would remember to take the medicine.

In the pasture, Jezebel, her horse, was kicking up his heels, nipping naughtily at the young foals grazing nearby. She called to him, and he ran at a fast gallop to the fence. Vanessa picked up the last of the fall apples from the ground and stood with him for a while using her fingers like a comb to straighten his mane, remembering their great adventure of yesterday in the fog and her meeting with Pierre Bonneau. Finally, she gave the horse a swat sending him back to his frivolous play and started home on the same route she came. Her pace slowed as she passed the overseer's house. The interior seemed dark. The porch overhang kept light from passing through the two windows on either side of the flimsy door that had blown open in the blustery weather. Why did she feel such a curiosity about Kirk Yoors—overseers were just overseers, not at all involved in her life directly.

A broken flower pot lay on the ground under his open window, and Vanessa took advantage of this excuse to enter the house. It was McIver property after all. And anyway, it was midday—he would be working with her father until well into the night, so there was no chance of being discovered. She picked up the pot and entered the house. Her eyes adjusted to the darkness. It was starkly furnished with just a chair, a table and, in a corner, a simple, large wooden desk with a hurricane reading lamp. Overflowing from the desk onto the floor

was a stack of books. One was lying open on top.
Vanessa moved to the book and peeked at it. Her mouth
dropped open. It was a picture of a naked woman. She
quickly averted her eyes only to encounter large
diagrams of a naked man and woman tacked over his
desk. She stepped back—shocked by the possible
salacious meaning of the drawings, anxious now to get
out of there as quickly as possible. She spun around and
bumped squarely into Kirk Yoors, who had entered the
room silently.

"Oh, you frightened me! What are you doing here?"

"It is my home, Miss McIver. I have a right to enter
when I please."

"Well, I wasn't intruding—I only came in to leave this
plant that had fallen to the ground outside your house."

"Did you enjoy browsing through my books?" He
flipped the open one shut.

At the mention of the books, she blushed. "I hardly
glanced at them—I was looking for a place to put this
down." Now she was getting angry—angry with herself
for intruding into his private life and angry with him
for not letting her exit gracefully. She felt cornered—
suddenly he approached her. Frightened by his move
and the look in his eyes, she swung around, moving
backward toward the front door, trying to maneuver herself to a position to run if necessary and at the same
time thrust the plant at him or fling it if necessary. But
her back hit the door, and a human skeleton hit her
shoulder and grazed her breast. A cry of fright sprang
from her lips as she jumped forward in fright, the pot
dropping from her hands.

"You are the most peculiar man I've ever met, keeping obscene drawings and human bones hanging about."
With that she dashed out the door and ran toward the
manor house. Kirk Yoors shouted after her, "When you
intrude on someone's privacy, Miss McIver, you must be
prepared for the worst!"

3

Amanda McIver, twenty-two, and as beautiful as a little china doll, walked slowly through the dining room. She was delighted with the exquisite silver, china, and glassware gleaming on the highly polished tables. She swirled one way and then another, trying to take it all in. Her violet eyes sparkled—it was as if all before her were Christmas toys waiting to be played with. She slowly moved to the far end of the room and passed through heavily carved mahogany doors into the glass-walled conservatory.

She was not aware that Hatfield stood on the threshold of the room and was admiring her graceful, diminutive figure. He watched her clap her hands softly as she surveyed her surroundings and smiled broadly as she furtively plucked a gardenia.

"Ouch," his voice mocked painfully.

She spun around and was doubly startled when she saw it was Lord Hatfield. But then she saw the broad, playful smile, and she relaxed as she coyly flirted:

"I just had to have the little ole flower for my hair, sir."

"The flower will not do your beautiful hair justice, mademoiselle. I regret there are not white orchids to adorn your blond curls."

"White orchids? Oh, sir, you turn my head with your compliment."

They eyed each other silently, Hatfield trying not to stare too openly at the ripe breasts pushed almost over the edge of her bodice and the full, cherry red lips now in a pout, just perfect to be kissed. Amanda in turn could not help but admire his well-built body easily defined in the snug-fitting trousers and long cutaway jacket. It always amazed her a man of his age could be so appealing. It was also his power and the way he gave orders which were so quickly obeyed, that impressed and excited her.

Suddenly embarrassed by her thoughts, Amanda said in a rush, "Vanessa has already left for the hall."

"Has she? I'm sorry I missed her. I wanted to wish her well. Perhaps I can go backstage before the recital and see her."

"Oh, she doesn't like that," Amanda said quickly. Too quickly. "Only her maid and manager are allowed. Something to do with internal preparations before she plays. Poor dear is such a slave to her music." She had said it with a smile on her lips and her eyes batting in a charming fashion, but he could read a bit of jealousy into it.

"Well, I shall have to wait to see her afterward. There is so much I have to learn about the McIvers—so much, their likes and dislikes. Our acquaintance has been so short, but where the affairs of the heart are concerned, time is irrelevant."

"So true, Jamie, so true."

She is a flirt he thought. "You look very lovely tonight, Amanda. That gown is very becoming indeed." Georgina had discreetly asked for a loan for clothing for the family, and he felt, looking at the effect in front of him, that she had spent the money well. The pale pink and violet dress was just right for Amanda's pale blond beauty.

Forgotten were the fears he had had just a short while before. The potion had calmed him, so he was relaxed and feeling in good spirits once again. The medicine sometimes made him feel drowsy and lethargic, so he didn't like to take it before an important occasion, but tonight the effect was pleasant and reassuring.

Kenneth McIver entered the empty library and poured himself a stiff whiskey. He was uncomfortable in the new evening clothes Georgina had the English tailor make for him. Men's clothes in London had taken a turn for the worse, in his opinion, and the new cutaway jacket that was *de rigueur* here was not to his taste.

He made a concession in ordering his other new suits in somber colors—black and gray or heavy brown tweeds, shunning the brighter and lighter colors popular in the South, hoping she would understand that he wanted to make things right again, and this was a good way to start to repair their uneasy relationship and begin anew.

Now that the plantation was becoming livable again and finances were improving, he was anxious to have members of his family home once more, but was aware that he would have to take time in wooing them back. But, God, he wanted the empty rooms filled with their life. Josiah, his son, who was nineteen, was no more ready to take on learning to run a plantation than Georgina was ready to pick up their life together. Tomorrow he would spend all day with his son to try and interest him in the plans he and his brother, Thomas, had for the McIver land and business back home. He really needed the injection of strength and enthusiasm that the young man could bring into his life.

He took a good look at himself in a long mirror, not displeased with the figure he cut. His face had color from the Southern sun and the long boat trip, which eased the lines of age and trouble. His sandy-colored hair had just begun to thin a bit on top, but was still full, framing his face. At forty-eight he was in good shape, but then life these last years had not been sedentary. In a moment of quick vanity, he thought he might even look as young as his future son-in-law.

The only defect his body suffered was the angry red scar that ran on the outside of his right leg from his knee to his foot. For weeks he had been in danger of losing that leg, but even more painful than the wound and the pain it caused him on occasion, was the memory of those last days of the Confederacy. He still suffered frequent nightmares in which he relived the hours spent lying on his stomach in the mud, immobile—his leg slashed by a Yankee sword. Only the dense thicket that hid him, saved him from another Union sword. He was lucky to be alive.

"Good evening, Kenneth."

He turned to face his wife and was pleasantly jolted. She looked beautiful, the peacock blue velvet gown com-

plimented her eyes and showed off her still tiny waist
and full desirable breasts. He liked the way she had
piled her pale blond hair on top of her head. There
was no sign of gray yet or lines, and if someone had
to guess her age, he was certain they would make her
out to be ten years younger. Still a Southern belle, although one fighting desperately to regain some position.
Her manner was anxious, and in deference, he let her
prattle on nervously while he drained his glass and poured
himself another drink.

". . . Jefferson Davis is living in London—has been for
several years and Judah Benjamin has a law practice
here, but I understand his wife lives in Paris. Isn't that
strange?" She caught herself and didn't pursue their living
in different countries any further. As she turned to the
window, her back to him, he noticed the long single
finger curl that fell from the coronet down to her
shoulders. After a moment she said, "Many Southerners
have made their home in England since the war."

"Have you seen Jefferson and Varina? I understand
he is having a difficult time trying to do business over
here."

"I haven't seen them at all. How could I when I
was shabby and living in that tiny house? The last few
years have just been dreadful. We've been poor as church
mice."

"I sent you what I could."

She didn't know how dismal it had been for him
during that time back in South Carolina. The labor from
sun-up to sun-down with precious little to eat.

"But Hatfield will straighten out our lives, won't he,"
he added snidely.

For the first time since she came into the library
and saw him standing at the fireplace sipping the lord's
very fine whiskey, she showed a spark of life and
enthusiasm as she turned to face him. "Let's be thankful,
Kenneth, and not act like he is some kind of poisonous
snake, as you are wont to do since your arrival."

"The expression is snake in the grass."

"Kenneth, stop it. You have been behaving uncivilly to
Lord Hatfield."

"My God, Georgina, he's an old man."

"He's exactly my age, Kenneth, and four years younger than you. Do you feel like an old man?"

"I'm not about to marry a girl in her twenties."

She turned to the window again as she spoke, "I'm sure you would if you could. I never was aware of your taking a middle-aged woman to your bed."

It was out, the first time she had ever spoken of his amorous dalliances. What could he say? You were always too stiff when I made love to you, enduring, until it was over—never yielding to my kisses and desires. Good God, Georgina, he wanted to say to her, I had to find satisfaction somewhere. Since his arrival a week ago, they slept in the same bed, but she kept her back to him. He pulled himself up to his full height. "All right, I can't stop the wedding, but I'm not for it." He took a long sip of his drink. "When I leave here for home after the wedding, I expect you and Josiah to return with me. I am tired of being without my family."

She made no response.

"Did you hear me, Georgina?"

"I heard you. I was thinking about my answer."

"And that is?"

"I don't think I'll be ready to return just after the wedding," she said quietly but firmly. "It will be too soon."

"Too soon? May I know why you say that? You've been here almost five years."

"My children are here, Kenneth, and they need me."

"And your husband doesn't?"

"He never seemed to before."

"Things change, Georgina. Haven't you heard a wife's place is with her husband?"

"Can't you stay in England longer?" she said rather tightly.

"No. With the traveling and the time I am spending here as it is it will mean that I will have been gone from the farm for over two months." He could swear the way her shoulders relaxed, she was obviously relieved he would have to leave right after the wedding.

"Are they called farms now instead of plantations?"

"Yes, they are. Would you mind looking at me? I'm getting tired of talking to your back."

"It seems a shame you can't stay on longer. After all,

you've only been here twice during the four years and such short visits. It takes a bit to get reacquainted."

Now his voice was strained as he spoke. "Before those four years we were married over twenty. How much reacquainting do we need?"

The fire hissed then crackled, sending angry sparks against the screen. A silent, grim-looking footman wheeled in a cart with a large cut glass decanter and a silver salver holding finger sandwiches.

After the footman left, Georgina ran to the cart happily. "Jamie is so thoughtful. This looks divine."

"Yes, divine," he said as he poured another drink for himself. His sarcasm was lost on Georgina as he added, "Jamie Hatfield is a prince of a fellow."

"You should see what has been planned for the reception."

"A large gathering?"

"Oh, yes."

"Then I don't suppose Hatfield will mind if Thomas brings a guest with him, a lady guest."

"Of course not. What difference will one more guest make in such a big house?"

"Not to say our Southern hospitality still reigns even if three thousand miles away," he retorted.

"Won't Jefferson and Varina be surprised when they see all of this. I sent invitations to other old Southern friends to come to the reception. Kenneth, we should be so happy tonight, not let anything spoil it. Who is Thomas bringing with him?"

She didn't wait for an answer, but continued in a happy rush. "I was so surprised when Thomas got off the boat. Of course, I know I invited him for the recital and then the wedding, but I just somehow never expected him to come."

"He's my brother."

"I know. You don't have to remind me."

"Why didn't you invite him and Josiah to stay here? You said Hatfield offered for all of us to stay at this house."

"He did. And it was terribly sweet of him. But Thomas has always been so disruptive in the past and from what I've seen of him since his arrival, he hasn't changed much. Still fighting the Civil War."

"It's a hard thing to forget, Georgina, and I would have liked my son closer to me."

"They are better off in the house in Chelsea. This way they are free to come and go as they please."

"What would they have been here? Prisoners?"

She went over to the cart and started to daintily munch on a finger sandwich. "Who did you say Thomas is bringing with him? Some lady he met since he arrived?"

"Not exactly. But it is someone from home."

She was all attention now. "Who? One of the ladies from Charleston?"

"Yes and no. She sometimes lives in Charleston. It's an old friend that came over on the boat with us. A neighbor from St. Helena."

"Harriet Bonneau!"

"You guessed it."

"That woman will not enter my house!"

"This is not your house, Georgina, and Thomas had asked her before consulting me. She is also to be at the recital."

"Well, you'll just have to tell him to take her some place else, I will not allow her here. How could you, after all that has happened. And with Vanessa! Why did you wait till now to tell me?"

"I didn't know you were going to have such a violent reaction. She did, after all, lend the money to get McIver Hall started again. Whether you like it or not, she has been our benefactress since the end of the war. Not with the most grace, I will admit, but when Thomas and I had nowhere else to turn, she came through—giving just exactly what we needed to barely survive at that point. So, I don't see how we can turn her out tonight."

"You never told me of her lending us money."

"I wanted to spare you the pain of what I was going through trying to rebuild a life for us back home."

He recalled in a graphic flash his return to McIver Hall after the war. Broken in spirit, still suffering from fever due to his leg injury, he was expecting the worst. He had heard the house had been destroyed. With dread, he and Thomas arrived early one misty morning and elatedly thought the information had been untrue. For down the long, overgrown live-oak avenue stood their home, their haven, seeming to be intact, but as they got closer, he saw the hazy morning had played a cruel trick on him, for much of the house was a mere shell, a rotted ruin. Old servants who still lived there came to greet them politely but coldly, informing they were freedmen now and the small crops they had planted on the land by rights belonged to them and not the McIvers. He knew they feared he and Thomas would try to become masters again. One toothless old man, a field hand ever since Kenneth could remember, yelled he had lived all his life with a cotton basket on his head and now that he was freed he would not put it on again. There was fright on both parts.

The biggest shock was when he and Thomas found out they had returned to the sea island just a day away from a final tax auction for their property. Penniless, with a rich Northerner's agent ready to bid on their home and land, they were in a panic—everything seemed lost. It was then that he and Thomas begged Harriet Bonneau's help. After hours of entreating her to the point of exhaustion, she lent them just enough to pay the taxes. They knew she only did it finally because she didn't want a Northerner for a neighbor. Her house and land had fared better, and she had no money problems. She had lost a lot, of course, but hers was old family money, invested wisely through the years in the North as well as the South, with large holdings in England. Paying the taxes was only the beginning for the brothers. The fields, acres upon acres, were a jungle of dank growth. Credit was prohibitive. Most were asking a fifty percent lien on a crop. Thomas had gone begging again to Harriet. Whatever he did, he got her to lend more money. However, she doled out pennies. But with it they started on a small scale, arduously doing work they were not used to, with little or no help. They slowly restored the land, the house partially, and brought in bigger and bigger crops each year, but still with small profit if any. As yet, they had not repaid Harriet, but Kenneth felt in a few more years, they would have some firm stability again and be able to pay back her loans.

Georgina was still talking, words spewing out as sharply as before. "I will not have it. I'll turn my back on Harriet Bonneau if she sets foot in the door."

"Georgina, she can call in the loan if she wants and take our land if she so wishes."

"Let her. We can live here."

"Georgina!" He was furious.

"That woman has been in London many times and always sent notes asking—asking hysterically, if we had seen or heard from Pierre. Why on earth would she think we would see or hear from him?"

"That's why she is here now. She received a letter from someone saying Pierre was living just outside of London. Has Vanessa heard from him?"

"Of course not! Why should she hear from that person?"

"A lot happened between them—"

"Please, don't bring that up. And I beg you, Kenneth, keep Harriet Bonneau away from me. Keep them both away from me. Stop her from coming here tonight."

He started to speak when Amanda swept into the room followed by Lord Hatfield. She was glowing and embraced her mother.

"Jamie and I have just had the most divine conversation in the conservatory. He knows so much about plants and flowers, Mama, and he's going to teach me."

Kenneth, still agitated from his discussion with Georgina, burned at the sight of the handsome lord, and mumbled under his breath "snake in the grass." He was certain that Hatfield was an expert in the teaching of the flowers and the bees to young girls.

The sign over the fancy shop said: SILLAR'S—French Millinery. It was located on the street floor of a small Italian styled house off Portman's Square in the center of London. Sillar, a well-known designer among the upper middle class and nobility, was just about to close when she had an idea that pleased her and sent for one of her salesclerks to carry it out.

"Denise, on your way home, would you mind delivering a package for me? It will not be out of your way—backstage at the concert hall off Piccadilly."

Denise assured her it would be no problem as she went right past the hall after she got off the omnibus and she would love to go backstage. She confided she had never seen that section of a theater in her life.

Her employer grinned, telling her she may get no further than the stage door man, but she could try.

Sillar had been deeply affected when she saw Vanessa McIver's picture in the paper a few days ago with the announcement that she was to give a performance in London and now that recital was tonight. How far Vanessa had come she had thought, and after all that had happened. Sillar hadn't seen any of the McIvers for almost five years. Taken for a Spaniard, an aristocratic one at that, the very fashionable woman was actually a black with Creek Indian blood—at one time a McIver slave. She had been sent along with the family to England, by Kenneth, for safety near the end of the war on the eve of the fall of Charleston. Georgina McIver had been furious when Sillar had been forced on her. She knew she had been her husband's bedwench for several years, and Sillar knew she knew. When she saw Vanessa's picture, she wondered immediately if Kenneth were in London. Her thoughts had been of him almost constantly since seeing the announcement—surprised that he would still have that effect on her. When she saw the young black behind Vanessa in the picture, she was also touched —dear JoJo. She knew she must be about eighteen now and still with her beloved mistress, Vanessa. The present she was sending was for JoJo, a black orphan from birth, who was always so afraid as a youngster, always giggling to cover her nervousness. She pulled herself out of her reverie and saw Denise waiting for further instructions.

"That hat I designed today—the apple green velvet with the plaid ribbons and bows . . ."

"Yes, Miss Sillar. The one you made especially for Lady Manley, one of the queen's ladies-in-waiting. It is ready. We are going to deliver it in the morning."

"No. That is the one you will deliver to the concert hall tonight."

"But Miss Sillar . . ."

"No *but*'s about it. We will make a copy for Lady Manley tomorrow."

"A copy for her? You know how she is. Suppose the two ladies meet wearing the same hat?"

Sillar threw her head back and laughed heartily at the idea. "If these two ladies meet wearing the same hat, I am sure one would giggle and the other would faint dead away."

The hat was put into a purple and white striped band box with the name SILLAR emblazoned in deep red. She quickly wrote a note, attached it, and Denise sped away.

Sillar went up the stairs to her private rooms above the shop and thought of getting dressed for the recital. She noticed it was just a little after seven, and she had an hour before her wealthy patron would arrive to escort her to the hall. She poked up the fire in her drawing room, sat in the silk velvet bergère chair close to the fireplace and stared into the flames.

A young maid in a heavily starched uniform stood respectfully near her for a moment without speaking, not wanting to disturb her thoughts. Then quietly, most respectfully, she interrupted. "Ma'am?"

"Yes, Clara." Sillar answered just as quietly.

"Shall I start bringing the hot water up for your bath?"

"Oh, I guess it is time. And Clara, place the tub near the fireplace in my bedroom. The night has become very chilly."

"Yes, ma'am."

Sillar turned back to the flames, but Clara did not leave. Timidly she started again.

"Begging your pardon, ma'am. Nanny said to tell you young Master Kenneth is asking for you to come up to his room. He says he wants his mommie to tell him a story before she leaves for the evening . . . a Bray Rabbit story."

Sillar's voice sounded as if it came from a long distance.

"Brer Rabbit," she corrected.

"Yes, ma'am."

"Folk stories of the South," she said as she looked at Clara absently, and then realizing the young woman didn't understand, she explained, "the South in the United States."

"Oh." And quickly in a rush of pride, "Master Kenneth is so bright. Wherever did he learn of stories about the South—in the United States no less, and him being only four years old?"

"You had better start bringing up the water, Clara."

"Yes ma'am. Right away." She left the room immediately, leaving Sillar with her thoughts and a broad smile on her beautiful face. Where did little Kenneth learn of the South, indeed. But it was strange, she reflected, that of all the stories she told him he loved the Brer Rabbit stories best of all. She wondered if his father, Kenneth McIver, would ever tell him a story, and if he did, what kind of a story would it be. She looked around the room, feeling as usual, deep pleasure: the fine Aubusson rug on the highly polished parquet flooring was a treasure, and the carefully selected early Chippendale furniture that filled the drawing room—perfect in her eyes. She questioned herself if it had been wise to ask her patron, the Duke of Blamford, to take her to the recital tonight. He was so clever, always seeing through any game she ever tried to play. If she and Kenneth met, would Blamford see? She knew now that what she had felt for Kenneth in the past, a powerful, overwhelming love, was still there. Buried, but smoldering strongly.

She climbed the stairs to the nursery on the third floor, still deep in thought, noticing all that she had attained. Evidence of the duke's wealth and influence was everywhere and especially in her demeanor. She now spoke two foreign languages, French and Spanish, fluently, and her English was smoothed and perfected. She was well-read and mixed easily with London society. Kenneth must never know that she bore him a son. At the door to the nursery, she stopped and studied little Kenneth from afar. With his very proper nanny at his shoulder, he stood at an easel blackboard trying to write the letters of the alphabet. He was a child who had an enormous curiosity about everything and was always eager to learn something new. The chalk squeaked harshly as little Kenneth pushed it laboriously up and down the board trying to form the letters properly.

"Bonsoir, mon tresor," said Sillar.

Running to his mother gleefully, he easily answered, "Bonsoir, Maman cherie," adding quickly, "tell me a story, a story of Uncle Remus. Nanny will bring us cookies and milk. Won't you Nanny?"

The woman looked at the small boy who was beaming with pleasure at having his mother close. Her heart melted. She could refuse him very little, and she went for the

cookies and milk. Sillar picked up her son and held
him high over her head as he squealed with delight.
Then she placed him on her hip and carried him to
the rocking chair near the window. She thought, I'm
carrying him just like an old mammy would. Little Kenneth also laughed. He loved his mother; she was always
so much fun to be with, she roughhoused him, tickled
him, and he loved to sit on her lap as she told him
marvelous stories.

JoJo had never seen so many flowers before a recital
or notes of good wishes, but then previous engagements
had been in much smaller out of the way halls where
they rarely knew anyone. As she waited for Vanessa's
arrival, she picked up a copy of Dickens' *A Christmas
Carol;* she was reading the story again because of the
approaching season and it was one of her favorite books.
Vanessa had given it to her two Christmases before while
they were in Rome. She had worked so hard at learning
to read, with Vanessa constantly pushing her to improve.
Now she loved to submerge herself in a good book.

There was a knock on the dressing room door, and
the stage door man handed her a round hat box with
a note. Her hands trembled when she noticed the name
"JoJo" written on the envelope. She quickly opened it,
being careful not to make the flap ragged and read the
message carefully.

"My dear JoJo. I was so happy when I saw your
beautiful face in the newspaper photograph standing next
to your Nessa. You've grown and changed into the lovely
young woman I knew you would turn out to be. Now
the pet name JoJo, that Nessa gave you, no longer seems
to suit you. I shall look for you backstage after the
recital this evening, my dear friend Jassime. I have
changed a lot too, so I hope you will recognize your
old friend—Sillar."

"Oh Sillar, my dear friend."

JoJo picked up the hat box and loosened the strings.
She squealed in delight when she saw the beautiful hat.
Sillar had sent her the most wonderful gift she had
ever received. Jassime, yes. That had been her name before
Vanessa changed it. She hadn't thought of her real name
for so long. It all seemed so long ago.

She was standing on the second-story veranda, nine years old, giggling and jumping up and down as she watched her new mistress walk through the gardens with Pierre Bonneau. Vanessa looked so demure and collected. Just a few minutes before, Vanessa had come into the bedroom out of breath, grabbed her by the arms and swung her in a wide circle as she told her to get out her prettiest afternoon dress. Pierre Bonneau, she announced grandly, had come to call.

"I was walking past the parlor and I almost died," she said excitedly. "Sitting there, talking to mama and Amanda was Pierre, asking where I was. Hurry, JoJo, get my lavender muslin dress. I peeked through the crack in the door and saw my sister making cow eyes at him."

JoJo quickly went about pulling down the dress and stiff petticoats and waist cincher, jumping up numerous times to reach the items hanging in the tall armoire, for she was small for her age. Vanessa stripped frantically, tossing her clothing all over the room. The black child giggled harder each time she jumped for each article.

Breathlessly, Vanessa also giggled. "JoJo, you're the happiest child I ever did see. Why are you giggling all the time?"

"I ain' happy, mistress, I jes' laughs . . ."

JoJo had only been given to Vanessa two weeks before for her seventeenth birthday. Vanessa had told her several times that she had looked over all the slave children very carefully and finally spotted her, attracted to her large, twinkling brown eyes, and flat button nose. She had first seen the frail girl in the slave nursery where JoJo had been tending newborn babies with several old slave women who were no longer capable of working in the fields. JoJo had clapped and danced like a gazelle when told she was to live in the big house, learn fine manners, and "spek correct like white folks an' tak care of the yung mist'ess."

An orphan since birth, never knowing the touch of love, she had so hated living in the filthy cabin with the old women. Her constant fear after coming to the big house was that she wouldn't please and be sent back to that dirty cabin. There was so much to learn and Mrs. McIver was so demanding.

Finally Vanessa was freshly attired and staring in the mirror.

JoJo giggled as she studied her mistress. "Oh Miz Nessa, you is so beautiful . . ."

"Are you sure, JoJo? I'm so scared. I look terrible to myself." She walked around the room like a caged lion, fighting for composure. "My heart feels like it will burst right out of my chest. Oh, JoJo. He is so elegant . . . what if I make a fool of myself when I talk or walk—I could trip and fall on my face."

"You'll do jes' fine, Miz Nessa . . . jes' fine . . . he's gonna love you a lot."

"How can he love me? He has fine ladies all over Europe. Well, here goes." Pinching her cheeks hard, she suddenly flew out of the room.

JoJo giggled hard at Vanessa's happiness and then started the task of cleaning up the room that was now in complete disarray. It was during her folding and making a bundle of the soiled clothing that she had stepped out on the veranda to watch her mistress and the awesome Mr. Bonneau. She ran back into the room to finish her work, as she heard Mrs. McIver giving sharp orders to Sillar the house slave, who was also the seamstress. She became anxious and tried desperately to reach the hangers to quickly put away her mistress' dress, wanting the room to look neater, and decided to stand on a small French chair. She was giggling nervously and straightening the pretty dresses in the closet when Mrs. McIver entered the room. She screeched at her for standing on the antique chair, scolding her so hard that JoJo's giggles turned to sobs and caught in her throat. As the severe tongue-lashing continued, big glistening tears ran down her face and her lower lip started to quiver uncontrollably.

"This child will go back to the fields or wherever she came from if she doesn't learn more quickly." Then she turned on her heels and left in disgust.

Sillar had been behind Mrs. McIver when she came into Vanessa's bedroom and remained after the lady of the house stormed out.

She tried to console JoJo, wiping away her tears with her finger, flinging one big one into the air.

"Go away, tear. We wan' only happiness here."

The child still continued to sob, not being able to control her crying, the corners of her mouth turned way down.

"Why Jassime, honey, you stop that crying. You Miz Nessa's pet."

"JoJo," the small child corrected.

"JoJo. What kind of name is that, suga?"

"Miz Ness geb me a new name."

"How come JoJo, chile? Why she named you dat?"

As the tears continued and little choked sobs were making it hard for her to catch her breath, she managed, "Cause I be so happy all de time. My mistress sez I be like a JoJo."

Sillar threw back her head and laughed.

"Honey, you is the most miserable looking happy person I ever did see! Get yerself a stool from the yard for when you have to stand on somethin', chile, and den yo worries will be over."

"Sometimes I knows I'll never learn how to be a house nigger. I jes' got no brains."

"JoJo, if you get confused you come runnin' to Sillar, and I'll help you learn how to get around."

"Oh thank you, Sillar, all I wants is to learn how to take care of Miz Nessa."

"Sweet JoJo, some day you'll want more and when that happens you will want to be called Jassime again."

"Oh no, Sillar, I likes the name JoJo."

"We'll see."

Vanessa came into the dressing room and saw JoJo sitting at the dressing table trying on the hat. She watched her reflection in the mirror, the small shining face all smiles as she turned first one way and then another. She hadn't heard Vanessa come in and Vanessa kept quiet enjoying JoJo's pleasure as she studied herself in the glass.

When she turned for a profile view, JoJo saw Vanessa out of the corner of her eye and ran to her, soft giggles coming from her throat. "Look at the present I got. Isn't it something?"

"It's beautiful," said Vanessa as she took off her rain-cape and hung it on the clothes tree. "It's one of the prettiest hats I've ever seen. Did you get it from a beau?"

"Oh, Nessa, you're always joshing me. Where would I get a beau? It's from Sillar." Vanessa looked at her puzzled and JoJo added excitedly, "Our Sillar. The seamstress from back home."

"Of course. Sillar. She made the hat?"

JoJo ran for the box and showed it to Vanessa proudly. "See. Doesn't that mean she is the owner of the shop?"

"It certainly does. My. I've heard of that place. But I never connected . . ."

"She made something of herself. I'm so proud. She was just a slave like me." JoJo held her head high and pranced around the room. "I'm gonna get me a fancy dress to go with my new 'chapeaux.'" Her black button eyes were twinkling and her arms outstretched as she strutted and swung herself around laughing happily. "It makes me feel so good to have this fancy pot on my head."

Vanessa was caught up in her gaiety and was laughing, too. "It's really a hat fit for a princess."

JoJo stopped, all concern, and went to Vanessa. "Oh Nessa, excuse me for getting excited. I was just so surprised to hear from Sillar and get a package addressed especially to me. It's the first time ever." She took off the hat quickly and carefully placed it in the box. "You got to rest and be quiet before you play."

"No. Don't apologize, JoJo. I would also be excited to get a gift like that and especially to hear from Sillar. I often wondered what happened to her."

"She says she saw our picture in the paper."

Her too, thought Vanessa. Someone else has also reentered our lives through that picture she wanted to tell JoJo, but it was all too personal as yet.

Vanessa dropped tiredly on the chaise. There was a small pillow propped against the back and an afghan was folded back. It was a lovely coverlet, one she and JoJo had made together during their travels. Each one making squares of various colors until they had enough, and one whole day on a train between Rome and Geneva they spent the hours putting the small squares together. Both treasured the woolly afghan, and it went wherever they did. JoJo was at her side immediately, bending down to help Vanessa take off her boots and then her dress. She got a woolen wrap for her and made her a cup of tea on the gas burner in the dressing room. Vanessa leaned back on the chaise sipping the tea as she prepared to rest before the performance. JoJo covered her with the treasured afghan and said quietly, "Sillar is coming to the recital. Isn't that wonderful, Nessa? I can hardly wait to see her."

"Nor I. What a reunion this is turning out to be."

"She must be some grand lady to own a shop like that."

"Maybe someday you'll own a shop . . ."

"Me? Why would I want to do that? I work for a pianist."

Vanessa put down the cup and took the soft, small hand in hers, holding it for a long moment, both women looking deep into each other's eyes. How far they had come together. And now, thought Vanessa, their journey together could be over, a turning point was here, and she didn't know her path. But JoJo had a life of her own to live and someday soon she should live it. She smiled and JoJo smiled back. A love so deep and strong was there, a tie so binding. Sometimes Vanessa felt the eighteen-year-old JoJo was her child in many ways, and beyond a dear, dear friend. The hours Vanessa practiced in various cities, with JoJo sitting in a corner mending or crocheting. The shopping she did in the strange towns, bringing back food to their small hotel room to cook or heat on crude burners to save money. The fears they shared while they waited for some word in small cities by critics or hall owners who felt a woman shouldn't be a pianist in public to begin with. The cold they felt on drafty day coaches, in second rate rooming houses, or shabby hotels. She is such a part of me, thought Vanessa.

"Did you notice all the flowers, Nessa?"

"Yes, they are so beautiful. I'll look at them more closely when I get up later." She didn't expect flowers from him . . . they cost so much. Vanessa leaned back and shortly after, saw JoJo slip out of the room. She tried to force all else out of her mind except sleep, or at least quiet rest, relaxing her neck, then her shoulders, her hands—beginning to feel drowsy and comfortable.

JoJo was outside the dressing room, putting on her cloak and gloves. She was going to leave the theater and go down the street to the fish and chips place to have her dinner. Vanessa never ate before she played, but JoJo thought that tonight she would bring her back some cookies in case she wanted just a snack with a cup of tea. JoJo froze when she approached the stage door and saw Harriet Bonneau arguing with the doorman. "Oh, no," she uttered under her breath. That woman must not be allowed to go to Vanessa's room before the recital. What is that horrid woman doing in London anyway? She didn't know exactly what she was going to do because she had always been terrified of the woman, but she had to do something.

George, the stage doorman, saw JoJo approaching. "This lady here says she is related to Miss McIver and wants to see her."

JoJo girded herself and in bold tones she had never before used to speak to a white person, scolded George. "You know Miss McIver has a rule of no visitors before a concert. Her manager, Mr. Bronsky, is gonna be very upset with you." Then turning to Harriet Bonneau, "I'm sorry, ma'am, but Miss McIver can see no one now."

Harriet would not be dissuaded however. "Girl, you just take me to her room. She'll want to see me. In case you don't remember, I am Harriet Sims Bonneau."

JoJo was trembling inside and at first her words were shaky. "Miss Vanessa tells me every time, 'JoJo, I don't care who it is, even if the queen comes 'round, you tell her I don't see no one before I play.'"

"You stop this nonsense and take me to Miss McIver immediately, you impudent girl."

JoJo placed herself directly in Harriet's path, pulling herself up to her full height and putting her hands on her hips. There was no doubt in Harriet's mind that the only way to pass JoJo would be to physically push her aside.

"If you were back home this behavior would never be tolerated."

In a mocking tone, she answered the imperious woman. "Mrs. Bonneau, we niggers have been taught one thing by you white folks: do what the master says no matter what. My mistress tell me no one comes to see her before she plays. That's my duty, and I'm gonna makes sure I obey her."

As Harriet spun on her heel heading for the door, she frustratedly shouted out, "You make sure your mistress knows I was here."

The door slammed shut, George turned to JoJo just in time to help her collapse into a chair. "You sure are something, JoJo. I never knew you had such spunk."

"I needs to sit in this chair a second—my spunk just up and run out."

Harriet was angry and confused as she stumbled to a carriage to take her back to her hotel. She hated to lose, and when she alighted from the hansom cab, she pushed open the hotel door, leaving the startled doorman thinking that this lack of decorum was what Londoners had come to expect as typical behavior from Americans.

Harriet went immediately to her bedroom—this misery—she shook her head trying to stop herself from being so overcome emotionally. It had been getting worse and worse since her arrival.

"Oh my God," she sighed as she recalled that sunny day in June. With Pierre there was so much hope and love and joy. She lay back on the bed and closed her eyes, trying to remember happier times.

Harriet woke on that special morning, June 13, 1861, the servants in her home in Charleston were already stirring. As she lay in bed the slight breeze from the harbor gently moved against her bedroom curtains. She felt like a bit of a fool lazing on this day, humming a tune that went with the spirit of the occasion.

Dinah tapped on her door and came in with the light breakfast Harriet always expected.

"My, my, Mistress Bonneau, you is happy. I haven't heard you singing a tune in a dog's age."

"Dinah, I swear this morning the garden flowers smell sweeter and the birds are chirping more melodically than I've ever heard them."

"Why anyone would think you was the bride."

"I guess I am being a bit foolish today, but I don't care. I can't remember being this happy since my own wedding."

Dinah drew back the curtains and busied herself about the room listening to the lady of the house go on about her excitement.

As the day progressed it grew stifling hot, weather every Charlestonian came to expect for that time of year. However, midafternoon surprisingly brought a lovely breeze off the waters surrounding the city, cooling the air, a welcoming comfort to the guests starting for St. Michael's Church for the 4:00 o'clock wedding.

Pierre came out of his room ready to leave for the church and was surprised to see his mother in the hall waiting for him.

How like his father he looked she thought, especially today.

"As I see you standing there, I can only think how proud your father would have been—he couldn't have asked for a better son and heir."

"You embarrass me, my dear mother."

"Well, you've made me very happy. I've dreamed so long of the day you would take a wife and settle down here. To show you how pleased I am, I want you to give Vanessa the pin your father gave me on our wedding day." She could see the emerald and diamond brooch had the effect she hoped it would on Pierre.

"It is very thoughtful of you and a beautiful gesture. I know Vanessa will be pleased, knowing this symbolizes your acceptance of her. So, there will be a new Mistress Bonneau."

Her heart skipped a beat, the thought that someone else was to be called Mistress Bonneau, a name she alone had carried so proudly for so long, stung, and a quick feeling of resentment toward Vanessa rose in her.

She gave Pierre a small hug, trying to shake off her pique, and she attributed his coolness to the normal groom's nerves. He took her arm formally, and they started for the stairs.

There were other girls she thought who would have been a better match for Pierre—more money and better social standing, but Harriet supposed their love was inevitable. From the foggy night Vanessa found her way to the Bonneau home, they were almost constant companions. She watched them riding their mounts along the ocean—Vanessa, back straight, sitting a good seat—Pierre's face, not gloomy for the first time since his forced arrival from Europe. Pierre showing her his treasured art books, improving her French. But she could not control the flush of jealousy when Pierre overtly displayed his pleasure when Vanessa recognized an artist's work or called various dishes by their French names. A long way from the young girl who a short while ago had not heard of salmon mousse.

And the piano. Vanessa would play endlessly for Pierre. The music relaxed him so much, he had said, and he even began to put his mind to plantation business. Well, Vanessa would do. She was attractive, and there was a strong but gentle spirit about her. They would have good children. The girl's lack of worldliness was actually an asset. Vanessa loved St. Helena and Charleston, and she felt sure Vanessa could persuade Pierre to stay in the South with their families, lessening her concern that he would find a way to return to his beloved Europe. Vanessa would do, and with a little work she could be molded into a Bonneau.

As they passed the garden on their way to the waiting carriage, Harriet was pleased with the effect of the colorful tents erected for the reception. A profusion of azalea plants edged the paths leading to the entrances of the tents and inside, huge pots of begonias had been hung. Hours had been spent covering the trusses with garlands of ivy, roses, and double ranunculas. Japanese lanterns were hung in the trees to be lit when the sun slipped from the sky.

She saw that the orchestra had already arrived and were setting up their stands beneath a special canopy decorated with potted palmetto trees and giant ferns.

Waiters were busy getting everything in readiness. Pierre had arranged for the best French cook, recently arrived in New Orleans from Paris, to come with three assistants to prepare the feast. The menu brought together the best of French and Southern cooking—Pierre saw to that. There would be two soups, and three different kinds of fish caught that morning, a hot quail pâté, oyster patties, and saddle of mutton with purée bretonne.

The ducklings were prepared a la rouennaise, and the to-
matoes were being stuffed to surround the chicken a la
portugaise. Chef Louis himself was overseeing the
decorating of the lobster a la parisienne with strips of
truffle dipped in half-set mayonnaise jelly. Huge vegetable
pots would be brought in shortly to begin heating the
water that would steam the freshly picked vegetables.
Iced bombe, strawberry tarts, with dried fruits and nuts,
and sweet biscuits would bring to a close this grand
dinner. Harriet knew the menu by heart.

As they reached the door to the street, Henry had the
servants lined up waiting for them. The gold embroidered Russian livery she had made especially for the
occasion, glittered in the bright sunlight.

Harriet did feel like the bride herself as she rode
beside Pierre in the new Silver Phaeton carriage to St.
Michael's just a few blocks away. They turned left onto
Meeting Street and passed the South Carolina Society
Hall with its handsome portico—strollers along the way
tipped their hats, calling out, "Have a happy day, Mrs.
Bonneau! Congratulations!"

Harriet enjoyed her aloof position in Charleston and
now that Pierre was at last settling down, things could
only get better. Business would expand, not that the
Bonneau fortune hadn't been well guided by her, but she
could have Pierre sit in on the male-dominated meetings
at the Agricultural Society and make certain the Bonneau
interests were protected even more strongly.

Ahead was St. Michael's with its handsome bell tower.
As they approached, she could hear the clear peal of the
church bells. She tightened her grip slightly on Pierre's
arm, remembering how this beautiful church had seen the
Bonneaus through their joyous as well as sad times.

Harriet walked along the church path, head erect, losing
her composure only slightly as she approached the small
cemetery. She paused, then went to the headstone marked,
GERARD BONNEAU, BELOVED HUSBAND OF HARRIET, BE-
LOVED FATHER OF PIERRE, 1810 TO 1840. Her son was
close behind her. "Pierre, you go on in, I want to stay
here a moment."

As he walked away, she couldn't help but remember
the joy and happiness she felt as she walked up this

path so many years ago to become Gerard's bride. Her grandmother's flander lace shawl wrapped around her shoulders, the same one Vanessa would be wearing today. Little did she know that her life as a young wife would last not quite five years. In that time Pierre would be born, her father gone abroad in government diplomatic service, never to return, and her husband dead in a hunting accident, leaving her at the age of twenty-three to run the two plantations by herself. Well, she had more than managed and now her life would be easier and fuller. She had missed male companionship over the years, but no one had matched Gerard and she couldn't give herself to less. He had been a difficult man to know, but there was always an excitement when he was around. Poor Pierre missed having a father, which she was certain was the reason that he was difficult at times and hard to understand. A boy needs a father's influence.

Harriet felt a hand take hold of her arm. "Come, Harriet, the young bride has just arrived. It's time for the ceremony to start. Let me escort you into the church," said Thomas McIver.

"Yes, thank you, Thomas, you caught me remembering." Harriet was grateful to Thomas for his attention. Even though she knew of whispered comments about his strange personal life, he was still an elegant and well-respected Southern gentleman.

She saw Georgina, all aflutter, alight from her carriage with young Amanda and Josiah. Georgina looks the fool in all those frills, thought Harriet, trying to compete with Amanda as the young belle. But Kenneth, what a handsome man. Good stock. Yes, she thought again—pleased—there will be fine children from her future daughter-in-law.

Harriet caught her breath when she saw Vanessa step down from the carriage, dressed in ecru silk embroidered with fine gold thread. The tucked bodice was topped with a lace mandarin collar and the wide-pleated sleeves were caught by the lace again at her wrists. She was exquisite. On her head she wore the flanders lace Bonneau shawl and carried a simple bouquet of violets in her hands.

She went to her and said warmly, "Sweet Vanessa,

you look so radiant. Pierre shall be a happy man with you as his wife."

Vanessa was moved to tears. "Oh, mother Bonneau, I already have too much happiness. I am the luckiest girl in all of Charleston if not the world. I promise that you will be proud of me."

They embraced and Thomas walked Harriet into the vestibule of the church. As the usher took her arm to escort her to her place, Sillar was busy arranging Vanessa's dress so the train would trail behind her gracefully as she walked up the aisle.

On her way to the front pew, Harriet nodded to the guests and to a number of Bonneau and McIver slaves craning their necks to get the first glimpse of the bride from their section of the church. The women's homespun dresses and bandanas of calico in bright flashy colors, contrasted sharply with the elegant attire of the cream of Charleston society at the wedding.

The church was filled with the perfume of gardenias and lit with bayberry candles. Large white silk ribbons were attached to the side of each pew. The altar was banked high with masses of summer flowers.

Harriet had a view of Pierre looking very solemn as he waited in the sanctuary. When the processional music began, he moved to the center of the altar and turned toward the back of the church, his face, instead of warming at the sight of his beautiful lady coming toward him, looked slightly disturbed. But only Harriet caught it.

Kenneth, escorting Vanessa down the aisle, looked wan. The time had come for him to give his daughter away in marriage.

Pierre took Vanessa's arm and as they turned toward the minister, the ceremony began, "Dearly beloved, we are gathered together here in the sight of God, and in the face of this company, to join together this man and this woman in holy matrimony . . ."

Pierre's somber gaze held Vanessa's strongly as the minister spoke, "Wilt thou, Pierre, have this woman, Vanessa, to be thy wedded wife . . ." His reply, "I will," was firm if not somewhat forced. Although Vanessa was never known to stutter before, she had trouble giving her promise. "I wi—wi—will." She again showed her nervousness by giving her right hand instead of her left when it came time for Pierre to put the ring on her finger. He smiled sweetly at her, helping her regain her composure. "With this ring I thee wed and with all my worldly goods I thee endow."

The final blessing was spoken and Pierre took Vanessa's face in his two hands and kissed each cheek and then his deep set dark eyes burned through her, blurring out everything else as he slowly kissed her mouth. The music swelled symbolically, filling the church.

As the young couple drove off in their carriage to the reception, Harriet's ecstasy was momentarily dampened by the sudden realization that she was alone now. Although Pierre had spent many years away from her, she always considered him hers. Now it was his time to make a family of his own. Thomas again rescued her, helping her into her carriage. "Come Harriet, can I ride with you? We are all family now."

The small breeze that made the tents billow softly, encouraged the guests to dance spiritedly into the night after they had supped.

Amanda caught the bouquet and was blushing almost as much as her sister when Pierre swept Vanessa off her feet—carried her out of the tent and through the front door of the house.

Harriet wandered through the Bonneau residence that evening, letting memories carry her from room to room. As she passed the bridal chamber she heard sounds that made her flush, the sounds of young lovers. She walked as quickly and as silently as she could past their door, only to have her heart almost stop when she realized that what she thought were sighs and noises of love-making, were really agonizing sobs from Vanessa. The heart wrenching cries stayed with her long into the night and kept her from sleeping, too afraid to sort out the reason for Vanessa's weeping.

The French porcelain clock on the fireplace mantel in her hotel bedroom clanged the hour, reminding Harriet it was time for the recital. She got off the bed and brushed her tears away as she picked up the ticket from the carpet where she had thrown it earlier.

She read the name, "Vanessa McIver." An ordinary name, McIver, no style or grace like Bonneau. She tore the ticket in pieces and held her hand out the open window, letting the wind carry the torn fragments down into the streets of London.

4

Josiah McIver held the key to Daphne's room in his hand. He had just let himself in and was excited. The place was as he imagined it would be for an artist's model: clothing strewn about, the unmade bed in the corner, faded wallpaper shredded in spots with rough sketches of her tacked up all over in a haphazard fashion, mostly nudes of her sensuous, plump body.

The scent of her was everywhere, filling Josiah's nostrils, exciting him further as he moved deeper into the room.

He spied a tiny table by the dormer window and placed the bottle of red wine he brought in the center of it, then searched for glasses as he took off his muffler and overcoat. All he could find were two cracked cups behind a screen that hid a small hot plate and several pots and plates. The screen stood on three wobbly legs and was decorated with picture postcards and more drawings of Daphne in various states of nudity. In one faded wash, Daphne was astride a huge white horse with only a long scarf around her hair, the silken ends billowing out like the wings of a great predatory bird. He wanted to take it to show to his school chums to prove to them what he had been telling them was true, but then thought he'd better not—it was probably something she treasured.

Josiah had met Daphne at Sir Robert Ashcroft's studio on a Saturday when he was down from Oxford. There she was, sitting in all her naked glory on a piece of blue satin, not the least embarrassed that a strange man had walked in and was staring at her wide-eyed. For

Josiah had never seen breasts quite like Daphne's. To be perfectly honest, at nineteen he had not seen many breasts, but these were beyond belief even in his wildest fantasies. They resembled two melons about to burst—the nipples were really nipples—long, erect, and ballooning at the very ends like small popcorns, just waiting to be nibbled on. She held her pose but gave him a quick wink as he continued to gape at her. A tall, well-built youngster, Josiah looked more mature than his years.

He walked her to the horse-drawn omnibus on King's Road after her sitting, giving some silly excuse or other to Sir Robert for his leaving right at the time Daphne was heading out the door. While they waited at the stop, he asked her if she wanted to have something to eat at a nearby pub. That was just over two months ago and every weekend since he had been coming down and taking Daphne to the rooms of a friend for lovemaking. The friend who was abroad had returned suddenly and Daphne suggested her room tonight if, she had pouted, he wouldn't be put off by the smallness or poorness of the place. She had no idea who he was or that he was still at school, and he was not about to tell her the truth of his identity.

He set the cups on the table next to the bottle of wine and flopped into a chair with its stuffings spilling out, and its springs scraping the bare floor. He hoped she wouldn't be too long because he was ready just thinking about her. Her vulgar grunts and screams as she had orgasm after orgasm sent such waves of thrills through him that he thought about little else since the first time they had sex together. He wished to hell she would hurry up. She had warned she might be a little delayed and that is why she gave him the key, but he had little less than an hour before he had to leave for the recital, and she demanded so much fanciful fingering and kissing before she would let him enter her.

Making himself think of his Uncle Thomas and the encounter they had just had at the house in Chelsea, cooled all ardor as he knew it would—it was a disturbing talk. One he knew was coming, not only from Thomas, but his father, about his returning home after the wedding and the rebuilding of the plantation. Thomas was

such a hothead, a militant who enjoyed being one of the
leaders of the Ku Klux Klan in South Carolina. His
father he knew was a different sort.

"The uppity ones are being taken care of," Thomas
had boasted. "We're organized now and fighting back
when the Yankees aren't looking. Of course, we let them
cut them down from the trees."

He had poured another large drink as he continued,
"Free the niggers they had said. Well, you should see
how they are still living in the same filthy quarters or
sleeping in the streets of Charleston—no better off as
free men—worse if you ask me, because no one is
telling them how to put one foot in front of the other."

Josiah had gotten away as soon as possible. Like his
mother, he also felt that London was now his home. He
had after all spent five years here, and this is where
he wanted to stay. Who wanted to be around anyone like
Uncle Thomas all the time. He shifted in his seat, Where
the hell was Daphne?

Under the hissing gaslight in the downstairs hall, behind the stairway, Mack Malone held Daphne roughly
by the shoulders. She wanted him to hold her close
and give her a kiss, but he would have none of it. He
was all business, trying to pound into her head what she
had to do with the young nob waiting so hotly upstairs.
Mack had seen Josiah come in and hid in the shadows of
the narrow hall until Daphne arrived to make sure she
carried out the scheme he had devised. A dockworker,
often unemployed, he was a brute of a man with piercing
steel-blue eyes and black hair that hung straight and limp
around his broad face. Mack believed vehemently a person had to snatch every opportunity, right or wrong, in
this world. He shook Daphne until her teeth chattered,
when she tried to grab his oversized manhood to divert
him.

"You silly bitch. You always got one thing on your
mind."

"No, Mack. Just with you. Honest. You make me feel
tingly all over. I can't help it."

"Bull. You can't get enough and you know it. When
you're my Mrs., it will be me and only me, or I'll break
your head. Pay attention to what I got to say and then

we can get some good money from that young swell upstairs. You wanna have your kid proper, don't you? Not in some charity ward."

She bobbed her head up and down, the hazel eyes misting over for a second.

"You sure he won't tell you who he is? Hell of a night to be following the bloke."

"No, Mack. He clams up proper when I try to find out."

His face looked ugly as he reflected on that, the wide mouth became surly. "If that's the way the nob wants to do it—we'll get him anyway."

To him the plan was ingenious, and this was the night he was going to put it into action. Daphne only half listened as he told her what she had to do. She had heard it all before, and knowing Mack, she knew she would hear it again and again. Her hands tugged frantically at his fly buttons as he talked. She finally opened the top two, exposing stiff, short black pubic hair that grew in a straight line right up to his belly button. She fingered the hair lovingly, curling it around her finger as she cooed in his ear, "Luv, just let me hold it for a sec before I go upstairs. It will drive me crazy if I don't." Without waiting for an answer, she quickly slipped her hand down the waistband of his pants and found what she was longing to caress. Daphne sighed and Mack, in spite of his intentions, started to moan lowly as they kissed and nibbled at each other's ears and lips, growing more and more amorous. Mack grabbed her behind in his two massive hands and pulled her hips to his pelvis roughly.

She spoke in gasps, "Hon, I love it so much. I want it in me, please." She lifted her skirt in the tight squeeze with her free hand and pulled down her long underpants. "Put it in me, Mack—please, darlin', I have to feel you inside." She raised her body, trying to position herself so he could enter her.

He was moaning louder now and gyrating his hips as he pushed against her body greedily. He came inside her almost instantly. She threw her head back in ecstasy gasping with pleasure as the warm semen filled her.

Josiah jumped up from the chair when he heard the key in the lock. Then Daphne came into the small, shabby room, her face flushed and her chest heaving. When she saw the eager young man, she looked at him demurely and said in a husky, lispy voice, "Hello, Luv. Ready for a little luvin'?"

5

The voice of Sasha Bronsky, impresario, guider of Vanessa's career, boomed outside her dressing room door as he gave strict orders to the doorman: "Remember, George, no one is allowed to disturb Miss McIver before the concert. My artist must have absolute quiet. Not a sound!"

Vanessa had to laugh at the noise he was making. "I do love the silence, don't you, JoJo? It helps calm my stage nerves."

"Yes, Miz Nessa. I'm practically fallin' asleep with the quiet."

The tall, heavy man whirled gracefully through the door. His fluffy beard and tightly curled gray hair framed his jowly face. Sasha continued to bark orders to George, ". . . and if anyone tries to see Miss McIver, one of the most brilliant pianists on this earth, it is your duty to throw him out bodily."

With that performance done, he turned full face toward Vanessa, who now sat calmly at the dressing table fully dressed for her appearance.

"Ah, bubeleh. You look wonderful. Beautiful! Hearts will melt when they see you." His face in an instant was full of concern, and he took hold of both her hands. "Are you calm? Do you have the jitters? Are you beside yourself with apprehension? Do not be afraid. Sasha's here to take care of you and to present you to London." In his nervousness he quickly ran to the door again and shouted to the empty backstage, "If you allow anyone back to disturb this great artist, I'll have your head."

"Sasha, what would happen if the Prince of Wales

decided to see me before the recital? Do you think George will throw him out bodily?" she asked teasingly.

"What? Bubeleh, do you think he will come back? I know he is expected for the recital—oh, goodness, let me tell George. Oh, that imbecile—do you think he would stop the prince?" Completely out of breath he added, "You are expecting the Prince of Wales back-stage?"

"Sasha, Sasha, I was only joking."

Sasha's nerves before a performance always helped to calm Vanessa. Since he discovered her at the Rome Conservatory, he had mentored her career and practically taken over her life in his own peculiar fashion. Suddenly he raised her from the chair and led her toward the chaise. "So, my darling, I want you to lie down and relax. You have a few minutes yet—take it easy—leave everything in my hands." Then as a quick aside to JoJo, "Save the flowers, they are beautiful—be sure to save the cards. It is important they are acknowledged. There is so much to think about—always." His attention returned completely to Vanessa. "Doesn't the room look nice? I had to twist the theater manager's arm to fix up this place. Now it is nice—no? Good. I knew you'd be pleased."

JoJo giggled as she spoke, "Mr. Sasha, come sit in this chair and relax yourself. You're a wreck."

Just as he settled on the chair, a loud rap resounded on the dressing room door, making him leap up and begin his nervous banter all over again. "Who is it? What do you want? I said no disturbances. My artist must not be disturbed."

"Sorry, sir," said George, "but a young gentleman just dropped this off for Miss McIver and said it was important that she have it right away."

Vanessa took the bouquet—Wind Flowers—her face turned crimson. "Thank you, George, that was very kind."

"Vanessa, my little rose, all these flowers and more. Who is this admirer?"

Vanessa did not answer him, but buried her face in the flowers.

"Should I be jealous? Is there a great knight who will come charging through the door and steal you away?"

"Sasha, you are being silly. JoJo, try to find a vase for these." Going out the door to see if she could find another container in the prop room where she had found others, JoJo wondered who sent the Wind Flowers.

"There doesn't seem to be a card. Aren't they lovely. At one time they were my favorite bloom. I really don't think I've seen any since I left America."

"I see. So, the sender remains a mystery."

"So it seems." She tried to be nonchalant and gay to cover her feelings. They must have come from him, but here in London, out of season, they would be so expensive.

"Some friend from back home no doubt."

"Yes, and the person thought I'd know." She tried to change the subject somewhat. "At the reception, afterward, you will meet many friends. In a way, that will be the nicest part of the evening—it's been so lonely."

"Lonely? My sweet dumpling, with your music and the audiences who love you, how can you feel lonely? And now the music world has begun to recognize you. Soon the name of Vanessa McIver will be synonymous with great music throughout the world. What a great gift you have. One not to be tossed away."

"Sasha, is music everything?"

He was getting very worried, his countenance belying his inner feelings.

"Of course not. But first we will work very hard for a little bit longer to make you the celebrated artist I know you can be. And some day I will put together a tour of the United States for you, including South Carolina. Then JoJo will have a chance to eat all that wonderful Southern food she keeps talking about. But she will be sorry—she will put on forty pounds just like I have since my mama came from Russia. Oh, how could I forget the best news of all. Mama wants you and your family to come for dinner. She has already started cooking. You see, Vanessa, your life is full. What more can you want?"

"Yes, Sasha," she said hardly listening as he went on and on like he always did, asking questions, not waiting for answers. The flowers in her hand held such meaning.

JoJo came back into the room with a metal container and took the flowers from Vanessa. Sasha was quiet. Could she be serious about someone, he wondered, as he noted her deep, private reverie. He contained a flare of anger. He had kept such a close watch on her, how could it be?

A knock on the door and George's voice saying, "Fifteen minutes before the recital, Miss McIver."

"I'll leave you now, bubeleh. JoJo, help our beautiful princess get ready for her greatest performance." He was very subdued and Vanessa was surprised.

"Yes, sir, Mr. Sasha."

The McIvers and Lord Hatfield were among the early arrivals at the theater and stood near the center doors in the lobby, very close to the easel that held the announcement of the evening's event.

Georgina nervously checked out the people arriving. Where was everybody? she wondered. But soon the lobby filled, and the gas chandeliers and candle sconces reflected the brilliance of the jewels worn by the ladies.

Georgina nodded to everyone as they came to speak to her, congratulating her, the many faces became confusing in the crush.

A great ahh! rose all of a sudden from the lobby crowd and all eyes looked at the sign being hung, which read THIS PERFORMANCE SOLD OUT. The McIvers noticed the young man at the box office with his ticket, looking uncomfortable at having been caught in the middle of the attention, not knowing he had not purchased the last ticket but was picking up one that had been left for him. It was obvious from his plain black suit that this was not his milieu.

"Thomas, who is that man?" asked Kenneth. "He looks familiar."

"Not to me, but he doesn't look like an Englishman—not in those clothes."

Georgina was put off by their trivial conversation, and she started moving them into the hall toward their seats even though the first bell hadn't rung yet.

"Amanda, you take Jamie's arm and start in. Perhaps that will persuade your father to follow." Kenneth gave in as Thomas excused himself to socialize a bit more in the lobby.

The sight of the grand piano with its large barley-twirled legs dazzlingly inlaid with ivory looked so solitary on the large stage, making Kenneth apprehensive for his daughter. He had seen her perform before, but it had been so long ago and only in their home or for the St. Cecilia Society in Charleston. He had felt a tinge of anxiety for her then, but now the reality of this evening set in and he excused himself to walk off his nervousness on the pretext of waiting for Josiah in the lobby. As he walked up the aisle, he bumped into the young fellow who had been at the box office.

"Good evening, Mr. McIver. You don't remember me do you? I'm Kirk—Kirk Yoors."

"Kirk, of course. We all knew you were a familiar face. I guess it is just that we never expected to see you in England that made us not recognize you. What are you doing in London?"

"I'm in residence at Guy's Hospital."

"A doctor?" The surprise showed on his face.

"Yes, Mr. McIver."

"Well, I guess a lot has happened to you. You must come to the reception afterward."

"I intend to. I've already been invited."

"Good. I know the family will enjoy meeting you again, and we can catch up on your life."

Thomas was off on one end of the lobby holding his own with the Southern contingent—rather impressive this evening. Jefferson Davis and his wife Varina, resplendent in her favorite white, and Judah Benjamin, who had been the Secretary of State for the Confederate states. Thomas signaled to Kenneth, and he joined the circle.

He was engrossed in Davis' conversation about Canadian copper mines and the possibility of a business venture, when to his shock he felt a hand brush past his buttock and give him a quick, but firm pinch. He was certain he was mistaken and pinned it on his nervousness since, when he turned around, the only people near him were a couple on their way into the hall. The lady was tall and dressed in a plum moire bustle dress and the gentleman, he was told on inquiring, was the Duke of Blamford. I must settle down, he warned himself, my imagination is running wild.

After the second bell, Kenneth moved into the hall to take his seat.

Georgina was fretting about Josiah's not having arrived

yet, but nothing could dampen the McIver's pride for Vanessa as they looked around the large hall and saw the elegantly dressed audience that had come to hear her play. Everyone stood and quietly applauded the entrance of the Prince of Wales and his entourage. The Duke of Blamford, sitting to the right of the royal box, greeted the prince, and Kenneth couldn't help but watch the cool, dignified movements of the lady with Blamford as she curtsied and conversed easily with the prince and his party. Then she turned her head in his direction and through the nose veil of her headcovering, he saw her eyes find his and give him a tiny wink.

Well, that was not my imagination, he mused. What a bold, but delightful lady, and why is she choosing me to toy with? He sat up straighter in his seat and smoothed his hair self-consciously.

As the lights began to dim, signaling the start of the performance, Georgina already had her handkerchief out to wipe away the first tears.

In the third row of the balcony, the people in the seats closest to the aisle showed the usual annoyance at being disturbed by the late arrival of a young man, who had to push past them, stepping on toes.

Pierre Bonneau, lost in private thoughts, took no notice of their disgruntlement as he took his seat.

There was a hush over the audience—all eyes seemed to be looking toward the stage, expectantly. Vanessa took a deep breath in the wings, squeezed JoJo's hand and waved to Sasha who stood on the other side of the stage in the darkened wing. He saluted her nervously, his other hand stuffed with a handkerchief wet from wiping his perspiring brow. She glided out, head held high, and moved directly to the piano on center stage. When she got there, she did something she never did before. Instead of sitting on the bench and positioning herself to play, she turned and faced the audience, searching the sea of faces. She could see the hall was packed and the applause increased at her gesture. She was searching for that one person. JoJo had gone to the ticket window just moments before and his ticket had been picked up. The knowledge of his presence somewhere close filled her with a strong vibrance.

Sillar caught her breath as she looked at Vanessa. She

was so lovely and regal. The last time she had seen her
she was a defeated, miserable girl. She started to applaud
louder for her.

Kenneth was amazed that it was his daughter standing
up there looking out at the audience. No longer the
gangly child that raced instead of walked, talked so fast
one had to slow her down and make her start over. Next
to him, Georgina wiped the tears from her eyes, and
Amanda clapped politely for her sister. Jamie Hatfield
was enthusiastic in his response, his smile was ear to
ear. Kirk did not applaud, he just stared at the beautiful
woman, his heart was beating quickly, and he had butter-
flies in his stomach. In the balcony, Pierre held back
the tears. Looking down on the stage, she looked like a
miniature princess, her pale blue satin dress gleamed in
the bright lights of the stage, her soft brown hair was
atop her head braided in a high cornet, small diamonds
glittered in her hair. He knew they were the diamonds he
had given her their first Christmas. He had found them
in a shop in Charleston. The small perfect gems were
set in silver hair pins. He sank lower in his seat and
just stared at her, trying to calm himself.

Sir Robert Ashcroft stood as he applauded. He loved
Vanessa dearly and was happy the hall was filled and
she looked radiant. He hoped she would play brilliantly,
she had to. Vanessa caught his eye in the box nearest
the stage and impulsively she held up her hands to him,
he threw her a kiss. He certainly remembered the first
time they met and she showed him her hands.

She moved upstage and sat gracefully, then placing
her hands on the keyboard she started to play, the music
filling the theater.

Kirk closed his eyes as he listened to his beloved play.
He thought of the day when he knew for sure that he
loved her and would always love her.

He woke with a start, the silence of the early morning,
surprising. Listening hard, he could hear no movement—
not even a bit of the wind and rain that had pelted them
for the past two days. Kirk pushed off the blanket and
sprang from the bed. He had slept in his clothes, and
only had to pull on his heavy leather boots. Picking up
his jacket, he started in a run for the big house, past the

ominously quiet slave quarters. The hands were probably
up and dressed, waiting for their fate to be determined,
perhaps this very day. A few had run off or gone into
hiding in the marshes, but for the rest, over the past
few days, there was no noticeable change in the amount
of work done, but the singing had stopped. They were
biding their time. His feet made deep hollow sounds, and
he could hear his breathing. When he reached the back
door of McIver Hall, he didn't observe the usual protocol
—no knock, he just entered and walked quickly to Kenneth's study, where he knew he had been sleeping since
the Yankee fleet first appeared in the distance off shore.

Kenneth was already awake, but he seemed for the
moment unwilling to make a move, knowing as Kirk
did, it was going to happen.

"So the time is here, Kirk. Then let's get to it and
have a closer look at this damned Yankee fleet threatening our lives."

Kirk was glad Kenneth had sent Mrs. McIver with
Amanda and Josiah to their house in Charleston. Young
Josiah, who had just turned eleven, kicked up a great
fuss declaring his right as a McIver man to help defend
their home. When the carriages were all packed for the
trip, Josiah had run into the marshes to hide.

Kirk had called out a few of the men to help in the
search and Thursday, on hand from the Bonneau plantation where he now lived with Vanessa, found him hiding
in a tiny cave they had played in together when they were
little. As a final statement of resistance, he refused to sit
with the ladies in the carriage, but climbed up next to the
driver and slung his gun across his lap. Kirk, helping strap
on the last piece of luggage, caught a glimpse of his lower
lip quivering, but his back stayed straight and he gave one
short salute as the carriage pulled out. With them out
of the way, it would be easier to do whatever would
have to be done in case there was an invasion. However, on this day in November of 1861, most Southerners
thought if there was a full-scale war, they quickly would
be the victors.

Kenneth rode next to Kirk, both silent. Tension filled
the air, even the horses felt it, spooking at the slightest
noise or flutter of a leaf. The neighbors had agreed to
meet as soon as the weather lifted at the Jenkins Planta-

tion, which overlooked the entrance to Port Royal Sound. That was the target. It was protected on one side by Fort Walker and on the other by Fort Beauregard. But Kirk wondered if the defenses were strong enough.

As they rounded the last turn in the road before the Jenkins place, they pulled up their horses, stunned by the fearsome sight of the Yankee armada, laid out so close before them. There at the lead was the flagship *Wabash*, reported to have forty-four guns on board, surrounded by fourteen men-of-war and backed up by approximately thirty other ships.

Kenneth and Kirk joined the small cluster of neighbors on the south porch. Soon Pierre arrived and then every few minutes another neighbor would gallop up, his horse all lathered from the frantic ride. The men talked nervously, trying for a show of bravado, commenting on how brave the men were in the forts and how strong the artillery units from Charleston were. But Kirk knew most were fighting in their first battle, and Commander Tappnall's "mosquito" fleet, which consisted of three small river steamers and a tug, didn't have a chance against the Yankee force massed before his eyes.

About nine-thirty the *Wabash* weighed anchor, and Kirk heard the sound of the drums calling the men to quarters. Suddenly the morning quiet was shattered by the blast of a gun from Fort Walker, followed by a large shell screeching over the *Wabash*. The men's anguish was at last released with the bombardment, and shouts of support rose from the small group on the porch.

Immediately, the bow gun on the *Wabash* fired at one of the "mosquito" fleet, which was quickly immobilized.

Kirk's heart sank as the Yankee fleet began to move ahead rapidly, first coming close to one fort and shelling them broadside, then on to the fort on the other side. He saw the faces of the planters, they were stunned by the sight of the battle and the might of the Yankee force. He stood with them dumbfounded and powerless. Shortly after noon the reality of their desperate situation took hold and the smell of food burning on the kitchen stove signaled that the slaves had run off.

Kirk watched the hasty emotional goodbyes. Men whose lives had been so tied together, some for many generations, did not know when they might meet again. Despite the threat over the past months of this attack, few families faced the reality of actually leaving their homes, their land.

Pierre was near the stairs, taking another gulp from a flask. He had been drinking all morning and was now pushed along by the rest of the men running for their horses. He stumbled forward down the steps and Kirk caught him before he fell. "Mr. Bonneau, I'll go back with you to the plantation to help get the women out." Pierre looked at him blankly. "We have to get Vanessa and your mother to safety."

He started to shout incoherently, "Let the Yankees take it and better luck to them with the blasted mosquitoes and yellow fever! Let them have their violence. I've had enough of this land, this so-called civilization."

Kirk tried to calm him. "Easy does it. Let's get on home."

Pierre shoved him aside and lurched onto his horse and held on to its mane with one hand and the reins with the other, galloping off toward the Bonneau plantation without heed for anybody.

Kirk was anxious to start off after Pierre, when Kenneth appeared at his side, very concerned. "Don't worry, sir, I'll see that Vanessa is safe. I believe they are planning to go to Wind Flower."

"Yes, I'm sure. Good luck to you and perhaps we'll meet again in easier times."

Kirk let his horse run full out, finally taking to crossing the fields. The narrow island roads were clogged with wagons filled with hastily packed possessions and weeping women and children, horses being flogged to escape the Yankee invasion.

The quiet of the Bonneau land and house was eerie after the scenes he had just passed through. Suddenly, a group of Negroes ran across a field, firing stolen guns in the air in celebration of their freedom. They disappeared quickly down the road toward a small village nearby. The sound of his horse's heavy breathing matched his own, and his ears still rang from the pounding of the bombardment at Port Royal.

When he rounded the side of the plantation house, he saw a handful of Bonneau house slaves milling about. For some time Harriet Bonneau had been moving out her prized possessions and most of the hands to the Sims-Bonneau rice plantation, Wind Flower, up the Combahee River.

Little Thursday kept pulling on JoJo's arm. "Come on, JoJo . . . you stay with Dinah and me. We is gonna be free. The Yankees is makin' us free, JoJo."

"We can't leave Miz Nessa. She's our family."

"Tell her, Dinah, tell her how we gonna be free."

"Enough of this foolishness," shouted Old Henry. "All of you, quickly help carry these things to the boats. We gonna go up the river to the rice plantation. Come on, Dinah, I had enough sass from you."

"It's like the boy says, Henry, I'm stayin' here and the Yankees is gonna free me."

Harriet Bonneau, dazed, came out of the house holding a suitcase. Old Henry took it and tried to lead her to the small dock and the waiting boat. "Come along, Miz Bonneau. These niggers wants to stay. That Dinah never had no manners. She better off bein' a Yankee." She looked at all of them not fully comprehending. It struck Kirk odd that in the moment of crisis, Old Henry had to take care of the imperious woman. JoJo and Thursday held on to one another, starting to cry hysterically. They had never been apart. When Vanessa married, they were the two slaves she brought with her.

"Please, JoJo, stay wid me. The Yankees gonna be here soon."

"I can't. Where's Miz Nessa? We gotta go."

Harriet was led easily, her eyes glazed over as she turned her head in all directions, but not clearly seeing. "My son. Where is he?" Old Henry quickly soothed her fears, "He's comin', don't you worry none, Mistress."

Kirk helped JoJo pick up her belongings. "I'll find Vanessa. It will be all right, JoJo. Just tell me in what direction she headed."

"I don't know. She ran to the outbuildings after Mister Pierre."

He got them into the boat and watched them go up river. Dinah's and Thursday's head hanging, went toward the slave quarters.

He moved quickly in the direction of the outbuildings—everything was silent and he espied other slaves hiding, waiting for the Yankees. Anxious, he hurried past the kitchen, then the dairy room, and headed toward the barns. In the corral by the stable he saw Vanessa struggling to saddle her horse. He called to her to wait.

"Oh, Mr. Yoors. Oh, thank God. Please help Pierre. He doesn't seem himself. He came riding in here and grabbed his rifle to go help Colonel Dane put down a slave rebellion on his place."

"Quickly, Vanessa, let's get a boat—we can reach the Dane place easier by water. The roads are too dangerous now. Don't worry, we'll find him."

Harriet Bonneau was long gone when they reached the dock. Their only hope of escape was in an old, small flat-bottomed boat, which was stuck on the bank in the mud. They took off their shoes and waded into the muck. Vanessa pushed from the back while Kirk yanked hard on the front, trying to free it and get it afloat. Finally it gave, sending Vanessa face down into the bank.

"Oh, look at me. I'm covered with mud," she sputtered as Kirk helped her into the boat.

He grabbed a long, sturdy limb lying on the shore and guided them out into the water. The boat was missing oars.

"Oh, Mr. Yoors, look, we've forgotten our shoes."

All of a sudden, everything was too much for her to hold in. She began to cry uncontrollably, the deep sobs and the cold wetness of her clothes plastered to her made her body shake.

"Vanessa—we'll be safe. Just lie low. The tide is with us, we'll move along quickly."

He took his handkerchief, dipped it in the water and wiped the shiny wet earth from her face. Then he took off his shirt and wrapped it around her. The smallness of the boat forced their bodies together, his arm remained around her shoulders to keep her head from lying in the filth on the bottom. Kirk was surprised at how delicate and fragile she felt. He always envisioned her strength, riding her horse at breakneck speed, running along the beach with JoJo and Thursday behind her. But he had seen very little of her since her marriage, and she seemed wasted away. The blinking of her lashes to hold back the tears and the movement of her lips letting out sobs against his naked chest began to excite him. Their bare feet touched, and he wrapped his other arm around her.

His lips lightly kissed her hair and Kirk wished this little boat could sail on forever.

The gentle waves rocked the boat lightly, but his reverie was abruptly broken by a gruff shout from shore.

"Lie quietly, Vanessa, it might be trouble."

"You there, we need help," came from the shore.

Kirk slowly raised his head, eyes scanning the sandy shoreline. He could see the Dane overseer standing close to shore holding up an inert figure of a man. Vanessa too sat up in the boat and as they approached the shore, they realized it was Pierre. The man on shore recognizing Vanessa, quickly reassured her, "He's all right, Mrs. Bonneau. Just a little woozy from being caught in between a runaway and his master."

Kirk pulled Pierre into the boat—he was moaning incoherently and immediately passed out. Vanessa held his head on her lap as the ocean water flowed into the Combahee River.

He tried but couldn't keep his eyes from Vanessa. The sight of her cradling her husband hit him with a spasm of jealousy, which surprised him; it was a pain stronger than any physical ailment he had ever known. "My God, I love this woman," he thought.

Melodious strains of Liszt's "Mephisto Waltz" filled the hall as Kirk came back to the present. The Faustian legend translated into musical form by Liszt had always been a favorite of Vanessa's, and it was one of the pieces he had heard her practice over and over as he listened at the window at McIver Hall and later at Wind Flower. How often he had gone to concerts or recitals of various artists in the past five years, sometimes using the last of his money to pay for the ticket, to feel closer to Vanessa—along the way, he had also learned to love and appreciate music. However, because of his exhausting medical studies—Toulaine immediately after the war, an intensive year at a medical academy, and then the grueling training at Charity Hospital in New Orleans—he would often fall asleep during the concert or recital only to be awakened by a porter or an amused member of the audience. No problem of that tonight he knew, although he was very tired from the draining day he had spent at Guy's Hospital, where he was receiving advanced training in surgical procedures. He tried to relax his tense body to let the waltz rhythm of the sonata fill his being. For a moment—a moment he fought to hold on to, because he was sure it was based on unreality—there was a sense of coming home.

There was applause as she finished the piece, and she moved into the composer's "Valse Impromptu" in the all-Liszt recital.

A few rows behind him, Georgina was getting concerned. Josiah's seat on her left was still empty. She hoped he was standing at the back, but craning her neck as politely as possible not to be too obvious in what she was doing, she couldn't see anyone standing in the darkness at the rear. He has to be here, she told herself. He would never miss Vanessa's London debut. She turned her mind away from the possibility that something could have happened to him and smiled when she saw how Varina and Jefferson Davis were so enthralled with the music. It relaxed her a bit, especially when she caught Jamie Hatfield's eye, and he nodded his head in firm approval. She then raised her eyes to the boxes and saw the Prince of Wales also quite attentive.

In her security that all was going well, she subconsciously reached for Kenneth's hand and held it lightly in hers, letting it rest on his knee. The music is lovely, she thought. Vanessa played with such strength and sensitivity.

Kenneth was surprised at Georgina's gesture. He did nothing to disturb their entwined hands. He was all the more sure now that their time had come and gone and they were doomed to a polite, empty relationship. A sensuous person by nature, he didn't know how he was going to live with a cold marriage.

Amanda stared hard at the back of Jon Hortz's head in the row in front of her, hating him and his simpering wife, Pansy, sitting so regally next to him, always the sweet aristocratic Southern belle. Jon Hortz was Swiss, raised in the Deep South. He had been forced to open a private academy in Chelsea to earn his keep. The poorly run school was attended mostly by other homeless Southerners licking their wounds. Josiah was sent to the school first, with Amanda following at half rate because

Pansy was, after all, an old family friend from Charleston. Amanda had spent three long years in its smothering confines before becoming an apprentice teacher for the noxious man who had sneaky hands and runny red eyes. But he was a good teacher in what he knew well, she had to give him that—forcing his knowledge into his students. As a result, Amanda spoke fluent French and was quite well versed in French and English history. But he was always trying to keep her after school or push her into a dark closet. How many times she had run home from the airless, dusty school in his home, where windows were never opened, to tell her mother of the nasty headmaster and his trying to get his clammy hands into her pants, only to find Mrs. Hortz sipping tea out of cracked china cups with her mother. The two Southern belles reliving the glorious moments of the past, the moments becoming more and more glorious with each remembrance. The tears she shed over the thought of having to spend her life teaching little girls drawing, sewing, and French.

The applause was loud and spontaneous. Amanda realized Vanessa had finished the "Valse Impromptu" and she also started to applaud politely, as jealousy pricked her heart for a moment because of all the attention Vanessa was getting, but in the next moment she was pleased for her sister. Her life had been just as hard, and if Amanda admitted the truth to herself, much more difficult. Tonight, hard-won success was hers, bringing a new life in the immediate future. The music began again, one of the Hungarian rhapsodies, and the audience became quiet instantly, wanting so to hear more from the brilliant young pianist.

The sputtering candle cast grotesque shadows of two heaving, grunting bodies on the wall behind the shaking bed. The copulating couple didn't hear the anguished cries of a choleric baby next door or the rain that had just started to beat on the cracked windows. A moan started to rise out of Daphne's throat and increased in sound until a shrill scream bounced off the walls of the tiny room. Josiah, reaching his peak a moment later, grabbed her long blond hair in both his hands and yanked hard as giant waves of ecstasy raced through his body. Daphne loved it as he continued to yank her hair, and she pumped harder with him until they were completely spent. Josiah went limp and rolled off her plump, perspiring body. She suddenly kicked both her shapely legs to the steeply pitched ceiling and loudly exclaimed in her lispy voice:

"Lovie, do me some more. You are the best. Built like a great big bull you are." It was something she said all the time, to all her johns, but was quite serious about Josiah. He was good. Much improved from their first encounter when he was inexpert and too quick. Eighteen-year-old Daphne, a street child since she was eleven, was a good judge in that direction. She had known many men. Raised until that tender age by an alcoholic father who worked off and on as a bricklayer and a grandmother who was also always into a bucket of ale, she desperately sought any kind of affection she could get, equating sex with love. But in her ignorance, she turned her back on real love. In Liverpool living with a kindly old woman there was an adorable two-year-old who needed to be loved and would give it back generously in return. Daphne tried hard to forget that two-year-old, her daughter, born in anguish and pain in a charity ward. She was now pregnant again, and in another couple of weeks, with her distended belly, she wouldn't be able to work as a model. She didn't want to think of that either. They had to get the money from Josiah.

"The best," she cooed again in Josiah's ear. "A regular bull. What you do to a girl. You make her crazy."

Pleased by her compliments, he kissed her deeply, something none of her other men friends did. Now, of course, she was mainly tied to Mack, it was his child she was carrying, but she was moved by the kiss and to add to the delight, Josiah was from the upper class. In gratitude, she moved her hands over his long, somewhat soft frame and lovingly caressed him.

"No. Not again, Daphne." He stumbled from the lumpy bed they had been sharing for the past hour and groped for his trousers. He didn't know the time but felt it must be late, and he had to get to Vanessa's recital.

Giggling, Daphne made a grab for his pants, managing to get hold of one of the trouser legs as he thrust his one, long, smooth leg into the other. They had a tug of war;

she playful and he serious, getting slightly annoyed as he hopped around on one foot.

"Daphne, stop it now. I've got to go. I'm late. You knew I had this important engagement."

"You can't leave me now, love. We're just getting started." She had already forgotten Mack's instructions—love him up good quickly, which she did do, and then make him promise to come back later for more. In the meantime, Mack would follow him, find out who he was, confront the young swell on his return that he was the father of Daphne's child, and demand a large sum of money by scaring him with the threat of blackmail. She moved seductively to him in her coarse, outlandish way, her naked hips swinging in wide arcs. Josiah could not take his eyes off her tightly curled blond pubic hairs.

"Don't you want to stay with your little Daphne?" she cooed. Puckering up her lips, she held her face close to his for a kiss. Josiah started to melt, but he was sore, and he knew his mother would never forgive him if he didn't make it to the theater. He gave her a quick peck on her full, ripe lips and tried to explain gently but firmly.

"Look, you've been swell. I really had a jolly good time, but I've got to be off. I'll come back tomorrow night. Is that all right with you? I'll be in London 'til Monday."

"Tomorrow night," she cried in dismay. "Why that's a whole night and day away. Come back to bed and we'll cuddle up like two little bugs in a rug. You don't want to go out in that nasty rain."

He managed to get his arms into his dress shirt and finish buttoning up his trousers. "Please—Daphne—I've just got to go."

She suddenly remembered Mack and then in a rush helped him finish dressing, even to giving him her large tortoiseshell comb to arrange his longish, sandy blond hair.

"All right," she said anxiously, now frightened that Mack had heard it all through the thin door. "You go to your fancy affair and then come right back to your Daphne. Promise?"

He was almost at the door. "Tomorrow night. We'll meet then."

She placed herself squarely in front of the door, blocking his exit.

"No, lovie. You've got to promise your Daphne you'll come back tonight—no matter what."

"Daphne!"

She tweaked the tip of his penis through his pants and a flash of painful excitement traveled through his nineteen-year-old body. He had to get out of there and quickly. She was a madwoman, he thought. A crazy, delightful madwoman. He couldn't wait to tell them of this latest escapade up at Oxford. His friends were already begging for her name and address.

"I'll be back," he said quickly. "I don't know what time it will be, but I'll be back."

"Promise?"

"Promise!"

He didn't at this point know if he were lying or telling the truth, but it did the trick. He was free. She turned his collar up and pulled his face close to hers as she whispered hoarsely, "You'd better, my Josiah, or little Daphne will become a great big tiger cat and come after you."

He became concerned for a moment as he had carefully hid his real identity from her, warning Sir Robert not to tell her who he was. Sir Robert assured him he never would. Josiah grinned sheepishly and took the remark in the spirit he thought it was intended and was out the door in the next instant saying again he would be back.

Mack was waiting for him, his fists clenched. He had been hiding in the garbage-strewn hall for an interminable hour. His squarish face had grown livid, and he was about to burst with hatred for the youth. He had heard snatches of what had gone on and he was going to make Josiah, whoever he was, pay through the nose until he was bled dry. Mack let him get down a flight of stairs, and then dogged him.

Josiah shivered in the doorway of the tenement as he studied the sky, deciding the best way to get to the hall. The heavy fog had turned to a chilling rain, coming down in slanting sheets. He pulled his scarf up around his ears and dashed past Soho Square onto Charing Cross

Road. Mack, cursing his luck to have to be doing what he was doing on such a night, stayed close behind. The only comfort he had was the thought of the end result—the money they would get from this young swell. His thin workman's jacket was soaked through, and rivulets of water ran off his limp black hair, down under his collar. He was forced to dodge in and out of doorways as Josiah looked up and down for a hansom cab on Charing Cross. In the entranceway to a shop where Mack ran to be out of sight, he felt a huge furry arm grab for him as it emitted a low menacing growl. Shocked, his eyes tried to make out the large shape next to him.

"Sorry, mate. It's just Oscar. He means no harm."

Unbelievably, what he finally made out, was a large bear and his keeper and a monkey dressed in a red jacket with gold braid who was sitting precariously on the bear's shoulder holding a tin cup. "Jesus," he cried as he got out of there just missing a sideswipe from the lumbering animal, who stood over six feet on his hind legs. "Sorry, mate," called the owner.

He was out in the road just in time to see Josiah get into a horse-drawn omnibus. Mack jumped on board just as the public vehicle was pulling away. He tried to hide himself from Josiah's sight as best he could. But he needn't have been concerned. Josiah was a very preoccupied young man at the moment, deep in private thoughts. He was again worried about having to leave England and was thinking how he could enlist the aid of Lord Hatfield. How lucky, he thought, that his sister landed one of the richest men in England. Sir Robert had told him that there was a chance Hatfield might follow Gladstone as prime minister. A queer duck he thought, very proper and didactic at times, but seemed a good sort, full of a sense of fair play and justice. Josiah at this time had no knowledge of his quick, strong temper. The best of all, he told himself, was that Hatfield was totally captivated by his sister. He prayed nothing would go wrong to change that.

Up until this year, he would have gladly returned to the States, but since he had been at Oxford, all that changed. He tried to ease his mind. So much had happened in the last months, he was nervous and on edge.

His friend, Binkie, up at Oxford, was teaching him mind control, telling him of a Hindu teacher he had studied with on his last trip to India, who could stop his heartbeat to appear lifeless, and start it again at will. This teacher had also taught Binkie exercises to relieve tension. Josiah applied some of the technique as the horse-drawn vehicle moved slowly in the inclement weather, but it didn't work. He just couldn't concentrate. He knew he had a major flaw in his argument to stay in England. Since he had met Daphne, he had failed most of his studies and had been placed on probation. He was sure his father was going to investigate his progress having mentioned only that morning that he was going to come up to Oxford for a visit.

The omnibus reached Cranbourn Street and was just about to pass it when he realized he was at his destination. He pulled the bell cord and the bus halted abruptly as he jumped off. Running across Leicester toward Haymarket, he thought there was someone following close behind him, but he paid little attention. Finally arriving at the hall, completely breathless, he pushed open the beveled glass door into the inner lobby and heard the music. He breathed a sigh of relief. He had not missed the entire recital, but he was sure it was near its end. He would tell his mother he wanted to hear it from the gallery to see how the sound carried, positive there would be a seat there—the usher would certainly honor an orchestra ticket. He dashed up the winding staircase to the gallery—there were no seats, so he had to stand behind the last row, at the moment not noticing Pierre, seated a few rows in front of him.

Mack waited outside in the rain. Soon he would know the identity of his prey.

Vanessa's fingers continued to work the keys. She was totally absorbed in the final piece. The perspiration trickled into her eyes, but she was unaware, filled with the interpretation of the sonata, emotionally rising with each swell. Wisps of hair curled damply around her neck and forehead, her arms and hands glistened with moisture. She reached a slow, quiet passage, and as she let the music lull her as she played, there was a sudden peace within her. A peace that comes with accomplishment. Quietly, she approached the finish, the sounds dwindling into a nothingness. After a beat, she raised her arms now heavy with exhaustion, and struck the final chord.

It was finished and only silence filled the air as she bowed her head humbly. She could vaguely hear shouts rolling in from the audience, but her mind was filled with sudden thoughts. It had taken countless hours at the piano and four long years, living and studying in foreign lands to reach this point. All the feelings of hopelessness, the loneliness—but being homeless these last few years had been the hardest for her to cope with. It had started very simply really. Sir Robert had said after her arrival in England, why not play the piano professionally. Those years of piano lessons as a youngster could pay off. She had been confiding in him about her need to earn a living. Pierre had arranged for her to have a monthly income, a small one, most of what he had at the time he had written her, that one and only time. But it wasn't enough unless she would be content to live very poorly, and she had to help her mother. Then, most important, she needed something to occupy her life, a life that could be over in a sense if she allowed it to be. You have the gift in your fingers, he kept repeating.

Sir Robert spoke to a friend connected with the London Conservatory. She was accepted and then spent an arduous two years studying. Next, Rome for advanced training on a scholarship. She thought work in the London Conservatory had been difficult, but her studies in Rome taxed her even further, draining her physically and emotionally. There was no time to think of anything else except on rare occasions. Life became blessedly blurred, music becoming her total commitment and existence.

She looked straight ahead as she sat, trying to see into the darkness of the backstage. Sasha was there, grinning from ear to ear. His fat cheeks crinkled into deep folds. She turned to look into the other wing behind her and saw JoJo. Large tears were running down her face, and she blew a kiss to Vanessa. They had shared a life for almost eight years.

The applause and shouts finally reached Vanessa's ears. She rose and walked downstage toward the audience, not quite sure, not fully aware. She had concerned herself with playing the piano. That was over. Now she concerned herself with whether or not she had played well, if she had been accepted. Sasha's ear-to-ear grin was an indication, of course, but that acclaim, rolling in like strong waves hitting the shoreline, was proof. They couldn't all be Southerners cheering for her, she reasoned, or friends of Jamie's. The whole experience was uplifting —rewarding. In the provinces they had been polite but not as enthusiastic. It felt wonderful all of a sudden to bask in the warmth of the applause, but for a split second she feared the warmth was without heat, a fickle fate, traveling on swiftly changing winds. Then she was afraid it, too, would be taken away like so many of the good things that had happened to her in the past—a string let out so far and then yanked back and away. It had been such a long hard road. She let the sounds of affirmation take her over. The sea of faces were shouting, "Encore! Encore!" They had been fired by a sense of discovery. The London debut of a young artist, and they were there. It flamed their enthusiasm. Vanessa stood simply, guileless. The applause rose to a higher level, her tiredness left her. She walked back to the piano and sat. Everything became quiet. They were waiting. She placed her hands on the keys, having no idea what she was going to play. She stared at her fingers, which suddenly took on the shape of Granny Claire's hands, all gnarled, full of pain. Granny had been her first taskmaster, making her practice her scales over and over again when she wanted to be out, riding, jumping, playing in the salt marshes, catching fish with her hands when the tides came in, digging for oysters to bring to her grandfather Angus, who so loved them before dinner. She recalled startlingly the last remarks Granny Claire made to her as she wrung her stiff, painful fingers. Her father told her that Granny was still alive, living on their land, a freed woman but still calling herself a McIver.

She started to play. A negro spiritual. One granny loved. One she had heard sung often at the Praise House on the plantation: "Let My People Go." Well, the Lord had answered granny's prayers—or had he? She played on— thumping loudly, so loudly it would be heard in heaven as granny had often directed her.

Thomas' back stiffened. He knew the song well and was furious with Vanessa. Next to him sat Jefferson and Varina Davis and on his other side, Judah Benjamin. "What the hell was she doing?" he fumed to himself. "The girl's gone mad." He sank down in his seat. "The next thing she'll be doing is playing a Northern song." There was a polite, confused response when she finished. Without hesitation she started to play another piece, again by Liszt. Sasha, who had been as perplexed as most of the audience when she played the spiritual he did not know, relaxed, but was not too happy at the selection. "Liebestraum," beautiful, of course, but played so often. Every student of the piano used it as an exercise. He paused in his thoughts as he listened, suddenly captured. This was different, very different. She was playing it with such feeling and sensitivity. He peeked at the sea of faces. They seemed completely enthralled. Well, he mused, when played well, the familiar is always successful.

Kenneth knew why she was playing "Liebestraum" and was touched. She was playing it for her grandfather Angus, his favorite piece. Angus McIver. He thought of his father as she continued to play. A man who had raised himself from humble beginnings in Scotland to become master of McIver Hall. How he had loved the land that had become his through backbreaking work, helped and encouraged by the woman he loved; a woman from Charleston of gentle upbringing who, although thirty at the time of their marriage, produced two strapping sons. After her untimely death, his father carried on alone, building it into one of the finest plantations in the Sea Islands.

He choked back his sobs, remembering the day of the Big Shoot, as it was now called on St. Helena. He had rushed back to McIver Hall after watching the Yankees take Port Royal, not knowing how soon they would be invading the land. He found his father dressed perfectly as if he were going calling, the long white hair neatly combed, his weathered face closely shaven, the white mustache just trimmed. The tall, reed-thin man was standing at the desk in the small office building behind the house, waiting for his son. When Kenneth entered and looked at him, Angus knew it was over. He had had a viral infection that he couldn't shake and had become weak, but he stood straight as he walked out to the lawn in front of McIver Hall, turning slowly in every direction as he surveyed the lands he had acquired and the lovely porticoed house that had been restored. There was a startling silence. None of the hands were to be seen. Even the chattering birds, so usual to the area, seemed to have flown away. He appeared overly fatigued all of a sudden, slumping to half his size. Kenneth watched his father as he walked back to the house, up the steps to the veranda and into the wide hall; asking his still-faithful servant, Conrad, to fetch his bible from the library. Kenneth tried to help him, as he had trouble climbing the flying staircase to the second floor, but he waved his son away with a weak gesture and told him in a formal manner, "I wish you well in this time of crisis. I'm sorry I will not be here to help."

Lying down on his bed fully clothed, holding on to the family bible, he said he was cold and old Conrad lovingly placed a down quilt over him. The eyes closed, Angus McIver just seemed to be asleep—dying so quickly, Kenneth was never sure when it happened. Together, son and faithful servant, buried him in the family plot. Conrad giving up a coffin he had been working on the past year for himself.

"Liebestraum." The German for "Song of Love." He was sure if it were possible, somewhere, somehow, Angus McIver was with them tonight, pleased by the tribute from his granddaughter.

Inadvertently his eyes turned to the mystery lady in the box. She was watching Vanessa, her bosom moving up and down more rapidly than under ordinary circumstances. He wondered why the strains of "Liebestraum" would so effect her. She turned her head toward him, and through her veil their eyes met for a moment before her gaze returned to the stage.

JoJo threw the warm cape over Vanessa's shoulders to protect her from the drafts as she came off the stage, and started to lead her to her dressing room when Josiah came running through the stage door.

"Vanessa! He's here. I saw Pierre in the gallery."

She was startled by the news. "Pierre? Are you sure?"

"Yes, it's him."

"Is he coming backstage?" Her heartbeat accelerated, and for a strange reason she became afraid. "Did he say he was coming back to see me?"

"He didn't say, but I don't think he is. He headed down the street away from the hall."

"Please, Josiah, run after him. Catch up with him and bring him back. We can't lose him."

"He didn't recognize me, Nessa. He just stared past me when I said hello."

"Quickly. After him before he disappears again."

Mack was confused. He had watched the encounter from outside the stage door, but could not hear what was being said. She was some kind of performer. Who was she to the lad? Was this good or bad? He rushed after Josiah as he ran out and down the street—the people were now pouring out of the hall, and he had to dodge in and out to not lose his victim.

Josiah saw Pierre pausing under a gaslight at an intersection. "Pierre," he yelled. The tall man dressed conservatively in a long gray coat and slouch hat pulled down over his eyes was puzzled by someone calling his name. He didn't know whether to wait for the young man or not, anxious to be on his way. Why, he wasn't quite sure, but he felt driven. He started to cross the road, when he felt the young man's hand on his shoulder.

"Pierre, don't you know me?"

"I'm sorry. But I can't say that I do."

"I'm Josiah McIver."

Pierre stared at the bright young face. "Of course. But you've grown. I never would have known you." He tilted his head to one side to study the youth more closely in the rain.

"Vanessa. She wants you to come backstage. She wants to see you."

"She knew I was there?"

"Yes. I told her. She sent me after you. Please come back with me."

His reply came in a rush. "I have an appointment. I'm late. Convey my apologies."

As he walked away at a quick pace, he called to Josiah who was still standing under the gaslight. "Tell her

she played beautifully." He was suddenly gone—a lost
figure in the rain.

It was an old pub just off Piccadilly. He hadn't had
any strong spirits for several years, the pint of bitters
sat on the scarred table in front of him. He was running
again, he told himself. He should have congratulated
Vanessa in person. A sleasy prostitute sat down next to
him and smiled through cracked teeth.

"Want a turn in the hay, m'lord?"

He fought his repulsion and looked into her eyes. They
were dimmed by alcohol, or drugs, one he noted had a cast
in it and gave that eye the appearance of being dead.
Like me, he thought, part of me is alive and part is
dead. He threw some coins on the table for the drink
and a pound note in her direction, then left hastily.

The crowd in front of the hall had thinned. He found
the alleyway that led to the stage door just in time to see
Vanessa being led out by a large man in evening cape
and top hat. In a thickly accented voice, he was yelling
directions to everyone as they rushed to a waiting carriage. Josiah was trailing behind. They came close to
him. He was standing in the crowd that had gathered
to see Vanessa. She brushed past, not seeing him due to
an angled umbrella held to protect her.

"Stand back. Don't crowd Miss McIver. Stand
back."

He wanted to call her name but couldn't. He stood
in the midst of her admiring fans and watched the carriage pull away. In a few seconds he was standing there
alone. Again he started for Waterloo Station, anxious
to get back to his small home in Kent, but suddenly
stopped. The long tapering fingers fished in his coat pocket
for a crumpled letter. A letter sent to him from his
solicitors in Charleston. It contained the information that
his mother was to be in London for a short time,
desperate to see him. Now, he thought. Why not now.
He had hid in the theater, in the balcony, that was
wrong. Why not face his mother now. He pulled his
hat further down over his brow and looked for a public
carriage. She was staying at Claridge's—he would have
known that without the letter. That is where his mother
always stayed. For many years she had been coming to

London to sell her precious cotton to the mills. Always, it was Claridge's and before it was called Claridge's it was known as Mivart's. One hotel, she had always said, that catered to people who would not have condescended to normally stay at a hotel.

The carriage got him there in a matter of minutes. The lobby reeked of Victorian magnificence, and the snide clerk told him that Mrs. Bonneau had retired for the night and did not wish to be disturbed.

"My good man, she will skin you alive if she finds out I've been here and was turned away."

The clerk was unsure. His eyes took in the man in front of him. He certainly was a man of breeding, American, but not the usual type in his opinion. Pierre told him again to ring Mrs. Bonneau. His imperious manner intimidated the clerk. He went to the switchboard. "Who shall I tell her is here?"

"Her son."

The old man, in a manner just as lordly, didn't bat an eye. "I shall tell her you are in the lobby, sir."

Pierre disregarded the clerk's suggestion that he wait in the lobby and walked across to the long curving staircase. The way to his mother's suite was familiar. The Bonneaus always stayed in Suite 127 through 129, a sitting room and two master bedrooms. He paused on the first landing to smell a bouquet of beautiful fresh flowers artistically arranged on the Regency table, gently touching the petals of a rose. That moment helped him collect himself. He was ill at ease at the prospect of seeing his mother again.

The last time he was in this hotel was after the war, filled with guilt for having hurt Vanessa and needing desperately to escape the heaviness of his life as a Bonneau of Charleston, St. Helena Island, and—Wind Flower. After weeks of isolation, he read of a lecture to be given by a holy man from India, the Ashami. The Ashami brought him what he needed—a peace, an acceptance of life as it happens and told him of a holy place in India. He spent three years there in meditation and study. Now he hoped he could handle this part of his life—his relationship with his mother. And Vanessa. Seeing her tonight stirred new fire in him—something that he had forced to be dead.

"Are you all right, sir? Sir. Let me help you. Your finger, sir."

His eyes focused on the young maid reaching out to him. "Oh, I've just pricked it on a thorn. It's all right. Here, I'll just wrap my handkerchief around it. Thank you."

He paused at the door to the suite, feeling the weight of his past upon him once more. Then he rapped gently. He hadn't seen a Southern black in a long time, so the sight of the young negress obviously just aroused from her bed by his unexpected visit, hastily tying up her hair in a bright calico bandana, caught him short.

"Good evening, Mr. Bonneau."

The lyrical sound of the Gullah dialect so reminded him of home.

He looked closer, "You're Dinah's daughter. Am I right?"

She smiled, big white teeth in her dark face. "Yes, sir, that's right, sir."

"You were just a child when I left. How's your mother?"

"She's jes' fine, sir. She's back working for Mrs. Bonneau for wages like all of us."

"You can leave now, Jubal." The cool tone of Harriet's voice was such a contrast against the pleasant singsong Gullah dialect of the young black.

She stood just inside the living room, the low gaslight not reaching her. He thought this room could have been back home—just her environment, the silk brocade walls in French blue, the black marble fireplace, and the floor covered with a fine Aubusson carpet. Finally, she started toward him, and he couldn't control the audible gasp that escaped at the sight of her thin body. Even the full moiré robe couldn't hide the fact that she no longer was a lady of impressive proportions. She was unattractively slender. Her hair was totally gray, and the once full face was now heavily lined.

"Well, come sit by the fire—this dreadful rain must have chilled you to the bone. Would you like something warm to drink or a sherry?"

"Nothing. I don't wish to have anything to drink, but I will sit by the fire."

"Of course. Jubal, take Master Bonneau's coat." The young girl helped him off with his outer garment and swiftly left the room. Harriet and Pierre settled in chairs opposite each other facing the glowing flames.

"It's good to see you, my son."

"And you too, Mother. Are you well?"

"Well enough."

There was such a wide breach between them—spanning it was so difficult. She went to a table and poured herself a glass of sherry.

"You sure you will not join me?"

"No. You go ahead."

"Did you go to the recital tonight?"

For the first time since he entered the room he spoke freely, "Yes, of course—she was wonderful. It was really quite extraordinary. There was Vanessa looking so beautiful, so tiny on that large stage. I felt very nervous for her, but from almost the first note I realized she had command, that she was up to the evening. She played like a dream—a true artist, never faltering. In a way it was all unreal. Since I last saw her, there has been so much growth. And she looks . . . ," At that moment Pierre realized with a little embarrassment that he was running on in a manner unusual for him. Harriet was obviously upset by his enthrallment.

"I'm sorry, Mother. I seem to have gotten carried away."

She just looked at him and moved to stand near the fire with her back to him. "Well, I couldn't go. I couldn't go for your sake. She has been so unkind to you—turned her back on both of us. At least she had the decency to not use the name of Bonneau as she tramped about the continent like some—some free woman, elevating her slave practically to a companion. It's a disgrace . . ."

As she turned back to him, she saw his eyes flare for a moment and knew she had done exactly what she promised herself she wouldn't do. Damn that Vanessa coming between them at this reunion. A reunion she was so looking forward to.

"I only say these things in your interest, my dear son."

"Mother, I've come to you so that we can end our own little war. The time apart has been good, and I also want to resolve things with Vanessa. She can't be blamed for the divorce—I forced it. She knew nothing about it until it was over."

"It was her failure."

"No, mine."

"I won't accept that, Pierre."

"Well, you must. My inheritance from Father is coming to me next spring, and I am going to give most of the money to Vanessa—the house in Charleston, my share of both plantations. I want her to have it."

He had never spoken with such calm resolve and this concerned her. It was uncertain ground, but she was determined not to be defeated in her aim to control him for his own sake to protect his fortune, and to have him back in South Carolina where he belonged. But now was not the time to play out all her cards—she would hold back some, but he would begin to know from this moment on that she meant business. "Pierre, things are not as simple as you think. The house in Charleston will go for taxes unless you come up with money to pay them very soon. You have very little money now, only property. You have a lot to catch up with—there is no rice farming, the freed slaves do one-third the work they did before, and the imposed wages make it impossible to break even. So, there are no shares of profit at the moment. No, it is not so easy."

"You will have to lend me money to pay the taxes so I do not lose the house in Charleston for Vanessa."

"Under these conditions, I don't think so."

"Mother!"

"Don't think harshly of me, Pierre. My generosity has been the only reason the McIvers still have the land and a home in St. Helena."

She had given him enough for now. She was disappointed that Pierre obviously still loved Vanessa, but if she had to, she would use that to get him back. The McIvers would be cut off unless Vanessa agreed to remarry Pierre. If it became necessary, she would threaten. No one in Charleston knew of the divorce and would never have to know—one good thing the war did was cover that over. Well, maybe she could right things to her advantage.

"Never mind, all this horrid business talk, Pierre. Let's talk about your time in India. Is the climate similar to South Carolina?"

6

The rumor in the back halls and downstairs was that one of the McIver daughters was to be the next Lady Hatfield—so the mother's behavior did not bode well for the future. Cyril and Miss Shields had worked a long time for Lord Hatfield—there were only a handful of other houses that had the same stature. Now they would be forced to put in an extra effort to keep the house up to standard. It was one thing to acknowledge among themselves that things weren't going well, but there was no way they would allow the employees of other great houses to look down their noses at them and make snide remarks about the sad business of working for an inelegant American mistress. Their only hope was that the mother would leave soon after the rumored event and the new mistress without the mother's interference would leave them to their duties.

Jamie's valet, Martin, stood in the outside vestibule watching through the long window for a sign of Lord Hatfield's carriage. The footmen, too, were at their stations, each with a large umbrella ready to keep the rain from the delicate dresses of the ladies who would soon be arriving. They periodically knocked one foot against the other trying to keep their circulation moving and had folded their arms across their chests to keep the chill of the night air from seeping through their jackets, continually grumbling about the "bloody rain."

Martin grinned at the sound of Cyril's voice, which had progressed over the past days from his usual sedate tone to a deep growl, a certain sign he had reached a state of total distress. Even a butler as experienced and respected as Cyril had a difficult time coping with Georgina McIver. She didn't know how to treat the staff, giving orders as though they were slaves, not trusting their abilities.

Downstairs, as they waited in this last moment of inactivity before the party began, several servants, full of excitement, sat around the kitchen table drinking tea from mugs, gossiping and speculating about the guests who were to attend the reception. The Prince of Wales, scandalous heir to the British throne, was expected, and that tickled their fancy the most.

"I wonder if old Bertie," said a scullery maid using the prince's pet name blithely, "will bring a lady of the theater with him?"

"Oh, is it Bertie, now," teased one of the footmen. "You on personal terms with the naughty darling of Victoria?"

"I ain't telling you my secrets," she parried back, enjoying herself grandly.

"I wonder what actress is his mistress this season?" asked an upstairs maid in all seriousness.

"Has to be a married one, that I can tell you," cried old Sarah, a veteran of the household who considered herself all knowing in these matters. "That way, if there are any 'accidents,' the little bastard won't be without a proper name."

"But he'd have the wrong father," boomed the jolly cook, adding, "I wonder how many of the upper class do have their proper fathers? They're very free these days, very free."

The footman's rap on the window brought Martin to attention, and he quickly stepped outside to escort Lord Hatfield and his sister, Lady Ardell Norton, the Duchess of Leighton, into the house. Her slippers were soaked through, and the duchess laughed as she kicked them off, telling the nearest footman to put them near a fireplace to dry. She enjoyed seeing her brother's arched, disapproving eyebrow.

"Jamie, don't be so prudish; no one will look down at my feet, not with these vulgar jewels I've draped around my bosom—and if they do you can be sure they will soon all be in bare feet for fear they were missing out on the latest fashion."

Anyone who saw them together could see the affection they felt for one another. If Ardell had been a man, she would also have held a high position in government, never intimidated, always speaking out on issues of the day of which she was surprisingly well informed.

Marrying the Duke of Leighton happened when she was barely eighteen years old. The duke was only ten years her senior, but he could have been her father in appearance and demeanor, being a person who seemed old from the day he discarded his short pants. Curiosity and snide comments ran rampant through London society when their engagement was announced. Why would sparkling, witty, attractive Ardell Hatfield, who could have had the pick of England's eligible titled men, choose the bumbling, stuffy duke? Granted he was among the ten wealthiest men in England, but the Hatfields were not far behind—if not possibly equal in wealth. Her peers were more than delighted to have her out of the running, leaving the field open to them, but what a dull life on the horizon for her, they whispered. And besides, the duke did not excel in any of the social graces—he didn't dance, his conversation was boring, and he could hardly be called attractive, with a largish nose and starting to bald at that early age. Of course they had to admit, he was very well versed in politics and sat in the House whenever he was in town during sessions, but left the decision making for the Empire to others.

The duke and duchess spent their honeymoon on a shooting trip in India. It was the last time Ardell shared in the duke's passion—hunting—and from the beginning he was gone on his trips most of the year. There were shoots in Scotland and Norway. Then Africa for big game, but he always seemed pleased to come home to Ardell and her wonderful gadfly life.

Soon after they returned from their honeymoon, their social set began to realize this odd couple was rather well suited to each other. She was free to pursue her own life protected by a respectable marriage, and he adored her—she was all his secret heart wished he himself could be and was content to let her way of life not spoil what they had together. More than once he was heard to say, "I would rather be married to Ardell with all her affairs and other carryings-on, than anybody else in the world. She is an exciting woman."

Ardell was discreet as much as possible in her romantic liaisons—of which there were many—but of course there were leaks. How could you stop ungentlemanly kiss-and-tellers. At times there was the, "Who is she bedding these days" game. High on the list would always be her latest "find," the poet from the Scottish moors or a new Italian painter or her on-again, off-again peccadillo with the Prince of Wales. It was rumored she couldn't stand it after he started to put on weight but was delighted to see him when he dieted. For her "finds" who became her paramours, support included financial aid and a room at the country estate for quiet contemplation, creative thought, and lots of physical activity.

The duchess was now noticeably shocked by the display at one end of the long buffet table. She stood absolutely still just inside the dining room in her stocking feet, her stature tall, the marvelous Roman profile thrust forward, and her hair, a smoky dark blond, was as usual pulled straight back into a tight bun, accentuating her long aquiline nose, strong jaw, and almost paper-thin lips. As the duke always proudly declared, "She's a handsome woman with thoroughbred features." She heaved a heavy sigh of disgust.

"My God, Jamie, do you expect all of London to show up here tonight?" The eyes narrowed as she turned to Cyril and Miss Shields who stood close by. "Really, I do think you two could have seen some restraint was used. Mounds of food aren't the least bit appetizing. I'm referring to that ugly, piled high mess at the end of the table."

"Fried chicken," said Miss Shields, so happy the duchess also disapproved.

"Oh," she responded archly, "one of those frightful Southern dishes. Ugh. It looks so greasy," she mused. "How do you eat it? With your fingers?"

"Precisely," informed Cyril, turning up his nose in imitation of the duchess.

Jamie was stern in his reproach.

"No more of this—it is inappropriate. Fried chicken is

a favorite dish among the McIvers and fellow Southerners
—there will be quite a few here tonight from that section
of the world—so enough said. Bring the champagne,
Cyril."

The orchestra was tuning up in the background as
Miss Shields disappeared and Cyril rushed to do Lord
Hatfield's bidding. A servant appeared almost immediately
with a silver tray holding crystal tulip glasses and champagne was poured.

"Well, dear brother, I see you are very taken by the
McIvers. Next thing we know we'll all talk 'jes' lak
them'—I think the Americans can be an interesting lot,
they are such a mixture, but I find it incredible that anyone would be the least bit interested in trying to acquire
a taste for their food. What is your attachment to this
clan—they're houseguests I understand."

"Wait and see, and I hope you will be pleased."

Oh God, she thought, he's been snared—trapped. Well,
he needs release, just like the rest of us. It never entered
her mind that marriage was in the wind. She raised her
glass in a toast, "Here's to us, Jamie. I'm so pleased to
be here with you tonight."

"Thank you, Ardell, it was good of you to cut short
your visit to the shires to come."

"You peaked my curiosity when I read your note
about this exciting young pianist. She was simply marvelous in her debut tonight, by the way. I became jealous
however. You know how I pride myself on knowing all
the talented artists in London before anyone else, and
here, Jamie Hatfield, a peer of the realm, so immersed
in the running of his land and politics, uncovers the find
of the year. Tell me all about this Vanessa McIver—
where did you find her and how did you get so involved
with this Southern family?"

Not willing to discuss the issue any further at the
moment, he tried to distract her. "Tell me about your trip
to the midlands and the Beresford-Pierces. Are they still
as crusty as ever? I want to know all the good gossip.
It's been so long since we've talked."

He was pleased that she moved on quickly to stories
of the parties and the many misadventures of the landed
gentry she had been visiting—he never noticed the determined way her stockinged foot kicked aside the short

train draped from her bustle to allow her to take his arm and walk regally toward the receiving area to greet his guests. The duchess was in control of the affair.

"I will steal you off for more of this later," he whispered as the arrival of the first guests was announced.

The music was playing, and the house glittered with light from the many chandeliers and wall sconces. Servants stood in attendance every few feet and the fireplaces blazed, filling the rooms with warmth.

Ardell's genius with people was very apparent as she and Jamie greeted the arrivals—never forgetting a name or when she had last seen them. Soon some of the McIvers arrived, Georgina rushing ahead, all excited, walking as though her shoes had springs.

Ardell was fascinated by this group. The father was rather handsome, someone Ardell would like to view more closely. Then the uncle, also good-looking, but a pompous ass, his neck constantly craning to see who was there, becoming so effusive when he heard her called by the title of duchess. She allowed him to kiss her hand and then turned her back to him as she said hello to the next person. But the group of them just milled near the door. Finally she said to the mother, "Why don't you and the rest of your family circulate in the other rooms— so many guests have already arrived—I'm sure they're just dying to meet you." She was pleased at her cleverness, she would be rid of them. Georgina McIver was off, quickly followed by her husband, the uncle headed straight for the dining room where, it seemed to Ardell, all the Americans had rushed, they were ever so fond of food since their Civil War, but the young McIver girl, introduced by Jamie as Amanda, balked.

"I'll stay here with Jamie," she piped boldly.

"Well, that will be all right, I guess," said Ardell, deciding to match this young woman's forwardness with a bit of her own. "But first do repair your face—you have too much rouge on your cheeks."

"Why your Ladyship, I have just taken care of my appearance. I didn't want to look like so many English ladies, sallow and aging in appearance. A little color always does wonders. You are a dear to be concerned."

Ardell had to smile—fancy her so audacious.

When Vanessa arrived, the applause began quietly then swelled to "bravos." She was surrounded by old friends and new admirers kissing her cheeks, holding her hands. Sasha was in his glory, ordering people about, holding them back in the crush.

"Patience, patience, she will have time for all of you. Careful with her hands. Miss McIver's hands are magical—her debut was a supreme event." He was genuinely delighted by the party, feeling this too was confirmation that Vanessa had moved into a new world.

Despite the adulation, Vanessa's eyes darted everywhere for a glimpse of Kirk and was disappointed when she couldn't find him. But she continued to be on the lookout as she was introduced to one person after another.

Georgina was shocked when she saw the Prince of Wales slyly put his finger down the duchess' décolletage and her quiet, amused rebuke, "Stop that, you naughty man. How's the new diet coming?"

The portly young man whispered something in her ear, and she squealed with delight. Then, "Why not. We are friends after all. Once in a while might be a lark."

Georgina tried to hear more, but they took some champagne from a passing tray and walked in the opposite direction.

The orchestra was playing a lovely waltz—the party was gay, the rooms filled to capacity. Jamie waited until Amanda finished dancing with a Southern gentleman, then took possession of her, steering her through the crowd.

"We will go into the library, my dear. I have something to give you."

He closed the massive doors, and they were alone in the hushed quiet. Amanda looked up at him expectantly.

"Are you ready to let the world know that you are to become my wife, Amanda? Think of all those poor young fellows, so jealous of me for having captured the most beautiful flower to land on our shores."

He tried to take her in his arms but she cleverly skirted him.

"Jamie, you make me blush. All those ladies will surely be jealous of me. I hope they will accept little Amanda, especially your sister," and with the sweetest Southern drawl she purred, "I know she doesn't like me, and I just wanna die."

"They will accept you . . . I'll make . . ." He fell silent in midsentence. Amanda tilted her head, puzzled by the slightly glazed look in his eyes, his open mouth hanging slack.

"Why Jamie, are you all right? Have you been drinking? Jamie! What's wrong?"

His eyes focused, "What?" She looked startled. "Are you tiddily?"

"Oh, no—er, yes, I had a drink or two," grabbing at the excuse for his spell, "but I've a right, have I not, my dear? Tonight is so special."

He turned toward the desk, and while unlocking the drawer, a grimace passed over his face, but he fought to force it away quickly; he was beginning to feel himself again.

"One moment, Amanda. Now that you are to be my bride, you shall wear the jewels belonging to the Hatfields. Stand in front of the mirror so that I can put my favorite necklace on you."

From behind he removed the simple pearls she was wearing and placed a ruby and diamond triple strand necklace around her neck.

"No ruby or diamond could ever ask to spend its life in a more beautiful setting," he whispered seductively, as he wrapped his arms around her tiny waist and then moved his opened hands on her body just below the small high breasts, finally cupping her in his strong hands as he kissed the back of her neck.

Amanda couldn't say a word, she was so taken by her image in the mirror. Somehow the jewels transformed her into the lady of the house; Lady Hatfield, a countess, and she liked it. Standing as tall as possible, she admired the effect—totally oblivious to Jamie and his fondling her.

The Duchess of Leighton's eyes were drawn immediately to Amanda's bosom as she entered the drawing room with Jamie. Twice before he had presented these jewels to the two women who became his wife. Now she understood her brother's remarks at the beginning of the evening and his anxiety when she mentioned the McIvers. Ardell's eyes scanned the room looking over the Southerners thinking—outcasts. "My God, Jamie," she thought, "you've gone the limit. This time I shall have something to say about who fills mother's shoes. You are so brilliant in so many ways—how could you make such a mistake. Why air your bedding needs in public?"

Josiah cursed under his breath at having been cornered by his mother and forced to dance first with Bronsky's mother and then with Pansy Hortz, the schoolmaster's wife. He gritted his teeth as he listened for the tenth time this night about how tall he had grown and what a fine young man he had become. "If only you could know, madam," he thought as her large bosoms careened off his chest, reminding him of Daphne. The dance seemed interminable, and finally he caught his uncle's eye and signaled for him to break in, grateful when Thomas picked up the cue. Josiah quickly crossed the room avoiding his mother and then darted into the music room at the front of the house. He threw open the tall windows and the rush of cool air felt refreshing— as he expelled his breath in one loud gasp, he attracted the attention of the footman standing in the rain at the curb. As he nodded recognition to the servant, his eye caught a movement behind the carriage parked just below the window. He strained his eyes, only the light spilling from the house illuminated the area. The figure stepped forward a bit, brazenly, and although Josiah still couldn't see the face, he knew the man was looking directly at him, the leer portending evil and hatred. Josiah shuddered at the bad vibrations he felt from the dark figure in the shadows. Quickly closing the windows, he caught the lace undercurtains in the frame but left it—and suddenly, afraid to turn his back on this obvious danger, backed across the room, arriving in the hall as Jamie stood high on the sweeping marble staircase announcing his forthcoming marriage to Amanda. With Georgina noticeably at her side, she grandly received the applause and cheers; Amanda was now the center of attention.

Sasha growled to Vanessa, "The man should not have made the announcement at this reception—this is your night."

"No, Sasha, it is a night for both of us—a McIver night."

Actually, she was glad to be out of the limelight, for

it gave her a chance to look for Kirk again in the crowd. Once or twice earlier, her eyes had caught sight of him—leaning against a far wall, alone, obviously uncomfortable. At one point when her mother, who kept a steady flow coming her way had again asked her, "Vanessa dear, you remember the Haywards from back home," she raised her hand at him indicating she would come over in a moment. He had smiled and shrugged, but now when she looked to the place where she had seen him before, he was gone. Her eyes darted about the room finally catching a glimpse of him near the door—he was leaving. Their eyes met and he waved goodbye.

Vanessa pushed through the small group standing around her and caught up with him as a footman was helping him with his coat.

"Kirk, you're not leaving yet."

"I must. I have early duty at the hospital. It's not good to stay out late and drink 'til all hours of the morning. Think how horrified you would be to see a doctor with shaky hands coming at you."

She laughed and felt happy at last to be with him, but disappointed that he was going. "Well, you haven't asked me to dance. You cannot leave until we do."

"I'm sorry, Vanessa, but some other time."

"When?" She was stunned by her boldness and so was he. Both were totally unaware of people nearby listening to their conversation.

"Well I—I don't know."

Feeling at a loss and confused by her behavior she quietly said, "Kirk, it's so good to have you back again. I guess I just want you to know that we all—no—that I would like very much to see you again soon." She couldn't lift her eyes to his for fear he would find her forwardness unpleasant, very aware of his hard, lanky masculinity.

He touched her arm. "Vanessa, I would like nothing more than just that, but the McIvers and the Yoors are still worlds apart."

She risked going further, suddenly she didn't want this man out her life and clasped her hands over his, holding his fingers tightly, looking into his eyes, relieved to see a tenderness there—wanting to push back the dark blond curl that had fallen on his forehead.

"No, we're not. Not any more. Things have changed, Kirk. I know I have. Now promise me you'll call on me."

"All right, I will."

"Soon?"

He laughed, the voice deep and resonant in its southernness, "Yes, soon." Kirk turned to leave then turned back and very quickly kissed her on the cheek. "You played brilliantly tonight."

She watched him out the door until the night covered his figure and blew a kiss in his direction.

"Au revoir, Dr. Yoors," she mouthed to herself.

"Now that you've said adieu to one of your admirers, may I claim you for a dance, Mrs. Bonneau?"

Mrs. Bonneau. She hadn't been called that since—

"Pierre?" she said softly, almost to herself.

"At your service, madame."

Vanessa turned slowly, and looked into the deep brown, mysterious eyes. She was surprised to see heavy lines at the corners of the lids, and although he wore a broad smile on the still very handsome face, his eyes were rapt in serious thought, the dark hair was longer, below the chin line, almost touching his shoulders, giving him such an aesthetic look, but silver was prominent at his temples and streaked the top of his head. He had aged, and surprisingly she didn't remember him being that tall, towering way over her. They had not met in six years.

"It's been a long time" was all she could say.

"Too long—" then very charmingly but overpoweringly in command, he said, "May I have this dance? It's a beautiful waltz and unfortunately I have to leave shortly to catch a train, the last one out of London in my direction tonight I fear, so I don't want to waste a moment of the music."

He walked her gracefully to the conservatory, guests parting to make way for the tall, good-looking couple. He was not dressed in formal wear, but his manner and bearing raised no question that he was a person of importance, one who belonged.

Ardell, standing at the edge of the dance floor, was immediately attracted to Pierre's imposing figure.

"Who is that devilishly attractive man?" she whispered

to Lady Manley, a lady-in-waiting to the queen, standing next to her.

"Haven't a clue," replied the matronly woman, "but I'm also dying to find out."

Pierre took Vanessa in his arms firmly, and they danced away, not talking for a few moments.

"You sent the Wind Flowers."

"Yes."

"Thank you, they were lovely. Why no card?"

"Did I need one?"

He gripped her harder as they waltzed on.

7

Kenneth knew she wasn't sleeping. Her breathing was shallow and quivery; afraid I'm going to touch her he thought. All day she was gay and pleased with everything, flitting about like a butterfly, the old Georgina. When Hatfield laughed, she laughed—so easily. The ride through Hyde Park this Sunday afternoon in "the lord's" splendid carriage thrilled her. She nodded grandly along with Hatfield and Amanda to others in expensive carriages or polished traps pulled by prancing ponies. A gracious smile never left her face until the evening's end, when that smile crumbled completely as she trudged up the stairs with him.

It was no use. Sleep was impossible, his old war wound throbbed, and he was feeling so displaced, desperately in need of affection and release.

He slipped out of bed and pulled on his robe. Slowly, he turned the knob and went into the hall, not knowing where he was heading, just knowing he had to be on the move. Wandering down the long corridor that led to the marble staircase, he couldn't deny it was a magnificent house. Even the paintings lining the upper hall were beautiful works of art, and Jamie, in spite of his poor attempts at humor, he now knew possessed a keen mind, especially when it came to law and politics. However, he still grew anxious when he thought of his daughter and Hatfield as a married couple. Jamie was very virile in manner but twice married and so much older. He hoped Amanda wasn't so impressed with Hatfield's position and wealth, she equated it with love. He did not want her to have an unhappy life for all the money and social activity.

Another disturbing thought was that she would be living life as a foreigner on alien soil.

He stopped when he saw the light under Vanessa's door. Lonely or not, he would welcome the chance of spending a few minutes with his eldest child. He knocked lightly and heard her very gentle feminine voice. "Who is it?"

He whispered through the door, "It's your father." After a second or two, she stood there—framed in the doorway—simply dressed in a pale pink wrapper. Her light brown hair was tied back, the ends of the ribbon trailing down her neck. There was a shy smile on her face, and Kenneth recognized that grin from when she was a little girl—that hadn't changed.

"I'm so glad you came to pay me a visit, Father. I couldn't sleep."

"Nor could I. I was just wandering around in the hall."

"Don't wander around—come in."

He followed her into the spacious bedroom, sitting room. There was a good fire going in the fireplace and they sat in front of it, opposite each other in small tufted velvet chairs. Needlepoint was on a table near her, and he realized she had been sitting there embroidering before he came in. Looking at the bed he saw it was still neat as a pin. So, she hadn't been to bed at all as yet, and it was well past midnight. Vanessa picked up the scrim and started to work the pattern. It was comforting to be there, and he relaxed, stretching his legs in front of him as he watched her doing such a homey thing as stitchery.

Vanessa looked up at him, feeling his gaze and smiled that shy smile of hers. She's content to be sitting here with her father, he thought—he was pleased. It was a good moment. One he would hold on to. How he missed these moments back on the plantation. It had been so desolate without his family. They were all facing a turning point again. First it had been the war, and now because of the effects of that war, instead of his family coming home, a dream that saw him through the severest of times, it had dispersed them like seeds thrown to the wind. He rationalized they would, at this age, have been going their own way, back home, but close enough for him to still be a definite part of their lives. He didn't know if he could control Georgina. But Josiah—he was especially determined that his son not remain in England. The young man needed to spend more time with men. The women around him had made him soft, self-indulgent, with no real purpose in his life. He was shocked when meeting him last week, he sounded and behaved more British than American to him. Not Vanessa though. An American still, in all her ways. Quieter, not as spunky— very reflective—but that had started back in Charleston before she left for England.

He sensed she wanted to talk but didn't know how to begin, and neither did he to tell the truth. There was no doubt she would never completely get over her marriage and all that happened to her while living with the Bonneaus. Then the shock of Pierre divorcing her. Georgina and Amanda had certainly felt the horrors of the war when they were living in Charleston, but nothing like Vanessa experienced.

Their eyes met for a moment or two, then she looked at him quizzically. It was as if each was trying to read the thoughts of the other.

"Have you found happiness and contentment, my daughter?" Immediately he thought what a foolish question. He knew life always doled out qualifiers in moments of success or happiness and added hastily to cover the silly question, "It must have felt wonderful to be so warmly received after the recital. Especially from these pompous, hard-to-bend Londoners."

She concentrated on her sewing again. "I was startled. I never expected such a reaction, especially since I didn't think I played exceptionally well."

"You did. I could not believe that was my child up there. My own Vanessa. The gangly girl who was always thumping on the piano when she wasn't out riding her favorite horse."

"I thought I thumped a bit the other night."

"Not to my ears you didn't. You are now what they call an artiste."

They laughed at that almost tentatively, as if trying to get to know each other again. Her blue-gray eyes sparked in the firelight, her lovely oval face was flushed from the heat of the crackling fire. To Kenneth she suddenly seemed so tender and vulnerable. He had a strong urge to protect her from whatever there was that might hurt her again. Reaching out to her unexpectedly, she dropped her stitchery, took his hand and rose. In one smooth movement she sat on the floor by him and put her head on his knee.

Her voice was so low, he barely heard her. "Pierre was at the concert hall."

"Pierre? During the recital?"

"Yes."

He felt threatened for her. "How did you know? Did he come back to see you or send a note?"

"No. Josiah told me. He saw him there."

"I don't know why I am so surprised. We came over on the boat with Harriet, and she said he was living just outside London."

"Didn't you see him at the reception here?"

"No, I didn't and no one told me."

"He didn't stay long—I wonder why he came to hear me play?"

At first he didn't know what to say, but he wanted to stop ugly memories, "He always loved your music, Vanessa."

"You're right. I used to think he loved my playing more than he loved me. If he ever did love me."

He smoothed back her already smooth hair. "I'm sure he did. How could he help but love you." He leaned over and kissed the top of her head.

"You say that because you are my father."

"I say it because it is true." There was a space of silence. "Did it upset you to see Pierre the other evening?"

"Yes."

He saw her eyes cloud over. "It was the times, Vanessa. The times."

"Not me?"

"Of course not. You were a wonderful wife." He had to change the subject feeling so inadequate in the discussion. "It was very thoughtful of you to play 'Lieberstraum' in memory of your grandfather."

"I felt very close to him at that moment."

"So did I. Almost as if he were there with us."

She wanted to continue questioning her father about her failed marriage, but she couldn't. So much was still locked inside her. Instead, "Grandfather was happily married, wasn't he? He always talked so lovingly of grandmother."

"I'm sure they had their problems, but it was an old-fashioned, good marriage all the way around."

"I've been thinking—that's what I would like. If I can get it—it seems so elusive." After a pause she added, "But that way of life just might not be my lot in life."

Kenneth feared all this was related to Pierre. He didn't want to see them try again.

"What about your music? You seem so involved."

"There's no other way with music except total involvement. It is a marriage of sorts—a form of slavery. Then you ask yourself—what is it really? Just living out of a suitcase with no real home life . . . alone. Nothing except the piano."

His spine stiffened. Of course she was not happy being first and only a musician, even with the success of the other evening. It wasn't really her choice, it had been forced on her. In his preoccupation with the rebuilding of McIver Hall and the land, he had grown to accept easily, he must admit, Vanessa's immersion into the world of music. In a sudden shock he came to grips with the reality that her total absorption was her protection from what had happened—a place to hide from real life and the involvement with people. He was saddened by the thought that he had probably always known it deep down but never allowed the truth to surface. It was so much easier that way. Then the revelation that this was the most open conversation he had had with her since she had grown or rather, since she married into the Bonneau family seven years ago, also startled him.

He loved his eldest child very much and wanted only happiness for her, but again felt his inadequacies, stemming from his own failures in human relationships.

"Here you are," he said quietly, "beginning to be an acclaimed pianist and what you really want in life is to be a loving wife and mother—not a musician."

"I don't know. That's my problem. I just don't know. The other day it was all so clear to me—what I wanted. Then it changed again."

Pierre—it must be him—seeing him again.

She went on, "How wonderful it must be to love someone and be loved in return—to share a complete life with that person." She couldn't tell him about Kirk at this time—what was there to tell really.

"Could I settle down, Father, after these five years of continuous study—five years of entrapment in preparing for one thing only . . . ?"

He sensed what she was really saying was that she was afraid of giving herself to love again. Damn! Was it Pierre? "I don't know, Vanessa, success can be sweet—a wonderful fulfillment to a man or woman."

"Yes. It can feel good and satisfying. Oddly, though, if I fail at music, which I do at times, it doesn't touch me like other failures. And the fact is, maybe music has really become my love, making me unfit for others."

"That is a possibility and perhaps you wouldn't be content any longer with another way of life. But—why not both?"

She laughed—that sweet, soft laugh. "You just said what I really want is to be a wife and mother—then you said, why not both? But, Father, being a concert artist, well, both would be an impossibility."

"Don't press so hard for answers. That may not be true and you have a whole life ahead of you. Your aims will straighten out."

"But what kind of life will I have, Father?"

"You are young yet, Vanessa."

"Not so young. I'm twenty-five."

"Young to me, and I don't think I had mature thoughts like you have until I was in my thirties. At least I think they were mature thoughts."

"But you married mother when you were twenty-four and she was only nineteen. She had three children by the time she was twenty-five. Were you very much in love?"

"Yes, very. Your mother was and still is a beautiful woman."

He had to change the subject. They were getting into areas he didn't want to burden her with, she had enough to cope with at the moment.

"Vanessa, have I told you how much I have missed you these past years, how much I love you and how proud I am of you. I've longed for my family."

"Now you have us all together again."

"For the moment, yes."

A sleepy JoJo came out of the dressing alcove. She was never far from her Nessa.

Kenneth stood and greeted her warmly, watching her rub the sleep from her eyes.

"I'm sorry to disturb you. I heard voices."

Vanessa went to her. "Come join us. My father and I were talking. He says he misses us back home."

"Yes, I do. Very much."

More awake now, she politely corrected him. "Not, JoJo, Mr. McIver. Jassime."

Vanessa shook her head in affirmation. "Yes, Father, we are to use the name of Jassime now—no more JoJo."

"That's my real name," explained the young woman.

"I remember," said Kenneth. "I remember it very well. But why the change all of a sudden? I though you liked the name JoJo."

"I did and I may never get used to Jassime again."

"It's because of Sillar," chimed in Vanessa. "You remember her, don't you, Father?"

He was startled at the sound of her name.

"She was at the theater also," said Vanessa.

Jassime said hastily and excitedly, "Sillar said she was going to come backstage to see me after the recital but instead she sent for me, and I saw her in her box. Oh, Mr. McIver, she was the most grand lady. You should have seen her."

"In a box? Was she wearing a nose veil?"

"Yes, Mr. McIver, did you see her?"

"I did. I did indeed."

"Wasn't she something?"

"She really was, Jassime."

"Get the hat she designed for you, Jo—I mean, Jassime. I will have to get used to using that name. But it does suit you."

He couldn't bring himself to talk and ask the questions he was dying to ask.

Jassime was back with the striped hatbox in an instant. He looked at it and saw Sillar's face as she had looked at the hall. In a haze he watched Jassime take out the hat and put it on her rumpled head. His eyes searched for an address on the box—there was none. Through his fog he heard Jassime say she would go get some hot

chocolate for them and Vanessa saying that would be
nice unless . . .

"Would you, Father?"

"What? I'm sorry, I didn't hear."

"Jassime is going to the kitchen for some hot chocolate unless you would prefer a brandy. She could stop in
the library for that."

"No. No. Hot chocolate will be fine."

Miss Shields walked down the long hallway stealthily.
In her arms was a fine velvet dress that she had just
brushed and steamed in the laundry room below stairs.
She heard the voices in Vanessa's room and paid scant
attention. She no longer was startled by what the Americans did. She loathed Amanda and Mrs. McIver, an
uncouth woman she thought, who was starting to tell
her what to do in not too subtle ways. She couldn't
bring herself to think of the forthcoming wedding.

At the end of the corridor, she used her passkey to
unlock a bedroom door. The candles were glowing and
the beautiful room was polished and gleaming in the
soft shadows, as if awaiting the momentary arrival of its
mistress. The velvet dress was placed carefully in a
French armoire next to other fine garments. Pleased with
the array and the aromatic air emanating from the wardrobe, she moved to the Chippendale dressing table between
tall windows facing the square and lit the white candles
in a tall candelabra. Finding the fine white cloth deep
in the pocket of her black dress, she endearingly polished
the already sparkling silver brushes and jeweled miniature boxes on the dressing table. This had been the late
Lady Hatfield's bedroom, and Sara Shields kept it alive
as a shrine to her ladyship as she did her lady's bedroom
at the country estate in Norfolk.

Lord Hatfield had never entered these rooms since the
death of his wife and was unaware of Sara Shields'
continued devotion. In the ten months since her untimely
demise, he tried to obliterate painful memories, therefore, avoiding contact with any of her personal effects.
Certainly her bedroom would stir up powerful images
that he wanted out of his life. Unbeknownst to everyone
except himself and her doctor, Cora Hatfield had been
dying for several years. He had taken her to the Italian

Riviera during the last stages of her illness when she became weak and feverish. Upon becoming catatonic, she suddenly knew death was upon her, for the truth of her sickness had been hidden even from her. Cora Hatfield died on the Riviera, not only tragically but violently by her own hand. Neither Sara Shields nor anyone else was told how it actually happened, but among the servants, the suspicions ran rampant. Only Lord Hatfield knew the true story of her death, and he kept the secret. Shields had been beside herself for days after the telegram arrived telling them of the death.

An unattractive middle-aged spinster, she came to work for the Hatfields in Norfolk fifteen years earlier, having been recommended by a cousin who had been a steward on the estate for some time. For years she had lived a wearisome existence with her elderly mother, catering to her because she held the purse strings of what little money there was. Her end was a blessing not only to the elderly woman tired of life but to Sara Shields as well. Although she would never admit it even to herself. Immediately awed by the Hatfields, landed gentry, whose regal mansion lay in a vast parklike setting with giant oaks, herds of deer in the surrounding forest, and peacocks strutting on the lawns, she set about carving a niche for herself. Her mother had been the daughter of a country vicar, and Sara had a fairly good education, so she was put in charge of household accounts and assisted the then housekeeper, Mrs. Higgins. Upon the old housekeeper's retirement to a small cottage on the land in Norfolk, she took over her duties and became indispensable to Lady Hatfield, eventually running two of their residences: the manor house in Norfolk, the seat of the lord's earldom, and the townhouse on Belgrave Square, where she personally came during the social seasons during the year to set it running properly. Now in her late fifties, she did not want her position usurped. She looked around the elegant room and was pleased, feeling she was its protector. Like the room, her ladyship was always so grand and imposing. She loved beautiful things and made sure they were tended to with the utmost care. Shields' brow furrowed deeply, that young snip of a girl, Amanda McIver, so messy, her clothes strewn about, magazines all over the floor and on her bed all the time.

If only it were in her power to stop the marriage. Her thoughts were broken by the sound of footsteps in the hall, and she tried to get to the door quickly to shut it but was too late.

Kenneth McIver stood on the threshold.

"Is anyone sleeping in this room?"

She was taken aback, frantic that he would enter. She moved to the door swiftly as she spoke, hoping he would step back into the hall as she approached so she could close the door behind her. He didn't budge.

"No. But the room is kept special. No one is allowed to sleep in here."

He was very tired and out of sorts from his tiredness. He and Vanessa had talked for a long time over the hot chocolate, stopping only when they spotted dawn peeking through the heavy sky.

"That's ridiculous," he said, surprising himself, "the room looks prepared for a guest, and if no one is expected, I'll use the bed." He stalked past the amazed woman, threw back the satin covers and started to take off his robe. He was about to drop from his exhaustion.

"You can't sleep here," she exclaimed excitedly. Horrified, she watched the robe drop to the floor, and gasped audibly when he slid between the covers. He was too dulled to care and overly satiated by the airs of some of Hatfield's servants.

She rushed to the side of the bed throwing caution aside, acutely aware she was drastically overstepping her bounds. "I told you this room is special. No one is to sleep here!"

The man was asleep immediately, and she could do nothing further. He had violated the room, and as she fled she vowed to keep the door locked after he left in the morning. She stood in the hall, her heart palpitating —the McIvers she felt had become a blight on her life, and her dislike turned into hatred.

Vanessa took up her needlepoint again after her father left, still not able to face bed and sleeplessness. After a time, she felt chilled and noticed the fire had died down. She got up and put another log on the dying embers, kneeling close to the hearth, watching, waiting for the log to catch and flare up so she could feel the warmth. While she waited, she stared fixedly at the logs, and unexpectedly thought of Wind Flower Plantation. Beautiful Wind Flower that was no more, like so many things in her life that were just no more. Burned to the ground—the old rice plantation with its gracious old pink mansion and exquisite gardens complete with tiny lakes. She remembered Mother Harriet, as she had called her uncomfortably during that time, telling her proudly, "My great granddaddy laid out those gardens and terraces, Vanessa. He wanted to have the grounds look like a perfect English garden. Took a hundred slaves ten years to carry out his plans." Vanessa recalled all the hands it had taken, daily, while she lived there to keep it perfect. How she loved walking down the paths, delighted by the profusion of colorful flowers, the heady scents, and the white swans floating on the lakes. There was an abundance of bright camellias in the winter months, brilliant azaleas brightening the terraces in the spring, and in the summer, beautiful magnolias and kalmia. Of course, the jewel-colored anemones were almost always in bloom because of seedings throughout the year. Pierre held one in his hand one day following their arrival from St. Helena Island just after the evacuation, and blew on its petals. It had been the favorite flower of the garden's planner, his great, great granddaddy, he told her, and the blooms didn't open unless the wind blew, be it a gentle or a strong breeze—that's why the favorite flower, anemoni, was also called Wind Flower, from whence the plantation took its name. As he continued to blow on the blossom, the petals slowly started to unfold, displaying its showy black center. When she received the bouquet of Wind Flowers with no card the night of the recital, she should have known who sent them.

There were sounds of hissing, spitting, and then crackling as the fire caught. The flames shot up crazily in front of her eyes, and it was mesmerizing, throwing her back in time, an agonizing time at Wind Flower—the burning, the sacking—death. She could see again the grotesque shapes of the flames reaching insanely toward the heavens only to suddenly turn into black smoke columns full of devilish sparks that would quickly set another blaze. She could once again hear the sounds of people running, horses gone wild, and accompanying it all, the sounds of a gruff voice shouting cold-blooded orders. The Yankee colonel in charge, a harbinger of destruction, was a fierce, gaunt man, with the deepest set eyes she had ever seen. He brought brigand, savage warfare, to the white families of the Combahee River as he raided and pillaged.

Words rang in her ears. Words she thought she would never bring to consciousness again. "Why are you doing this?" she had shouted at him in utter pain and panic.

In a calm, lethal way, the bearded, thin-lipped man answered her, his terrorizing eyes taking her in coldly, "I aim, ma'am, to bring this war home to the civilian population. If it takes burning these rich homes and lands, I will burn them."

Wind Flower had been put to torch, only ashes remained amid blackened chimneys, and the hundred years of hard labor and love that went into the building of the magnificent plantation was destroyed. She winced as she thought of the library, which not only contained priceless first editions, but a silk copy of the Declaration of Independence. The thousand-year oak on the lawn was left a black skeleton. And most painful—the unmarked grave. The memory of that, numbing. She was caught up in it all again as she sat in front of the fire in Lord Hatfield's house on Belgrave Square, chilled to the bone by reminiscences. The reunion in London was the reason, she thought—some of it had been planned and some of it was fated. Kismet. Something must have started it in motion—how could so much of it just happen—this coming together, triggering deeply buried emotions to rise to the surface to be examined once again. Like the bees and the flowers, she thought further, there were attractions, somewhere, somehow, making it happen. And that day in June in the year 1863 came back to her vividly— a day of many endings and—beginnings.

She had awakened from a fitful sleep with a fast-beating heart, twisting and turning all night in the June heat that hung damply in the air, waking periodically in a panic, expecting something terrible to happen at any moment. She looked at the mosquito netting that formed a great white cloud around the huge mahogany bed, and tried to calm herself. She couldn't.

"JoJo, you come here quickly and fetch me some cool

water. My body is burning up from this heat." She called louder, "JoJo!" Surprisingly, there was no answer. Annoyed, she hurried to the alcove off her bedroom where the girl slept, only to find it empty. Her cot was still rumpled. JoJo never left her bed unmade. Vanessa stamped her foot and hastened back to her room, going to the washstand. Luckily, there was some water in the pitcher. She poured it into the china basin and sponged herself off as quickly as possible. She pulled a pale violet morning dress out of the armoire and threw it over her head, then grabbed her long hair, pulled it back and arranged it hastily on top of her head. After a cursory glance in the mirror, not too pleased with her appearance, she slipped her feet into kid pumps and rushed out onto the upstairs veranda, taking two steps at a time down the outside staircase, bounding gracelessly onto the lawn. She saw nothing and no one. It was amazingly quiet for a work day. Something was wrong, she just knew it—she could feel it, but as she whirled around she could see nothing out of order, but that did not stop her fear. The war was coming to them here on the plantation, she felt it in her heart. Just a few days before she had been so happy because she could suddenly feel life inside her. How she and JoJo had laughed. "The baby's kicking," she had shouted. They were alone in the garden, cutting flowers for the dinner table. She made JoJo put her hand on her stomach, and the young girl jumped when she thought she felt activity in Vanessa's belly. She hadn't told Pierre as yet about the child growing in her womb, and certainly not Mother Harriet.

In the year and a half they had been at Wind Flower, things had not gotten better between them. And the past few months, Pierre had become more and more aloof, rarely coming to her bed. In her naivete, she felt the child would bring them closer together, and she was delighted about it, so looking forward to holding the precious infant in her arms. In secret, she and JoJo had started to embroider pieces of cloth to be used later for the making of sheets for the crib and nightdresses—they stitched only the last initial, a big round B, the first to be added later.

Pierre was such a puzzlement to her. At times the most kind and tender person, listening to her music, patiently trying to improve her French, and at other times a total, closeted stranger full of anger and bitterness, reeking of brandy. When they were told about the raid the other evening down river and of the fearless Colonel Montgomery who was the leader, Pierre wanted to evacuate to Charleston. But Harriet was adamant. They chased her from her plantation on St. Helena Island, and she'd be damned if she'd be frightened away from Wind Flower. This home and land, she declared, had been in her family for over a hundred years. Pierre had tried to reason with her, adding they had stayed way beyond when it was safe for health reasons. The summer heat was upon them and several cases of swamp fever had broken out among the hands who worked in the watery rice fields. Vanessa knew she couldn't hide her pregnancy much longer because she was starting to show, and Harriet had been eyeing her suspiciously, but she didn't want to leave without Pierre, and if they knew, they would make her go. She started for the house.

It was early, about seven she guessed, and she was in need of breakfast. She turned to look at the river once again when she got to the veranda steps. The house stood on a rise, and she had a clear view of the Combahee. The heat shimmered on the water as the morning mist continued to rise—the hands were hard at work ditching, hoeing, and hand picking the weed grasses in the muddy waters. All seemed normal and quiet, too quiet, but the familiar view gave her a sense of security for the moment, allowing her to enjoy as she did most days, the sight of the gardens terraced down toward the river and up and behind both sides of the house.

On the veranda she rested her flushed face against the cool stone of one of the masonry columns, trying to think of other things. She must answer Josiah's letter today. He was soon to be thirteen and desperate to be an active participant in the war. How she hated it all and wished it would end. He had written about Lee's great victory at Chancellorsville and of Uncle Thomas' trip to Richmond for Stonewall Jackson's funeral. Can you imagine, Nessa, he had written in his youngish scrawl, Jackson was mortally wounded during that battle by his own soldiers! They had been told about it at Wind Flower, but Josiah had given additional details. A North

Carolina regiment had mistaken Jackson, with mounted aides, for the Yankee cavalry they were expecting. It was night, and they couldn't be blamed, Josiah had added. Then he went on to tell of Uncle Thomas' account of the funeral in the Confederate capitol—church bells tolled, flags at half-mast, and guns fired in honor of the great Major General Jackson, Uncle Thomas admitting he wept when he looked through the glass lid of the coffin as Stonewall lay in state. He ended the letter with a plea: "Please, Nessa, when you write or see father, (mother said you might be coming to Charleston soon because of the fever season), tell father I should be in the home guard now—so many of my friends have joined, and the streets here are full of boys my age or younger in uniform."

She was shocked to awareness by the sound of a man's voice.

"Good morning, Mrs. Bonneau. Are you feeling poorly?"

She realized she had slumped against the column and how awful it must look. Immediately she straightened her blossoming figure and turned to him, flustered, "I'm fine, Mr. Yoors. It's just this heat, and it's still so early in the day." He stood tall and straight in the bright sunlight, a few feet away from her on the gravel, holding his large brimmed hat in his strong hand. There was a serious look of concern on his face. She never noticed the sharp and clear cut of his features before or the deep blueness of his widely set eyes. The blond, tightly curled hair on his arms glistened with small beads of perspiration, and rivulets of moisture trickled down his long, muscular neck.

"Well, take care," he said in his deep but rather flat voice. There was a tightness there, she detected. They saw very little of each other. She went out of her way whenever possible to avoid meeting him, never having gotten over the embarrassment of their escape together from St. Helena Island. Now he was the Bonneau overseer and she couldn't help but wonder why he stayed at such a remote place like Wind Flower. There were rumors of a woman who came to visit him in the dark of night—a white woman from a nearby village she had been told, and once Vanessa thought she had seen her.

Well, he had a right, she had reasoned—a man has certain needs. But somehow it was disturbing to her.

"If I were you I would stay indoors today not only because of the heat but for other reasons. It would be a good day for you to practice at the piano, and it would also be good for such beautiful sounds to come from the big house."

"You can hear my playing down by the river?"

"Sometimes—if the air currents are right."

"Well, there's no wind today, that's for sure. It feels like a thunderstorm is brewing."

He looked up at the hazy but cloudless sky. "Could be. But sound carries even when there's no wind. So why don't you go in and stay at the piano today?"

"Are you giving me orders, Mr. Yoors?"

He smiled at her, a great big friendly smile. "Sounds like it, doesn't it."

"I've been playing the piano almost every day since I was six. Sometimes it gets boring."

"It's not boring to my ears."

It dawned on her that his speech was not uneducated. There was the New Orleans intonation of course. Odd, she reflected, in all this time, she had never noticed his speech before. But admittedly, she had never had more than a few words with him at any given time during the year and a half they had all been at Wind Flower, and practically never spoke to him when he was her father's overseer.

He was talking again, she realized, and was startled when she heard, "I'll be leaving at the end of the week. I've just told Mrs. Bonneau." He paused to look at her, then continued, "If I don't get to see you again before I go, goodbye and I bid you well."

"You're leaving Wind Flower, Mr. Yoors?"

"Yes, ma'am."

"Where are you going?" She was strongly affected for some reason, filled with a new anxiety.

"I'm to join a medical unit. They told me yesterday to report at the end of the week."

"My goodness, Mr. Yoors. A medical unit?"

"I've had some training in the area, ma'am."

The words came out in a rush. "There's no reason

for you to go, Mr. Yoors. What you are doing here is important—the troops need food, and I believe there is an exemption given for it."

"I know, ma'am. It is my choice to go. Your husband can look after things with his mother."

Her panic grew, and she didn't know what to say. "Where will they send you? Will it be the hospital in Charleston?"

"No. My orders are to join General Lee's army in the field—somewhere near a place called Gettysburg."

"Gettysburg? I never heard of it."

"I'm told it is in Pennsylvania. I'd like to write you from time to time, Mrs. Bonneau, if I may."

She was shy as she looked at him, embarrassed by his strange request and judging from his sincere, determined stare, he was waiting for a straightforward answer from her. Instead, she gave him a stupid reply because she felt inept in the situation.

"Of course. We at Wind Flower would like very much to know of your fate in the war and will answer your letters promptly, giving you all the news that might interest you."

"Thank you kindly, Mrs. Bonneau. When it's over, I'll be back. You can count on that."

There were sounds of furtive footsteps on dry leaves. Kirk jerked his head in the direction of the muffled noise and noticed a strange black figure moving through the bushes obviously coming from the slave quarters. Before he could run toward the man to find out what he was about, there were shrill pipings of gunboat whistles coming from the direction of the river.

JoJo, at the same instant, turned the corner of the house, with the expression of a startled deer on her face. "They've come," she screamed. "They've come! The Yankees are here!" Then she screeched the high wail of a banshee, unable to move. The freshly cut flowers she held in her arms dropped to the ground.

Negro scouts, there to get the slaves, ran in the open now as they crisscrossed the lawns yelling, "Come on, brother—be free—free as the winds of heaven—run to get your liberty . . ." And one shouted at the top of his lungs, "There is a white robe for thee, brother, join the North for your freedom."

They came slowly at first and then with speed, the stable hands, gardeners, women and children. Havoc was taking place around them. "Get into the house, Mrs. Bonneau, and lock the door behind you. They're only after the hands and supplies." He started to go but she, like JoJo, couldn't move. Kirk grabbed her firmly by the arm and shoved her roughly into the hall, using his lank frame to cover her. Once inside, still holding her tightly, he looked around, taking in the hall with its rear entrance and the windows facing the lawns and gardens. "Oh, my God, the whole downstairs is wide open. Get to your room and lock yourself in."

She looked at him dumbly.

"Do you hear me, Vanessa? Up to your bedroom, bolt the door and the windows and stay there 'til this is over."

He was shouting at her, trying to snap her into awareness.

Pierre, hearing Yoors' voice, lurched into the hall from the dining room, his white jacket and trousers were wrinkled, the coffee cup he held in his hand reeked of well-aged brandy, the dark eyes bloodshot, and his mouth twisted in a snarl. Suddenly he sprang at Kirk, "Get your hands off my wife, you filthy lout."

"Pierre, don't." She had never heard him speak or act this way before.

Kirk was struggling with him trying to hold him off. Pierre, with great strength, swung at him, the coffee cup flew out of his hand, smashing into bits on the floor, as he continued to throw punches wildly. Kirk held him at bay as best he could while he frantically pleaded with Vanessa. "Get upstairs, quickly! Damn it, girl, get upstairs!"

The sounds of running footsteps on the gravel in front of the house were louder, a gunshot tore the air. Everything was happening so quickly. Mrs. Bonneau's voice could be heard—she was yelling at the running slaves, threatening them with death if they didn't return to their quarters.

JoJo ran into the hall. "Miz Nessa, it's terrible out there, everyone is running away to be free and Mrs. Bonneau is shooting in the air."

Pierre looked at them, suddenly comprehending what

was happening. He shook his head and tried to get his tongue to function properly, "Is it the raid to get the slaves? Good God, let the Federals take them and leave us be." He stumbled out onto the veranda and Vanessa started after him.

"Pierre, don't go!"

Kirk grabbed her furiously, "I told you to go upstairs, now you get." She looked at him—startled by his fierceness, then he gentled his tone as he urged, "Please, Vanessa, do as I say." Then he was gone.

She started up, but midway turned to look back at JoJo, who was just standing there in the hall, lost, staring up at her, her black button eyes filled with fear.

"Go, if you want, JoJo. Go. Run off with your people."

"I don't know. I don't know what to do."

She rushed up the stairs and grabbed Vanessa's hands, pleading with her. "Tell me, Nessa. Tell me what I should do. I just don't know. I'm a house nigger. I don't know where I belong."

"Dear God, I don't know what to tell you."

"Please, Nessa. Tell me."

There was torment for both of them, a deep searching moment for Vanessa.

"Run. Go with your people, JoJo, that's where you belong. I can't ask you to stay."

"Miz Nessa, I'm so scared."

"So am I, JoJo, my dear friend. But run, run quickly. You'll always be close to my heart. Always. Run to your freedom." She turned quickly and dashed up the rest of the steps to the landing. Once inside her room, she did what Kirk had commanded her to do and locked the door and the floor to ceiling windows leading to the veranda.

She stood by one of the windows looking out, the lawns leading to the river were full of slaves. The drivers, Mrs. Bonneau, and now Kirk were among them trying to get them back. She searched but could not see Pierre. He so hated violence of any kind, she was still so amazed at how he had sprung at Kirk in the hall. A few moments and all this had happened. A world turned upside down, her world. The June day was rent with confusion as she watched the screaming women dragging children, some hanging on to their skirts as they rushed to get to the gunboats waiting midstream. The field hands in their dirty sack clothes had dropped their hoes when they saw the boats and were already on board. Vanessa wondered where the Confederate troops downstream were, supposedly protecting the river that fed into the Atlantic, for there was absolutely no resistance. She remembered being told of the 2nd South Carolina Volunteers made up of freed blacks and their leader, a white man, Colonel Montgomery. The attack must have been guided by those very familiar with the river territory, men who knew how to get around the Confederate soldiers posted along the way. All the able-bodied Sims-Bonneau slaves fleeing would be trained to fight against the South, like the men of the 2nd South Carolina Volunteers.

The black troops with drawn guns were suddenly on the lawn, emerging from the terraces on both sides of the house and up from the river. To her dismay, she heard the tread of heavy footsteps on the outside staircase. A shattering of glass sent her into a frenzy as a black hand reached through the broken glass of one of the French windows on the other side of the room and was trying to release the lock. She rushed to the hall door, struggling to unlatch it, running out just as she heard the heel of a boot smash the lock impatiently. Then men entered her bedroom as she stumbled toward the back stairs. Why were they in the house? She had been told several times they were only after the slaves and supplies.

Vanessa tripped on the last few steps and couldn't catch herself, taking a bad fall into the empty kitchen. She yelped with anguish when she felt the stab of pain in her abdomen, accompanied by a hard pulse in that area of her body. Picking herself up, she moved with difficulty into the yard, gasping for breath as she fought to reach the stables. "Oh, my baby, my baby," she cried out in despair, "don't let my baby be hurt."

The horses were whinnying and kicking at the stall doors. There was no one there, and she didn't know what she was about, just rushing, blindly, for some kind of cover, holding onto her stomach as if it would ease the pain. She screamed in terror when she saw a heavy rope with a noose at its end dangling from a beam—it was swinging as if someone had just left.

"Pierre!" she shouted, looking around desperately—did he try to hang himself? "Pierre!" He had often said at drunken moments that he felt so trapped and smothered at times, he would find it easier to die. "Pierre!"

"Get her out of here . . ." the voice was hard, with a noticeable twang. "Then burn the outbuildings along with the house."

Vanessa wheeled around and came face to face with a tall weather-bronzed white man surrounded by black soldiers. Gunfire rented the air outside the stables. He looked at her through deep-set hazel eyes, "Colonel Montgomery, miss. Now if you will clear out, we will get on with our business."

Her pain was so strong, she was doubled over as she fought to keep on her feet.

"Why? Why are you doing this? We are not fighting you."

He answered her grimly in his flat midwestern voice, "I aim to bring this war home to the civilian population. If it takes burning these rich homes and lands, I will burn them. Hit you people where it hurts. I am weary of it all. Now," he said menacingly, "are you going to get out of here or do you want to burn with the place?"

"The horses. You will free the horses?"

"Open the stalls," he commanded roughly. The horses snorted and reared on their hind legs, sensing the danger all around them as they were let loose, running blindly, bumping into each other until they found the opening and freedom. The colonel drew his gun, turned on his heels and walked out without a backward glance at her. Vanessa grabbed the mane of one of the horses and with all her remaining strength, pulled herself onto its back and took off into the stable yard, horrified to see the house being put to the torch. Behind her she heard the hissing and crackling as the hay in the stables and barns caught, immediately bursting forth into giant flames.

On a pinnacle back of the plantation, she looked down and saw the raging inferno and the tall columns of black smoke in the sky. The gun boats were starting to fall back, just escaping the searing flames. The sluices had been opened and the rice fields were completely covered by water, totally destroying the crops. Not being able to hold herself upright any longer because of the severe cramps, she lay prone on the horse's neck. The animal carried her into nearby woods where she fell off, too much in pain to even cry. Blood was running down her legs, oblivion mercifully engulfed her as she lay on the mossy ground. Her screams pierced the stillness as she came back to consciousness, the twinges gripping her, rendering her incapable of lifting her legs or arms. She knew she was losing her precious baby. "Oh, God, no!" The final tortuous contractions made her float into a gray outer limit of time, and then the fetus lay between her legs. The tears finally came along with the tears, loud wracking sobs that shook her body.

Hours must have passed as she lay there, calm now in the churchlike silence around her—her heavy sorrow contained in a deep well of her being. The sun was high overhead, sending strong rays through the thick leaves. It was fuzzy at first, then a bit clearer—voices from way off—they were coming closer and closer and now she could make out what they were saying.

"She's lying over yon. It looks like the young mistress from Wind Flower."

They stood over her. A not too young woman and an elderly, bent man. Poor farmers she thought. White trash, Mother Bonneau would have called them.

The old man knelt down by her and was startled when she tried to speak. The woman said, "Praise the Lord! I took her for dead."

Vanessa's voice was a faint whisper, and they both knelt closer to try to hear her.

"Help me . . ."

"What's that, Mrs.?"

"Help me. I can't move."

"Are you wounded?"

She told them with heaving chest about the baby. The woman understood about such things and lifted her skirt and tore the ripped cord easily in her strong hands.

"What do you want me to do with the baby?"

"Wrap my baby in my petticoat, please. I have to have a proper burial. I beg you."

"Yes, Mrs." They were simple country folk but understood life and death.

The elderly man left and came back with a piece of canvas.

The woman handed her the small bundle wrapped like a cocoon. Vanessa took it gratefully, holding her dead baby very gently as if it would break.

The old man mumbled a few words and then the woman told her they were going to roll her onto the canvas and take her to their wagon a short distance away.

The smoke-filled air stung her eyes, and she knew they were nearing Wind Flower. The wagon wheels jostled her, and she tried desperately to hold the bundle so it wouldn't be tossed about. The wagon stopped, and the woman got down from the seat in front. In a few moments Vanessa saw the ash-streaked face of JoJo looking at her over the sideboard.

"It is you, Miz Nessa," she cried. "We been searching and searching for you in the rubble. Mr. Yoors, Mr. Yoors!" she shouted excitedly. "Here's Nessa."

Vanessa heard running feet, and heavy hands shook the wagon as they grabbed the side to look in at her. "Thank God. I thought you were dead."

In her haze, she could hear the woman talking, probably explaining, for she could make out Kirk looking at the bundle in her arms and she heard the sobs of JoJo.

His voice was low and soothing, "Mrs. Bonneau, do you want to have the baby buried in the family plot?" His eyes stayed on her face intently as he tried to take the bundle gently from her tight grasp.

"Yes please." She let him have her valuable parcel. Her voice was no more than a hoarse whisper. "Are there any flowers? Can you gather some flowers for my baby?"

"I'll try."

JoJo's little face was a mass of wrinkles as she fought to control her sobs.

"Nessa. Ole Henry is dead, too. He done had a heart attack. We got to bury him, too."

"Of course. Poor Old Henry. He will also be buried in the family cemetery. You're still here, JoJo."

"I couldn't leave, Nessa. You're my family."

Kirk was noticing the widening stains on her skirt. "As soon as we take care of the burials, I'll get you to the nearest hospital."

"Pierre."

"His mother and some of the house servants are out looking for him. He's disappeared."

". . . or has been hurt."

"Possibly," was the curt answer.

Propped up in the wagon, she watched the parched earth being turned and her aborted baby being placed in the shallow grave. It would have to do for now. They made a pitiful group on the blackened earth, as simple prayers were said by the woman and JoJo. Then the woman looked toward the heavens and raised her voice in song— "What A Friend We Have In Jesus"—it was a lovely pure sound. JoJo placed scorched roses on the grave and then Old Henry was laid to rest, wrapped in the canvas from the wagon, stained with her blood. He was the first black man to be buried in the family cemetery. Old Henry was now a member of the clan through eternity. JoJo placed bruised Wind Flowers on his mound.

8

A watery sun was trying to poke through a thick layer of clouds on this damp, early Monday morning following Lord Hatfield's Saturday night reception. London's working classes made their way to employment. Work, duty to the queen, country, church, and family were undeniably the keynotes for most Britishers, the very components that made England the "Empire," and in their minds, England carried the world and was greatly imitated by others.

Victoria had reached her fiftieth birthday in May and had been in painful mourning for her beloved Albert for almost eight years, just now, slowly coming out of her morbid seclusion from public life. She would have preferred to become a private person, feeling more comfortable tending to personal matters and pressures, of which there were many, rather than matters of state.

If possible she was present for the births of all her numerous grandchildren, being in attendance at times to rub the brow of the mother, pat her cheek, or hold the flailing hands during the "pitied" time. But Victoria was not fond of newborn babes. She was called Gangan by her grandchildren, and supplied knitted quilts made by her own hand for the newborn, arduously keeping track and distributing essential supplies from hot plates to bassinets, making sure when they were not needed any longer they were passed on so there would never be any waste.

She was having a love affair with the lower classes in the sixties, oddly ignoring the middle class, which unbeknownst to her, were perfect Victorians in her imagined image, firmly steeped in her self-righteous morality.

The queen was very disturbed at this time by what she termed the "fast set," members of that special upper strata of society of highborns who spent the majority of their time in idleness, which was a sin to her. It was also her firm belief that they kept her son, the Prince of Wales, away from his mother's company. Their horrible vices, according to Victoria, included gambling, racing, smoking, and the association with Americans and Jews.

It was no great surprise then to those around her when she expressed shock and indignation upon hearing the tidings of Lord Hatfield's forthcoming marriage to an impoverished American. The news had been quickly sped to her by one of her ladies-in-waiting, Lady Brigette Manley, who had been at the reception when the event was announced, adding juicily in her breathless telling to the queen (whose head bobbed under her widow's cap as she digested it all), that the intended was very much younger than Jamie and possessed a brazen, flippant nature.

Lady Manley was fully aware of Victoria's quick judgments and hysterical outbursts, and was smugly satisfied by her outrage, heightened by the fact that widows and widowers were almost a preoccupation with the aging queen. She was always sending sympathy notes far and near on these sad occasions, and although she didn't know Mrs. Abraham Lincoln, she dispatched a personal letter to her immediately upon hearing of the assassination, offering condolences and then adding, citing from her own experience, sorrow for the plight of being a widow. The most satisfying deaths she knew of occurred when a husband or wife followed the other within a short period of time. But alas, she always bemoaned, that was not her lot in life.

Jamie's wife had been dead less than a year, so she was also horrified at the lack of respect for the dead, this being compounded by the news that the young woman was a foreigner and of questionable background. In her own case, Victoria, after all these years, still slept with her late husband's nightshirt and kept a cast of his hand on her night table. She was not one for letting the dead die. The queen was very fond of Jamie Hatfield, the Eighth Earl of Raleigh and considered him a close political ally. He had worked closely with her, to her great relief, on the problems of the disestablishment of the Irish Protestant

Church during the previous summer, and she felt he also believed with her and Disraeli that the working classes would soon educate their masters.

Victoria wanted no more misbehaving by the upper strata, greatly desiring that society be reformed. To her way of thinking, Jamie must be kept pure in the public's eye. Then, like her other involvements with relatives and close associates (some would more honestly say interference), she would not sit idly by but try to do something about correcting things she felt were amiss. She conveniently overlooked one of the biggest offenders of misconduct—her son, Bertie, who would one day become king of the Empire. To her, that was something else again.

Lord Hatfield sat in the firelit library this Monday morning just finishing his breakfast tea as he reread a note from the queen. The black border around the heavy white paper was almost an inch thick. There had been a narrow black band put on the queen's stationery when her mother died, but since Albert's demise, it had grown to this wide, gloomy width. It was a brief note in her hand saying, "I heard some surprising news regarding your Lordship and request you come to tea at Windsor next Saturday to discuss this matter."

He was no fool and knew what it was about. His first inclination was to write back declining, using some excuse or other, having reached the stage in life where he felt he was entitled to do what he pleased in his personal affairs, since, in fact, he had paid high dues in many respects to queen, duty, and country. Damn it, he thought, what right does she have to meddle? His sister, Ardell, had left Victoria's court of her own volition and survived grandly. No one questioned, no one pointed a finger, but that was Ardell, the Grand Dutchess of Leighton, excused because she was thought of as a rich eccentric. She was also not in government, he had to honestly admit to himself. He started to boil inside. His stiff wing collar dug into his Adam's apple as he continued to stare at the note. He was not going to be trapped by the queen's narrow conventions. He knew at the outset there might be some problems when his marriage was announced, but he certainly didn't expect or want to be advised that it would be judicious to stop the union due to appearances.

"Damn it! Damn it to hell!" he uttered audibly.

To his consternation, Miss Shields entered after a quick tap on the door, her hatchet face agitated and red. She immediately went into a tirade about the violation of his late wife's bedroom, and how she was going to stop it from occurring again. He could see he startled her when he said quite tartly, "Miss Shields, I have no idea what you are talking about. What violation? I have no intention of keeping a 'living' shrine to my late wife. She is respectfully and properly buried. If there is no other bedroom for my guest and he wishes to retire there, so be it."

The pulse in her neck was throbbing visibly, and her voice conveyed a shortness of breath, "But, your lordship, it's sacrilegious. There's all of Lady Hatfield's clothing, her personal effects, just as she left them," adding in a higher pitch, "It's as if she were still with us, m'lord."

There it was, he thought. Victoria being copied, her susceptible subjects following her actions, feeling closer to the dead than to the living. Hell! He would not have it.

"My good woman, we will not have some kind of death chamber in this house. Is that understood?"

The tall, thin body stiffened, and her razor-sharp mouth pursed in an ugly line as she spoke in an hysterical tone. "Lady Hatfield was one of the finest women that ever lived. She was a true lady and her life on this earth should be respected and remembered."

The remark reached him as intended, and he softened a bit, feeling he was seeing his housekeeper with fresh eyes. He knew of her devotion to his late wife but never suspected it was so strong. The woman was trembling, and he turned his anger at himself where he thought it rightfully belonged. There was no reason to jump at her, the occasion obviously had been a trying one.

"Miss Shields, I want to assure you her ladyship's memory shall always be honored and respected in this house. In no way will I permit anything else. Is that quite clear? But I repeat, I will not allow a death chamber."

She nodded painfully.

"Good. I am advising you to pack Lady Hatfield's personal effects properly and carefully, as I know you will, and have them shipped to the country house to be stored." Then his voice rose in volume and authority, "As should have been done, Miss Shields, after her death!" He wanted

to be rid of her but she replied in a rush, fearful but determined.

"With due respect, there is another bedroom not in use,
your lordship. I could have it prepared quickly in case
Mr. McIver is in need of another bedchamber."

His eyes narrowed as he fingered the sheaf of papers on
the large oak desk, and his broad shoulders hunched forward in his extreme impatience.

"The townhouse is quite full, Miss Shields. To my recollection there is no other available sleeping chamber."

She took a step closer. "The third floor, sir. It's a big
comfortable room overlooking the square. The one above
your room, your lordship."

He sighed deeply, "Is that room clear and ready for
use?"

"It could be in a matter of a few hours."

"And Lady Hatfield's bedroom?"

"Oh, that would take days, my lord." Her rigidness relaxed slightly, a smile played around her paper-thin lips.
"All her things are just as she left them when she was last
there. Her silver brushes, her clothes . . ."

He interrupted her curtly. "That room above me has
not been in use for many years, it would be musty and
dank, most unpleasant. Start packing Lady Hatfield's things
immediately and make the room ready in case my guest
has to use it this evening. I suggest you do the personal
effects lying about first and take care of the wardrobes in
the very near future. That will be all Miss Shields unless
there is urgent household business you wish to discuss
with me."

He lowered his head again to the papers on the desk and
started to study one.

"No other matters that can't wait, my lord."

He heard her quick light step until she reached the
door. It was closed in a second with a slight slam.

He got up quickly and stamped about the room, circling it several times.

"Martin," he called loudly.

His valet was in the library in an instant.

"Have them bring my carriage around immediately."

He then took the royal-crested note and tossed it into
the wastebasket. When he looked up Amanda and Georgina were coming into the room.

"Jamie, you are scowling. Is there anything wrong?"

"No. No. Nothing at all. Nothing to bother yourself with, my dear."

"But you are leaving. I heard you order the carriage. I thought we were going to have breakfast together?"

"Some dastardly annoying business has come up. I must be off," he said quite severely.

Amanda was concerned, Georgina wisely held her tongue for once, as Jamie did look very perturbed. She pressured her daughter's arm lightly as she started to rush forward, but Amanda didn't take the hint and rushed to him anyway.

"Nothing serious, I hope, Jamie. My, I've never seen you angry before. You look like a fierce bear. Your brow is creased in a thousand folds."

He looked at the doll-like creature in front of him and his countenance softened, but he was fuming inside and it was growing not subsiding. How had the queen heard so soon? he pondered. The announcement was made Saturday night and here it was only Monday morning.

"Jamie, are you sure nothing is amiss?"

The china blue, almond-shaped eyes searched his face, and there was a winning pout on her small bowed lips. All of a sudden he felt very old in her presence. She looked no more than sixteen in the pale library light. Her tightly bodiced dress of light gray complimented her blond curls, making them look like silvery puffs.

"I'm sorry to be in this foul temper. Forgive me." My, God, he thought, I now feel like her father. He knew full well that the jolt of the queen's note, whether he would admit it to himself or not, had thrown him into this tizzy.

"Is it something I can help you with? I want so to become a good helpmate."

"I'm sure you do. But this is something I have to take care of myself."

Martin was back with his coat, top hat, and cane.

"Will you be here for midday meal? I'll come back from shopping to be with you, Jamie," Amanda said sweetly.

"No. No. You go about your shopping. I'll take lunch at the club after I see my sister this morning, then off to Parliament for the rest of the afternoon and evening." He buttoned his coat hastily, and Martin handed him his top hat and silver-topped cane. The carriage could be heard coming around the corner from the stables in the mews behind the house.

"The duchess? You are visiting her so early in the morning?"

"Yes. Something unexpected."

He was leaving and she ran after him.

"Please pay my respects to your sister. I so liked her when I met her the other evening. I hope we will become friends in the future."

"Possibly. Don't expect too much from Ardell. She is not the easiest person," and then over his shoulder as the footman held the door and Martin was struggling into his overcoat to accompany him, "Don't you think you have too much color on your cheeks, Amanda?"

He was gone, and Amanda rushed back to the library and her mother.

"There's something wrong, Mama. I feel it. He never criticized me before. What would happen if he didn't go through with the marriage?"

"Don't be foolish and don't say such things. How can he not go through with the wedding? He proposed didn't he and made the announcement to all his friends."

"He can change his mind. I jus⁺ have this terrible sensation in the pit of my stomach—ever since I came in here and saw his face. He never acted like that before in front of me. Usually he lights up when I come into a room."

"Well, just get used to it, darling. Men have many moods and we women have to live with them."

"Do I have too much rouge on my face, Mama?"

"Lord no. You look pretty as a picture."

As Georgina moved to the desk she saw the royal crest on the piece of paper in the wastebasket. Picking it up quickly she exclaimed, "He received a note from the queen. Look at this—inviting him to tea. We must speak to Jamie to have us presented at court as soon as possible—I wonder what she wants to see him about?"

Hatfield pushed aside the footman and sprinted up the curving marble staircase to Ardell's private sitting room and bedchamber when he was informed his sister wasn't receiving. Madame de Rochmont, the duchess' social secretary, who had been in the library writing letters on

Jamie's arrival, was right at his heels, explaining as she rushed after him that her ladyship was still asleep and had asked not to be disturbed.

"It's approaching nine A.M.," he exclaimed, "time she was up and about."

He entered the sitting room and was startled—it had been a long time since he had been there, and the decor had been very different. The walls were decorated in loose red silk, coming together in the center of the ceiling to form a giant tent. A black lacquered lantern hung in the middle of the billowing drape and was barely lit, shadowing the room as if it were the middle of night. For a moment he felt he was in a sheik's tent in the Sahara Desert—all it needed, he thought, was sand strewn about. There were oriental rugs scattered over the black floor, and a strong odor of incense stung his nostrils. An empty champagne bottle lay like a dead soldier on a tiny gilded table and fragments of broken glass littered the fireplace—probably thrown after a toast, he suspected.

Large, poufed ottomans dotted the room, and Ardell's Pekingese dog, Chin Chin, sat in the center of one of them chewing on its golden tassel. The silky haired, snub-nosed creature looked at him with disdain as she continued her destruction. He failed to notice her litter of recently born puppies lounging lazily on another overstuffed pillow by the fireplace.

"Ardell!" he yelled out. "Get up. I wish to speak with you. Ardell!"

Chin Chin started yapping at the gruff disturbance in between chewing on the silken cords.

"Who the hell is making that noise and whoever it is, go away." The voice was husky and filled with sleep.

Madame de Rochmont took a small step toward the darkness, "I'm sorry, your ladyship, but your brother insisted on coming to your private rooms."

"My brother? Tell him to get the hell out. I'm tired. Furthermore, I'm sleeping."

"I'm right here, Ardell, and I will not budge until you show yourself."

"What's wrong? Did somebody die?"

A male voice grumbled, "Get rid of them for Christ's sake."

"Now, now," Ardell purred, "go back to sleep."

Jamie turned to Madame de Rochmont and asked in a surprised whisper, "Is that his lordship?"

The woman flushed to the roots of her thinning hair, and her thin hooked nose quivered in embarrassment. She excused herself incoherently and fled from the room.

Chin Chin, suddenly jumping around and barking hysterically, set off mewing howls from the puppies languishing on the large pillow near the fireplace. The male voice from the other room cried out, "Can't you stop those things from yapping. Have pity, man, my head is splitting. What kind of dive is this?"

"Ardell, come out here. I have to talk to you."

He heard a deep groan from his sister and then the rustling of bedding. Chin Chin was tugging at the bottom of his trousers now in between yaps, and the puppies were crying all the louder. Jamie was surprised at himself for being here. He had never invaded Ardell's private rooms before and had very little talk with her in recent years relating to his personal life. But he felt he had to discuss the matter of his forthcoming marriage with her. Suddenly, Ardell was there. She had thrown on a bright red and yellow sheik's robe, the long wide sleeves touching the ground.

"Jamie, I can't say how pleased I am at seeing you because I'm not. This is a devil of a time to come calling." As she talked she walked to Chin Chin, picked her up and placed her on the large cushion with her puppies. "There you little beast, stop yapping and tend to your babies." The dog obeyed her mistress' command and the puppies cuddled up to their mother immediately, pushing each other to get to her lush full nipples.

Ardell's natural hair was so curly, it formed corkscrews around her head, giving her the appearance of having received a severe shock. That was the reason she pulled it back tightly into a chignon when it was dressed. At the moment in her bright colored robe and wild hair she looked like a great ruffled bird about to take flight. She sank to the floor, yogi fashion, next to the dogs, fondling the puppies and patting Chin Chin's head, who was wincing because of the tugging on her sore nipples.

"It's the plight of mommies, my dear. It will soon be

over, and they'll forget all about you. Now, Jamie, what's all this about?"

He was looking around for a chair, but could not find one.

"Ardell, I am not an Arab. Where can I sit?"

"On your behind like everyone else, my dear. There's a perfectly marvelous cushion right over there, next to the door."

"I don't want to sit on the floor. I want to sit on a chair."

"Did I invite you or did you come all by yourself?"

"Never mind. I'll stand."

"Good idea. But then you always were a wise one. Until recently."

"What do you mean?"

"Jamie. Your marriage, of course."

"What's wrong with my marriage plans?"

"They are so inglorious."

"Ardell, what are you talking about? I am being very serious."

"And I am not? That's why you've come, isn't it? To talk about it?"

"The McIvers are a fine family from the South. They were just victims of a war and lost everything. They are not inglorious."

"Why do you have to be their savior?"

"I'm marrying Amanda, not the family."

"That's what you think. You've got yourself a crowd of poor relatives."

"I've never heard or seen you act this way before. Was Amanda rude to you? Of course, that I can't imagine."

"Well, do imagine it. There's a deeper well there than you think."

"She's a lovely girl. Always trying so hard to please. Really, Ardell, behave yourself. I have to speak to you seriously about a note I received this morning from the queen."

"Good God. Has the old biddy gotten mixed up in this?"

"The queen is the queen, my dear sister, and don't forget it. She has a great deal to contend with—she is not a biddy."

"Sorry. In the future I'll hold my biting tongue with regard to the queen. Well, what has her serene highness med 'ed in this time?"

"I received a note from her this morning—rather cryptic."

"Brigitta."

"What?"

"Brigitta Manley must have raced to her with the news."

"That old gossip."

"That old gossip is about your age and probably green with jealousy." Ardell rose and swung in a wide circle holding her sides in glee. "Victoria must have split her stays. I can just imagine what Brigitta told her."

"What on earth could she have possibly said to get this quick reaction?"

"A young girl is threatening to all we middle-aged women, and probably Brigitta thought you should either not remarry at all, be in mourning your entire life, or pick one of your own kind. After all she is a widow . . ."

"Brigitta and me? That's ridiculous."

He started to look a bit dazed and subconsciously loosened his tight collar a little, his speech was tinged with a slight slur, "Why do these things happen? I don't want Amanda to be slighted or offended by those around me. What am I to do?"

"Are you asking me or going to tell me?"

"I'm asking you."

"Don't marry her."

"Ardell!"

"She's half your age, and her zestful energy will run you ragged. Keep her as your mistress if you must. Put her up somewhere, why not one of those small houses in St. John's Wood. Everyone who is anyone is doing it. That way you will only have to face all that bloom of life once or twice a week."

"She's a good girl with a good mind and belongs at my side."

"Oh, Jamie, you're a public figure and getting more important all the time. You can't be made to look foolish."

He was angry again. "You're the one to talk. You have one . . ." He stopped in midsentence, somewhat befuddled, then, coming to, quickly, he pointed toward the bedchamber. "That's not the Prince of Wales in there—is it?" His eyes started to roll slightly.

"No. We finished our little affair a while ago. He was getting too fat for me." She studied him for a minute, he looked disoriented. "Jamie, are you all right? You're so white." But he didn't hear her. He sank to one knee. She was at his side and tried to hold him up under his armpits, but he was a heavy man and she was losing the battle. Frantically, she called toward the bedroom. "Sean! Come here quickly, I need your help. Sean, please!" she screamed.

A huge naked figure dashed into the sitting room. He was at least six feet five and his surprisingly milky-white body was covered with a thick mat of black hair. Sean Loughery was Welsh and had been a coal miner, now he called himself a poet, one of Ardell's finds.

"Get him to a chair."

"What the hell is wrong with the bloke?"

"Never mind that. Grab him. His weight is breaking my arms."

Sean lifted him like a broomstick. Jamie was starting to come to.

"Where the hell can I put him? There ain't no chair in this damned tent."

Ardell was back in a second with a chair from the bedroom, and Jamie was put on it. Ardell hovered over him, loosening his tie. "Get out of here, Sean. He's coming to. Get out! You're lewdly naked."

"Sorry. It was you who called me. Remember? Shall I go out the front door or back to bed?"

"Back to bed," she hissed authoritatively.

"Yes, Duchess. At your service." He was gone, Jamie's half-opened eyes followed his big lumbering frame.

"Jamie?" There was slight foaming at the corners of his mouth, and Ardell wiped it away with one of the sleeves of her robe. She was all concern. She had not seen him having an attack in so long, she had forgotten the horror.

"My dear brother, I'm sorry."

He was all right now—but upset, feeling he was having attacks much more frequently than usual.

"Does Amanda know?"

"I've discussed it with her mother. She foresees no problems."

"I see. She was going to tell her daughter?"

"More than likely."

Feeling somewhat responsible for bringing on the attack, she tried to make up for it. "I'll speak to Brigitta to see if she can sway the queen in the opposite direction. But, are you sure, my brother? You are taking on a great deal with this spirited girl and her large impoverished family. After all, an announcement is just an announcement."

"She brings so much into my personal life."

"That may be true, but think it over—don't let your heart lead you foolishly."

"All right, Ardell—perhaps you are right. I will give it further thought."

"She can always say she misses America too much, and you do have a fat pocketbook to smooth it over. Think about the mistress idea. It would be ideal in my opinion."

"Be like you, Ardell. Keeping people on your whim."

"It suits me."

"What of your husband?"

"It suits him also."

They had never talked this personally.

"My needs are different."

"You said you would give the idea of an arrangement hard thought. Do that. She is a beauty and bright as you say, but you may be happier with smaller doses."

She went over to Chin Chin and moved her warm body, taking one of the litter from her tits, a sleepy puppy with long, silky blond hair and a wet black nose.

"I shall send Amanda one of my treasures. Beautiful Peony, pick of the litter, and I shall invite her to tea."

"Ardell."

"Do not fear, my brother. She shall see the most charming side of my personality."

9

Kenneth was relieved that Amanda and Georgina had left for a day of shopping. He needed this time for himself. It was ironic how happy he had been planning this trip, to get away from the daily pressures of making the plantation function again. So many of their neighbors in Port Royal were destitute and their destitution was oppressive. He thought this trip would bring relief and he could relax, surrounded by his family's love. But that is what hurt and confused him the most. Except for Vanessa, he had experienced what amounted to total rejection from the others. He realized his view of the world had been narrowed by his struggle back home, while theirs had been broadened by living in another country with different views and motivations. He no longer was in tune with what they wanted from life and that disturbed him. He came to London expecting to meet his family, just a bit older, but familiar. But nothing was simple any more in the quickly changing times. He wished he could pass on to them the wisdom these last few years had brought to him. Be gentle with each other—love, understanding, and family being the most important things. He could no longer be severe or demanding with them, or anyone in that regard—the war took that away from him.

Thomas had invited Kenneth to join him at the Royal Exchange. His brother spent part of every day there trading financial and political news with their old friends from the South. Kenneth found Thomas amazing—he still functioned as though the house in Charleston with all its beauty was still theirs, and McIver Hall, perfect and producing like in the old days—never allowing that the North had conquered.

The carriage was approaching the Strand. "Cabby," he yelled, "I'll get off here." He wanted to walk to try to push away a bit of the tension. Besides, he enjoyed mixing with the people. On the plantation he loved to walk his land, feel the earth, talk to the workers.

The damp air was heavy with soot from the chimneys, but the cool November weather made it pleasant and he breathed deeply, feeling his body relax.

He turned onto Wellington Street so that he could walk through Covent Garden market. Although most of the activity there happened before dawn, the roadway was still choked with vans, carts, and barrows of all sizes and shapes. As he entered the market area, the din hit him like a wave, with shouts and oaths being freely exchanged, animals adding to the noise. One donkey gave a prolonged bray and was immediately followed by a score of others, plus squawking chickens and grunting pigs. Men bearing baskets and cases on their heads dodged each other with a dexterity developed over years of experience.

Trying to avoid a load of cabbages ten feet high, he was nearly knocked over by a burly porter coming up from under a load of cauliflowers. He apologized, smiling, for being in the way—the man cursed him out.

Moving on he noticed all the beggars and loafers standing about, and was fascinated by a butcher in a long white apron, his waist slung with a wide leather belt that held his knives and cutting tools. In front of him was a large basket of steaks and other pieces of meat. He waved a large cleaver in the air, yelling, "Buy, buy, buy!"

Women selling flowers kept pressing their goods on him, but he resisted until one tiny girl of about fourteen approached him, smiling seductively. She wore a wide-brimmed hat with feathers, a plaid shawl over a tattered dress, and high-heeled lace-up boots. She cajoled him, "Come on, duckie—brighten up your day. You are too gloomy for a good looker." She pinned the carnation boutonniere into his lapel and kissed his cheek. Placing some coins in her hand, he reddened as she squeezed his fingers suggestively.

He came out of Covent Garden and passed through Christopher Wren's beautiful gateway known as Temple

Bar, and entered onto Fleet Street. The streets were crowded, but here the mood was abruptly different—the atmosphere subdued. Interspersed among the great printing and newspaper offices were shops along both sides of the street. Next to the TELEGRAPH building was a small chemist shop. He stopped and stared into the window studying the bottles—one containing poppy heads, it said on the label, to rid toothaches and two plaster of paris horses set in the back indicated that horseballs may be had within. He looked about and saw St. Dunstan's projecting clock—it was past eleven. He boarded an omnibus advertising Bovril, crowded with bowler-hatted men, and rode up the hill toward St. Paul's Cathedral and the financial district beyond. He heard the Bow Bells ring out—it was said their peal carried over a six mile radius and those born within the sound of the bells were cockneys.

He reached Threadneedle and Cornhill, where the Royal Exchange stood imposingly, and entered the building.

Kenneth located Thomas excitedly conversing with Jefferson Davis and six other men, most of them friends from home. Jefferson was close to putting together a Canadian tin mine deal, and Thomas was in his glory advising him. Kenneth quickly found himself involved in a conversation about politics at home and the effect it would have on their taxes. This was something he avoided in Charleston, because being on the scene of Reconstruction somehow didn't allow a rational discussion of such matters. One of the group suggested they move on to lunch at his club. Time had slipped by, and he was delighted to feel his adrenalin pumping and his mind stimulated. He excused himself from joining them, noting he was due for a fitting for the tails he would wear when he gave Amanda away.

Swears and Wells on Regent Street was considered the finest outfitters in London, and Mr. Ashwood, who took care of Jamie's wardrobe, was assigned to look after Kenneth. Ashwood, whose clothes fit so tightly, without a crease or wrinkle, made Kenneth extremely uncomfortable as he flitted about so quickly, checking the trouser legs, the ease across the shoulder blades, the width of the shoulders, and through it all, the short, overly thin man hardly spoke a word, just "See here," pointing out flaws to the browbeaten tailor.

After the fitting, Ashwood ran down a list of accessories, making certain everything was taken care of. His mention of a top hat reminded Kenneth of Sillar.

"Tell me, Mr. Ashwood, is there a listing of establishments that make ladies' bonnets?"

"Most certainly, Mr. McIver, we have a directory right here and would be happy to suggest a milliner for Mrs. McIver if you wish."

"The Duchess of Leighton mentioned a shop run by a woman named Sillar." He couldn't believe he was coming out with a boldfaced lie but hoped the mention of the duchess' name would cover his nervousness. "We need to know the location of the shop."

He gave Kenneth the address off Portman's Square, saying that she was known for her imaginative creations. "Many of the best-dressed ladies patronize her shop. Madame Sillar is an aristocrat herself from Spain. I'm certain you will be delighted with her work."

Kenneth had a moment of delight at Sillar's passing herself off as an aristocrat from Spain. This brought clearly to mind how he always enjoyed her sense of humor and her delightful boldness. He knew he had to see her again. It would help wash away some of the gloom of the years since they parted. He still bedded a woman now and again, but there was never any magic, only physical relief.

He took a carriage to Portman's Square, remembering the last night they had spent together on the plantation.

The family had retired early that night, all weary from the emotions of the past few days and anxious about the real threat of a Yankee invasion. The Union naval fleet had been visible on the horizon for days. In the morning most of the household slaves, including Sillar, would make the move to the Charleston house with Georgina and the two children, Amanda and Josiah. Kenneth had a difficult time thinking of sleep, his mind ran over the uncertain future and the safety of his family. Finally he ordered a brandy brought to his study.

He took off his shirt and stood in front of the fire letting its warmth seep through his bare chest. He was lost in a trance when he realized arms were wrapped around his waist and hands were unbuttoning his trousers.

"Massa, I'z jes' here to check if your buttons is sewed on your trousers proper like. We wouldn't want you scarin' the lil' girls down in the slave quarters when you ride through," the woman's voice was pitched high and speaking in a heavy Gullah accent common to the slaves of the islands.

He teased back, going along with her playacting, "You are a good servant, always doing your job day and night. Now come 'round girl where massa can have a look at you."

Sillar moved into the light of the fire, showing off her beautiful high cheek bones and blue-black hair that she now wore hanging straight down to her waist. Her skin was a deep olive, combining her Creek Indian blood with that of her black ancestors. Her wrap dress of simple cotton accentuated her beautiful breasts and clung to her round hips. Kenneth couldn't resist touching her as always, untying the side opening and letting the dress slowly drop. His desire was always heightened by the sheer undergarments embroidered with lace that Sillar wore made by her own hands. Her nipples were dark against the white fabric and as he ran his hand from her neck down between her breasts, they became hard.

"Sillar, you are the strength and comfort I need tonight." Kenneth laid her down on the rug in front of the fire and very gently removed her underclothes, and she slid her hand over his buttocks helping him take off his trousers. While stroking her body quietly, he dipped his fingers in the brandy, touched it to her lips, and licked it off. He did the same to her neck and the inside of her knees and thighs, then sucked her breasts hungrily, his hands moving all the way up her inner thighs.

"You are taking too long, Master."

"I can feel the heat of your desire, Sillar," he said, as his fingers reached the warm wetness between her legs and laid his body on hers, rocking back and forth until his penis found its way into her. That wonderful sigh came from her lips the way it always did when satisfaction was near, and when he came, it washed away all of the heaviness of the day.

Before he knew it, he faced the shop. In the window were several hats, most very elaborate. The tiny bell jingled as he opened the door, and he hesitatingly entered the room. There were a few tables with velvet stools charmingly set about, and on top of the tables were three-sided mirrors. All the places were now occupied, making him feel out of place. A young salesgirl approached, "Good day, sir, I'm Miss Denise. May I help you?"

"Well, I, ah, I want to surprise my wife with a new bonnet," he stammered, realizing it was his second lie in a very short time, "and I don't have anything particular in mind. Perhaps if I could see Sil—Madame Sillar. I was told to see her personally—she would know what to suggest."

"Madame Sillar is busy right now, but I shall tell her you are here. Who was it that recommended Sillars?"

". . . uh . . . The Duchess of Leighton."

Sillar had been standing with her back toward him tending a customer. She knew it was Kenneth by the sound of his voice. At first she wanted to run, feeling unable at the moment to handle facing him. The other evening she had felt brazen and flip—confident, but not now. The only relationship she had ever had with him had been as his slave. This unexpected encounter frightened her.

Kenneth followed Denise with his eyes as she moved to the back of the shop.

"Miss Sillar, a gentleman would like to see you personally. He was recommended by the Duchess of Leighton. I don't believe she is a customer."

"Tell the gentleman I will be with him shortly, but please warn him that I must finish with Lady Ferguson before I can help him." The young woman started to go to do her bidding, but was stopped by Sillar. "Denise, the gentleman might be more comfortable in the drawing room upstairs with a cup of tea. Attend to that please."

Denise was surprised by the suggestion. Only very special clientele were escorted to her private quarters. "The drawing room?"

"Yes, the drawing room. Gentlemen feel uneasy in a ladies' shop."

She never turned around or acknowledged him, and he was grateful that he didn't have to greet her in this room filled with frilly hats and gossiping ladies, curious about his presence. She began to get control of herself realizing she could now greet him on her grounds and on her terms. Let him wait, he could spend the time absorbing the new Sillar. The drawing room would speak well for her.

He drank the tea from the fine china cup and was very taken with the beautiful room—glad for the moment's repose before facing her. She had accomplished so much.

He crossed to a side table and took a closer look at two miniature portraits on small gold easels. One was of the man who had escorted her to the theater—Lord Blamford he had been told was wealthy and of great prominence in the political and shipping worlds. The other portrait was of a young child, curly dark blond hair, a mischievous smile on his face, so engaging and somehow familiar.

The tinkle of a bell followed by the sound of a voice, "Bon soir, madame. Merci. Au revoir," called his attention again to the downstairs shop. Then he heard the light cadence of a woman's footsteps climbing the stairs. Her face came into the arc of light made by the weak sun peeking through the beveled glass windows. He looked at her fully, there was no veil to cover her beauty.

She showed no expression for a time, but then her wide smile burst forth. "Well, Mr. McIver, how nice of you to come visit my shop and home." As she talked on he had to look at her face to keep reminding himself it was Sillar. How extraordinary, the voice was different, a suggestion of a Southern drawl, but for the most part her accent and tonality was close to being upper-class British. Her hands were calm, with none of the broad gestures he had loved to see her make. He noticed she was looking at him quizzically, and he realized she probably had asked him a question. He was too embarrassed to ask her to repeat herself so felt safe in saying. "I came because I thought Mrs. McIver would be pleased to own a hat made by you. But I must admit I didn't realize what I was getting into. I mean, all those ladies trying on bonnets—I never felt so uncomfortable in my life."

"Worse than leading off the reel on Christmas Day?" They laughed remembering how awkward he was on the dance floor, which was surprising since he was so well coordinated in everything else he did. It was as though he had made up his mind he wouldn't dance well, and never mastered the art.

"I can't tell you how happy it makes me to see you like this—your home—your shop. You should be very proud." She accepted his compliment and started moving gracefully around the room, touching objects, as though she were taking him on a tour of the possessions she had acquired.

"That portrait, Sillar, of the young boy. He is beautiful. Who is he?"

Her heart skipped a beat as she answered quickly, "The son of a very good friend."

"And the other. Is that the gentleman who escorted you to the concert?"

"Yes," she answered stiffly, "he is my patron, Lord Blamford."

She stood absolutely still, looking at him blankly, her only movement was deep breathing. He felt he had offended her by questioning her about Lord Blamford. The awkwardness of the moment lingered, but neither seemed to have the energy to change things—they had both become exhausted by the small talk.

Kenneth felt uncomfortable staying with her any longer. He knew what he wanted was their old relationship and now he felt that wasn't possible. She had her life, her lover and patron, and all he could offer her was another short interlude until he left England for home. It was presumptuous even thinking that she might want to spend any time with him on any basis. "I'll say goodbye, Sillar. It was good seeing you again. I'm pleased you are doing so well."

"But the bonnet for your wife? Isn't that why you came?"

"I seemed to have lost my enthusiasm for choosing plumes and ribbons. Goodbye." He started for the stairs.

"Goodbye, Kenneth McIver." She knew that was how it should end, but she ached, her body longed to touch the South again (as hateful as it had been at times) for that's what he also represented—the wonderful sandy earth under her bare feet, the warm, blessed sun, the salt air, the wonderful shell food taken from the ocean, and her black friends, the only family she knew. He brought all of this rushing back into her mind. She watched him descending the stairs and as he reached the bottom, she called out, "You are being very decent—very kind by leaving." He stopped and listened. "You don't have to go on my accord. I have been able to live very well since I left you, as you can see. I can do well with or without you. Shall it be with you for a while?"

His hunger for her was so evident—without words she took his hand and led him to her room. She drew the heavy wine colored draperies and they were bathed in darkness until she lit a candle. The etching on the hurricane glass sleeve threw tiny dancing figures on her as she undressed. He lay naked on the bed watching, each layer stripping away more of the unfamiliar English lady, returning to him his Sillar. First she removed the fichu, and he saw the upper part of her bosom about to pop from the neckline. Slowly, she unfastened the lacings running down the front of her dress, stepping out of the bustled skirt, leaving her standing in her favorite style thin chemise, more elegant than those she used to wear. This one was an off-white gauze, embroidered with silk so fine, her body glistened through it, exposing the shadows of her pubic hair and the dark shading between the high breasts. Finally, she unlaced her high kid boots and rolled down her fine lisle stockings.

He loved the way she was taunting him, the oh, so gentle touching of herself as she undressed, but his desire made him rise in one swift movement and lower her body onto the bed sideways, entering her before they came to rest on the mattress.

10

Vanessa dismissed the hansom carriage and stood at the entrance of Guy's Hospital. It was so large she wondered in what section she would find Kirk. Or should she say Dr. Yoors. In thinking about him in the last few days, she realized how much they had lived through together: the big shoot when they fled St. Helena Island and headed up the Combahee River to live at Wind Flower, the burning of the rice plantation by the marauders, and the loss of her precious baby. She had, subsequently, called him Daniel, and even though she only held the remains of his body wrapped in her tattered petticoat for such a short time, the memory would live with her always. Why she named the baby Daniel she never could figure, but it was a name that pleased her and gave her son a real identity. To this day only Kirk, JoJo, and Sir Robert, whom she had told one evening, knew of her pregnancy and aborted baby.

Dr. Kirk Yoors. So natural a profession for him she thought—remembering the tenderness and gentleness he displayed as he cared for her after she lost the baby, getting her to a doctor and then a hospital, staying with her until he was assured she would be all right. Now he was a doctor himself, she mused. It must have been a tremendous struggle for him.

She climbed the steps of the hospital still not sure what to do except she knew it was very important for her to see Kirk, lying to herself that in a way it was a courtesy call. Guy's, she had heard, was one of England's finest teaching hospitals—well, it looked imposing enough. She made her way to the information desk and asked for him. There was some confusion and finally she was told he was in the dispensary. Either she could go out the building around to another street and come into the clinic that way or go through the hospital corridors. She chose to walk through the old halls and was amazed to see unkempt food and drink peddlers trying to sell their wares in the various wards. She came to a dead end at one point, seeing a large ad on the bulletin board: "Rags—bring your rags to the hospital to be used for bandages."

A nurse in a starched white cap and apron queried her and then put her on the right track again. She came upon Kirk—he was bent over an elderly woman as he seriously listened to her heartbeat. He looked up and was amazed—then smiled, and she smiled back. He spoke quietly to the old woman, then came to her, taking her arm without a word, guiding her into one of the hospital corridors away from the clinic.

"This is ridiculous I know, to bother you here."

"No," he said warmly, "not ridiculous at all. I'm just surprised." Concern shadowed his face. "You are not here seeking professional help?"

"No. Not at all."

"Good. You look well. Very well."

"I was passing by and thought—I'll visit Dr. Yoors. Can you take luncheon with me? It's just about that time."

"Well—I don't think so."

"The clinic? You work straight through?"

He started to stammer and then cleared his throat, he was acting like a schoolboy, he thought. "I have work, yes, but it's also that I am a poor man and there is no proper place in the vicinity I could afford."

She started to say she would pay, but didn't. "I see."

"Do you?"

"It was presumptuous of me to come by . . ."

"An answer to a dream." He smiled broadly at her, a lock of his blond hair fell forward on his forehead. "Perhaps we can arrange something else—some evening, an afternoon—the Tate Gallery."

"Dinner," she said excitedly. The idea came to her in a flash. "I'll make you dinner."

"At Lord Hatfield's house?"

"No. The house in Chelsea. My mother's house. Come, I'll fix you dinner."

"I'm delighted."

"Tomorrow night?"

"I'll be there."

She gave him the address, instructions to get there, and they set a time.

"I have to go back. There are always so many."

They said goodbye, and she walked down the corridor the way she came. She heard running footsteps behind her.

"Vanessa."

"Yes."

"Could you fix fried chicken and cream gravy? I've been dying for that for so long."

"Of course. That would be my pleasure, Dr. Yoors."

"How about potatoes beaten till they are as light as air?"

"Certainly."

"Corn bread?"

"Now that's carrying it a trifle too far." They laughed together in their happiness.

She was out on the street, wanting to run and swing in a wide circle. She stopped short. My God, I can't cook, she cried to herself. All these years and she had never learned to cook. She breathed deeply. JoJo would help her—also glad that she had decided not to use Jassime—claiming she preferred JoJo after all—but she stopped again. JoJo didn't really cook either. Tea, eggs—things prepared on small burners while traveling—only helping out when they were at the house in Chelsea. She'd work it out, she convinced herself. Happy again that she and Kirk would spend a pleasant evening together. But how was she going to learn to cook by tomorrow night?

They rushed around the small kitchen bumping into each other.

"JoJo, how come we got to this old age without learning to cook?"

There were giggles from the young woman, as she tried to pick up after her.

"We were always doin' other things."

"I hope it comes out right." Vanessa was dredging the chicken in seasoned flour. "I never remembered them putting the chicken through flour back home."

"There's lots of ways, I guess." She giggled again, her

bright saucerlike eyes dancing merrily, "I was chased out of the kitchen all the time back home."

"It would have been nice if one of us had learned. This chicken looks very messy."

"So does the kitchen."

Vanessa looked around as she brushed wisps of hair from her flushed face. There were pots and pans all over the counter and working table. The giblets were boiling over on the stove and most of the cupboard doors stood open. JoJo went around the kitchen shutting the doors and picking up the used pots and pans to put them into the sink.

"How can I be so organized in other things and so disorganized in this?"

"Beats me. And you is just cookin' for two."

"No, three. There's plenty for you."

"I don't know," she said as she playfully wrinkled her button nose. "How do I know you ain't gonna' poison me?"

"JoJo. What a thing to say. I'm following the cookbook for American recipes."

"Yes. But it's written by a Frenchman."

They laughed. A small bird outside the window tilted his head at the sound. The weather was still damp and heavy as night approached. Vanessa, overheated from the stove and the preparations, stuck her head out the kitchen window and smelled the wet earth of the small overgrown garden at the back of the house. Her mother had tended the garden laboriously until she went to stay at Lord Hatfield's. She used to say working and tending the garden, even though it was just a small patch, gave her some peace from all her worries. She'd put on big cotton gloves to protect her hands and was very pleased when one of her blooms was good enough for prominent display in the parlor. Vanessa looked further down past their garden and could see the edge of the Chelsea Physic Garden botanical research station. It always seemed ironic to her that it was there that the cottonseed was developed and sent to the United States.

They carried a small tea table from the window facing the garden and placed it in front of the fireplace. The parlor was small but had a pleasantness due to the efforts of Georgina, who had worked hard to change the oppres-

sively dark room into the charming room it had become.
She had seen a picture in a magazine of bleached oak and
worked one whole winter to get the oak wainscoting
around the room the whitest possible, then painting the
walls above, a pale blue. Fortunately, the dominant color
of the Persian rug on the floor, picked up the wall
color. The "find," as they called the rug, had been purchased secondhand from a Southern family that had decided to leave London and chance life back home again.
The damp weather was the main factor, they had told
Georgina, but gossip had it that they were penniless and
sold everything they had to scrape together money for
passage home. Hopefully, the talk went, they would be
able to carve out a life for themselves with the help of
relatives and friends back in Charleston. After all, Georgina had said at the time, their very prominent name
should stand for something. The British professed to like
and support Southerners, most had rooted for them at the
beginning of the Civil War, but to give them employment
or a helping hand in business was another matter.

The paintings around the room were lovely watercolors,
mostly using the blues and whites of the room with touches
of pale pinks and greens. They had been done by Amanda,
who had a certain flair in painting bowls of roses and
fragile bits of china or dolls in still life. Amanda had always adored and collected bits of china and dolls. One of
the saddest partings for her when they fled on the eve of
Charleston's downfall had been her dolls, one especially
carved for her by grandfather Angus. The rest of the
makeshift furnishings consisted of a rocker and footstool
and two blue and white striped love seats (upholstered by
Josiah) on either side of the room facing the hearth. The
small tea table, which JoJo and Vanessa had just moved
from the garden window, was usually surrounded by two
very old wicker chairs made comfortable by fine needlepoint cushions. These, done by Amanda and Georgina, de-
picted bouquets of violets tied in flowing pink ribbons. It
was in this window area Georgina entertained her genteel
but mostly ragged group of friends at tea. They talked of
old times and shared their dreams of the future. Dreams
they just had to keep alive for their survival and dignity.

The dining room was mostly taken up by Vanessa's piano, an old battered one bought from a church where it

had been used for choir practice. She had practiced vigorously on the instrument while she was a student at the London Conservatory and still did when she was in London, except for the times the conservatory allowed her to use a free room.

JoJo placed a lace cloth on the tea table. She had borrowed it from Miss Shields at Hatfield House saying Miss Vanessa needed it for a tea she was having. In her nasty way, the housekeeper had told JoJo she could use one they were about to discard, but to JoJo, it was lovely and trailed to the floor gracefully. Vanessa brought in a single white candle set in a china holder and placed several flowers around it. While shopping they had bought some hothouse roses and a few sprigs of fern. Then they turned down the gaslights on the walls and prepared to light the fire. They were pleased by the effect.

The clock struck seven, and Vanessa ran up the narrow stairs to the attic room, which was hers, and started to get dressed. The pitched roof made it look like an overly tall wardrobe, but the smallness suited her, especially when they first arrived in England four years before. She wanted to look her prettiest tonight and went through her dresses. JoJo knocked and poked her head through the door.

"Want me to help you dress, Nessa?"

Her desire was to be alone—alone with her happy thoughts. Everything in the kitchen was in readiness and now she needed only to get herself together.

"No. I don't need help, JoJo, why don't you go to your room and rest or take a walk—do what you want to do. Have fun. I'll also serve."

"You sure?"

"Yes. I'll try not to drop anything. Got to learn sometime."

She hesitated at the door—there was something she wanted to discuss with Vanessa and didn't quite know how to put it. She had been thinking about it ever since she saw Sillar that afternoon, but Vanessa had been too busy shopping and cooking to talk about it. She also hadn't mentioned seeing Mr. McIver there—he was leaving just as she was arriving. Luckily he hadn't noticed her. She knew Sillar had been his bedwench back home. No one ever told her, but she heard things behind doors and snatches of talk that stopped when she came into a room. They had said she was too young to know when she had questioned.

"You ever think of back home, Nessa?"

She hesitated for a moment. "Why do you ask? Are you suddenly homesick?"

"Is that what I am?"

"I don't know. You don't usually mention home."

JoJo didn't say it was because she didn't want to remind Vanessa of painful things—that had been the reason. Then seemingly out of the blue, "I saw Sillar today."

"You told me. You said she had a most beautiful house and shop."

"Yes. But it was something else. Got me to thinking."

Vanessa started to wash in the cool water in the basin, sponging her flushed face and neck. JoJo went to her automatically and raised the loose hair that had fallen around her neck.

"Sillar was talking about the sun, the soft winds off the ocean—the birds and flowers—digging for clams with bare toes on the sandy beach. Do you feel comfortable here, Nessa? I mean all the time?"

That gave Vanessa pause, "I haven't allowed myself to think too much about back home—until just recently."

JoJo was talking to her as she never quite had before— revealing her own inner thoughts. Vanessa liked that. She slipped into a lovely square-necked dress of deep rose.

"Here, let me do these buttons in the back."

Vanessa turned to allow JoJo to use her nimble fingers.

"Do you think Dr. Kirk knows of folks back home? Maybe he's seen or heard of Thursday."

"I don't know. He's been here almost a year. Why don't you ask him?"

"I will. My! A doctor. That's importnt. And Sillar, such a fine lady. It wouldn't surprise me if Thursday isn't doing good, too. He was getting a lot of ambition when we left home."

"You're doing well, too, JoJo."

"Me?"

"Yes, you. You've traveled through most of Europe, have become a beautiful young woman, and in my opinion, you're as smart as can be."

The girl beamed—her big smile lighting up her face.

"Wait till I go back one day and let those folks see me strut my stuff. Will they be surprised."

"And proud," added Vanessa.

They fussed again with the table. It was getting on to eight. Finally, Vanessa lit the single candle on the table then sat by the garden window. It was pitch black by now, and the low light gave the room a cozy look. That pleased her, but she started to worry about Kirk's time of arrival. She rose and used a match to start the fire. There was a chill in the room and she wanted it to be warm and inviting when he came. She then went back to the wicker chair and waited.

The clock on the mantel ticked slowly—each minute after nine seeming an eternity. After a long while the candle on the table sputtered and went out. JoJo was there in a second to replace it.

"Don't put in another candle. He isn't coming."

"Something must have happened, Nessa. He wouldn't just not come."

"There are ways to send a message if one wants to." A pall filled the room, then the anger that had been building in her the last hour flared up. At first she vented the rage at herself, "I threw myself at him. He must have thought I was some kind of idiot. I can't believe what I did. I walked into that hospital, crowded with people, like a brazen hussy and practically begged him to see me. What could he say or do?"

She started to pace up and down the small parlor, running her strong hands through her hair.

"Do you want me to bring you some chicken? You should eat."

"How could I have made such a fool of myself? I thought—I've got to come out of my snail's shell—live again like a normal person, find companionship. I tried to make something happen and made a fool of myself. But why would he do this? He should have said he was too busy —or just plain no. This is not fair of him, JoJo. Not fair at all." She bowed her head on the mantel. "Forcing myself like that. I'm so humiliated. I know if I ever meet him again, I'll just die from embarrassment." The hurt was there again.

"You did nothin' wrong, Nessa. I'll bring your dinner, and you'll feel better. We'll eat together—here in front of the fire. Just the two of us."

The small figure bent down and poked up the dying embers until they flared and brightened the room.

"There. That will make it warmer—feels real good to me."

"I went into that hospital seeking him out—what possessed me? He never made an overture—gave any sign. He didn't even ask me to dance at the reception." She broke into a quick stride again.

"But this is wrong. No one with any sense of breeding would do anything like this. I'll never speak to him again. This is an out-and-out insult."

She stopped short at the sound of carriage wheels and horses hooves coming down Cheyne Row.

"He's here, Nessa. He's come."

She took a deep breath and straightened her body. "All right. But be calm. Don't act like anything out of the ordinary has happened."

There was a heavy tap on the door, and JoJo took a second before she went to answer it. There was another heavy demanding knock as she opened it. Sasha Bronsky stood there beaming but also a little agitated. He immediately went to Vanessa.

"What are you doing here—at this place? I went first to Belgrave Square."

His quick eye took in the small table set for two in front of the fireplace and the implications made his stomach turn. Lately he worried about Vanessa and romantic involvements, she was so beautiful, especially this evening.

"So. I am disturbing a party?"

"No, of course not. Please sit down. I'm happy to see you."

She was honestly glad for the distraction from her confused painful thoughts. She went to him and led him to the striped sofa. But he was too excited to sit.

"I'm not coming by too late?"

"Of course not. I'm delighted, but why did you come?"

He was so full of his news he could wait no longer. "Ah. You want to know why Sasha came by at such an hour? It is for a good reason. I could not wait until tomorrow to tell you."

"What is it? Please."

"You were going to eat?"

"Sasha! You are such a tease. Good news?" And she added hastily in an involuntary aside, "I could use some."

"There is something wrong? You are upset, bubeleh?"

"Sasha!"

"All right. I'll sit and tell you."

He placed his huge bulk on the sofa and crossed his hamlike legs in princely fashion.

"Your dream, bubeleh, is not only to play recitals in the capitals of the world but also in concert with famous orchestras. Am I not right?"

An apparent sadness came over her as she answered slowly, not noticed by Sasha as he was so caught up with the dispatching of his news.

"Yes, my biggest dream."

"You got it!"

She looked at him in surprise as she sank next to him on the sofa. He slapped her playfully on the shoulder.

"You're amazed. Speechless."

"What happened, Sasha?"

"Brussels! After your recital in Paris, a small hall but still very respectable, then Antwerp—Right?—again not too big but still important. And then, my little one—are you ready? You are to play as guest soloist with the Royal Symphony Orchestra in Brussels. Isn't Sasha making you into a great international artist?"

She smiled weakly at him and rose, moving almost numbly to the mantel where she stared at the fire.

"You said it was after Antwerp. Will I have to be gone a long time?"

He jumped up and went to her. JoJo who had stayed in the background, retired unnoticed from the room. She went to the kitchen and stood by the stove, which was still heated to keep the chicken warm.

Sasha was ruffled, "Why do you ask such a question? Jump for joy! Such a thing would take a year ordinarily and for some—never."

"How long, Sasha?"

"Five extra days. We arrive over the weekend from Antwerp, and you will have three days rehearsal with the orchestra. Not full days of course, but enough time."

Three days. She was relieved she would not have to

be away from London for more than ten days in all, but the concert—suddenly she was horrified. "What am I to play? Is it something I am familiar with?"

"Bubeleh. It is a blessing. Would Sasha let you down? It is one of your favorites. You say you play it in your head all the time."

"Chopin?"

"Do I arrange it good? Of course. Actually, it was already arranged for another. Fortunately, or unfortunately, depending from where you sit, the artist broke his finger and they need a replacement. An opportunity, a big opportunity for us." He eyed the table again as he tried to read the concerned look in her face, hoping it was her anxiety at such an important appearance and nothing else.

The murky atmosphere again turned into rain, which grew heavier and heavier after midnight. Then the wind started to blow, rattling the windows as if its velocity over the channel had invaded London. Vanessa still tossing, unable to sleep, sat up with a start when she heard the front door slam open, but on recognizing the cursing and stamping of feet, relaxed as much as she could under the circumstances, knowing it was her Uncle Thomas coming home. She had asked him as a special favor to stay out this evening—but had not asked him to stay out until this late. He stumbled up the narrow stairs and into her mother's bedroom. She wondered if her mother would ever use that room again. She seemed so ensconced at Hatfield's house on Belgrave Square.

Vanessa winced when she thought again about Kirk, the hurt deeper than she suspected at first. All the past years of protecting herself from just such a happening—why did she ever allow the invitation to such a hurt. She punched the pillow, trying to get comfortable—pushing aside as best she could these thoughts—hopefully forever. Tomorrow was a busy day, she kept telling herself.

Sasha, with everything else, had arranged for her to see her old music teacher to get help with the concerto she would play with the Royal Orchestra in Brussels. Actually she was looking forward to seeing her old teacher, Madame Dworski. Vanessa tried very hard to concentrate and was somewhat comforted when the notes of the concerto were spinning in her head—she could hear the sounds—but as much as she tried, she could not get rid of the longing in her body, which ached from the need to be loved. She had known no man since Pierre. In Rome, a few had tried, but her aloof demeanor scared them away. Lately her body had been tingling, but her foraging had brought only pain again. Music never failed her, she reflected, and fought valiantly again to fill her head with nothing but the notes of Chopin's concerto.

The rain continued into the morning, but Sasha appeared at the appointed time with a carriage and they went off to the conservatory, first dropping JoJo at the house on Belgrave Square to get the packing done for the evening's departure. They were to take the train from London to Dover and then the boat to Calais—from there on to Paris by rail.

11

The small ivy-covered cottage was set high on the white cliffs of Dover overlooking the English Channel. It was an old house full of nooks and crannies, formed by the many extensions and additions by loving rather than professional hands.

Pierre, still in his silk dressing gown, stood by a tall wide window, a recent addition by him, looking out at the choppy gray sea. The heavy rain had passed, leaving in its wake an overcast, but there was a brightening in the far sky promising a partial clearing sometime during the day. He imagined he could see the coast of France beyond the horizon. Calais. Vanessa would be going by boat to Calais then taking the boat train to Paris for her next recital. Paris and Antwerp and then back to London all within a week's time she had told him while they danced.

Vanessa. She hadn't been out of his thoughts since he saw her the other night, realizing now she had always been a part of him during his retreat from life these last few years, but thoughts of her lifted his cover, the protective cover needed to cloak his guilt. How beautiful she had looked as she stood on stage and while he held her in his arms during the waltz. So statuesque, the finely chisled features, the blue eyes tilting at the corners, always earnest, searching, still the same. But she was much more reserved, something she had never been before. Still the sweet smelling body he remembered, but feeling much harder in his grip, no doubt from the arduous life demanded by her music.

He had almost come to a decision during the night and

was trying to sort all the pieces together. He had to be sure—as sure as a human being could be, he didn't want to intrude on lives again, only to fail and disappoint.

Suddenly, as he continued to stare out the window at the turgescent waves, it was there again—the noise filling his ears—the screeching, hysterical cries ripping from the throats of frenzied chickens. The same sounds that had plagued him, causing nightmares for several years. His eyes widened as the sounds ballooned, echoing in his head, then compounded in his mind by other noises. As quickly as they came, they were gone—a bitter remembrance, the sounds of fury and war.

He had enlisted after the Federals burned Wind Flower, and wore the Confederate Gray until the end. The recruiting officer looked at him with loathing when he told him he would do anything except be a part of actual combat. The man knew of the Bonneau family and the great statesmen and heroes it had produced, but held his usual sharp tongue. He assigned the tattered young man to the morose commissary general, Colonel Northrop. Pierre worked until totally exhausted to help keep the Confederate Army fed. A moving regiment, he was told, had to have a full belly. For a time in that first autumn, he labored in the fields of Tennessee side by side with infantrymen from General Bragg's army. The men had been enlisted to bring in the bumper crop of wheat that had ripened, for there were no farmers available to harvest it. The wheat provided the troops with desperately needed flour.

Lieutenant Bonneau went wherever the need for food was greatest. He had been bringing in supplies behind enemy lines during a decisive battle at Missionary Ridge, high in the mountains of Tennessee, when the Federals broke the Confederate skirmish line. He witnessed with great sorrow the drunkenness among the Southern officers and the veteran Confederate soldiers running to the rear in fear when they saw twenty thousand Yankees storming up the ridge. The battle was lost, and the Confederates retreated toward Georgia with the enemy nipping at their heels. Grant's victory at the ridge meant the South had lost Tennessee and so much of their food supply. Pierre and his men scoured the countryside for eatables.

It was in the harsh backwoods of Georgia on a cold day in January 1864, when he was scrounging for food for the tired troops that were beaten, sick, and hungry that he killed a man—that act would live with him forever.

12

Georgia - 1864

A nagging wind had chilled his body, and as he dis-
mounted from his tired horse, he flung his arms repeat-
edly across his chest to increase circulation. It had been
raining for days, stopping only this morning—but Pierre
knew it was just a short break in the weather—any moment the heavens would open again to send down another
icy cloudburst.

His cracked boots sunk in the red mud as he approached
the chicken house and heard the wild clucks of the fowl.
He thought the man he had sent to gather them was doing
his job. He had just paid the farmer for the chickens
they were about to take, allowing no stealing by the men
under his command—taking without payment only goods
on abandoned farms. In the last miles of the retreat that
led them from the Tennessee mountains into Georgia, he
had been sickened and amazed at the number of blacks
lying dead along the road and in the woods—blacks who
no doubt had fled to join the Federals and perished on the
way. Turkey buzzards swarmed over the area, some waiting for new prey, others feasting savagely on the bodies.
He tried to have some buried decently, only to realize the
reality of priorities—their time had to be spent dealing
with the needs of the living during the retreat.

When he got to the chicken house, the fowl were flinging themselves around wildly—hitting the side slats of the
flimsy structure. A Union soldier was rolling on the floor
with the young private he had sent in to collect the fowl.
The soldier in blue, caked in mud and filth, had the obvious advantage of height and weight as he pinned the

rebel to the ground, raising his cocked gun against the young soldier's temple. The eyes of the young rebel looked to him, pleaded for him to make a move to free him. In an involuntary gesture, Pierre abruptly grabbed the gun at his hip, never fired by him before, and killed the Yankee. The startled expression on the young man's face as he turned to him was imprinted on his mind forever. The saved soldier under the dead man pushed the body away and when free, hunched into a ball and sobbed. The frenzied chickens screeched louder, their feathers filling the dank air.

Pierre walked outside and fell to his knees sinking in the mire. Dry heaves racked his body painfully. He had performed, for him, a heinous act, one against all his principles. He had watched the act of killing in combat, but this was different. He did it. Face to face he killed a human being, not a faceless target.

The young man he saved came out of the chicken house and spoke, his voice full of emotion, tears running down his dirty face, making grimy tracks. "Thank you, Lieutenant, thank you for my life. I'll never forget it. Bless you, sir." He then helped him to his feet and handed Pierre his gun, dropped after the fatal firing. Pierre studied the young man and then wondered what the parents of the dead soldier would say to him. There were no winners here, only survivors. His voice was hollow. "Go get those chickens, Private. They'll probably taste like hell after what they've been through—but the men are hungry."

"Yes, sir." As he turned to carry out his orders, Pierre could see the young man's body was still shaking—so was his.

"Private." The young man turned, a weak smile on his face.

"Pull out the body so it will be found. If there's one Yankee around, they'll be others. Let's hope he'll get a decent burial."

He rode at a slow pace behind the supply wagon, now half filled with the dead chickens. The young soldier had wrung their necks. Pierre's eyes were almost sunken into his head as his thoughts went back to Wind Flower and Montgomery's raid up the Combahee. Drunkenly he had stumbled out into the marshes, watching the fleeing field hands climbing into the gunboats, and had fallen into the swampy rice fields, then passed out. When he came to the next morning, his head barely above the waterline, he staggered back to the house to see the charred ruin and his mother sitting in a daze on the blackened ground. She ran to him and they embraced. After the emotional re-union, she told him Vanessa was alive. One of the slaves hiding, too scared to flee, had seen her in a wagon being driven away.

"You must never leave me, Pierre. Never again!" his mother had cried in her anguish.

As gently as possible because he was too drained for anything else, he told her, "I am your son, Mother, not your husband. I have a life of my own."

But she clutched at him, and it took all his remaining strength to free himself as he started for the road behind the house—at that moment he had no idea where he was heading. She chased after him, imploring him to stay with her, but he kept on walking and finally she let him go.

"You'll be back, my son?"

He didn't bother to answer.

The rains came now, and his body became colder and more numb on this January day. The supply wagon sank into a rut. He got down and put his shoulder to the wheel—the dead soldier's startled face appeared in his mind's eye vividly—to haunt him. He glanced down at the gun again on his hip. He hated the weapon—hated all guns—he had been witness to the gun accident that took his father's life when he was five. He wished he had it in his power to get rid of all the guns on this earth.

Shortly after, he decided to divorce Vanessa. He was so filled with loathing for himself, how could he expect anyone to live with him. She deserved a chance at life—not to be saddled with the shell of a man.

But here at Dover, five years later, a soul-searching five years, he reversed that decision about himself and wanted Vanessa back.

He had always been a lonely person, and he did not know how to accept love. Instead he had always been so suspicious of relationships—afraid they would entrap and enslave him. The cold domination of his mother since he was a boy and his fight against it had been at the core of his behavior since his father's death, making him a poor companion for any woman.

He now felt he knew how to love and accept it in return. He cringed as he remembered his wedding night. Drunk, he had taken Vanessa roughly, rolled off with an insulting remark and passed out. Most of their coming together had been the same.

In the spring he would come into the bulk of his inheritance but until then he was somewhat strapped, the monthly payments of his trust fund had been shared with Vanessa, so there hadn't been much. He would need a chunk of money for what he definitely decided he was going to do. He knew it meant going to his mother—he wished there was another way. There might be, he reasoned, the bank that handled his drafts was a possibility, but his mother would be simpler. So be it.

As he pulled the sash of his robe tighter, he turned and was surprised to see Geeta standing there. She was wearing a sari of a small print, gayer than she usually wore. Her bright, dark eyes filled her small face, and were staring at him intently. The daughter of his manservant whom he had brought from India, she had grown in the past five years from an awkward unattractive child into a budding young woman of pure ethnic beauty.

"Sahib,' she said in a low pitched girlish tone, "do you wish more tea or perhaps your breakfast to be served?" She knew something was different from other days that had been filled with an aura of serenity, and she shivered, feeling the new threatening vibrations coming from the sahib, knowing that their days of tranquility were possibly at an end.

"No. Nothing. Ask your father to go to the storage room and get one of my larger traveling cases. I am going to London for a while and will send for more things as I need them." He walked from the room without a further glance at her. Usually she rushed to fulfill his wishes but this time she stood rooted, cold drafts, like suckered arms of an octopus, seemed to creep through the cracks between the panes of glass, trying to engulf her—she hugged herself to stop the entrance of the frigid chill into her childlike body.

13

The footman opened the door to the tapping, but saw no one. He felt a tug on his livery jacket and when he looked down, saw a small boy soaked through from the rains that lingered over London.

"What do you want, child? Deliveries are made at the basement door."

The ragged child carefully took an envelope from under his shirt, the paper was wet in spite of his careful efforts. He tried to protect it further as he explained in his heavy cockney accent.

"This 'ere is fer Miss V. McIver. A very important message."

The footman took it, trying not to touch the dirty hand. He noticed Guy's Hospital printed in the corner of the envelope. The boy spoke again urgently, "A doctor give it to me to deliver."

"I'll see Miss Vanessa McIver gets it," and he closed the door on the sooty face. The letter was placed in a silver bowl on the hall table, then the footman went below stairs to change. It was his afternoon and evening off.

Mack Malone paid scant attention as he saw the ragamuffin go to the door, deliver an envelope, then scurry down the street. He was so involved with the anger that had been growing inside him over the past few days, he paid heed to little else. Having watched the fancy reception in the heavy downpour the other night, later following the young nob, Josiah McIver (he now knew his name from one of the servants), to the small house in the Chelsea section, Mack was still confused as to his actual wealth—it was gnawing at his guts. So he kept coming back to the house on Belgrave Square, telling himself there had to be money there, especially after learning about the engagement of a McIver to the fancy lord. He had a heavy cough from the cold he caught that night, and after a painful fit of hacking this wet afternoon, decided to have another pint of bitters at the Nag's Head—a pub he found in the mews behind the Square. It was there he had the luck, he told Daphne, to meet some of Hatfield's footmen, and now he hoped he would encounter one or two of them again to garner more information while warming his innards with some strong brew. The more he dwelled on his plan, the more he was positive the money was due him—blackmail some would say—but to Mack, after all the tossing the nob had done with his Daphne, it was only rightful payment. Then in a year's time, he reasoned, pleased with himself, he would get more out of this Josiah McIver and on and on—as long as the young bloke thought the kid was his.

He entered the Nag's Head and went down the steps to the bar below street level, eyeing the few afternoon drinkers to see if one was from Hatfield House. None looked familiar as he stepped up and put his foot on the rail, so he stood alone, watching the barman draw his pint. He intended now to stay there the rest of the day in the hopes of making a contact.

Kirk moved hand over hand up the wall to help himself to his feet. Three hours before in total exhaustion he had leaned back into the corner of an empty room next to the ward he had been working in, sank to the floor and slept in that awkward position. He had not felt such exhaustion since he was an overseer on the McIver plantation during the cotton-picking seasons—when he thought he would drop because of lack of sleep and then during the War, especially toward the end, as a medical assistant attending the wounded in the field. Somehow though, these days at Guy's Hospital were the most draining. Part of the difficulty was he felt so excited by what he was learning he couldn't pull himself away.

But no matter how tough it was, he knew he had made the right decision to scrimp and save back in the States, enabling him to come to London for further study. At home the medical standards and surgical advances were far below those of England and the rest of the Continent. Many became doctors without having seen the inside of a hospital. Here in England the medical college was a part of the hospital, and it required dissection of bodies, the study of clinical medicine, and practical anatomy among other courses—and finally, before a license to practice was given, there were rigorous examinations.

This was a particularly innovative time for surgery in England and Scotland and that was Kirk's interest. Great advancements were made every day to the point that some operations were becoming "routine." The use of anesthesia was improving, first ether and now chloroform. And Dr. Lister's famous paper, which he gave in Dublin a few years before on the prevention of bacteria by sterilization of instruments, the operating room, and in fact anything that came in contact with the patient during the operation, was beginning to make inroads.

Kirk had become a doctor of medicine back in New Orleans but on his application to Guy's Hospital asked to be put in training as a student, and for a small salary practiced in the hospital clinic. He was doing double duty and would for another six months. His love of medicine and healing went back many years. As a small boy he carried the satchel of the doctor who owned the plantation where his father was overseer, and as he grew older, assisted the learned man in his operations on fistulas and hernias done in the infirmary in the slave quarters. Once he helped at the age of eleven in an emergency operation in an open field, with the patient doubled over the shaft of a wagon, screaming for death as he was sewn with horsehair without the aid of any painkiller.

His mother and father were proud of him, especially his mother, a German immigrant, calling him the little healer, as the doctor grew very dependent on him.

Hilda and Will Yoors had a deep love for each other, always delighting in each other's company—they danced together often, with Kirk on the sidelines clapping the rhythm or hopping along as they did the polka in the small family room of their house. They traveled to nearby Lake Pontchartrain for picnics and sang joyously, then they munched on the food prepared lovingly by Hilda Yoors.

Her two men, she used to say as Kirk grew—"my two big, strapping men, Yoors stock, it is good!"

The walls had been thin in their house on the edge of the slave quarters, and often, young Kirk fell asleep hearing the sounds of their coming together, secure in their love.

He was not allowed in the room to assist the good doctor when his mother at age forty gave birth to a stillborn infant and died herself shortly after. He had felt utterly helpless hearing the pitiful screams during the long labor, and his father, when told of his wife's death, was eaten with remorse, blaming himself, and never again drew a sober breath. Kirk covered for him as best he could as overseer, but in a year's time he followed his wife in death, having no strength to combat the swamp fever that raced through his emaciated body. Kirk had tended his father day and night during this sickness to no avail, leaving soon after the burial feeling defeated by death and painfully alone.

He forced himself awake and saw a nurse at the far end of the ward working her way along the beds, wiping a forehead, fluffing a pillow. Everything seemed quiet and in order. He walked quickly in the direction of the apothecary shop on the ground floor, which held the telegraph machine hooked up to the police headquarters, then went out the door to the courtyard where the ambulances waited. On his mind was the note he had sent Vanessa, and he was anxious to know if she received it. Only one of the three ambulances was standing there. "Good morning, Doctor. Emergency?"

"No, I am looking for little Harry. Do you know if he's come back?"

"No, Doctor, but I'll tell him to look you up when he does."

"Do that."

Kirk turned slowly and headed back toward the wards.

14

Pierre settled in comfortably with his friend, Sir Robert Ashcroft, in his house off the river embankment on Tite Street. It was a smallish house designed around a large painting studio. It had all of Sir Robert's unique touches and was usually filled with other artists, models, people of the theater as well as those of the upper class. Despite his wealth and fame as a portrait painter, Robert never wanted to move to a more fashionable part of London, preferring to live in the center of the creative life in Chelsea. Whistler lived nearby and several other famous painters had lived in this very house before him. He felt his talents were fed from the richness of the neighborhood, and whenever he was asked why he stayed, he would always answer, "I don't have to worry about what I wear when I take a walk or have to hide my lady for the night under my cloak. I would also have to get a whole new set of servants, ones who wouldn't abuse me. No. This keeps me in touch."

Sir Robert belonged to the upper class himself. His father was a famous admiral who married the daughter of the Fourth Earl of Burnington—on both sides there were distinguished dukes and earls, but that was not the life for him. After Harrow and Trinity College at Cambridge, he rented a room in Paris and became a painter, completely immersing himself for the next ten years in the excitement of that French city. He studied with Courbet and Delacroix, and returned to London in the late 1850s to become a sought-after portrait painter of his own set. He never married, enjoying the frequent changing of love mates. Lately he delighted in the sweet fruits of the freer morals of his own class—bored matrons, forced into planned marriages by their families, now desirous of a romantic fling with no attachments, following the new moral code set by the Prince of Wales. Sir Robert, not overly handsome, but witty, virile, most obliging, knew how to please a woman.

His friendship with Pierre had started during his days in Paris, and he was pleased but somewhat surprised when his old friend asked to be his house guest.

Pierre had slept in Ashcroft's studio, and the north light streaming in from the skylight awoke him early. Even after his eyes focused on the day, it took him a while to recall just where he was.

Robert, dressed in a deep brown velvet dressing gown, came in carrying a tray with a large pot of steaming coffee, two enormous cups, a small pitcher of milk, and a bowl of sugar.

"Well, good morning. The roosters have long since crowed and here you are stretched out still dreaming."

Robert poured the coffee, "I've never been able to understand the awful habit of you Americans starting the day with strong coffee."

"Drink your tea. I'll join you."

"No, you're a guest. I'll drown the bitter brew in sugar and cream."

They settled down in front of the studio windows overlooking a small overgrown garden. After a few sips, Robert, never comfortable with an uneasy silence, looked his friend firmly in the eye, "You are going to hate me for what's coming, and you'll probably be rude and tell me to mind my own business, but I cannot."

"Don't struggle so, Robert, you want to know why I am here. I'm sure you've guessed it's Vanessa."

"What are your intentions?"

"You sound like her father."

Robert crossed his ankles revealing his cracked leather slippers, stained with dabs of paint, obviously longtime favorites. "Despite my appearance, which might lead one to think I could be her father when standing next to her, I rather fashion myself as her possible suitor sometime in the future. It's conceivable for me to settle down, you know."

At first Pierre's instinct was to chuckle, but then he no-

ticed Robert's face was serious, and prepared for the hurt
he felt was coming.

"I mean, she's a very special woman, who has pulled
herself through abominable times."

"That she has."

"But I must say when it comes to men, she is the
most naive person I have ever known. Do you know she
has no idea that half the men who meet her, if given
half the chance, would fall madly in love with her?"

"I know. She is a beautiful woman."

"Also a very vulnerable one. It would be too easy for
you to hurt her, and I won't allow that to happen again."

Robert felt silly having gotten so quickly overwrought,
but he felt a great need to protect the girl. "Now that
some of the secrets of my heart have been exposed, why
don't you tell me your real feelings, and I promise I shall
listen like the rational man I am."

Pierre gave in to his friend's charm. "Well it's really
rather simple in a way."

"I've come to the conclusion nothing is simple."

Pierre's handsome face was full of concern, trying to
make this man understand that which he didn't understand
too clearly himself. "I want to see if it can work again. I
still love her, and I can honestly say even more so now
than before. The war stripped away all the ruffles and
frills of our lives, leaving us exposed, seeking a place to
hide. God, we are pitiful creatures some of us, and I've
been one of the most pitiful."

"Join the club, my friend." Robert poured more coffee
for the two of them. Pierre talked on, released now that
they had found a way to start.

"But Vanessa, when the Southern trappings were
stripped away, only a genuineness remained. I remember
the shock that ran through Charleston society when our
engagement was announced—she's so plain they said—no
grace and on and on. Well, what she was then and is now,
is real and honest—not a manipulative bone in her body."
Then with a grin, "You must admit I have good taste."

"No one will deny that. But what of her, Pierre? She is
all the things you say. But now she's more. Her music has
been her life since you left her, and you can't expect her
to trade off again—you for the music."

"Maybe the one who's changed the most is me. I have

no urgency left in my life. The peace I found in India defined my needs and left no doubts. I only want to lead a truthful life. Vanessa can have her music—I'll support her in any way she needs, financially and emotionally—traveling with her and making a home wherever she wants—just as long as you're willing to water my roses and orchids while I'm away."

Robert passed over his levity, "Now you are being naive. She is a simple woman in some ways, but very complicated in others. Maybe she won't be happy with you—did you ever consider that? You on your white charger saying 'whatever you want, dear.' I'm sure she's done some defining of her life over the past few years—come to some conclusions regarding her needs. As for me, there is nothing that makes me angrier than a person who constantly says, 'whatever *you* want.' "

"I think you're being unfair, Robert. And in any case all of this will be worked out slowly over months—not nights."

"You've forgotten one thing, Pierre—Harriet Sims Bonneau. Don't you think she'll have something to say in this?"

Pierre was surprised that the mention of his mother in this way could still make him defensive, and he spoke with a touch of annoyance. "I know what Harriet wants above all else—me. And she can have me this time but only on one condition—that she accepts Vanessa and whatever life-style we choose. Otherwise nothing."

Robert didn't know what more to say, he idly started sketching a charcoal of a woman's figure—an abstract of Vanessa.

"You're hurt, Robert, I'm sorry."

"No, no, I'm thinking of Vanessa. I can't ever rid my mind of the picture of her standing in my doorway, so forlorn. I expected her at some point. Luckily some of the letters got through. She had written of the steady bombardment of Charleston and of the devastation, the yellow fever epidemic, saying one day they would have to leave and her father was planning on their making it to London. Then one day there she was—she never spoke about you—not a mention."

"Did she know I arrived in London after the war?"

"Possibly. I can't be sure. Then you were off to India.

I never told her about that. I felt she wanted to forget the heavy past."

Robert's Siamese curled himself comfortably in Pierre's lap, and he stroked the silky fur, talking for the first time about his experiences in India. He described his tiny whitewashed room in a house high above the Hanuman-ghat in Benares, the most holy of all Indian cities. At sunset he could faintly hear the voices of pilgrims bathing in the Ganges, the most sacred of all Indian rivers and nearby was the temple to Hanuman, the monkey god. Then each day the small bell sounded, calling the worshippers together, fresh and clean from the river, carrying flowers.

He told Robert of the simplicity of his life, his day starting at dawn, the pure moment of the day. He would bathe in the river and pray and perform the holy rites of the Hindu religion, then wash his utensils and clothes. In the beginning he had felt caught between two worlds. He had been trying to take stock of himself in an attempt to find his place in the chaos of the fast world. He meditated daily and tried to follow the principles of equality, purity, and universal love—to come out of himself, to be less self-serving.

Eventually, the maid interrupted, bringing Sir Robert the message that Lady Whiting had arrived for her sitting. He rose to change, and Pierre felt obliged to again state his feelings about Vanessa.

"Robert, I'm grateful to you for letting me talk. I am perhaps too voluble about my desire for Vanessa, but you must know that I love her deeply and there is no way for me to hurt her any more—it is against my very nature now."

Robert thought about what was just said, "Do we ever really know ourselves, my friend? And do we ever stop hurting those we love?"

Then he put his hand on his friend's shoulder, "I want you to know that there are wounds there, deep ones, and she has been unwilling to talk with anyone about it. While you were finding yourself, the woman you say you've always loved, was left to flounder in frightening, muddy water." Pierre turned white and bowed his head. "Since you seem determined to entwine your life with hers again, then you must know what her struggles have been and weigh them against your own desires before you open her heart. Please, if you marry her again, it must be because you feel you can make her life happier. And then you cannot forget the baby—that was a painful loss, and it still lingers sharply, contained like a volcano within her."

"What baby, Robert?"

Robert saw the stunned look on his friend's face.

"Why, your baby, Pierre."

"Quickly, tell me. I don't know what this is about."

"I'm sorry. I thought somehow you were told. When Wind Flower was burned by Montgomery, Vanessa lost the baby she was carrying. It was a boy."

For a long time Robert just watched his friend bent forward, head in hands strained white, his anguish expressed by an occasional heaving of his shoulders and the shaking of his head in a silent "no," trying to push away the sadness.

Vanessa was standing at the ship's railing watching the turbulent waters churning in the English Channel. Her mind continued to run through the music she was to play the next night, each note clearly flowing forward. Suddenly the music in her head stopped and she became overwhelmed with fear—looking down at her fingers she imagined them frozen on the keyboard. She shook her hands vigorously, trying to rid the image of herself unable to continue playing. It's my life, she screamed inwardly my only life—my hands. She stood there frightened and then pulled her heavy cape closer around her shoulders and walked to the upper deck, trying to shake off the sudden anxiety that overtook her. The Strait of Dover was becoming more and more treacherous, the boat pitched and rolled as it bucked the high waves, leaving no doubt who was master here. There was a very good reason the boat had so few passengers, only fools traveled these waters in winter. Poor Sasha and JoJo had been ill from the second the boat slipped away from the pier. Vanessa, however, felt invigorated by the power of nature, and she looked up at the moon beaming its arc of light on the rampant black water of the North Sea.

The night had seemed an eternity, and dawn came as the train at Calais jerked forward, starting its journey south to Paris. JoJo spread herself out on a seat at one end of the train, still wan and weak, apologizing to Sasha and Vanessa sitting across from one another. The train picked up speed as they rolled on, and for a time none of them spoke, only staring out the window at the tiny, picturesque farms along the way. Now and again the steam from the engine hindered their view as the train maneuvered a long, arched curve in the track.

Vanessa broke the silence as they entered the first tunnel. "Sasha, I have a new determination to become the greatest pianist the world has ever known. And nothing will stand in my way."

The train reached the end of the tunnel, and her eyes blinked at the sudden rush of light that filled up the car.

"There is no doubt, my darling—that is what I've been telling you and that is what you will be. Trust your Sasha."

15

Kenneth sent two notes to Sillar asking to see her. Both times the messenger was asked to wait for a response and both times he returned empty-handed. Fortunately, Georgina was so involved in planning Amanda's trousseau and the trip that the family would soon take to Jamie Hatfield's country estate that she never noticed his distraction and would certainly not miss his presence today. He had decided he would go to Sillar's shop and confront her himself.

Since their first meeting, he had gone through moments of elation, then frustration, and finally when he was met by total silence on her part, he became angry—angry at himself for needing her so, and angry for her treatment of him now. He acknowledged that he had no right to make demands on her, but surely she had some feeling for him, must feel a bit of the same emotions he was experiencing, and she did reopen their former relationship, putting him in this agonizing position.

Fortunately, there were only two patrons in her shop, and Sillar noticed him the second he walked through the door. In the polite tone used on customers, she greeted him, "Good afternoon, Mr. McIver. Come with me and I'll show you the work we've done on your wife's bonnet." She then took him to the drawing room upstairs and in a quiet firm voice informed him, "I prefer that you not come here unless invited."

"You didn't answer my notes, and I had to see you. Surely you must want to see me, too. It was you who said, 'shall it be together while you are here?' "

"I was wrong the other day. I know that now. What we had before is over, and we mustn't try to revive it."

"You have a right to want to turn me away, and I accept that. But I won't give up seeing you easily and it's because I know we have so little time left that I am anxious to spend as much time as I can with you. Please, Sillar, don't cut me out of your life."

"Now you are making me feel mean and unkind. I want to see you, Kenneth, but you are jeopardizing my life and my home."

"How?"

"That I can't tell you."

He could see the pain on her face.

"I beg you—if we meet, it must be on my terms."

"It will be on your terms, Sillar. Whatever way you want it. Just don't shut me out. I need you."

"Then meet me at the Queen's Gate in Kensington Gardens this afternoon. I shall be there as close to four 'o'clock as I can make it—we will talk."

As Kenneth left the shop, a large, elegantly appointed carriage drew up in front of Sillar's and the footman unfolded the stairs, helping a little blond-haired boy climb down to the sidewalk. He was laden with all sorts of gifts.

"Au revoir, monsieur, merci bien," he gaily shouted back at the carriage.

"Au revoir," returned the thin male voice. The man was sitting too far back in the carriage for Kenneth to make out his face. The little boy scooted past him, thanking him for holding the door to the shop open for him.

Blamford wondered about the identity of this strange gentleman. It was peculiar for a man to patronize Sillars by himself, and he had the appearance of someone in an emotional state. He felt a quick stab of jealousy, a not unfamiliar feeling when it came to Sillar. He loved her and she was the only person he had ever known with whom he could relax, to express some of his inner feelings and even at that, she teased him about being a stuffed shirt. For an old bachelor it always amazed him that her son had grown to be such a joy to him. Whenever one of his many ships docked at the East India ports, he would take Kenneth with him, While he went over documents with the captain, young Kenneth would scamper over the deck, conversing easily with every manner of hand on the ship and always ended up laden down with souvenirs from all the exotic places the ship had visited.

Blamford delighted in watching the relationship of mother and son. Sillar held the child often, got down on the floor and played games with him, tossed him in the air, played tag and catch with him, then shocked the new nanny by dining with her son at least once a week. She was not intimidated by her servants, perhaps it was because she had been one herself. He so wished he could be open and unrestricted like her, but his own childhood was so severe, raised by a strict governess, hardly seeing his parents, sometimes only just before bed to say good night—and those occasions were rare.

He remembered when he met Sillar. He was a house guest in the country, and when his personal valet became ill, she was sent to his room to repair a rent in the sleeve of his dinner jacket. Not expecting him to return to his room for several hours, she decided to do it there, instead of the dark room below stairs set aside for sewing. She had pulled a small chair over to the French doors leading to the balcony that overlooked the gardens and was just sitting there contemplatively when he entered the room. He stood quietly by, so enthralled by her beauty and serenity. Finally she finished the sewing and bit the thread with her teeth. When she turned to pick up a hanger from the wooden valet, she was startled, "Oh forgive me, sir, I shall just rehang your jacket and be off."

His stern face had intimidated her, and she quickly left the room, taking, he knew, a great deal of him with her. The moment he returned home, he had his solicitor contact her, offering her money to set up a shop as a seamstress. He thought having her own business would intrigue her. She insisted on meeting this patron before accepting his offer, and he would never forget how she looked when she came to his solicitor's office to meet him. She was nervous, but her manner was proud. He admired her dress, the very latest style, but of cheap fabric, and was taken by her directness as she spoke of the business offer, then asked him what he really had in mind. He told him quite as directly, and she looked him square in the eye, telling him that she knew that was the reason and made a good business deal with him in return for what he wanted. Six months in Paris to study millinery—she didn't want to do dressmaking. What will I do in those six months, he had asked her, really amused by the gall of the woman.

"Spring is almost here, m'lord, and they say Paris is very pleasurable in that season."

And it had been a beautiful spring. Her son was always with her and in time he gladly promised her that when it came time, he would use his best efforts to get little Kenneth accepted at the finest schools in England. His love never waivered, it only grew, and he often cursed his reserved manner, wanting to tell this open, warm woman how much she meant to him. He also could not curb his jealous nature when it came to her.

Sillar was dreadfully shaken by the confrontation with Kenneth. Since their first meeting she had been apprehensive, not certain she could control her emotions and now she felt as though she were drowning. She went to her bedroom and stretched out on the chaise, pulling a coverlet up over her legs, feeling drained and chilled.

The nurse brought in young Kenneth, still bubbling from his outing and bringing her a gift.

"Ma'am, it is time for his nap."

"It's all right, leave him here. Come Kenneth, lie on the chaise with me, and we'll have a tiny rest together."

The warmth of his tiny body comforted her as his little voice told of the adventures he had on shipboard—finally drifting off in midsentence in a pleasant sleep. She laid her cheek on his soft curly hair, lulled by his light breathing and the lovely smell of him. She closed her eyes and thought of the joy she felt when she knew she was pregnant and then the horror when Kenneth told her she must leave for England with Georgina and the children. She never dreamed she would have to go away from him. Thoughts of running off to keep her from going entered her head, but the war had spread devastation all over the South and to protect her unborn child, she allowed Kenneth to send her away. After the flight from Charleston as the city fell, they fought to get to Nassau, where they boarded a steamer for Liverpool. Georgina finally felt safe and became her old self, returning to the relationship of mistress/slave. She used every opportunity to abuse Sillar, and when England was sighted, Georgina called Sillar to her and told her she would no longer be needed by the McIver family.

"When your foot touches English soil, you will be a free woman. Now, doesnt that please your heart, Sillar? I know the master will be pleased when he learns of my generosity, although I'm certain he, more than any other member of our family, will miss you."

There it was—for sure—Georgina knew she was her husband's mistress or bedwench as she would call it. There was no point in pleading with her to keep her position until she could find a way to earn money. She was free whether she liked it or not. Amanda, Josiah, and Vanessa were confused and upset, leaving Sillar standing on the dock as they loaded their belongings into a carriage for the train station.

"But mama, we'll have no servants," said Amanda. "Who will take care of us?"

JoJo was only Vanessa's charge.

Sillar started walking toward the center of Liverpool and finally came across a pawnshop. She fingered the small, gold engraved disk hanging from a chain around her neck, then removed it. The money she collected she figured would pay for the train fare to London and the rental of a modest room. Kenneth had given her the necklace on their last night together, and her promise to him was that she would never take it off, but their unborn child needed it, and that promise would have to be broken.

She managed to obtain temporary sewing jobs in London, and every spare moment she had she made simple but warm clothing for her soon-to-be-born infant.

The old couple, the Doyles, who owned the boardinghouse where she found lodging, were very kind, and when the baby was born, they brought her food and presented the newborn with a cradle a past tenant had left. When Kenneth was six months old, she finally had to take a position as a live-in housemaid and baby Kenneth stayed with the old couple. Every spare second she had off, she would run back to the boardinghouse to see him, so upset when the family she worked for moved to their country estate for the holiday season. It meant weeks would go by without seeing her young son.

It was there she met Blamford. She always felt the encounter was a stroke of extraordinary good luck. When she returned from Paris, he helped her set up her shop. He didn't hide her off in a corner as his mistress, but supported her new identity as an aristocratic Spanish lady who had become a milliner. He showed her off in society, taking great pleasure in bringing her to all the major cultural events in London and to all the upper-class parties. She blossomed before his eyes, and he had never had so much fun in his life catering to her needs and putting her on display.

Through him she met the ladies who became her clientele, and they accepted her without question because he escorted her. But most important, he pampered her overindulgence of her son. Sillar suspected that he loved young Kenneth. She knew he was jealous and in the past she never gave him any doubts. But now Kenneth McIver was threatening her peace of mind, and she disliked the deceit she felt she was partaking in with Blamford. She also knew he had a vicious streak in his nature—a part of him she hoped she would never see.

16

Vanessa did not play well in Paris, and Sasha went into a depression, blessing God it was a small out of the way hall —an engagement set long before her success in London. They headed on to Antwerp, the diamond-cutting capital of the world, and the perplexed man kept asking her what was wrong, hoping to correct the problem before her next performance. He had never heard her play so badly and hoped it wasn't a pattern. Finally, he gave up; she was becoming withdrawn from the prying, hardly talking at all. They settled into a grand old hotel on the waterfront, too expensive for them at this stage, Sasha sighed, but now, he said, their image was important.

The morning of the recital in Antwerp, a wet snow was falling, and Vanessa sat alone in the hotel dining room having breakfast. As she looked out the window, trying to see the Schelde River through the weather, she fought to forget her troublesome thoughts and to think of pleasant things. She wished she could see the river of the great seaport more clearly and the big boats that were docked. The city fascinated her, and she was amazed at the number of paintings by Rubens throughout Antwerp. The day before, she had visited the cathedral where two of his masterpieces hung. One located in the choir area was called *Assumption*. She had studied the painting for over an hour, appreciating his superb treatment of light on the canvas, the work touched her deeply with a calming effect. She planned to visit Rubens' home after practicing at the hall later that day, sandwiching the visit in before she rested in her room prior to the performance that evening. She had been told at the cathedral by a young priest who stopped to discuss the paintings with her that there were a number of his works at his home as well as those of his students. Vanessa was also interested in seeing where this great master had lived and worked, described to her as opulent, and the studio done in Italian Renaissance style.

How Pierre would have enjoyed seeing it, too. Then, she reflected, he probably had. All those years he studied art and art history in schools in France and Italy. He must have enjoyed it so—but what does it prepare you for in life—in a career, unless you are going to be a painter—but the appreciation—that was such a joy. She vowed when she traveled in the future, she would try to see the great art works in each city. Before, she and JoJo just tried to survive as they got in and out of the small towns as if only passing through to make train connections. She hoped that aspect of her music career was over.

She twisted in her seat looking toward the door. Sasha was to have joined her for breakfast, and it was the first time in her recollection that he had ever been late. She had gone ahead and ordered not knowing what to do when the waiter kept hovering over her. She knew he was upset because of her sloppy playing at the small hall in Paris. Well, now, her music had failed her. No, she told herself honestly—she had failed her music. Her concentration had been off and her fingering therefore suffered. The big concert in Brussels next week was worrying him she knew, and her too. She hoped it would go well that night, to give them both courage. She drew her cape closer to her neck—she was cold—the dining room was not properly heated and her cloth cape not very warm. She had been threadbare so long; it had become a way of life with her. The little money she had been making went into the essentials of living and for the purchase of the gowns she wore for the recitals.

She felt eyes on her again—bold prying eyes, but she willed herself not to turn in their direction. She had seen the gentleman when she entered and sensed he had been staring at her since her arrival. The intensity was so strong she felt as if a hole were being burned through her. Taking a deep breath, she tried to interest herself now in the kippers on her plate—she had looked out the window long enough.

A waiter approached, not hers, and spoke to her. His language was Dutch, an amazement to her that such a small country like Belgium had two native tongues. In the southern section near the French border, they spoke that language, but in the northern section where Antwerp was, they spoke Dutch. He then handed her a business card. She thought it might be from Sasha, but the embossed card said, "Aram Van der Veer," and underneath, "President, World Diamonds." She noted several addresses in Antwerp, Paris, Johannesburg, and Rome. Slowly, hesitantly, she turned the card over: "To the beautiful lady sitting alone by the window. May I join you?" It was written in French, and she knew it was sent by the man who had been staring at her.

She looked over at him, and his riveting greenish eyes, so outstanding, locked with hers, almost draining her will. His skin was dark like an Arab's and his dark curly hair was streaked with gray. The upper torso of his body was thick but showing no evidence of fat through his jacket.

The man then nodded and smiled invitingly. Her face flushed a deep red, and she looked down at the table shaking her head negatively to the waiter and quietly murmuring: "Tell monsieur I am expecting someone momentarily."

The waiter delivered the message and Aram Van der Veer made an elaborate face of disappointment that she observed from the corner of her eye.

Vanessa took a last sip of coffee and was gathering her gloves to leave when he was suddenly standing there beside her. His voice was deep and commanding.

"Mademoiselle, you are alone. I am alone. Can you give me one good reason why we should not share a cup of coffee together?"

She looked at those eyes and felt alarm for a fleeting second.

"We do not know each other, sir. This is not proper."

He shrugged. "Who makes up the rules telling us what is proper and what is not proper? Do you?"

She shook her head no.

"Nor do I. Now, would you not enjoy getting to know one another?"

"My dear sir!" Her eyes flared widely and her indignation made her an inch taller.

He had to laugh—showing perfect white teeth, then soothingly he tried to convince her, "Do not be afraid to live, mademoiselle. Life can be a great adventure if you allow it to happen."

She frowned, nonplussed.

"All right. I can see I am upsetting you. We will do it *properly*. I will get myself introduced, Miss McIver."

"You know my name."

"Of course, and also that you have a finicky appetite." He looked down at her plate with the food hardly touched.

He was a terribly virile, forceful man, something she had very little contact with so far in her life. It was exciting, but it was also frightening.

He flagged the pompous maître d'hôtel and asked to be introduced to her. The man nodded. With no expression on his florid face, he turned to the young woman at the table.

"Mademoiselle, this is Mr. Van der Veer, a very well known, important man in Antwerp."

Aram brushed him aside. "That will do, Henri, we don't want to overdo."

"Yes, sir."

"Will you have the waiter bring us fresh cups and coffee?"

She plopped in her chair and Aram sat opposite her. His mischievously wicked grin captivating her—in spite of herself—she returned his smile, although with great restraint, and after a confused moment she grabbed her gloves again and started to rise.

"I'm sorry, but I must be going."

Quickly he placed his strong hands over hers.

"Please. At least just a cup of coffee together." The hazel green eyes danced, and the white teeth flashed in the deeply tanned face.

"Do you always get your way?"

"I try. And I must admit, I usually do."

The waiter came and poured them fresh coffee. Aram lifted his cup and toasted her.

"To a very interesting relationship." He then took a long drink of the hot brew as he studied her lovely face over the rim of the cup.

Sasha scurried into the dining room looking frazzled.
Amazement appeared on his face when he saw Van der
Veer. He knew who he was immediately and was delighted
at his presence.

"Mr. Van der Veer. This is a great pleasure. Good
morning, good morning. You two know each other?"

"Miss McIver and I have just met."

"Ah, I see." But he didn't see.

"Vanessa, this gentleman is one of the great patrons of
music in Brussels, Paris, Rome . . ." he waved his hand in
a sweeping grand gesture, "in all of Europe." He sank
into a chair with a thud. "Of course you are coming tonight?"

"Tonight? What is taking place?"

"Vanessa," he said in astonishment, "she is to play
Liszt at the Royal Hall."

Aram turned to her, surprised. "You are a pianist?"

"Yes."

"A good one?"

Sasha beamed, "A good one? She will be the world's
greatest—take my word."

He continued looking at Vanessa. "Are you a great musician, Vanessa?"

He alarmed and fascinated her. "Why don't you come
and decide for yourself?"

"So young and beautiful. It is hard to imagine you
choosing this lonely life. Unless you have learned how to
live with it."

She was feeling braver with Sasha there. "You have a
recipe, sir?"

"Perhaps." He quickly looked at her ring finger.

"Are you good? I hate bad playing."

Sasha broke in, "Is she good? I just told you."

"I am asking Vanessa McIver. An American, I take it."
He studied her intently as if undressing her. A shiver ran
down her spine. But she rose to the occasion.

"I don't think you will be disappointed."

"Then I shall be there."

"This is marvelous." Sasha was so pleased with himself,
thinking he engineered it all. "And you must come back
after to tell us of your enjoyment."

"That I will do, and you shall have my candid opinion."

He rose and shook hands with Sasha, bowed to Vanessa and was gone.

Sasha leaned back in his chair as he lit his cigar. "With a man like that behind you, Vanessa, you would be on top of the music world in no time."

17

It was a small hall, and Sasha stood in the rear. Disappointingly, there were a number of empty seats. He blamed it on the heavy snow that was now falling. Scanning the hall again, he did not see Aram Van der Veer. Sasha had not offered to give him a free ticket at breakfast because the man was rich and plenty of seats were available for purchase. Vanessa appeared on the platform and there was a smattering of applause.

She went directly to the piano and struck the first chord. Sasha took a back seat to listen. After her performance in Brussels he would be off to Prague to attend a concert of his great violinist, Dmitri Leondoff, an old man who still commanded much respect, but he needed new blood under his banner and was counting on Vanessa's success. If it went well for her in Brussels, word would reach the music world as if by lightning and he would be able to book her with famous orchestras throughout the world, starting in the middle of Europe while he was there. Besides Prague, there would be Warsaw, Budapest, Berlin, Vienna, cities that loved great music and gifted artists. He also would arrange to fill in dates between the great cities with either smaller well-respected orchestras or special recitals.

At the end of the first piece the applause was polite. Sasha could never read the Dutch. A man walked down the aisle and took an end seat. It was Van der Veer. Sasha was relieved. He now had a purpose beyond Vanessa's performance. The man was an important barometer. Moving to a seat near Van der Veer, he never took his eyes off him, willing in his heart for Vanessa to play brilliantly.

What he couldn't do with the diamond merchant's money behind him! He had heard all the rumors of his flamboyant nature and of his mistresses, but his only concern at the moment was his wealth and patronage of musicians. This was the first time he had ever traveled with Vanessa, usually she was booked by him, and she played the dates only accompanied by JoJo. But she was getting important, and he would be spending a great deal of time with her on tour in the future—*if* it went well in Brussels.

The recital was over and while Vanessa was nicely received, it was not overwhelming. Sasha thought she had played well but not as inspired as she had played in London.

Vanessa buried her head in her arms on the battered desk. The hall did not have a dressing room and the performers had to use the small office in the rear. JoJo was rubbing Vanessa's arms and the back of her neck dry before she changed into her regular clothes. She was worried and felt totally drained. She had played correctly, but there was just no spirit there. Energy had always been a part of her—but not tonight or in Paris. She had made no mistakes this evening but that certain something eluded her, and during the recital her concentration went again—she hoped it wasn't going to be a pattern. Even in the beginning, when she first started, she never lost concentration, she was always deeply immersed in what she was playing. It had been a total protection from her past. Now, ever since the reunion in London, with all the people unexpectedly coming back into her life, she had been off—except the night of her debut. She had never played so freely or spirited before.

Vanessa lifted her head from her arms and looked around at the shabby room. The paint was peeling, the window heavy with dirt; the damp cold licked at her like icy fingers. I don't really want this, she told herself. Being so lonely, spending the nights in hotels, cold beds. She remembered back to the talk she had with her father a few nights before. She only suspected then what she knew as a certainty now. This was her life. Paradoxically, she did enjoy some of it, she had to admit. Before this loss of concentration, she soared inwardly when she played, losing herself completely, making the experience very rewarding for her. Also, at times she was very attracted to the little fame that came her way. Well, there had to be a lot more fame to make it worthwhile, she thought.

JoJo moved to the old coat tree and took down her dress. It was shabby, just like the room, she admitted to herself. That has also got to stop. Shabby rooms, shabby clothes. She rose wearily and slipped out of the gown just as there was a tap on the door. Sasha's booming voice informed her he was there with a guest. JoJo waited until she was in her street dress, then opened the door. Aram Van der Veer stood there, with Sasha, dressed in a rich topcoat trimmed in dark mink and in his hand was an ornate gold-topped cane. He looked around the ugly room trying to hide his distaste before resting his eyes on her. Vanessa pulled herself to her full height, becoming the statuesque beauty he had seen on stage. Her pride would not let her be humbled because of the seedy surroundings. It was evident that she attracted him as a woman— his eyes swept her body. Sasha was babbling on about something—Van der Veer interrupted.

"Miss McIver, I would be honored if you will be my guest for a late supper."

Sasha answered for her, and she could see the disappointment on Van der Veer's face.

"We would be delighted. A great pleasure indeed."

Vanessa demured. "Sasha, please, I don't feel up to supper. If you and Monsieur Van der Veer would excuse me, I am tired and tomorrow we leave for Brussels."

Van der Veer was quick to reply, "Of course. You must be exhausted after the performance."

"But, Vanessa, it is because we are leaving we should have supper with Monsieur Van der Veer."

"No, no. I am also going to Brussels on business in a day or two." His wicked eyes looked at her meaningfully. "We will meet there."

"How delightful," said Sasha. "We are staying at the Grand Palace Hotel."

"Good. If I can't wine and dine you, my dear, can I at least give you a lift to your hotel this evening? The snow has become heavy."

"Thank you," replied Vanessa. "That is very kind of you."

The voice was smooth as velvet. "My pleasure, mademoiselle."

She did not ask him for a candid opinion of her performance, and he did not offer it as he took her threadbare cape from JoJo and placed it rather intimately around her shoulders.

18

His long legs were tired as he rushed through the streets of London. He knew he had lost a great deal of weight in the last few months and looked only quickly in the mirror when dressing not to be reminded of his gauntness. If he were advising one of his patients he would tell him or her to take a vacation, eat regular meals, and get plenty of rest. In his own case, he didn't fall asleep, he passed out when he hit the bed—heartsick that he had overslept the other evening when he was to have dinner with Vanessa. He was so looking forward to the evening. He didn't allow his mind to go any further than that, as he had in the past few years tried to keep her in a special place in his mind and not let himself have false hopes.

There had been other women, and recently a nurse who had been an on and off companion of his since his arrival in London some months ago. He had no idea Vanessa or the family was still here after their escape from Charleston, having lost all track of the McIvers during the disastrous end of the war and his long walk back to New Orleans and the plantation where his father had been an overseer. The family had taken him in. Childless, they treated him as a son coming home and helped him to rebuild his life. The doctor eventually encouraging him to seek further education, guiding him into what he had always wanted to be—a man of medicine.

Upon reaching Belgrave Square, he studied the house for a while before going up the steps to knock on the highly polished brass trimmed door, disturbed when the footman told him that Vanessa was abroad. He then asked to see a member of the family.

Georgina received him in the library, and she covered her hostility to him very thinly. Kirk asked her if she knew if Vanessa received a note he sent her a few days before. She told him curtly she had no idea. Vanessa had a very busy schedule she informed him and received many notes and letters. He persisted and asked when she was expected back. Again Georgina was vague. It was obvious she wanted him to leave.

"Mr. Yoors—I'm sorry to be so abrupt . . ."

"Dr. Yoors."

"Yes, of course. This is a very busy household. There is to be a wedding in a few short weeks and there is so much to do. My daughter Amanda is marrying Lord Hatfield, the Eighth Earl of Raleigh."

"I know. I was at the reception when the announcement was made."

"Then you understand why I have to say good afternoon. I'm sure you do not know that the wedding is to take place at Lord Hatfield's estate in Norfolk, and we are journeying there shortly for all the grand celebrations—there is so much packing, last minute preparations—" She started to lead him to the door.

"One moment longer, if you please. I want to write another note to Vanessa."

"Her name is Miss McIver or Mrs. Bonneau, Mr. Yoors. You must have also seen Pierre at the reception."

"Mr. Bonneau?"

He hadn't seen him the other evening and the fact he was around was a jolt. He quickly took out his pad and scribbled another note to Vanessa. Georgina stood by very annoyed.

"Would you make sure Miss McIver gets this on her return?"

"I'll try, Mr. Yoors . . ."

"Dr. Yoors."

She completely ignored his remark, "As I said—we are so busy here . . ."

"Try your best. It is important."

After he left she rushed up to Vanessa's room and found the note she had seen on the dressing table earlier, but never suspected who the sender was. She took the note and the new one he had just written and hid them in her sash. As she was crossing to the door, she saw the hat box and

was stunned. It took her breath away . . . Sillar. So many
bad pennies showing up to threaten her. Did Kenneth
know, she wondered? As she went to her room she was
breathing heavily from all the sudden upset. Trying to
gather her wits, she read the contents of the notes from
Kirk, giving an audible gasp when she discovered they were
to have dinner together at the house in Chelsea, but
breathed a sigh of relief on learning he never made it.
That was providence, she thought. Even if the man had
become a doctor, he was still white trash. She had noticed,
after her first shock at seeing him, how Pierre had been admired at the reception. After all, he did come from a fine
social family. The name Bonneau stood for something on
both sides of the Atlantic. If only it would work out once
more between he and Vanessa. She had been dead set
against their coming together again, but no more—their
reunion would be perfect.

Georgina also had other worries. Jamie had not been
the same recently. He seemed aloof, estranged in some
ways. She hoped to God he was in no way cooling on his
marriage to Amanda. The man needed an heir—she kept
bringing it up as discreetly as she could under the circumstances. If the marriage took place, she would make
sure Amanda worked on getting pregnant immediately.
There were ways these days for men to use protection
she had heard—well, she would talk to her.

The other note from Kirk had asked Vanessa to get in
touch with him at the hospital as soon as possible upon
her return, and mentioned his prior note. She went to the
fireplace and poked it until it was blazing. She tore the
papers into shreds and let them fall into the flames. Then
she went to the bellpull and rang for a maid to bring her
tea. Her heart started to race and her face flushed. With
everything else at this time, she was now sure she was
going through the change, starting to weep as she fumbled
with a bottle on the bed table. Shakily she put a Parr's
rejuvenation pill in her mouth, following it with a large
draught of water. She fingered the crystal goblet now
empty of water—fine glassware, she always loved the
French crystal they had back in South Carolina. She
flicked the rim of the glass lightly and the ping of the fine
stemware rang in her ears. Throwing herself across the
high Chippendale bed she cried, the racking sobs shook

her body, "Oh God! Daddy, please help me!" She saw
him, big and portly from his high living, but such an
authoritative figure, over six feet, called the Big Man
when referred to by all but his family. They always
called him Big Daddy. She had blurry visions of running
along the Mississippi to get to their wharf where Big
Daddy was overseeing the loading of the cotton on the
river boat, and his holding out his strong as iron arms
as he saw her approach. She always rushed into them to
receive the great big bear hug, relishing his saying in his
booming voice, "Are you daddy's girl?"

"Yes. Yes," she would squeal as she tried to get breath
in her body, the hug was so tight. He was the largest plant-
er for miles around—King of Cotton in all Tennessee.

She beat her fist in the mattress—all gone—not a shred
left. Flinging her arm wildly she heard the crash of glass
and saw the fine crystal goblet laying shattered on the
floor. Like her life she thought—shattered—and unless
she put back the pieces with a fine glue, what would become of them? She did not admit to herself that no matter
how fine the cement, the lines, the damage would always
be there.

How wise had the decision to leave Charleston been in
the first place, setting them adrift in a strange land. What
if they had stayed and took their chances with the enemy
approaching the city? It was their last home—all they
had left. Big Daddy's land long since gone. She hadn't
wanted to leave; it was Kenneth. She fought not to leave.
The city is falling, he had screamed at her. Savannah,
Atlanta, the railroad—all cut off. They will be here at any
time.

Georgina watched the approaching figure of Thomas
riding wearily toward their townhouse. She knew he was
bringing the news they had all been expecting.

A mood of impending disaster had gripped the city for
months, increasing with each new report of Sherman's
"march to the sea." She pulled her shawl tighter around
her shoulders, protecting herself from the gale winds that
blew through the long French windows. Heavy paper
patches had been used to replace the panes that had been
blown out by the naval bombardment that had rocked
their home over the past few years, but the paper was

no protection from the stormy weather. In the distance, sounds of shelling could be heard. She thought she could live with that sound forever rather than think of the Yankees taking over her city and everything that was her very life.

Thomas was almost to the door now, so close she could see the lather on his horse's neck. He had always been an optimist about the war, disguising the bad news with prospects of impending victories, but even he had to admit in recent weeks that Charleston might fall. Thomas had served the South and especially Charleston well, raising money for ammunition and weapons, carrying bonds to Major Huse in Europe to purchase them. He arranged blockade-runners that brought in the precious cargoes, and assured Kenneth he could arrange their escape to England if it became necessary. Thomas knew the time was here.

He was barely through the door of the drawing room when he asked about Kenneth.

"I don't know where he is, Thomas—he left two days ago with the home guard and there hasn't been a word. I can't let myself think anything has happened to him. Do you know where they've gone?"

"Well, the home guard is gathered near the Buck Hall Plantation at Graham's Creek. A major attack is expected there, but for now the firing is sporadic and with the gale weather, we have a few days. I'm sure he's fine."

Kenneth had joined the unit in January, 1863, when Beauregard urged every citizen to give their all for their beleaguered city. At first he would be gone only part of the day, then Georgina began to experience bouts of fear as his time away grew, day extending into night and then days strung together without him. Each time when he was gone and there was a knock at the door she expected to hear he was dead.

"Georgina, you remember I promised Kenneth I would arrange safe passage to England for you and the children if it became absolutely certain the city would succumb. I've kept my word. Today Beauregard sent evacuation instructions for the troops. You must all be ready to leave this evening. Pack enough food to sustain yourselves for a few days, dress warmly, and for God's sake, try to keep everyone as calm as possible."

"I won't go. I can't leave without Kenneth. He won't know where we are. No, we have to stay—our home must be protected—it's all we have left."

"There is no time, Georgina. We are doomed. You must leave immediately or stay to bear the wrath of Sherman and his men. Atlanta was just the beginning—the stories of what they are leaving in their wake are terrible, and I needn't remind you they are black troops that will hit Charleston first."

"Give me time, Thomas, I beg you. Give me a few days. As soon as Kenneth comes I promise I'll do what he tells me to. I can't leave without seeing him. Please. . . ."

"All right, only a little while longer, but if you don't go of your own free will, I'll have to force you."

For the next few days Georgina spent the time moving from one window to another on the top floor of their home searching for a sign of Kenneth or one of the men in the same home guard. She watched the movement of families and troops leaving the city. For a change she welcomed the bad weather—it gave her time. Thomas came once to report no troops could land because of the forceful winds and rain. On the evening of the seventeenth of November, Vanessa came to her.

"Mama, we must go—Daddy would want it. You have to think of Josiah and Amanda—they have to be given a chance. Daddy wants us to go to England. Do that for him."

"I can't leave here, Vanessa, this is my home. Let me stay and you take the children. You go."

"No, Mama, I won't leave you. You don't want to stay to see the end of the city. Let's leave it while it's still in control of the people who love it. We'll come back— Daddy always said so—we won't be gone long."

Georgina privately had experienced over the past few days an hysteria that was so quiet, yet paralytic, that it frightened her. Vanessa was right, it would be harder for her to stay and watch the final destruction.

"We'll leave tomorrow afternoon whether or not your father is here."

"Get some sleep now, Mama. We have a hard journey ahead of us. I'll tell Uncle Thomas to make our plans."

Georgina fell asleep dreaming she was rocking in her father's arms.

On the morning of Saturday, February 18, Sillar was busy sewing all that was left of Georgina's jewels into the hem and cuffs of her green velvet dress. She formed tucks and gathers cleverly disguising the hidden booty. Georgina selected this dress deciding that Thomas be damned. He had persuaded Amanda and Vanessa to dress in young boy's clothes, but she would not allow herself to surrender that part of her dignity. No neighbor would see her slinking out of town looking like a field hand. And what if they were captured?—she shuddered, putting that thought out of her mind. While she was waiting in her petticoats for Sillar to finish, she packed the last few items, a miniature of her father and the silver brushes from her grandmother in the one bag Thomas allowed each of them to carry.

The sound of Josiah hooting and yelping sent her running for a wrap. She raced to the head of the stairs, her heart thumping with fear that the Yankees had arrived. "Josiah, what's the fuss?"

"It's Daddy, Mama, he's here."

As Sillar helped her lace up her dress, she heard her children greeting their father, Amanda and Vanessa babbling with sounds of tears in their voices and Josiah asking questions excitedly. Then his steps sounded on the staircase.

Georgina was stunned at the sight of him. His boots were gone and his clothes were unrecognizable, shredded and ripped, caked mud covered what cloth was left. Her eyes searched every inch of his body and was happy to see that he bore no physical wounds.

Her concern was interrupted when she realized Kenneth's attention had settled on Sillar. Sillar, she noted, was painfully staring at him, eyes brimming with tears. Anger grew in Georgina that even now when his family would be split, he was still ogling his bedwench.

She snapped at her servant, "Sillar, go downstairs quickly and take my case with you. Then you are free to go wherever you wish."

"Sillar is going with the McIvers."

Georgina whirled around, her ears not believing what they heard. "No, Kenneth, I won't have her. Do you hear? I don't want her near me any more." She glared back at the slave woman as she spoke and became more angered that she stood taking the verbal abuse without so much as a flinch.

"She has been a loyal friend, Georgina. Besides, you and the children will need her help. Sillar, prepare to leave."

As Sillar left the room, Georgina faced her husband—her neck veins were clearly visible, pulsing against the taut skin. "You are being wretched, Kenneth McIver. I am to take that . . ." she couldn't say the word to describe her feelings, "sneaky, dishonest whore to my bosom and bear her across the ocean with my children—protecting her—for what, Kenneth? What are you saving her for?"

"There is no time for this, Georgina. She is going—it is settled."

A look on his face that she had never seen before, shut her up. She would bide her time, accept Sillar and then when three thousand miles of ocean separated them, she would see that his whore woman was finished with their family—forever.

The gale winds beat against them as they left their home. Georgina couldn't believe the wagon. Floor boards were missing and those that remained were encrusted with horse manure and debris. It stank. "Kenneth, let's use our carriage. I can't ride in that."

"Don't be foolish, Georgina, this simple vehicle will be a better cover in traveling through the difficult terrain."

With that he grabbed her around the waist and hoisted her into the cart. "This is no Sunday ride."

As she plopped on the floor, she cried, "My dress, oh my Lord, just look at my dress."

Amanda and Vanessa comforted her. She stared at her home as they pulled away in the dusk—the winds whipping at them all and shaking the loose boards of the wagon.

Georgina lifted her head at one point, "Poor old Charleston, deserted, only a few stragglers left to see you raped by the Yankees."

They passed by the Northeastern Railroad Depot that had blown up that morning, the accident caused by several boys carting handfuls of the stored gunpowder to throw on a cotton fire. Their trail ignited and doubled back to decimate the building. Houses nearby were still burning. Wherever they looked, sadness and destruction greeted their dazed eyes.

Sillar and JoJo huddled together in the buckboard; Kenneth and Thomas riding on top encouraged the worn horse to bear its burden a little faster. Vanessa and Amanda continued their efforts trying to comfort their distraught mother, and Josiah sat straight—staring ahead blindly—his face red with anger and frustration.

As they approached the center of town, the women were further shocked by the devastation. For several months they had confined themselves to the house with the servants, and Josiah scrambled for what meager foodstuffs could be bought or more importantly what they could afford. They hadn't realized how bad things had become. In the public squares the cadets from the Citadel, young brave boys, were putting to fire the enormous piles of cotton and bushels of rice so the Yankees would be prevented from profiting from their stores. Everywhere vehicles of all kinds were filled with people trying to leave, pulling aside only to allow the retreating troops passage. Vanessa put an understanding arm around Josiah's shoulder, knowing the longing he felt to join in the defense of his country and home. Weapons that couldn't be carried were blown up. Then the earth shook—the gunboat *Palmetto State* was blown up, sending a huge spray of water toward the sky. Georgina watched the hull sink as if it were a symbol of all that was happening to them. This was the gunboat built from funds raised by the ladies of Charleston. It had done proud service against the Union blockade all this time.

She was suddenly so weary—she bowed her head to rest and prayers came to her lips. She prayed for the city that now seemed to be ablaze from river to river and only the black fire companies were left to hold back the flames from totally taking every building in its path. Finally, they reached the edge of the city, crowded in by the other vehicles trying to escape. The bridge over the Ashley had burned down, so this one over the Cooper River had to bear a double burden. Panic showed on everyone's face, even Kenneth's as he goaded the horse into a fast-gaited trot not able to stand the suspense of a slow walk across the rickety bridge, groaning under the weight of so many panicked people in the exodus.

When they were safely on the other side, Thomas took his leave. He was heading for St. Stephen's Parish to join troops that had pulled back from Charleston to board the train from Columbia. That train was carrying the last of the troops from that beleaguered city and they would head toward North Carolina to try and regroup, to pool what strengths they had left.

Thomas handed Kenneth a paper with the names of the contacts for the small boat at the Santee River that would take them, hopefully, to the blockade-runner off the coast and then to the larger boat waiting to pick up people wanting to get to Nassau.

Passage to England from there would be paid by fifty bales of McIver cotton stored on that island.

"Good luck, McIvers," said Thomas stoically. "Remember we are a proud family. I'll see you all very soon." Then he was gone without looking back.

The darkness soon overtook them as they continued on, but the sky over Charleston flared as large balls of fire exploded in the air.

They traveled through the night, getting out of the wagon at times and walking to ease the horse's burden. They were glad they had taken food so they could avoid the risk of going to a farmhouse for something to eat. The houses were locked up tight and not a light could be seen as they passed. As dawn started to break in the sky, they had to abandon the horse and wagon as they approached the dense thicket leading to the marshes along the river bank. Georgina stumbled along cursing her vanity for wearing her fancy dress. They walked through large pools of water from the winter flooding, drenching their feet and clothing before they reached their rendezvous. They waited all day—watching. During the night, Kenneth swung the lantern almost continuously to signal the boat as to their location. Finally, in the darkest part of night, they heard a boat and then a rough voice coming from the tall bullrushes.

"Ahoy! Give us your name!"

"McIver—the McIver family," stated Kenneth in a hoarse cry.

All Georgina's courage left her. "I can't, Kenneth. I would rather just stay here and die. I'm not strong enough —please let me stay with you."

"Georgina, we've been through all of this—there is no time."

"Come on, mate. Get them in—this is no party. We'll be lucky to get out of these waters alive." They could make out the boat now as it came about twenty feet from shore.

She continued to weep and now Amanda picked up her mother's distress, the hysteria spreading, "Please, Daddy, don't leave us."

"Shut them up or we'll get on without you."

The gruffness frightened them into silence and with that Kenneth kissed his wife goodbye and carried her into the freezing water to the boat. "You are a Pickett and a McIver—think of your daddy. He would rather die than live under the Yankee boot. Now go, Georgina. You are a survivor. Take care of our children."

He then kissed the children goodbye as they waded out to the boat. JoJo looked so hapless as she said her humble farewell. Sillar came and got into the boat silently, not looking at him. As it pulled out into midstream, Georgina watched the shore, able to tell Kenneth's whereabouts by the low light of the lantern. She saw Sillar also following him with her eyes—the light flickered in and out of sight in the heavy thicket—then was gone. Though surrounded by her children, Georgina McIver felt deserted and alone.

19

———

Inside the concert hall on the Rue Royale in Brussels, Vanessa sat rigidly at the grand piano on stage, concentrating on the very tall man leading the orchestra—waiting for her cue—that is, she thought, if he ever got to that section. The man was an ogre. His longish, white hair flew around his leonine face, as alert, black as coal eyes darted menacingly from one musician to another as he furiously waved the baton to get the overly quick tempo he desired. At the same point as before and several times prior, he threw both his hands toward the heavens in horror, stopping the music to shout, "No, no, no! It is terrible! Unbelievable! You call yourselves musicians?" He glanced murderously at them, then hit the music stand with the stick for attention, which in Vanessa's mind was ridiculous as they were riveted to him anyway, scared to death. Telling them which note they were to begin with, he raised the baton majestically in the air, holding them poised for a moment like racers at a starting gate and suddenly, down came the baton and they began again at the furious pace the famous conductor deemed proper for the concerto.

Vanessa waited again for her cue. The place was cold, but she was oblivious to the temperature. Her eyes were now also riveted on the maestro as they were fast approaching where she would enter. She made up her mind when she left Antwerp she would indeed try to become the world's greatest piano player, devoting all her time and energies to her art. No longer would she suffer any makeshift dressing rooms like the backstage office she had in Antwerp—promising herself she was going to live well, at the top. It would be her obsession.

The time came and his head nodded toward her as if she were a bird on a perch being told to take off. Her hands hit the keys. There was no question of concentration any more. She played forcibly. But she heard his yelling—all had stopped except her, and he was hitting the music stand furiously, shouting again, "No, no, no!" She looked up almost dumbstruck, her hands stopped in mid-air.

"You are lagging behind. You must keep up the tempo. Again, please."

They took it over, and she sat perched, waiting—it came. She struck the keys and played frantically, the pace was killing but she kept up. Sweat poured from her forehead; her hands, shoulders and arms ached. Finally, a rest period for her, and she took a deep breath, looking up at the great lion face. He was wooing the string section to play more melodically—romantically. Then there was a crash of cymbals and she entered again. He threw his baton up in the air and screamed at her. "You were late! You have got to come in on time. This is not a music school, miss. This is the Royal Orchestra of Brussels."

She didn't say a word—she waited. He was handed another baton, which he arbitrarily snapped in half. Another was presented and after whipping it in the air a few times, his eyes swept the whole orchestra including Vanessa. He raised the reedlike wand—the moment was almost holy. "From the second coda if you please."

"Maestro?" She spoke loud and clear.

"You interrupted?" He was aghast.

"Yes, it is all too fast."

"It is not too fast. It is the way it should be played."

"It is not a race to see if we all can finish together."

"A race?"

There was a churchlike silence all around them.

"It is so fast, the beauty of the notes do not have a chance to be fully heard and appreciated."

"My dear young woman. You make excuses because your awkward fingers cannot keep up."

"Maestro, I'm telling you the concerto would be more melodic and fulfilling if played a little slower—the tempo is killing it."

Sasha rubbed his hand over his face and sank lower in

his seat. What is she doing contradicting the famous conductor? He will throw her off the stage. But the concert was tomorrow he reasoned, who would they get to replace her? And she is right—the tempo is too frenetic. But what had gotten into her? She never acted temperamental before. Just after their arrival she asked for the theater manager and told him the dressing room assigned to her would not do. She wanted a better one—he told her the one on the side of the stage, a bigger one, had been reserved for the other soloist, a famous violinist. She marched right to it and took possession. When he arrived she was firmly ensconced and the manager had filled her dressing room with flowers, and now this.

Sasha had not noticed Van der Veer, who had entered just before the blow-up and was standing in the aisle watching. To everyone's surprise, the conductor gave a curt bow in Vanessa's direction:

"Miss Macintosh . . ."

"McIver. Miss McIver, Maestro."

"Oh, yes. The English girl . . ."

"The American woman—from the South of the United States."

"Oh, yes. We will convenience you and play a little slower for your stiff fingers."

"Thank you, and it will also sound better that way."

"But not too much slower. The subscribers will fall asleep." He hit his baton on the music stand and told them to go back to the same place. The orchestra watched fearfully as they waited their cue. Vanessa surprisingly was relaxed, enjoying the challenge—she was like a primed racehorse ready to hear the signal to commence. It came and she went—her body was fired with the experience— the music filled her being. She matched the power of the musicians and the conductor in her verve. She was inspired by the old man—in his way he was pulling great music out of her. They played through—a crash of cymbals—her last section, a difficult passage—she played it so loud she felt her ears would split, but the sound was not harsh, it was overwhelmingly powerful.

Sasha sat in his seat dumbfounded.

The maestro's baton slit the air crisscrossing a number of times for the finish. He then threw the stick to the floor and walked off the podium. The musicians turned to her, some applauded while others lightly hit their bows on their instruments. Her chest swelled with pride.

"Thank you, thank you very much. But I couldn't have done it without the great maestro." They smiled approvingly.

When she got to her dressing room, Van der Veer was already there. She showed no surprise—just looked around the flower-filled room smugly. He watched her, knowing why she was doing it and smiled. She hadn't realized what a really attractive man he was.

"It suits you better. They will be grander and grander."

"You like my playing?"

"Like? Hardly. I love your playing, Vanessa. You are on your way to becoming the world's greatest concert pianist."

"Will they yell and shout for encores?"

"My dear young woman. The world will be at your feet. Will you dine with me this evening?"

"Only if you will take me to the finest restaurant in all of Brussels."

"You will be wined and dined in the finest restaurant. Eight o'clock?"

Arbitrarily she flung at him, "Eight-thirty will suit me better."

Vanessa's face was shining as she sat on the sofa in the hotel suite and listened to the news Sasha brought her. The maestro had asked him to come to his dressing room after the rehearsal, and Sasha was all prepared to defend Vanessa's behavior when the great conductor waved that aside, telling him he was to be guest conductor in late summer at the Berlin Philharmonic and wanted to know if Miss McIver were free to be his guest soloist.

"Imagine, you are to play with the Berlin Symphony Orchestra!"

"It is wonderful, Sasha. All too wonderful."

"Two performances—not one, but two. In Berlin."

JoJo brought in a great box that had just been delivered. She opened it as Sasha and Vanessa talked. JoJo still saved string and tissue paper, packing them in her suitcase and leaving them in the house in Chelsea when they returned, so it took time to get to the contents. The young woman gasped.

"What is it, JoJo?"

"Look at this, Nessa." She took out the most exquisite sable cape. Handling it as if it were a priceless, fragile object. It was the most beautiful fur piece any of them had ever seen.

"The card says, 'From one of your admirers. I'm certain I shall always want to shout Encore! Encore!' "

Aram Van der Veer looked at his pocket watch, then dismissed his secretary. He had just finished a letter to his fifteen-year-old son, a student at Eton in England. It was a ritual each week no matter where he was. His daughter, a precocious nine-year-old and an unceasing delight to him, expected gifts when he returned to his home in Switzerland, no letters for her. He knew she was going to be a vixen when she grew to womanhood—already an expert at wrapping people around her small fingers. His wife of sixteen years, a French woman of aristocratic heritage, took him as he was, pleased to see him when he arrived at the chalet in Lucerne, and she felt happy to see him go after a few days time. Although their lovemaking was satisfying—most French women knew how to please a man—he suspected she had a lover who waited for his departures. She was too blooming and vital to be content with their life, which had many separations due to his business.

His main office was in Antwerp, where they maintained a home seldom used, his wife preferring Lucerne. When he insisted, they went to his family's home outside of Cairo, built next to a small oasis with a view of the vast desert lands and majestic pyramids on the far horizon. His mother lived there most of the year, leaving only in the extreme heat of summer, when she went to a small lakeside house also in Lucerne to be near her grandchildren and her son. There was a polite distance between her and Aram's wife; one always seemed to leave the room when the other entered, with some excuse or other. Never remarrying after his father died ten years before, her physical needs were taken care of discreetly by a young man, an Arab, who lived in, conveniently, as her social secretary. Although he was also no longer young, but approaching fifty years of age to her sixty.

Aram was still very impressed with his mother, a remarkable woman in his opinion. An Indian of pure Aryan strain, she was of the upper Vaisyas caste, the majority of whom were traders. It was in India that his father found her while doing business with her family at their summer residence near the Nepal border, with forests so lush with orchids, his mother often told him, the blooms were used at times for cow fodder.

Lala Van der Veer was to him the epitome of womanhood. He was not in love with his mother in the sense he wanted to go to bed with her sexually, but she had given him his taste for women, and he hoped he would eventually find someone with her qualities. He had been mistaken in his wife, who displayed the desired qualities at the outset—so good at the pretense, knowing perhaps that was what he was seeking. Like an actress, she played the role but without heart.

His mother had been taught by his father, he knew, but this sensuousness had to be inherent, only waiting to be aroused—stimulated. The chemistry between them must have been perfect. He could remember just how they touched fingers, his father's brushing a wisp of hair from her face with such tenderness, sexuality—the looks they had for each other. As a youngster he had been so jealous.

When he saw Vanessa in that depressing hotel in Antwerp, he had been attracted more than he had been in a long time. He sensed there was something to be awakened in her, and he wanted to be the one to do it. His mistress, an opera singer in Rome, was a tigress. Her lovemaking more like aggressive attacks, lacking any finesse or true sensual enjoyment. In the beginning it had been exciting, but it wasn't what he really wanted. It was always hurry, hurry, hurry; I am ready, come and then we will do it again and again and again. When he tried to slow her down to more artful lovemaking, more foreplay, she screamed, "I want to feel the peaks, my love." He had been with her a few weeks ago to take her to the premiere of *Aida*, written by her friend Verdi to commemorate the opening of the Suez Canal. He couldn't wait to get out of her clutches and felt smothered by her possessiveness and excesses. There was no real enjoyment. No. Vanessa

McIver was growing stronger in his thoughts each day. She was so beautiful, as tall as he, fine thin bones in the lovely oval face framed by soft brown hair. Her almond-shaped, blue-gray eyes gave her away when she tried to be other than what she was feeling—that delighted him. Thinking about her excited him, and he felt his blood rush to the tip of his penis, throbbing, expectant, eager for sensual pleasure.

He laughed out loud when he thought about the sable cape. He could imagine the stir it must have made. Vanessa would not want to keep it—of that he was positive. But Sasha, her manager, a man of avarice, would convince her. Aram loved to give outrageous gifts. It had been intended for his mistress, but he was really concerned with the shabbiness and the thinness of her outer cloak in this foul weather. In Belgium, he was sure it rained three hundred days of the year. He left his hotel suite, one he kept permanently, and started for Vanessa's hotel. He was hoping to woo her back to his rooms and after dinner to start her awakening. His excitement was in high evidence beneath the fine cloth of his trousers.

She came out of the lift wearing the sable cape regally —heads turned and as she walked past him, haughtily, she whispered, "The cape will be returned in the morning."

Aram followed her in mock deference to the door and courteously helped her as she entered the luxurious carriage. She sat looking straight ahead like a queen as he adjusted the lap robe. It was raining hard and the rawness of the weather sent icy chills through the both of them. But she was wrapped like a cocoon in the deep pile of the rich fur cape and rug, and that pleased him. He fought taking her in his arms and kissing her on her soft wide mouth. He would have to move slowly with this American, becoming surer each moment, that behind that propriety lay a warm, passionate nature, just seething like a volcano, needing the right pressures to burst forth hotly. Aram also sensed she was terribly vulnerable to life and seriously wanted to know the reason why.

The restaurant was very grand, and in the background there was a very good string orchestra playing chamber music. For the first time, Vanessa was wearing one of her working dresses in her private life. The blue satin with a low scoop neck, the one she wore at her debut in London. She kept her few stage dresses apart from her regular, skimpy wardrobe, but she was glad she had worn it—it gave her confidence with his worldly, debonair man. He was teasing and playful, trying to find out things about her, and she tried to be just as playful and teasing in not telling him. He also kept filling the tall tulip-shaped glasses with champagne—she had several and was feeling the effects. It reminded her of the night she met Pierre—for some reason she raised both her hands to Aram and said, "What do you think of these hands, monsieur?" She had also done that same thing that night, she recalled.

He took them and kissed the fingertips—she blushed and looked around her but no one seemed to notice, so she relaxed a bit—it was all so enjoyable. She was tingling, then startled when he sucked on her index finger for a quick second. She pretended to herself that she did not feel the sticky moisture between her legs.

He started to tell her about the house where his mother lived outside Cairo. Their desert castle, he said.

She was very interested—it sounded so marvelous, she told him honestly. Egypt, a place she hoped to see some day.

"You will," he said assuredly.

His father, he confided, on a selling trip, came off the road from Alexandria to Cairo and it was one of the most impressive sights he had ever seen—rising behind the city were massive pyramids and seemingly an endless sea-blue sky. He fell in love with the land and built a castle in the desert for his bride of a year. They rarely lived elsewhere except when forced out by the heat in summer.

"Were you a little boy in Egypt?" she wanted to know.

"Yes, until I was nine and sent to school in England, but I couldn't wait to get back to the land of treasures and wonderment during holidays—and my horse, Majesty, a wonderful beast that carried me over the great shifting sands of the desert."

"I, too, love horses," she said languidly.

"You, Vanessa. You are a horsewoman?"

"Didn't you know all Southern women love their horses and their daddys?"

"I didn't know. Do you love your daddy?"

"Of course," she giggled at his wicked eyes, "but not the

way you are thinking." She looked at him through half closed eyes. "I know what you mean."

"You do? What do I mean, Vanessa?"

"You are very devilish, do you know that?"

The room was empty except for them. The hour was late; they had taken long to dine. She reached for the cape to put it around her shoulders. "I can't keep this, you know. What an extravagant gift."

"I want you to have it. You must accept it, and when you are wrapped in its warmth, I hope it will make you think of me."

She teased him with her voice along with a demure look, "Who did you really buy it for? That is before you decided to send it to me. Come on, confess."

"The little elves and fairies sat up all night making it just for Vanessa. The new queen of the music world."

She toddled slightly as she walked out of the restaurant.

In the carriage lined with the finest leather, she sank back luxuriously and sighed, very conscious of his warm body as he sat close to her. She had nowhere to move as she was already in the corner, distressed because actually it was exciting. She felt alive, like a woman. He removed his top hat and slowly pushed back the hood of her cape, so he could see her lovely face, he said. Her body tensed as she waited for the next move, hoping and yet horrified. He spoke softly, murmuring in French as he suddenly nibbled on her ear.

"Please don't," she moaned.

But he continued gently, his tongue lightly touching and circling the hole in her ear; she was too naive to understand the signal, but it excited her. His hand went to her cape and found its way inside, she tried to push him away, but he was too determined and persistent. In the next second she felt his hand on her breast and she screamed—the fire of sex causing her to force her thighs together.

"Chere, just enjoy, enjoy. I want so to make love to you. Beautiful love."

"No!"

He uncovered ripe breasts, and before she knew what was happening he had his mouth on her nipple. The sensation sent her reeling as she tried to protest more forcibly but was overcome by her own emotions.

"Touch me, my darling—please—touch me."

She couldn't—weakly she tried to push him away again.

The sucking on her nipple got faster. Uncontrollably, she felt the heat of orgasm start. She looked around frantically and only saw the leather of the carriage, the heavy rain, and heard along with his heavy breathing, the clop-clop of the carriage horses.

"Stop, stop, you've got to stop."

His teeth gently dug into her nipple and it started to roll in—a great wave of passion—she tensed—he knew she was coming and increased the sucking, and tried to get his free hand under her skirt.

"You've got to stop—please . . ."

Her strong hands fought with his, but he was a powerful man and she was powerless.

"Let me out of here—you've got to stop."

His fingers crept inside her. He was surprised that she wasn't a virgin. She gasped for air and kept begging for him to stop.

"Help! Help!" she yelled.

He gave a long, hard suck on her breast, and his hand moved more urgently.

"Oh, my God," she yelled. "Stop it."

"I want you to enjoy, my darling," he whispered hoarsely as his lips left her breast and sought her mouth. "Enjoy, my darling."

She could feel him unbuttoning his trousers. Suddenly she felt the flesh on her flesh and was powerless to stop him. The thrilling flames shot through her—she had never known there could be such fathomless feelings.

Like a crazy woman she flung herself from side to side, trying to get him off her. She felt him between her legs. She was almost at the peak and hated herself, but was no longer in control of what was happening inside her. She was being raped and couldn't stop it.

As he entered her, she started to come fully. She came again—the sensations of ecstasy flooding her being, but in spite of it all, she continued to fight him off. Finally, he came with her, grunting and groaning with such an ecstasy, calling her name over and over in his heated passion.

He did not remove himself from her when it was over, but sought her mouth and kissed her deeply, as if draining out of her the last spark of her life.

At last the carriage came to a stop in front of the hotel. She sat there dumbfounded. He tried to read her face. He knew immediately that he had behaved irrationally—after the warning he had given himself.

She found the power to rise and moved out of the cape now flung on the seat of the carriage, away from her body, and pushed open the door, then ran under the canopy of the hotel into the lobby.

An hour later as she lay in bed mortified, although her flesh was still excited, a note was slipped under her door— it was from Aram.

My Dear Vanessa,

I sat in the hotel lobby after you left me so abruptly trying to reason with myself the best way to explain my behavior—and how foolish it is for a man my age to try to put my feelings in a letter. But you bring the foolish out in me, and I must confess that I find it quite pleasurable.

My dear, something wonderful happened between us. Perhaps not the appropriate place, that was my fault and for that I apologize, but what we felt together is something to be cherished and when felt so gloriously, especially on my part, one should be grateful and not apologize for that. We are given so many burdens to carry on our shoulders in this world, we forget to enjoy the gifts of pleasure also given, if only we allow them to happen. As you can see, I am not a Victorian. Please let us look upon what has happened with thoughts of pleasure.

Alas, my dear, I didn't get to tell you I will not be able to attend your concert tomorrow evening. I leave Brussels in a few hours for Africa, not my beloved Egypt, but the southern tip, where in recent years great discoveries of diamonds have been made, and we must find a way of forming a union to protect the value of their export. See, how close I feel already, telling you about my business.

However, I will find out where you are going to play next and try to be there. Perhaps it will be our luck in life to meet in the capitals of the world. Wouldn't that be wonderful? You asked me in the hotel dining room in Antwerp if I had a recipe for the loneliness of being a concert artist—I have just given you my remedy.

Play well tomorrow. You are magnificent, but so like the sphinx to me as yet—a puzzlement, a riddle to be solved. My first discovery, however, Vanessa, you are a very genuine and desirable woman.

I want to ask a favor—think of me and enjoy life. It can be glorious.

Au revoir,
Aram

20

During the light lunch of soufflé and green salad, Blamford talked freely about the business he had conducted that morning. He enjoyed coming to Sillar's for the midday meal. She always had her table laid beautifully. Today a sheer cotton tablecloth, lightly embroidered in white with touches of yellow in a Chinese motif complimented the pale blue china. Small, cut glass vases held fresh flowers informally arranged, as though just plucked from the garden. The effect was charming as always. He made a quick mental note to bring her a new set of bone china dishware he had seen the other day, clusters of deep purple violets against a white background. She would be pleased and it suited her.

Blamford was a smallish man, overly thin with good bones. Hollows of strain were always under his eyes, and his high cheekbones and high-bridged nose gave the impression he was looking down at you, like a high court judge about to pass sentence. In his transactions he always used that look to advantage. He continued his discourse, feeling content. Sillar sat quietly, listening to him talk about his business. He was an early riser, convinced that you could always outsmart the competition by being two hours ahead of them. She knew his reputation in business. His decisions were made quickly and once made were irreversible, although he often said, "I accept the fact that I'll make a mistake now and again—everyone does. The difference with me that gives me the edge on my competition is I don't waste time reconsidering, since ninety-eight percent of the time I would arrive at the same answer. My decisions are made rationally with a full set of facts before me, so there is no reason to reconsider." He was also ruthless in his revenge on anyone who had wronged him, had shirked on a deal, or cheated him. Up front he would lay out all the terms, the good and the bad and made it clear if you accepted his money, you were into the deal all the way.

It was hard for Sillar to reconcile this image with what she saw of him. His lovemaking was gentle—most of the time she was the active partner. At times she could feel him weeping when they were through, but she knew better than to acknowledge the tears or to question their origin.

For the first year of these fairly regular luncheons, Sillar never made a comment, but listened well, her face glowing with pride and excitement when he told of his ships returning from some faraway port full of prized goods and then the sympathy and concern offered when he talked of a ship that sunk, a cargo broken or rotted when it arrived. Strangely, he never spoke of the men lost at sea or of their pain. She went with him only once to the docks, expecting to be excited to see in person the world he regaled her with, but instead when she saw the men carrying the heavy cartons on their backs, their faces haggard, beaten by the burden of their lives, she couldn't bear the sight. To her, it was returning to the slavery of the South. Though these men were paid for their labors, it was still a kind of bondage—just enough to pay for food and a roof. She never went again. Young Kenneth didn't see what she saw, his life wasn't tainted like hers. His view was of the powerful beauty of the sailing ships, their exotic goods, and thrilling stories of the ports visited so far away.

Blamford never knew that first year whether Sillar understood the intricacies of the business he described. At least not until the day she finally spoke up. He was troubled by an old friend seeking advice about selling his business. "I don't like advising people," he had said. "They are never as adventuresome as I—their concern is for the few pounds they will make while mine is the power struggle, outsmarting the competition. I know my friend—he will only waste my time and in the end go against my advice. Then he shall fail and mourn his losses."

"Then charge him for your advice."

"Sillar, he is my oldest friend—our families have been entwined for years."

"If you charge him, he will feel he was given something of value and since he has paid for it, he therefore will use it."

He loved her bold approach and afterward they laughed at his friend's chagrin. Blamford's advice was only one word, "Sell!" and for that he received a handsome fee.

From that moment on she contributed in various subtle but meaningful ways in his business decisions—holding off with any comment until he had unraveled the complications of a business venture. Then she helped him define what he needed to make it work for him. In a way it was a talking it out between them.

She too began to discuss her business plans, though they were very modest compared to his. Her shop was successful, the returns were not nearly enough to even begin to pay for the life-style she lived. She dreamed of expanding to include dress designing, and then entire wardrobes for the fine ladies of London. She wanted to dress them head to toe, she confided. He enjoyed hearing her spin out her dreams and offered her the money to expand, but she wanted to do it on her own.

This day like most when they were finished dining, they moved to the large chair by the fire in her small sitting room, bringing their half-empty wine glasses with them. She sat in his lap and with her arm around his shoulders, she cuddled against him. He gently ran his hand along the satin skirt, feeling the outline of her leg and then he kissed her under the chin. "Sillar, would it be nice to lie with one another?"

He felt her stiffen slightly. "If you wish, Blamford—you know I will if you wish."

Her resistance annoyed him. His sexual demands on her were few, and until very recently she never made him feel as though he was buying his sexual pleasures. For the past few days she responded in a way that was unusual for their relationship. Today's strange response added to his growing concern that there was someone else in her life. Until only a short time ago he never doubted her faithfulness to him. At the beginning of their relationship he was all doubt—never believing she would keep herself only for him. He had even followed her at times, and then to his embarrassment, but relief, she would turn into a fabric shop or scoot into a pastry shop for one of her favorite sweets. Soon he began to relax his fears, and on the occasions when he would feel pangs of jealousy, he found it was more and more easy to stifle. He hated himself for this flaw in his character, but she and her son were central to his life and he was determined to guard his interests.

He stood up suddenly, almost dumping her on the floor. "I must be going. I have urgent business to attend to, and then I don't want to miss the session at the House of Lords today."

Sillar was relieved that he hadn't pressed his needs. Since the House of Lords met from 2:30 P.M. until 10:30 at night, she knew her evening would be free and had agreed to have dinner with Kenneth. All her resolve not to see him again, when they met in Kensington Gardens, flew away after a few minutes of walking with him down the paths past Elphin Oak, with its carved gnomes and animals. They so enjoyed the sight—she didn't tell him it was one of Kenneth Jr.'s favorite spots. At the Round Pond they sat close together in the chilly weather watching the stout-hearted sail their model boats.

He called for her in a hired carriage, and they went to a small restaurant close to the neighborhood where she boarded when she first arrived in London and where their son was born. She remembered passing this restaurant and peering through the café-curtained windows at all the elegant diners, her mouth drooling at the food. Now she smiled, realizing how far she had come. What had seemed so elegant then was really quite ordinary to her now.

She was finally relaxed with Kenneth, able at last to throw off the remains of their former relationship and the fact that he once owned her. After their meal, he took her home and followed her in.

Kenneth sat in the same chair that Blamford had been in only hours before. She knelt down by the side of the chair and wrapped her arms around his knees. The knock at the door startled them, and Sillar rose so quickly as the door opened she caught her shoe in her hem. Clara let out a short gasp at the sight of her mistress off balance, suddenly aware she had intruded on a very private moment.

"Pardon me, madame. Nanny asked me to tell you not to be alarmed when you go into Master Kenneth's room tonight. He has a slight bump on his head, but he is all right. He wanted you to know he was very brave and shed only two tears."

Her heart started to flutter—she hoped Kenneth wouldn't put it all together.

"Thank you, Clara, you may go."

"Yes, madame. I hope I haven't intruded, but Nanny did want you to know."

Kenneth was standing behind her, and she could feel his breathing on her neck.

"Sillar. Sillar, look at me."

She turned slowly.

"You have a child?"

"Yes."

"The young blond-haired boy I saw running into the shop?" He moved to the portrait on the piano. "This boy, Sillar. The child is named Kenneth."

She hated the way he was dragging it out.

"He's mine isn't he."

"No, Kenneth. Just mine."

"But, I'm his father."

"You are the man who impregnated me if that's what you want to hear, but he is my child—alone. I bore him alone; I raised him alone; I take care of him, love him . . ." She began to weep.

"Why didn't you tell me?"

"When? As we were fleeing Charleston with me carrying your wife's belongings? Say to you in front of Georgina, I've got happy news—there soon will be a new McIver, a black McIver? Now, after all these years, what's the point?"

Her words stung him. "Please, please, Sillar, let me help. Let me know my son."

"I want you to leave me now. I need time."

He saw she was very distraught, but he wanted his son. "All right, I'll go, but only if you promise to see me again."

"Yes, yes, now leave—please."

When the sound of his footsteps faded on the marble stairs, Blamford stepped out from the hiding place he had taken behind the draperies. Even the sight of her heaving shoulders, the defeated, broken look of her body did not stop him from angrily giving his ultimatum.

He was brief and firm. She must never see the man again. If she did, he would expose her for what she really was, and the child and she would be removed immediately from their elegant surroundings.

21

Georgina was pleased that Thomas was coming to dinner and would bring Josiah; he was acting strange of late, disappearing for long periods of time, and she couldn't get him to discuss his work at school. If Kenneth wouldn't deal with Josiah, then she intended to speak with Thomas about his having a long talk with his nephew. This was men's business—they could communicate better and anyway, she had too much on her mind concerning her daughters.

Georgina chatted on to Kenneth about the wedding arrangements and the country trip, while they waited in the drawing room for Thomas and Josiah. They were to leave at the end of the week, she gushed.

"I know," he answered glumly.

The arrival of their guests gave Kenneth the opportunity of having the new footman—one more to Kenneth's liking—bring him another whiskey. It was unusual for Kenneth to drink like this. He had several earlier, and Georgina showed her tacit disapproval by raising an eyebrow.

Thomas, however, picked up on it, "It's all right, Georgina, he suffers from not having the McIver hollow leg, but I'll help him up the stairs and put him safely in your bed."

She couldn't bear his sexual references, and knew that he did it to fluster her. Despite her annoyance, she recognized that he relieved the sullen mood that hung over the room, and as usual she could rely on him to keep up a spritely conversation.

Harry, the new footman, remembered Cecil's instruc-

tions—he stayed at his hall station on the stiff chair waiting to be beckoned and when in the room, appeared as
though he were not listening to the conversations. He had
never been asked to oversee anything before; his services up until this evening had only been in large parties
under strong supervision. Normally, Cecil would never allow a footman with as little experience as Harry to be
solely responsible for an evening such as this, but Cecil
had very little respect for the McIvers, especially the
mother, who always managed to vex him in every contact they had. He decided this would be a good learning
experience for Harry, a distant cousin fobbed off on him
by a dear aunt.

So far, in service, Harry had proven himself to be a
clumsy oaf and had been warned that he had one more
chance to prove himself capable. The McIvers would be
the perfect testing ground. They were provincial in his
opinion and knew as much about social behavior as Harry
—they deserved one another, in Cecil's opinion. He took
the opportunity of his lordship's stepping out for the evening—dinner at the Duchess of Leighton's—to relax himself. Sara Shields had already departed for the country estate to prepare the staff for the coming event and
that was also a blessing to him. Besides, he rationalized,
his room was just off the kitchen so he could still keep
his ear open to make sure the house was running smooth-
ly. He planned to reread George Meredith's *Ordeal of
Richard Feverel*, one of his favorites—a new copy given
to him as a gift had been sitting on his bedside table for
weeks, waiting for just such a moment. Although he would
never verbalize his negative attitude toward the Americans, he knew the rest of the staff felt the same way. He
could hear the cook grumbling and telling Clara to ask that
oaf Harry if the Americans were ready to eat—it was
past time.

Despite her husband's glum mood Georgina decided
to press on, "Thomas, won't it be thrilling to go to Lord
Hatfield's country estate? They say it is one of England's
showplaces."

"Yes, Georgina, it will be like the old days back
home."

"But, better, Thomas, better than before. This is high society and royalty—we've come so much further than Charleston. Oh, London is much more elegant and exciting than Charleston ever was. I've never been happier in my life. I never want to leave."

Kenneth watched his wife's exuberance in utter fascination. So, she thinks she is definitely going to stay here. Kenneth's voice was so quiet that she had to bend toward him to hear, "Well, Georgina, you had better enjoy it while you may. We will have Amanda's wedding at Christmas and then our ship will be sailing a few days later. That leaves you a little over three weeks to get your fill of this lovely city and glorious countryside. When you get home, you will be surprised at how quickly you will move back into your old world."

Georgina pretended to not quite understand.

"Of course I'll be coming back to Charleston, but Amanda needs me here—she's just a child. You see how she can't make a decision without me. I would never desert her, Kenneth." She rushed on quickly, hoping she could persuade him. "I have a wonderful plan in my mind. I'll follow as soon as I feel Amanda is settled and perhaps I can even enthuse Vanessa to return home for a visit. We could come together. And Josiah, he should go back with you, Kenneth!"

She was desperate. "Won't that be nice, Josiah—you and your father need time together." She was offering Josiah in her place—a part of negotiation.

Before Kenneth could respond, Josiah walked up to his mother and stated flatly, "I'm not going back to Charleston. I want to stay here."

Disturbed at his resistance complicating her staying in London, she dismissed Josiah quickly, "Hush Josiah. This is not a matter for you to decide. It's your father's decision and if he wants you to go back with him—so be it. Now, that is that."

Harry had been trying to find an opening in the conversation to tell them dinner was served—he was a tall, ungainly young man, with blotchy skin on a pointed face like a mongoose. Three times he started, "Excuse me, madame . . ." each time raising the volume of his voice, trying to be heard over the loud exchange the Americans were having. Finally, just as they all stopped talking he shouted out, "Excuse me, madame . . . ," for the fourth time, so loudly that Georgina jumped around to look at him.

"Well, for goodness sakes, Harold."

"Harry, madame."

"Harry, Harold. There is no need to shout."

"Yes, madame, the cook says dinner is ready to be served."

She saw that Thomas was only half finished with his drink, "Tell the cook we will be ready to dine in twenty minutes."

"I'll try, madame," but the remark was lost on Georgina.

"When Vanessa goes back for a visit, we should arrange for her to play at the St. Cecilia Society. Wouldn't that be wonderful—what an affair we could have after— like Hatfield's reception here."

Kenneth leered at her. "Where would we hold this reception? In the streets?"

"The Bonneau mansion is still there, and I have a feeling in my bones that Vanessa will be Mrs. Bonneau again before long. Anyway, I won't accept they are divorced. Why the State of South Carolina doesn't allow it. And my feeling is if you're married there then you can't be divorced. So it's not legal."

The logic escaped Thomas, but he saluted her with his glass and went on drinking.

"Did you see how he danced with her at the reception, Thomas, how he looked at her? They are the perfect pair."

Kenneth couldn't believe his ears. Before the recital she didn't want to hear the name Bonneau—now she was scheming to have Vanessa acquire it again. There was a certain kind of madness about this woman tonight.

Thomas interrupted, "Harriet won't permit it."

"Won't permit it. What are you saying, Thomas? They'll get married and Vanessa will come back to Charleston with Pierre. That's what Harriet wants. Then Vanessa can play only when she feels like it."

He persisted, "Harriet won't permit it."

"Thomas, why are you being so disagreeable?"

"Georgina, I have talked it all out with Harriet. Not

only does she not want the remarriage, but has threatened me saying if we do not persuade Vanessa to stay away from Pierre, she will call in her loan. I might add she was also going to advance us the additional money we need to pay this year's taxes—that too would be denied."

Georgina looked helplessly at Kenneth who was staring in bewilderment at Thomas.

Thomas continued, "It seems to me we must make a firm effort to persuade Vanessa to abide by Harriet's wishes or the McIver family shall lose their only worldly asset, the partially rebuilt homestead."

Georgina started to cry. She hated this fault in herself—whenever a situation required strength and reasoning, her tears started and all control and composure was then lost. Since her menopause, it was worse than ever.

"Kenneth, do something, I don't want us to have the stigma of a divorce in our family. You've got to figure something out."

Just then Harry came in and announced dinner—firmly.

Georgina turned on him. "Dinner? Who can eat dinner, you fool. Tell the cook to take it back. We'll ring when we want you."

Harry reeled from the room. Never had he heard a servant talked to in that manner in front of others. When he timidly approached the cook with the news, she threw the sauce pot at him spattering the front of his shirt.

There was a surliness in Kenneth's voice as he addressed his wife, "There is no resolution. We are poor, Georgina, only scraping by and Harriet is our only salvation. I shall speak with Vanessa, but, I'm afraid, the ultimate decision is hers alone."

"How dreadful all this complication now—just when everything was going so right." Facing Kenneth squarely, she blurted out, "And you asking me to return to that—to that poverty. I won't leave here."

Josiah had positioned himself near the windows, trying to fade into the background for fear the subject of his returning would again be brought up. He was determined to stay in London, but this obviously was not the time to press his point. Charleston did not hold anything for him.

Thomas stood, weaving a bit—his good-looking face wore a broad grin. Fighting was his fuel. "Well Kenneth,

Josiah, Georgina, now that we have all aired our concerns, let's have something to eat; I am ravenous. Since
the war I have never let a good meal go to waste."

Harry entered the room just pulling the cuffs of his
new shirt into place when he was told they were ready.
He descended the stairs to the kitchen mumbling to himself, going over a list of other occupations for which he
would be better suited.

While the family was dining, Daphne appeared at the
front door. With Mack standing in the shadows of the
park across the street, she didn't dare go against his
orders. They had lucked it, he had told her, as they
watched the mansion that night, to see Josiah go in with
another man. They waited a while to see if he would
come out to confront him, but when time passed, Mack
made her go to the imposing entrance and ring the bell.
She was in pain from the beating he had given her earlier
in the week when he was drunk and ugly, blaming her
because Josiah was not paying her any visits. The baby was
growing in her womb, and she was so worried about it,
she allowed Mack to move her around like a puppet on a
string, and of late was in dire fear of him.

The footman stood there looking at her in total dis-
belief, informing her the service entrance was in the
mews at the back. She stood there determined, knowing
Mack was observing every move. and demanded to see the
young man called Josiah, who had entered the house earlier.

When Harry went into the dining room, he was unsure.
He tried to get the young McIver's attention, but the lad
was more interested in his food. There was a strange silence in the room as if this volatile family had talked
themselves out for the moment or was resting before the
next bout. Finally, he went behind Josiah's chair and
cleared his throat until the young man looked up at
him perplexed.

He bent down trying to get *his* ear only, but suddenly
Georgina was all attention.

"Begging your pardon, sir. I didn't know what to do.
I'm sorry to disturb you at dinner, but there is a young,
eh—lady at the entrance wishing to see you."

"A lady? To see me?"

"You could say that, sir."

"Whoever could it be, Josiah?"

"I don't know, Mother. Did she give her name?"

"No, sir. She didn't." In a low whisper Harry took it upon himself to tell him more, trying to warn him as to the type of woman who was at the door.

"She's a bit of a rough type, sir, if you know what I mean, but she wouldn't go away."

The chair scraped the highly polished parquet as he rose and excused himself. When he saw her, he was very disturbed, looking around in the vestibule to see if he was being observed. She was very forceful in her demands. She wanted him to come to her place immediately. He told her that was impossible. She threatened she would yell if he didn't come. He assured her that he would definitely be there Saturday, only a few days away. After a moment, she seemed satisfied and turned sweet.

"I'll make sure you have a good time when you come, luv. I've been lonely for you."

He watched her go down the steps and into the shadows of the night, trying to figure what he would say when he went back to the dining room.

Mack grabbed her violently when she reached him in the darkness of the park on the Square.

"What happened?"

"Ough, you're hurting my arm."

"You'll get more than that if you don't give me an answer."

"He's coming—he'll be there."

"When?"

"Saturday. For sure."

"Good. I'll get him then."

When Kenneth approached Georgina's bedroom later in the evening, he was fully prepared for a continuing onslaught from her, and he felt it was necessary for them to get it out of their systems. He was surprised to see her sitting at the vanity brushing her hair and smiling at him in the mirror.

"You'll never guess, Kenneth, I have it all figured out.

Jamie. He will help us financially. I'll speak with Amanda and explain everything. She'll see that he helps."

"No, we can't seek help from him. He's not one of us. Our neighbors are closer—we understand each other. I wouldn't allow Jamie Hatfield to help nor even let him know our desperate straits."

"That's foolish. He'll be a member of the family in a few weeks."

"That's how I want it, Georgina."

Now what he had been expecting started anew.

"Sometimes I think you hate me. You just want to see me suffer. Can't you see what I can have here now—a glorious life and you are going to take me back to live with the ravages of war. I can't do it, Kenneth. You can't make me."

"Only a few years ago you were begging me not to put you on that boat to England—to let you stay at home in Charleston. You'll survive, Georgina—you're very good at that."

"I won't. You don't need me—I'm just in the way. Silly old Georgina. If I'm around you'll have to start sneaking about again bedding Negro women in the barn. I'll bet you've had a fine old time since I've been gone. Have you taken them in my bed? And don't think I don't know that Sillar is near. You've probably had her a few times since you arrived. Am I right, Kenneth, am I?"

Her nasty mention of Sillar infuriated him—the last image he had of her was painful—so distraught, and the boy, his son, a love child, being taken from him. His ire was fierce as he turned on Georgina and shook her until her curls straightened and hung down her face. "Shut up! You are going to do what I say. You and Josiah are going back. There is no more pushing me around and no more arguments!"

His anger frightened her, but excited her, too. His strength, his firmness reminded her of her father. She had never enjoyed the act of sex. It had always been unpleasant, but somehow this evening she hoped he would come to her bed. Kenneth's next remark dispelled that.

"If you are not on that boat with me, Georgina, we will have a divorce of our own."

With that he left the room, not seeing the look of sheer shock on her face. She comforted herself almost immediately. He is only trying to scare me, a ploy to make me go home, she told herself. Well, he would not win, and she would not let any of this stand in the way of her enjoyment of her daughter's marriage to the Eighth Earl of Raleigh.

22

Vanessa hired a carriage at Victoria Station to go directly to Hatfield's house. Surrounded by luggage, she and JoJo tried to look out the windows at the street activity. The sky was clear over the city, rare for a December day in London, and the feel of Christmas was everywhere. The merchants had put up decorations, trees on display were trimmed with glitter, and the sidewalks were crowded with midday shoppers. She was happy to be back. Sasha, busy on the continent booking her in various cities while he made his way to Budapest for the concert of one of his other artists, had given them packages to take to his mother, adding to their excess baggage.

The lace she brought from Brussels at her mother's request, rested securely on her lap. It was for Amanda's veil and there was a great amount so it would trail well behind her as she walked down the aisle to the altar. The fragile work, handmade on so many wooden bobbins in the age-old tradition, was about the only material thing the McIvers were contributing to the wedding. Hatfield was paying for everything else.

Giggles came from JoJo as a box tumbled on her from the rack above their heads. "Lordy, Lordy, how did we collect so much in such a short time?" She, too, seemed to be more open and positive since Brussels. Revitalized, perhaps confronting the past before they left had been painful in some instances, but good for them. Then again, because of their close relationship, Vanessa's attitude was always catching.

From Brussels they had gone to Paris to catch the boat train for the coast, but Vanessa decided at the last moment, something very unusual for her as she was always most anxious to get back to the only home she now knew, London, to stay on in Paris an extra day to do some shopping for themselves and buy Christmas gifts. They planned to leave for Lord Hatfield's country home almost immediately with the family, and didn't know how much they could do in London beforehand. In a whirlwind spree, Vanessa purchased yards and yards of beautiful material to have dresses made. Amanda had told her of a very good seamstress recommended by Jamie's sister, the Duchess of Leighton, and she was going to treat herself to some new clothes. A very special dressmaker was making the wedding dress for her sister, and she and JoJo were looking forward to seeing it. They knew Amanda was going through the final fittings.

The traffic around the station was snarled and they sat for long periods of time, then moving slowly at best.

The concert in Brussels had been so successful. The maestro himself applauded her at the finish. Great bouquets of flowers had been brought down the aisles as she took her numerous bows. The flowers, she felt, must have been from Aram—there was such a display. Oddly, to her, since receiving his note, she had been happier, more sure of herself than she had been in a long time, and had a new sense of freedom.

Aram. After the incident in the carriage, she immediately had gone to her room. Grateful no one was awake in the suite, positive they would be able to read what had happened on her face. She buried her head in the pillows on her bed—wanting to crawl into a hole somewhere, not knowing how to handle what had happened to her, especially since her body was still vibrating from the ecstasy she had experienced. She couldn't fathom what his letter meant really, or reason how it all took place at all, but a peace seemed to come with the note—a peace within herself. Another turning point where her life again could never be like it was before. However, she was positive that she could never face Aram Van der Veer again.

Her mother and Amanda were delighted to see her, they were bubbling. The small puppy, Peony, danced all around her—a gift for Amanda from the duchess. They were full of talk of the wedding and their departure for the country the very next afternoon; she was, after all, a day late. Pangs of remorse and jealousy struck her as the wedding talk continued, but she vowed for the sake of her family and Amanda to be gay, to push her own problems out of her mind.

She watched her sister whirl around in the beautiful flowing white satin dress, overlayed with beaded tulle and silk flowers. Vanessa handed her the package from Brussels, and Amanda tore it open—both she and her mother gasped at its fragile beauty. Daisy, one of the upstairs maids, who was helping with the boxes and clothing, stopped to look at it more closely and asked if she could just touch it for a second. Her coarse hand gently stroked the fabric.

Amanda draped it over her head, and they all admired the doll-like creature dressed in her wedding finery. Daisy, in her cockney accent, remarked that she looked more like the little figure that would decorate the top of the wedding cake—it was all so beautiful.

Georgina talked on and on about the festivities to take place in Norfolk, the location of Hatfield's estate—thousands of acres, she bragged to Vanessa, villages, towns, mills, all on his land. The whole village near his home was coming to the wedding reception. A fair was being planned to honor the bridal couple—a horse race, too—she was beside herself saying over and over, isn't it just like it used to be back home.

In between her outbursts of excitement, Vanessa had asked if there had been any messages for her, and after a slight hesitation her mother told her no, nothing at all. Daisy's head popped up at that because she remembered bringing a note upstairs addressed to Miss Vanessa and placing it on her dressing table. She would check, possibly it was still there, that is if she were remembering correctly.

When she and Amanda were alone in the bedroom, Vanessa could not help but speak of Jamie.

"Are you very much in love, Amanda?"

"Of course, Jamie and I are talking of redecorating this house when we come back from our honeymoon in Italy. He likes all of my suggestions. Then we will entertain here on a grand scale. We had supper at the duchess' home the other evening followed by some readings by new poets. Ardell is the patron of many writers and some artists— she is so witty and gay. If you like I'll ask her to invite

you to one of her salons when she has a special evening
—especially by one of her up-and-coming poets. The other
night the man was Welsh, so divine looking, but really a
rough type. Jamie said he found he and his work stupid,
and there was another—Swinburne was his name. He was
awfully tiddly and is so scandalous—Vanessa, he prefers
men to women. Can you imagine!"

She ran to the dressing table and brought Vanessa a
thin leather-bound book, "The duchess gave me this by
Tennyson—he's the Poet Laureate of England—he writes
for all of England's special occasions, the deaths of well-
known men, royal weddings, like being the spokesman for
the country."

She flipped the pages of the volume and Vanessa just
watched her with a smile, happy to see her sister so caught
up and excited by her impending wedding. "I'll have to
read this. I'm sure she will want to discuss it with me. He
lives near Ardell—in Sussex. Oh, Vanessa, I'm dying to
see her country house, too. So magnificent I'm told, rolling
countryside, with a superb view across the downs to the
channel, and do you realize, I've never seen Jamie's country
estate either? I'm to be chatelaine of a vast mansion
I've never seen." She ran and grabbed Vanessa by the
shoulders enthusiastically. "I know a secret. I peeked. There
was a large box in Jamie's room. It must be one of my
Christmas presents, a Persian lamb cloak with a huge sable collar. I tried it on—it's divine. I can't wait to wear it."

"That is all truly wonderful, and I'm so pleased for you.
But do you love Jamie? Really love him?"

The doll-like woman was perplexed, "Of course I love
Jamie. I'm going to marry him."

"What I mean is, does Jamie make you feel all goose-
fleshy when he's near you?"

"Jamie? What a thing to say. He's a very important man;
he doesn't go around giving me goose pimples."

"What I'm trying to ask is how do you think it will be
between you and Jamie in bed?"

"You should know, not me—you've been married, you
know what it's like."

"That's just it, Mandy, I never felt anything when I was
married. I just became rigid, and endured."

"Oh, it's nothing but a bother. You just hate what you're
forced to do. That's what Mama says."

"But there can be something between a man and a woman. Something that can be pleasurable and when it grows out of their love for each other, it must be wonderful."

"Vanessa, whatever are you talking about? Did something happen to you while you were away to make you talk like this?"

"What happens when Jamie touches you? Do you feel all liquidy inside—like you want to melt?"

She was indignant. "No."

"What does it do to you?"

"Nothing. It feels like Jamie, my future husband, is touching me. Vanessa, you are being insufferable. Ladies don't talk like this."

"Maybe they should, Mandy. We might become more fulfilled."

"If Mama heard you carrying on like this, she would just die."

Vanessa had made up her mind that instant to go to Guy's Hospital once more and try to see Kirk. She had to know her feelings on seeing him again even though he had been ignoring her. She had tried desperately to push him to the back of her mind, but he kept coming forward—his image would not be buried.

Amanda pulled on a pink silk kimono over her corselette and lounged on a chaise in front of the fireplace. Peony jumped up and settled comfortably in her arms. She made a very pretty picture as she pursed her lips in a pout.

"Pierre is such a handsome man, why don't you try to win him back. Mama said several people at the reception asked who the dashing fellow was. It would be such a disaster, Vanessa, if our new friends in England should ever find out you are a divorced woman. Mama is going to invite him to tea. Thomas says he is staying in London."

She jumped up excitedly and grabbed her sister. There was a big difference in their height. Vanessa so tall, like the McIvers, and Amanda like her mother, so petite.

"Wouldn't it be grand if you remarried, in secret of course, and also lived here in London? Forget that old piano playing."

"Everyone keeps forgetting that Pierre divorced me. I didn't want it—it was his decision. But I would like to

see him again—so many things have changed; it would be
interesting to get to know him on another basis."

Amanda misunderstood, "Good. We were afraid you
would object. Mama and Uncle Thomas are going to be
so happy. The Bonneaus are an important family—even
here in England. And doesn't Pierre come into all that
money soon?"

Georgina hadn't told Amanda that Harriet Bonneau was
now set against Pierre and Vanessa coming together again
and how going against her decision would effect the Mc-
Ivers.

Kirk wasn't in the clinic—it was closed. Vanessa tried
to remember the maze of halls she went through the last
time to get to the main entrance where she could get information, but was stopped by an orderly who told her to
go back to the street and then around to the main gate to
make her inquiries.

She hurried down the road on the side of the building;
it was approaching four o'clock and the afternoon was
turning to dusk. A man and woman came out of a side
entrance. The man was tall and lean-boned; it was Kirk.
She started to run toward him when the woman at his side
took his arm possessively and they turned in an opposite
direction. Vanessa halted and let him get away. No doubt
it was his lady friend, and she had no right to interfere.

Later that afternoon, she instructed JoJo to get their
things together as they were moving back to the house in
Chelsea. It would be empty soon, with Thomas and Josiah leaving with the family in the morning. Vanessa did
not think she could be around such gaiety as the wedding
got closer. In facing her mother, she told her she would
arrive a few days before the big affair using the excuse of
her music and practicing with Madame Dworski. Josiah
also begged off until the last week with the excuse that he
had so much reading to do for coming examinations. So,
Josiah would be living with her until the appointed time,
when they would go to the country together.

23

Georgina placed the Christmas gifts she had made for the family in her hand valise. Amanda was to receive a sampler with a replica of McIver Hall on St. Helena, along with the date of her birth and the date of her marriage to Jamie. Embroidered in pale green silk thread, which snaked across the bottom in a ribbon effect was the motto of South Carolina, "While I breathe, I hope."

She was relieved at last to be leaving for the country—the past few weeks had been exhausting physically as well as emotionally, preparing for Amanda's wedding and the many reunions that took place for her. The duchess—she must learn to call her Ardell—and her husband, who had just returned from a hunting trip to Norway, would be joining them in a few days followed by other wedding guests. She was looking forward to it all, as it would show Jamie how capable she and Amanda were together in running Ashby Manor. Everyone said it was one of the most magnificent homes in all of England. She felt Amanda was very fortunate to have such an efficient mother. It was clear to Georgina that Amanda just couldn't manage without her—surely Kenneth would start to see that she couldn't just desert their daughter in such overwhelming circumstances. She was used to organizing the trips from the plantation to the Charleston townhouse for the season, but even Georgina had to admit she was a bit thrown by the enormity of the move that had gone on. A few days ago Mrs. Shields, the cook and two of her assistants, three housemaids, and the stillroom maid had left for the country. They had worked for days packing the Hatfield heirloom serving pieces and candelabra and decorative pieces, which were brought out on very special occasions, to be added to the country estate's already grand collection. Each piece was carefully packed in specially fitted cases to avoid breakage or denting.

The maid helped her on with her heavy black wool coat with fox trim. Kenneth and Jamie were already at the entranceway, and Amanda came bouncing down the staircase moments later. The footmen assigned to each of them were in traveling livery, fawn-colored coats and black pants tucked into high leather boots, black silk top hats with rust feathers and fawn-colored heavy leather gloves. Three of Lord Hatfield's private cars would be attached to the regular train—one would hold the servants traveling with them and the valises and hand trunks, the second was a sitting room, and the third was partitioned into four sections, with comfortable chaises.

Each footman saw to carrying steamer rugs and robes to put over the knees and feet of the family and also hot water containers for their feet, to ward off the cold of the unheated compartments. They were also responsible for the hampers filled with sandwiches, cold meats en gelée, fruit, breads, and serving pieces and china cups for the tea that would be kept warm over the small alcohol burners. Next to Lord Hatfield's chair was placed his wooden case bearing the crest of the Hatfield family. It held crystal decanters of brandy and Scotch whiskey, a selection of cigars, and several decks of playing cards. Reading material would also be provided.

Cecil was responsible for the Hatfield heirloom jewel case containing valuable jewelry, which was being transported with them. The case, with a chain attached to his arm, would remain locked and at his side for the entire journey.

Thomas joined them at the station, along with Vanessa and Josiah who were there to see them off. Georgina all aflutter, tears of excitement and concern welling in her eyes, kissed them goodbye and embarrassed Josiah by reminding him to eat well and to listen to Vanessa, giving him enough instructions to last several years. A few minutes before the train was to depart and everyone was safely and comfortably on board, a footman sent a telegram to Ashby indicating the time of their arrival.

Georgina and Amanda kept their footmen busy refilling

the footwarmers and serving them hot tea. After four years neither one was yet accustomed to the damp, cold English weather, and as the train traveled further north and toward the North Sea, they passed through pockets of heavy fog at times mingled with light snow.

Kenneth and Jamie sat together and enjoyed stepping off the train for airings at stations when the holdovers were longer than a few minutes. This was the first time they had been alone. Kenneth had avoided being with Jamie—from their first meeting, he felt an instinctive dislike for his future son-in-law, realizing now it was for jealous reasons.

The conversation was slow in getting started. They touched on mundane subjects at first—talking about the weather, and then Jamie began telling Kenneth about the wonderful hunting on his land, about his love for his country home, the tiny village of Ashby at the foot of his estate, about his tenant farmers, able to recall each name, as well as their children's, and the important events of their lives. Kenneth listened quietly, finding himself liking this man who, up to now, seemed so foreign to him, realizing he had many problems that were similar to his own in running his land. As a matter of fact, Jamie reminded him in many ways of himself—he was a gentle man, cared about people, and was willing to extend himself to find out about them, to share their human journey. He thought sadly that his daughter, Amanda, probably would never see this wonderful side of her future husband. He had to admit that Amanda was too much like her mother—he felt it was ultimately the wealth and the power that she was marrying. There was the chance that this man, so much older than Amanda, so much further along in life than he was when he married Georgina, might be able to keep a rein on their life together and hopefully shape her into a loving, unselfish companion.

When the train arrived at their station, their three cars were pulled onto a side track, and immediately the housemen of Ashby Manor boarded and started loading the luggage onto a large wagon. The first servant on the train was a bent old man, decked out in the full livery of the manor. He greeted Jamie warmly, and Kenneth could tell that Jamie felt a genuine affection for this old man, almost as though he were an old uncle or even a grandfather. "This is Archie, one of our 'odd men.' ". Archie bowed grandly when introduced to the future Lady Hatfield, then winked at Jamie obviously approving of his selection. Then he said to Amanda in his growly voice, "On behalf of his lordship's staff, we welcome you to Ashby Manor." With a touch to his hat in salute, Archie quickly departed to help with the rest of the luggage and Jamie explained that he was born at Ashby Manor to a housemaid and had lived his full seventy-three years there.

"We have several men like Archie, but none as sprightly and enjoyable. He's called an 'odd man' because he was never able to master his duties well enough to move along the hierarchy of servants. He is given odd jobs, laying the fires, carrying luggage and other menial tasks, but he goes about his day as though he were the butler and is well loved by all for the dignity and care with which he carries out his duties."

The footmen saw them into an enormous carriage drawn by four gray horses and emblazoned with the Hatfield crest. Two rode behind and another climbed on the box with the groom. The midafternoon was still light, so they had a good view of the countryside, the long rolling hills, the rich valleys, and finally, when they were nearing their destination, a magnificent view of the North Sea.

When they passed through the town of Ashby, many of the inhabitants, anticipating his lordship's arrival, were standing by their doorways, nodding their heads and occasionally waving in respect and affection. Many of the women stretched their necks as far as they could in hopes of getting a glimpse of the future Lady Hatfield. Amanda satisfied their curiosity. Unrestrained in her delight, like a child forgetting her dignity, she gaped out the window, craning her neck, freely pointing out things with her finger, so excited about her first trip to Ashby Manor and pleased that she was already being looked upon as the lady of the manor—and the future Countess Raleigh.

It certainly was so much easier here than in London, where she sometimes felt she would never be accepted. After the town, the carriage started a gradual climb, and at the plateau they turned north again with the wild sea on their right. It was difficult to see too well through the trees on the other side, but now and again at an occasional opening, Amanda would espy in the distance a tiny stone cottage of one of the tenant farmers, and at one clearing she saw columns of blue smoke rising.

"Oh Jamie, what is that? Is something on fire?"

Through a wider opening in the trees she could see cooking fires and a number of painted wagons decorated with flowers and fruit, vivid against the overcast day. A large group of brightly dressed people watched the procession go by.

"Jamie, who are they? They are so colorful."

He explained they were the Lande family, Romany gypsies, and twice each year at about the same time, they would suddenly appear. Then after a month or so they would leave as mysteriously as they came, without a trace, leaving behind only handwoven baskets and other objects they had made as gifts of thanks for the use of the land.

24

Rupa stood arrogantly next to his uncle, the old chief of the gypsies, watching Lord Hatfield's carriages wind along the long drive up to the manor house. He was next in line to become the chief—his older sister, Zena, was already the Bibi, the queen. Her wagon sat at a privileged distance from the others, and she was believed to have special powers and insights, attending the birth of each child and helping erect the ritual tent, which would be burned when the baby was delivered.

Rupa resembled his uncle in appearance, the same curly blue-black hair, olive skin, wide brown eyes, bulging muscles and, though he was as tall as his uncle, more than six feet, his frame was slighter but still powerfully built. Rupa's eyes, vividly alive and observant, were entranced by the face of the young lady staring at their camp as she passed, her blond curls falling from the hood of rich fur encircling her face like a halo. He was certain their eyes had met, for she drew her head back into the carriage suddenly out of his sight, but her image was etched on his mind.

Rupa's uncle, too, watched the lord's caravan, but not as intently as Rupa. He was more concerned with his nephew's rapt interest in the new arrival, so preoccupied that he didn't hear a few of the women talking excitedly in Romany about the play they would prepare. They were certain they would be asked to the manor to entertain for the many guests who would be arriving to celebrate the wedding—also, they speculated about the gold coins they would receive as payment.

His uncle worried about Rupa's wildness. Frequently he

253

would be missing from camp for days, and twice they were threatened by townspeople when mishaps happened and Rupa was seen only moments before. Over the centuries great myths and superstitions had grown up around the gypsies—often being accused of kidnapping children, of killing and eating the dogs of people who had wronged them, and of inflicting curses. So the gypsies kept to themselves in their camps, leaving only when they went together into towns to buy what they needed or to fairs and weddings to earn a bit of money selling their wares or telling fortunes.

Rupa was an expert horseman, working as one with his animal, able to command him with only a slight movement of his legs or feet. He was also a well-known fiddler and was often invited to play at festivities, while Zena read fortunes. There was a magic in his fiddle—whether plaintive melodies in a minor key, which moved one to tears, or gay rousing rhythms that made people want to dance.

Zena, the Bibi, had watched her brother staring fixedly at the young girl in the carriage and felt a foreboding. As if by second nature, she shuffled her tarot cards as she went back to her wagon, and there dealt out the grand star formation. Her long bony fingers laden with gold rings, some set with rubies, touched the cards, drawing from them some kind of message. There was the Emperor card, a sign of power and nobility, with the Ten of Cups next to it signifying a good marriage, but too closely followed by the Ten of Wands, portending difficulties and emotional disturbances. Her eyes moved to the card picturing a man walking with eight cups, predicting a marriage with a fair woman, but the moon was gazing down, and the card lying next to it, depicting the moon shining on the water with beasts rising from the sea, portended—disillusionment—peril. She slapped down the Eight of Pentacles, signifying a young man, a worker, and the Wand's card, the Knight, a warning of alienation, loneliness, and loss of roots; and the Eight of Wands, domestic disputes. Her fingers moved along the cards, the Ace of Swords, what would it mean to these people? It could either be great misery or great prosperity in the future. The next two cards troubled her as they came together and she never liked seeing them in this order. The Magician came up next, with his great potential to accumulate vast amounts of knowledge and to use it in a beneficial way, but oh, never to be trusted completely; and his friend the Fool, his head held high lost in the clouds, lips pursed as though he were whistling, walking toward the edge of the cliff certain to fall off, impulsive, foolish, heedless. She was relieved to see the King of Pentacles, the dark man, influential head of his group, who could perhaps save them all.

Amanda shivered as she moved closer to Jamie. "I don't like them. They give me the chills. They are so strange, living in wagons, moving about all the time. I don't like their being here." They reminded her of the old voodoo lady on their plantation on St. Helena. A black woman, an outcast, who even frightened and controlled the hands. She was said to have magic powers and could conjure up the devil. With a look, it was said, she could change your fate. Her cackle was shrill, and as a child, Amanda would walk miles out of her way to avoid coming in contact with the hag. Vanessa used to challenge her powers by walking past her, head held high and even blurting out, "Hello, have a good day." Nothing awful had ever happened to Vanessa, but still Amanda didn't feel it was wise to tempt fate.

Jamie enjoyed her pout and vulnerability. He could tell she was nervous and shaken. He slipped his arm through hers, patting her hand.

"There's nothing to fear, Amanda—they are really not a bad people and very dignified in their way. For centuries they have been maligned unfairly. I shall invite them to the house to entertain our guests when they all arrive."

Amanda continued to be unnerved until the carriage rounded a long inclining turn in the road and then passed through two, tall columns adorned with fierce stone lions rising on their hindquarters. The roadway narrowed slightly, and they were immediately in a sumptuous parklike area. As the carriage slowed to allow some peacocks to pass, Jamie told them the grounds were designed by the famous "Capability" Brown, considered by all to be the master designer of parklands for the most famous estates in the country. He then went on about the house—it was six centuries old and had always been in his family. Each head, as the title was passed on, added to it, the last addition was the Georgian front constructed two centuries before. Suddenly, there, straight before them, stood Ashby Manor.

The facade of red brickwork, with stone dressing, was broken only by the six great stone columns that formed the entranceway. The columns reminded Amanda of southern mansions back home, but none of course built on such a majestic scale.

The estate manager, the steward, the gillie (the guide attending to all the hunting and fishing), and Miss Shields were at the entranceway, along with a few local well-wishers. Miss Shields was cool, stiffly formal, in her welcome to the McIvers but overly pandering to Jamie, hoping to make up for the dissonance in their relationship of late.

Amanda was very pleased when she looked down the line of greeters to see the smiling face of a young woman obviously not a servant, who appeared to be about her own age. She could tell right away that they would get on. This very fair-skinned, red-haired young woman was Emma Jenkins, the daughter of the vicar, the Reverend Philip Jenkins. In addition to his church duties, her father ran a school for the local town children, and Emma assisted him in his teaching.

Suddenly realizing how exhausted she was from the day, Amanda was appreciative that Miss Shields had arranged for supper to be brought to their rooms, and she so informed the housekeeper who was startled by the compliment. Jamie promised her he would take her on a tour of the manor first thing in the morning. As she climbed the winding oak stairway, she could barely breathe from the excitement of knowing this would soon be all hers, she would be the chatelaine of this grand house.

25

The sound of the wood being brought through the halls for the fireplaces at five-thirty in the morning woke Amanda from her heavy sleep, but the darkness was still at the windows and the coldness of the room made her snuggle down in her bed euphorically. Peony whimpered at the disturbance, resettling herself on the pillow closer to her mistress. In her slightly awakened state, she had a difficult time separating dreams from reality. She felt like a princess, and in just two week's time she would start living the life of one as Lady Hatfield—countess being more proper as Jamie was an earl.

When she saw this room for the first time the previous night, the Pagoda Room she learned it was called, she disliked the decor intensely, partly because the style was so foreign to her and partly because it was the last room Jamie's late wife had decorated. Miss Shields made sure she was aware of that when she came in to turn down her bed herself. His wife had loved decorating, and Miss Shields told her smugly she particularly liked giving a theme to each room. This bedroom was well named with its Chinese wallpaper of lovely scenes—Chinese pagodas on ponds surrounded with beautiful flowers and birds, all done in muted golds and peacock blues. The red-laquered chinoiserie bed had exquisite silk hangings embroidered in gold thread. She had seen a few Chinese pieces before, but never an entire room done like this. It made her feel as though she were on an exotic journey, transported from her previous life into a magical kingdom, where nothing could tarnish her joy.

Shortly after nine-thirty unable to contain herself, she

bounded into Jamie's study insisting he take her immediately on the promised tour of Ashby Manor. They started
in the Great Entrance Hall which extended from the front
to the rear of the house and was several stories high.
From there they moved to the Long Gallery, with its fine
paneling and mullioned windows, lined with centuries of
family portraits, some painted by Gainsborough and Van
Dyck.

The library held thousands of richly tooled books and
only its egg- and tongue-molded ceiling distracted the eye
from the rich collection. There was a librarian in charge—
a small slip of a man with watery eyes and a long hawk
nose. He bowed low when he was introduced to Amanda
and told her he hoped to learn her preferences in books as
soon as possible to keep her well supplied for her reading
enjoyment. The balcony that ran around the double-height
room was done in wrought iron by Tijou, famous throughout the continent for his delicate work.

Amanda squealed with delight on seeing the music
room, and she couldn't wait until Vanessa saw it. The
walls were decorated with trompe l'oeil musical instruments and a lovely Flemish triptych hung in one corner.
Jamie pretended fear as Amanda marched before him
with the breastwork of a Spanish sailor taken from the
Armory Room. It was part of the booty saved from a
sunken armada. He was having as much fun as she, showing her her future home. Everywhere there were Italian
marble fireplaces, each different, each beautiful; tapestries
from Russia, priceless objets d'art from the Gobelin fac-
tories, and furniture rich in Aubusson coverings. Finally,
they came back to the Great Hall, the focal point of all
the centuries of Hatfields who had occupied the manor.

A footman appeared at the door and announced that
Miss Jenkins was waiting for Miss McIver.

"Oh, I almost forgot, Jamie. I invited her to come by—
I thought it would be fun to get to know her, she's so close
to my age."

"Emma's a fine girl and will make you a wonderful
friend. There is much more to see, but you've seen the
important parts—and there will be a great deal of time to
explore the rest."

Emma was waiting for them in a smaller reception
room. "Good morning, Lord Hatfield."

"Emma, I think it would be very good of you if you show Amanda the grounds. You probably know the gardens and park as well as anyone at Ashby Manor. Make sure that Amanda doesn't miss one branch or bird."

A petite girl, still retaining what one would call baby fat, she blushed slightly, having been caught so often hiding behind bushes watching the hunting parties, the picnics and festivities of the house, but she was all smiles as she said earnestly, "I would be delighted."

Jamie kissed Amanda on the cheek and saw them off, two young girls running and giggling, already fast friends.

He recalled the tea he had with Queen Victoria. She had invited him to her favorite blue room at Windsor Castle, explaining it was cozier, but he knew she also wanted their discussions to be private. At first she was all disapproval, but for the first time in their relationship, as statesman and queen and, most assuredly she informed her, as friends, he spoke from personal feelings—his emotional needs—the necessity for an heir—even using romantically, the wanting to hear the sounds of pattering feet. All this she understood, but couldn't understand why he didn't choose an Englishwoman. But then, her head bobbing under her widow's cap, she gave her sanction, although Jamie knew Amanda would never be totally accepted at the palace. He turned and saw Martin, who was never far behind, but Jamie was pleased, quite positive, he hadn't had any kind of an attack the last few days. As a matter of fact, he hadn't felt this young in years, hardly being able to contain himself until the wedding night. He saw Sara Shields watching the girls and knew what she was thinking—the future lady of the manor frolicking about for all to see, having no sense of decorum. Well, Sara Shields be damned, he thought. The poor girl was entitled to some freedom after the years she spent so displaced and constricted. The rules of society befitting her station would come later.

Amanda and Emma ran through the gardens until they came to a tunnel created by yew trees. When they reached the center, Emma excitedly began to tell her her memories of this great estate.

"As a little girl I used to glide through here, pretending I was a bride and these were my soldiers, my protectors, swords raised over my head, leading me to my prince. Oh,

Amanda, you are the luckiest girl in the world. Lord Hatfield is so grand." Part of her ease with Amanda was the knowledge that she did not come from wealth.

"Why Emma, I think you are stuck on Jamie."

She was embarrassed, but blurted out, "Why everyone is, Amanda. He's powerful and rich and all the girls in town always dreamed someday of catching his eye." Then she remembered that this young American with whom she felt immediate rapport was not really her equal and perhaps she had overstepped her bounds. "Oh, forgive me, I've spoken out of turn. I am sorry."

Amanda looked cross for a second, then smiled, "I'm pleased to hear that Jamie is so popular. Can we get a horse and cart so we can ride through the park land?"

Relieved, Emma was her exuberant self again. "Of course, the stables are over yon."

The grooms attached a small chestnut mare to a two-seater and they rode off. Wildlife abounded everywhere, guinea fowl strutted about, deer, all sorts of beautiful pheasants, and on a large pond swans floated gracefully.

At the top of a knoll they paused, and Amanda looked back at the house. She was delighted that although it was massive, it didn't look austere and forbidding, and when inside she felt a quiet, unhurried mood, not aware as yet that the smooth running of the household by the experienced staff made it so.

As they rode further they came upon the Hatfield cemetery. Two graves caught her attention—they had headstones of large angels similar in stance, a great sadness chiseled on their faces. It gave her the chills thinking that someday she would be laid to rest there—the third Lady Hatfield. All of a sudden the loneliness of being in a strange land gripped her as it had a few times in the recent past. "Tell me about them and about this house."

"Oh, I shouldn't, Amanda—that's for his lordship to do."

"Please, please, Emma, I feel so strange here—it's all so overwhelming. I want to fit in and yet I know it will take time, and I have so much to learn. You can be a friend and help me."

"I don't remember much about the first Lady Hatfield, but the second one was very energetic—not very beautiful but she was regal, and Lord Hatfield adored her, as did his sister. Her skin was so pale and her bright red hair gleamed like a new copper penny. Lady Hatfield gave the most elegant parties, very proper, but still lively, with many exciting guests. I was allowed to come to some of them when my father was invited. I would always end up sound alseep and being carried to our carriage."

"And Jamie, Lord Hatfield, what of him?"

"His lordship is such an important man—yet moves among the people like one of them. He's done many great things for England. They say the queen is his close ally, and he could someday be prime minister. A great gloom hung over the village when Lady Hatfield died. They say she had a brain on her and was a great aid to him in politics. We were all lifted to hear he was to have a new wife. The manor would become gay again—you know the life there is the center of our village, and when it is gloomy so are we."

Although the mention of the virtues of the late Lady Hatfield caused her pangs of jealousy, Amanda was delighted to hear that she had made such a difference in so many people's lives and especially Jamie's.

They entered a small pine grove letting the horse have its head, and they both heard the plaintive melody being played on a fiddle.

"Oh, Amanda, come—let's ride through the gypsy camp."

"No, I won't." She was immediately afraid. The music had suddenly stopped and there was a strange hush in the woods.

"Oh, come, Amanda, they won't bite. We'll just ride around the edge. They come every year—they're harmless."

"I don't care what you say. I am not interested in meeting up with them. If you wish, you go on and I'll wait here." She stepped down from the cart.

Emma didn't quite know what to do, but she was anxious to see the camp and possibly get some baskets she and her father needed.

Amanda stood in the grove watching Emma go off with no timidity whatsoever, envying her lack of superstition. She decided to walk a bit to keep her feet from freezing. Time seemed to drag as she waited, walking first this way and then circling back. As she rounded a large pine she saw him.

He was sitting astride a tall horse, like a statue, chin held high, his large nostrils flaring like his horse's—the dark eyes staring at her, holding her transfixed. She had never seen a man so strangely beautiful and yet so terrifying.

"Don't you want your fortune told, Lady Hatfield?"

She was shaken by his boldness and his knowledge of her. "I am not Lady Hatfield . . . yet."

He laughed, enjoying her disoriented moment.

"I don't like fortunes and in any case I know what the near future holds for me, and that's all I'm interested in."

"The Bibi's cards can be very interesting. They can show you all the loves and heartaches your life will bring and the ways to deal with them." His voice was deep, smooth as silk—seductive.

He got down from his horse and stood next to her—his strong muscles strained against the fabric of his open-necked shirt and trousers. He wore no jacket in the cold, raw morning, yet showed no sign of being chilled.

"My name is Rupa. Let me help you onto this nice high rock so you can rest while you wait for your friend to return." Before she knew what was happening, he picked her up—held her close to him for a second and placed her on the flat surface. In the distance she saw Emma approaching. Without a goodbye she scrambled off and made a dash for the cart—his laughter rang in her ears as they rode off. Emma was excited—the bearer of portentous news.

"Amanda, the old queen said you must come to have your cards read. It's very important. Was that Rupa you met? Isn't he dashing and handsome? Wait until you see him ride. He does all kinds of tricks on his horse and they say when he plays a sad tune on his fiddle, he can make you cry. The young girls are just mad for him and secretly wish he would charge in and carry them off."

Amanda realized she was still trembling. She didn't like the strangeness of all this and decided to ask Jamie not to invite the gypsies to the manor. She had had enough, having been properly terrified by Rupa.

26

During Vanessa's time abroad, Pierre had set about trying to locate a place to live in town. He considered himself lucky in immediately finding a small house in the southern end of Chelsea, a stone's throw from the Thames. From the parlor there was a view of the river and a covey of houseboats. The house had been unoccupied, so he moved in right away, working day and night to get it in shape. Early mornings and evenings the walkways along the river were usually uncrowded, so he enjoyed long strolls along the embankment watching the swift currents bearing a great variety of water traffic. Like Ashcroft, he felt more at home in this section of London than in any other.

The cottage had once housed several well-known painters, and off the low-roofed dining room was a studio almost two stories high, with a large skylight. It was this room that pleased him the most, with its tall ceilings and large windows that overlooked a small garden. With the aid of Ashcroft he had secured a loan from a bank, giving as collateral his future inheritance. In April he would come into the bulk of his father's estate and would then be a very rich man.

After living in the house only a week, he felt he would eventually like to own it, feeling content in this place. Pierre had no taste for social life, especially the Prince of Wales' Marlborough set, so the cottage would suit him fine no matter what his monetary status. He had it whitewashed inside and out, and the broad plank flooring stained a dark umber. He purchased several oriental rugs for the studio room and filled the whole house with plants and flowers. Ashcroft lent him several outstanding paintings until he secured his own. The house took on a charming air very quickly.

Hoping it would be used by Vanessa in the future, he splurged on a small ebony concert piano, which he placed in the studio surrounding it with tall palms. Across from the piano was a large walk-in fireplace and when lit, it radiated warmth throughout the room. At the far end he had installed a greenhouse, purchasing it complete and then having it transported and attached. Carefully, he and his Indian servant moved some of his roses to the new greenhouse, and he was in the process of tending them, helping them over the trauma of being transplanted to a new environment.

Harriet came to visit him a few days after he settled in. She walked through the rooms, a short train of material from the bustle drape sweeping the floor majestically. A small hat was perched on the top of her graying hair, with a stiff nose veil protruding. She still gave the appearance of arrogance. He had also been told that about himself many times—a family characteristic.

Again, he was surprised at how fragile she had become. The flesh on her once full face sagged, forming hanging jowls. He asked about her health, concerned about her extreme weight loss, and she informed him that her doctor back home had put her on a strenuous diet. Also, he must be aware of the many anxieties she suffered during the past years. Besides, she no longer had any appetite. Pierre also told her that many people had the same anxieties and worse sufferings. Mother and son had the same deep-set dark eyes. He thought as he studied her face that his mother must have been a beautiful woman. What a shame she never remarried. Cordially, he led her into the studio and lit a fire to offset the chill of the day. The gray sky on view through the skylight looked like it would open up any minute. He sat next to her and in a surprise gesture, he took both her hands in his. She shook at the touch.

"You will stay on for Christmas? I plan to put a big tree here in the studio—Sir Robert has already accepted my invitation and there might be others. You could help me plan the day."

"I have booked passage for next week, planning to spend a lonely Christmas on the high seas."

"Well, change your booking and spend not a lonely Christmas, but a happy one with me here in London."

"Are you sure you want me? After all those years of silence, I thought you wanted to get rid of me."

He took one of his hands away and placed his slender index finger on her lips to hush her. "Let us have a new beginning. Let the misunderstandings of the past lie buried where they belong. We were both at fault in our relationship."

The moment was too strong for her, she rose and moved slowly about the room. She so loved her son and now this display of kindness, the first she ever had known since he was a small boy had shaken her. She hadn't expected it.

"Why didn't you get a grander place? I could have lent you the money?" After the words were out she could have bitten her tongue—old habits were hard to break.

"It suits me."

"A Bonneau should have a place in Mayfair, Berkley Square, Belgravia—"

"This Bonneau prefers Chelsea. Come, I'll show you my greenhouse, it was attached only a few days ago." He in no way wanted to become ensnared in an argument with his mother (as in the past) due to her domineering personality and his rebellion toward it. His enslavement was over, and he felt he was ready to come to a new understanding with her on a positive basis—if only she would allow it to happen.

He showed her the glass structure.

"You must visit the house in Dover; there I have many greenhouses—here I have only this one for my special experiments."

She was very impressed, this was something she understood and admired. Her specially grown cotton came from the many years of experimenting on her husband's part and then hers, with various specialists brought to the plantation on St. Helena to test the soil and seeds. She told him how taken she was as she walked down the aisle looking at the beautiful roses.

Pierre pointed out a group of hybrid tea roses. "This strain took a long time to develop to get just the right blend of light pink petals with the pale gold center. I've named it 'Vanessa's music.'"

"So, it is still Vanessa."

"Yes and for always."

"Then why did you divorce her?"

Her tone was of one who was curious, not accusatory.

"To give her a chance at life—I was destroying her in a way, enslaving her. I turned around and did the same thing to someone else—someone I loved."

Harriet knew he was also inferring other things with that remark. She had been doing a great deal of thinking of late.

"The McIvers want to borrow more money. The house on the plantation had been almost totally destroyed during the Union's occupation. Kenneth and Thomas have reconstructed part of it, but half the house still has no roof. They have spent most of their time cultivating a small section of the land to bring in money."

"Give it to them. Whatever they need to make it their proud home once again. You are a rich woman."

"Rich or not, I have to make sure it will be put to good use—too much at once in some hands can be very destructive."

"Learn to give with grace, my mother—why do you keep wanting them to beg for it?"

She loved her son very dearly and suddenly she was aware of so many mistakes she had made—foolish mistakes from hatred inside her due to loneliness, a loneliness she had brought on herself. Embarrassed, she walked a little further and saw the yellow roses.

"These are exquisite, Pierre."

"They will be some day. Like every rose fancier, I am trying to grow the perfect yellow rose and when I do, I will name it after my son."

She looked at him startled, "You have a son?" Her heart started to quicken.

"I have only recently been told that Vanessa and I conceived a child."

"Where? Where is the child?"

"The child is dead; she aborted when Wind Flower was set afire."

She moved closer to him and placed her hand on his arm affectionately, "I am so sorry, my son. There is a small unmarked grave at Wind Flower. Now I know to whom it

belongs. When I return, I shall have a proper stone made
for it."

"Thank you. Mother."

"What was the baby's name?"

"I don't know. When I find out I shall let you know."

"Does Vanessa know you served in the Confederate
Army?"

"No. When the time comes, if it is something she
should know, she will be told."

"I will delay my trip back home. Pierre, and we will plan
a lovely Christmas together. Thank you for asking me.
One day you should return and restore Wind Flower."

"Perhaps one day I shall."

A few days later while working on his roses, he was
told that the person he was watching for, a few streets
away, must have returned as there was music being played
in the house.

The young Indian girl watched him intently, knowing
the news would please him.

"Geeta, you will take a note and wait for an answer."
He quickly put down his pruning shears and went into
the studio room to the tall Chinese Chippendale secretary
he had just bought at an auction and wrote a note to
Vanessa asking her to tea the next afternoon.

That evening he and Sir Robert were going to the opera.
He wondered if she would like to join them, then reasoned
she would have just returned and be tired from her journey. He would have to hold himself in check for another
night.

JoJo answered the door and informed the young Indian girl that her mistress was practicing and could not
be disturbed. The sound of the music filled the house as
well as the street, and the girl bowed and said she would
come back for an answer the next day.

In the morning she was told that Miss McIver could not
accept the invitation that day—she was going to be with
Madame Dworski at the conservatory all day.

Pierre accepted the message glumly—stewing about it
for over an hour. Then he donned his cloak and cap and
rushed over to the house only to find that no one was at
home.

It was Saturday evening—Christmas and the wedding were just a week away. His parents had only left the day before for Hatfield's country estate, and he thought with them out of his hair, he would enjoy his freedom, but he was feeling out of sorts. It was hell being nineteen with no money.

Josiah snapped the book closed; he couldn't concentrate anyway. In an hour's time he was due at Daphne's. He would have to get rid of her, she shouldn't have come to the house on Belgrave Square the other night, but he was sorely in need of her companionship.

Vanessa was practicing, and JoJo was off visiting Sillar, so there was no one to talk to. Most of his chums from school were off on holiday on the continent or at their family's estate in the country. He had wanted to go with Binkie on his trip to Switzerland, coming back in time for the wedding, but there was no way to get the money. It was one thing to go to Oxford, but another not to be able to keep up socially with his schoolmates due to lack of funds, having to constantly use one excuse after another to bow out of events and excursions. Lately, very few invitations had come his way because he had turned down his friends so often. His father had managed to pay for Oxford and the bare essentials, but how was he going to pay for the next few years if his father refused because he wanted him home. Recently he had come to the decision that when and if he finished at Oxford in two years time, he would like to read law. Hoping that the firm where Judah Benjamin worked would consider him, he was sure with his family pull (especially Uncle Thomas', who had done so much for the Confederacy in Charleston, training troops and carrying important messages to various people during the war), Benjamin would help him. He had discussed it briefly with Vanessa the night before, and she asked him if he didn't feel he would be better off back home where he wouldn't be caught in two worlds like he the life over here and felt like his mother that things were was now. No. He wanted to stay in England. He liked finally coming their way. The marriage between Amanda and Hatfield would put them in a better position, and there was another hope—he was praying that Hatfield would help him out financially, but it was too early to mention that to Amanda who was much concerned for herself at this time.

The rain was coming down, but he decided to start off for Daphne's; it would take him some time getting there. After putting on his rain cloak and hat and finding an old umbrella, he went to the room where Vanessa was practicing—Liszt's Concerto No. 1 in E flat major; she had been playing it over and over all day, so he knew what it was—it was the piece she would play at the concert in Berlin that summer as well as in Budapest and Warsaw after that. Sasha had sent her a wire that morning informing her of the new engagement. She would be famous soon, and he was pleased for her but still depressed about his own future. He watched her for a moment. "Golden fingers" the review from Brussels had said, "a gift from the heavens."

"Vanessa," he said loud enough to be heard over her music, "I'm going out for the evening. I don't know what time I'll be back."

She ran to him and ruffled his hair, "Where are you going? Don't you want to have supper together?"

"No. I'm going to visit a school chum," he lied, "and we are going to a pub for a bite to eat."

"Well, don't stay out too late. The streets of London are rough in the wee hours."

"Ah, Vanessa. You keep treating me like a child."

She kissed him on the forehead. "I'm sorry. You have a good time, but be careful. I'll be home for the evening."

In a way he was now sorry he was going. He suddenly didn't feel like having Daphne tonight, but he was so alone. Lately in his mind she had become dirty, unpleasant. He would try to tell her tonight that he would not see her again, using some excuse perhaps that he was going away. He hoped she wouldn't check at Hatfield's. It was getting to be such a bother, he would have to think of something. She had been almost threatening the other night.

Daphne sat on the lumpy bed watching Mack walk up and down the small garret, growling like an angry bear.

He had been drinking ale most of the day, and she was becoming increasingly frightened. Her face was still bruised from the beating he had given her the week before, and she had hunger pangs, not having eaten since early the day before. She was in her fifth month of pregnancy, and whereas before she looked like she was just getting plump, now the protrusion of her belly told the truth. She had not worked that week; Mack was supposed to have given her some money, but from his state, she knew he must have spent what wages he did receive on drink. The blond hair tumbled down her swollen face, and she felt ugly and unwanted. Mack grabbed her hair and pulled it, his thick cockney voice was hoarse from drink.

"You look like a pig. Do you know that?"

"Don't pick on me, Mack. I don't feel so good."

"You sure your young swell promised to be here tonight?"

"That's what he said when I went to that house."

"What did you tell him?"

"Just what you told me to, Mack."

"Go fix yourself so you look decent. You don't want him to run soon as he sees you."

He kicked a chair across the room. It hit the wall and splintered. "Soon as I get my hands on him, he'll cry for mercy."

"You're not going to hurt him. You said you would just get money from him. He's only a lad."

"He's older than you."

"You know what I mean."

"He's got to pay. Then we can get some place decent to live."

"Can you wait till he takes me to supper? I'm awfully hungry and the baby is growling in me belly."

He struck her, and she fell back on the bed.

"Always wanting food—you're so fat—best you don't eat."

She was crying, curled up in a ball.

"Please, Mack. The baby. I need nourishment for the baby."

"It's almost time. I'll wait in the hall in case he comes early. You fix yourself up. And wash yourself. You stink."

He slammed the door as he went out, and she slowly

picked herself up off the bed and stared at her image in the cracked mirror over the basin. A young puffy black and blue face stared back at her. She was a mess. She tried to straighten her hair and applied a cold cloth to her face—then yanked at her curls to cover her bruises and rouged her cheeks and lips. Washing her body as best she could with the cold water, she thought she should have gotten rid of the baby when she first learned about it. What kind of life would the child have? Mack had become so ugly lately, drinking heavily. Fleetingly she thought she should warn Josiah not to come; something inside her told her there would be a fight and Mack was such a savage bull, Josiah might get hurt. It was all too much for her; she sank into the ragged armchair and waited, wanting to stop what she knew in her heart was about to take place, but she didn't have the strength to do it.

Daphne heard him coming up the stairs. She wondered where Mack was hiding. Again she had the conviction that something dreadful was about to happen. What else had her life been but one bad thing after another? It seemed to her she was born under a bad star; it never occurred to her that to some degree she could control her destiny. She didn't want Josiah hurt, but she also would do nothing to stop it.

He tapped on the door and pushed the warped door open. "Daphne?"

The gaslight was low, and he barely saw her in the semidarkness.

"Hey. Are you all right?"

The voice was fluttery, "Right as rain, ducky," then with great effort, "How are you, luv?"

Mack bounded into the room and grabbed him by the collar and raised him off the ground.

"This the one, Daph? Is this the bloke that knocked you up?"

Josiah was stunned. "What's going on here?"

Mack smacked him in the mouth, and Josiah's head reeled from the blow.

Daphne rushed to Mack and tugged at him desperately, "Don't hurt him, Mack. Remember the baby."

The big man was breathing heavily, dancing Josiah around the room as he shook him roughly from side to side completely out of control.

"Is this 'im, is it?"

Frightened, Daphne screamed, "Yes, that's him."

Josiah was scared; the man was a huge brute and could easily snap him in two. "Let me out of here, please."

"You know you made her pregnant? The little lady is big with your child."

"What are you talking about? I've only known her two months."

"You gotta make it good. The girl needs money to take care of the babe."

Using all his might, Josiah broke his hold and pushed Mack, who hit the wall and bounced back at him. His fury now knew no bounds.

"You sonofabitch!" He swung with all his power. Josiah was lifted off his feet. Daphne screamed and screamed as Josiah went down hitting the floor hard. He didn't move. Mack, swaying in his drunkenness, hovered over him.

"Come on you bastard. Get up so I can knock you down again."

"No, Mack, let him be. Just let's get the money." She knelt over the still body on the floor. "Oh, my Gawd. Oh, my Gawd, I think he's dead."

Mack panicked, "Are you sure? Dead?"

She rocked back and forth wailing, "Oh, my Gawd."

"Holy Christ, I gotta get out of here." He bent over the body and started to go through his pockets.

"What are you doing?"

"Seeing what he's got on him." Finding the wallet he emptied the contents. "What a cheap bastard—almost nothing." He threw it at Josiah and started for the door.

"Where are you going? You can't leave me with the body."

He was at the door and did not turn. He was hell bent on getting out of there. "Take my advice and get your arse outta here. You don't want to be caught with no corpse."

"But it's my place. They'll come looking for me."

He slammed the door. She ran after him yelling as he sped down the crooked stairs.

"Come back! You can't leave me with him."

She looked around aware of what she was saying, but there was no one in the hall. She went back to the room, shut the door and did a wide circle around the motionless form. It was then she noticed the breathing.

"You're alive—thank Gawd you didn't die on me." She bent over him and shook his head roughly—his eyes fluttered.

"Come on, wake up—you can't just lay there."

He was still again, and her relief went back to panic. She started to wail once more as she rocked back and forth on her heels.

"Don't die on me. I didn't do nothing. It was Mack that did it. Come on, luv, wake up and get out of here. He might come back and finish you off."

Josiah tried to raise his head. He opened his eyes partially, trying to understand the reality of the situation.

"Wwwwa—llet . . ."

"Empty, Mack went off with your money."

"Wallet," he slurred again.

She grabbed it from the spot where Mack threw it and showed him the pocket. "See, empty—there's nothing—I didn't do it. I didn't take your money."

"Vanessa . . ."

"It's me, Daphne. Not Vanessa."

"No. His voice was weak, but he was trying to make her understand. "Go—for Vanessa."

"I can't. I don't know no Vanessa."

"Wallet. Address," and he trailed off into blackness again.

"Don't do that. Wake up. I don't know what to do with no dead body."

"Vanessa."

She stared at the brown leather wallet in her hand and saw writing on a card in one of the pockets. Her reading was very poor, but she made out his address in Chelsea. "Is this where you live? Is this where Vanessa is?" His eyes fluttered, and she shook him to get an answer. "Oh, my Gawd, you look dead again. Wake up!" She studied the address, grabbed her shawl and went out into the rain to get help. She didn't reason, she just went, yelling for a hansom cab in the deserted streets. She ran all the way to Oxford Street and saw someone getting out. The cabby questioned her and she roughly got in and gave the address saying not to worry about his money, he'll get paid.

Vanessa was still alone when Daphne pounded on the

door and went with her immediately, horrified by the news
and the appearance of the bearer. The poor creature
rambled on and on, exonerating herself of any blame.
When they got to the broken-down tenement, Vanessa gave
Daphne money and told her to continue on to Guy's Hospital to find Dr. Kirk Yoors and bring him to Josiah. She
didn't want to waste any time because it sounded so bad.
The cab went off into the wet night and she stumbled up
the stairs to the room, finding it almost impossible to
fathom what was happening and the surroundings completely baffling her.

She found Josiah sitting up on the floor, slightly dazed
but in better shape than when Daphne had left. She told
him to sit quietly as she had sent for Kirk who would take
him to the hospital to see if he was all right. She was appalled as she looked around the room but didn't say
anything. She could find out the details when they were
out of there—he was dizzy and she hoped he was not
seriously injured. He looked so young and scared. He wanted to get off the dirty floor. She led him to the broken
chair.

"Sit still—try not to move until we find out the extent
of the injury."

She went to close the door and gasped when she saw
him there. His large body filling the frame.

"Who are you?" he asked as he lunged into the room.
Mack had had a few more drinks with the paltry money
he had taken from Josiah and was weaving as he tried to
pin her to the wall with his body.

Josiah tried to rise but fell back into the chair. "Be
careful, Vanessa, he's the one who hit me."

"So, you're not dead. I'll do a better job next time."

Vanessa tried to squeeze around him, but he grabbed
her roughly by the arm.

"Where are you going? I ain't finished with the swell
yet. He's got to give me some money for what's he's done."

"I didn't, Vanessa. He's trying to get money out of me."

Mack turned angrily and went for Josiah. Vanessa was
after him. "You're gonna pay, you bastard."

Josiah cowered back into the chair. "I don't have any
money. I'm not rich."

Vanessa pulled on the big shoulders as Mack grabbed
Josiah out of the chair.

"Leave him be, he's hurt." She beat on the broad back, but he was anesthetized from the alcohol. "Don't touch him. I have help coming," she screamed.

He turned at the words and grabbed her by the neck.

"What are you doing here?" He looked at her, taking stock—her face and manner suggested class, but the cloak she was wearing and the rest of her attire was well worn. His fingers tightened around her neck, and she started to gasp for breath.

"How did you get here? Answer me or I'll squeeze the life out of you."

Josiah was struggling to his feet. Waves of dizziness kept coming over him. He knew Vanessa could be snuffed out by this brute in a matter of minutes. "Vanessa, try to run away—run."

"Listen to the nob. No one gets away from me."

Josiah grabbed a bottle from the nearby table and feebly struck Mack across the back of his head. It was enough to make him let go of Vanessa's neck, but he grabbed her arm firmly in his big powerful hand while he got the bottle away from Josiah. The grip as he pulled her along, hurt, and Vanessa struggled to get out of his grasp.

"My arm, you're breaking my arm!" she moaned.

The brute tightened his hold. "You're liable to get two broken arms if you don't stay still and answer my questions."

He looked at her horror-stricken face twisted with pain.

"I have to get money. You understand?" Her head shook up and down. "You related to this nob?" She shook her head again, the smell of his breath and the pain he was inflicting was making her faint. Josiah stumbled to them again.

"Leave her be. Don't hurt her arm—you mustn't hurt her, she is a musician—I'll get you money if I can."

Mack growled at him, twisting her arm further, realizing in his drunken stupor he would get more out of them by hurting the girl. "You can get some money? I want a lot."

Vanessa's arm was becoming numb, the hold was so painful. He was completely irrational and Josiah, too weak to fight, had to make promises.

"I'll get you a lot. Just let her be."

"Go get it fast, and I'll hold on to her 'til you get back."

"No. I won't leave her here with you."

He twisted Vanessa's arm more, a piercing scream tore the air, she was in utter agony.

"Go, Josiah. Go . . . get out of here."

"I can't leave you, Nessa."

"Go get the money, you bloody bastard. I'll kill her if you ain't back in the hour."

There was noise on the stairs—Vanessa strained to hear. "They've come. The help I sent for has come."

Mack grew frightened, but did not leave go of her arm. "Who did you send for? Is it the bobbies?"

Vanessa knew Kirk could not be there that soon, but whoever it was was still climbing the stairs. In an instant, Mack flipped her arm and the crack was heard across the room. The arm hung limply at her side as she looked at it in a dazed fashion, unbelievingly. Mack bounded out of the room and up the short flight of stairs leading to the roof.

"My arm, he's broken my arm," she whimpered as Josiah staggered toward her, crying.

"Oh, Vanessa, your music. I'm so sorry."

They were startled further by a crash—it sounded like Mack's body breaking the stair railing. They listened fearfully for a few seconds, but there was complete silence. The person they heard on the stairs before was no more, probably someone who lived below. They sank to the floor slowly, Vanessa's arm below the elbow hanging by her side like a torn rag. I'll never play again, she thought.

She held Josiah's head in her lap; he had passed out again. Her body started to convulse, she was going into shock. Time passed—there was not much pain in her arm, but it was turning a deep purple. Shivers came, her teeth were chattering—her arm was gone; there would be no more music. What would she do? She stroked her brother's head—where was help? It seemed an eternity. She was still wearing her cloak though it was hanging twisted from her body. The threadbare cloak—one that prompted a man to give her a sable cape and another just now to become violent. Whatever had Josiah gotten into—poor boy—caught like a spider in a web. He just didn't know where he belonged. She heard a door open in the next apartment. Whoever it was, looked in briefly and hurried away not wanting to get involved in any trouble.

There were quick, running steps on the stairs. Voices. One was Kirk's, asking directions from the girl she had sent to fetch him and then he was in the room.

"Oh my God, Vanessa." He was staring at her dangling arm.

There were cries of anguish in the hall from the girl. She ran in—frenzied. "Come quick. It's Mack. I think he's dead."

Kirk got off his knees and ran with her. Vanessa could hear their voices.

"He's dead all right. A broken neck. There's nothing we can do."

The girl started to scream and wail. He came back into the room. Josiah was stirring again. Kirk bent over him and pushed back his eyelids. Vanessa tried to talk to him. It was so good he was there, taking over.

"The ambulance is coming any minute, and we'll get you both to the hospital to take care of you. Don't worry. I'm here."

A few stragglers gathered around the entrance to the tenement building in the damp air, drawn by the possibility of some disaster to be witnessed—moving in closer when an attendant and the driver appeared with a stretcher followed by another. Kirk pushed them aside as he jumped into the wagon to make sure the conveyors were properly secured in the special frames.

Vanessa worried him—she showed the first signs of going into shock—her complexion was pale and as he felt her forehead, there was a slight cold sweat. Rolling his jacket in a ball, he placed it under her feet for elevation to keep her blood circulating properly. He wished he could question one of them to find out what had happened so he would know better how to treat their injuries. Josiah was semiconscious now—he had responded well to stimulus —his reflexes seeming normal, not exaggerated, and his pupils were not dilated, but he was in no shape to talk or be questioned. He rushed out and climbed onto the box in front next to the driver. The horses, sensing the urgency, responded immediately to the crack of the whip and charged toward the hospital. Kirk rang the hand bell and when that wasn't heard above the din of the London traffic, he shouted as loudly as possible at all obstacles in their way to clear passage—at times they drove straight onto the sidewalks to get around traffic blockage in the roadway. Kirk's mind ran through the procedure he would follow once they reached the hospital; he was fighting his own fears because of Vanessa.

Once they reached the hospital, Kirk quickly instructed the attendants to rush her into the operating room and to take Josiah to the emergency room for a more careful examination.

27

JoJo had come back to the house disturbed. She had spent the evening with Sillar who had taken to her bed, suffering from a bad cold she had said, but to JoJo she looked like she was suffering from something in her heart. The weakened Sillar had given her a letter, in secret she told her, to deliver to Mr. McIver as soon as she saw him. JoJo thought she was acting just like a white woman, and when she inquired why Sillar had closed the shop, all she would reply was, "It's Christmas time."

She was further disturbed not to find Vanessa at home, and searched all around for a note. When it got to be ten-thirty, her anxiety could not be denied. Something was very wrong. Running to the hall, she searched the table frantically for Pierre's note to find his address; he would know what to do.

He came immediately when told who was at the door. JoJo was drenched, having run the few blocks in the heavy rain, never bothering to put up her hood, and allowed him to move her blindly into the studio to the blazing warmth of the fire as she spilled out her concern. Together they went to the police station and hours later they were at the hospital, waiting. Josiah they were told had a concussion and was resting—Vanessa was in the operating room.

She lay on the table trying to remove herself mentally from what was happening—to escape the horror that surrounded her. She was afraid if she thought about all that had happened and the momentous change it possibly could make in her life, she would lose control.

The room was large and oppressive—there was an open viewing area with heavy mahogany chairs, several sinks on one wall, and many basins. Five attendants were moving around the immediate space, and she wondered what their responsibilities were. Why were so many needed? This also was very frightening—and nothing like she had imagined an operation to be. Traveling doctors had come to the plantation and had performed surgery—everyone was always told to stay away from the infirmary located in one of the outbuildings near the main house, when an operation was to be performed, but screams could be heard piercing the air, and the subdued conversation that ran through the house for days after told of the seriousness of the treatment. When anyone broke a limb, it was usually removed—amputated—and then quite often fever and death followed. Vanessa looked down at her arm, twisted and dark purple in color. Tears filled her eyes and through her distorted vision she saw Kirk moving knowledgeably about the room. His obvious professionalism and confidence made her begin to gain some control. He went to one of the sinks and began washing his lower arms and hands with soap and water, carefully scrubbing his fingernails as well. A woman in white came to him and poured a douche of a strong-smelling solution over his hands and arms—all of the attendants followed suit. By her side, a tray of instruments was being cleaned with the same liquid, and a reel of heavy thread in a corked bottle filled with a cloudy fluid was placed nearby by another nurse. Were they going to sew up her arm with that black thread on the reel?

The nurse—the same one Vanessa had seen with Kirk that day she came to the hospital—approached him and helped him on with a white smock to cover almost all his clothing. Then she walked to the table and began to wash down Vanessa's arm all around the break and where the bone had punctured the skin on her forearm. She was pleasant and cheery as she held a one-sided conversation with Vanessa trying to make her relax, "Now isn't this a lovely bath, and you'll be draped in all these clean towels soaked in carbolic acid to stop infection. Wait until you see the beautiful needlework Dr. Yoors will do for you. He's quite the master stitcher."

Kirk approached the table, "Vanessa, don't be frightened. Everything will be all right."

"You mean I'll survive?" she asked in a monotone, "but will I live?"—feeling at that moment that without the use of her arm her music was gone. What would there be to live for?

"Yes, you'll live, and we have a very good chance of repairing your arm. So much more can be done these days."

She studied him for a moment and realized how hard he was trying for her sake; beads of perspiration stood out on his face, his deep-blue eyes were clouded with concern. She wanted so to touch him, but he was standing on the side of her useless arm, surrounded by strangers all staring at her. "I trust you, Kirk, and I'm glad you're the one taking care of me. Thank you."

As she looked up at the faded gold-colored ceiling, the nose mask was applied and the chloroform administered. For a brief moment she tried to fight the numbness overpowering her mind—with a great effort she tried to focus her eyes, but then her body relaxed and gave in to this miracle anesthetic that would keep her from suffering the awful pain of the operation.

Kirk moved swiftly—he no longer saw Vanessa in front of him, but instead, a patient lying there waiting to be administered to. He made his first incision, cutting the flesh carefully—his fingers gently probed the opening—two bones in the forearm, looking like a fork, were cleanly broken. He found no bone splinters or foreign objects, and he manipulated the bones into place, then started sewing the incision. As the plaster of paris was applied to the cloth wound around her arm, he breathed more easily—there was more than just hope that she would mend quickly and regain normal use of her arm. It would, of course, require a close watch for infection—the next few days being the most important, and then weeks from now, when the cast was removed and massage begun, only then would he know for certain if she would have full use of her arm.

Kirk walked along side the table being wheeled to the ward where she would be placed, making sure she was put at the end near a window, and her metal bed surrounded with dividers for privacy. She was pale, her face drained of blood, her breathing shallow, but he was optimistic—she had come through the operation beautifully. Too often he saw his patients die of shock on the table. There were so many things that could go wrong. He always felt a great frustration when he lost a patient. There was so much they didn't know, and yet each day something new and exciting was attempted. Now he would have to watch and wait.

As she was placed in her bed she began to come out of the anesthesia. "I'm thirsty," her voice was weak and her words dragged out, her lips hardly able to form the sounds.

Kirk took a clean white towel and poured cold water from a pitcher onto the cloth. "Here, Vanessa, draw some water from this."

After several sucks from the cloth, she immediately lapsed back into oblivion.

Pierre entered the room and sat by her bed, taking her hand in his. He remained there through the night, and JoJo slept in a straight-backed chair outside the divider. Kirk checked on her several times during the long vigil, pleased that she slept soundly and her temperature remained normal. He and Pierre hardly spoke—only a few words about her condition. Toward daybreak she awoke and was conscious that someone was holding her hand.

She smiled feebly at him, "Pierre?"

"I'm here, Vanessa. I'll take care of you."

Her head rolled to the side away from him, and she gasped several breaths at the shock of seeing the heavy, large cast on her arm, and again drifted off.

Kirk, who was standing at the door watching the scene, left distressed by the closeness of Vanessa and Pierre. He had felt after their chance meeting in front of the concert hall and her offering him a ticket to the recital, that fate had brought them together. It was the first time he talked to her as an equal, the first time they were thrown together in a sweet moment—no Civil War, no running, just two people. He again regretted missing the dinner she had planned. But as he watched them—once husband and wife —they were better suited. Pierre could offer her money, comfort, and position. He could only offer her meager surroundings at first, more struggle. His heart ached—she was so lovely even in her illness.

He stopped in the hospital corridor, looking around for a moment at his world, the people who relied on him. He saw Nurse Piercely near the apothecary shop. "Come on, Piercely," he said curtly, "let's make the rounds. Our patients are waiting."

She started off after him. "Kirk, I've been meaning to ask you something, but with your being so busy especially with your friend, I . . ." She slowed down to a walk, trying to find a way to get his full attention and not show her real feelings. Before the McIver woman had reentered his life, he seemed very interested in her and they had been intimate for several months. He never noticed that she had fallen behind, that also was annoying, so she hiked up her long skirt with both hands to avoid it wrapping around her ankles as she rushed to catch up to him. "Kirk," she raised her voice, "will you come to the Christmas party with me?"

He was distant as he responded, "Christmas party?"

"Yes, a few of the nurses thought it would be nice. We all work so hard and so many of us are away from our families, we thought it would be lovely to have a little fun together for a change—it will be on Christmas Eve."

He didn't answer at first, but walked more slowly and then again picked up his pace.

"Kirk?"

"Of course I'll come with you."

28

In the late afternoon Kirk stopped at Vanessa's bed. Pierre had gone and JoJo was still seated in the straight-backed chair.

"Why don't you go home and rest—I'll stay with Vanessa for a bit. She won't be alone."

"Maybe I will, Dr. Yoors, and I'll bring her a fresh nightgown for tonight. That hospital one is sure ugly. Nessa's gonna be all right, isn't she?"

"Don't worry. I'll take very good care of her. Now you go."

The little figure picked up her things and walked wearily down the long corridor.

Kirk touched Vanessa's forehead and was satisfied that her body was continuing to fight off a fever. Then he sat quietly watching her—there were no thoughts in his mind other than looking at her. She was covered with a sheet and a light blanket, her arm weighted heavily with the cast. The light brown hair fell casually about her head, but her face wore a troubled frown, almost a scowl. Her lips moved slightly as though she were conversing with someone in her sleep. He took the hand of her injured arm to see if there was swelling, and then continued to grasp her fingers, working them back and forth. Her eyelids fluttered, her uninjured right hand unencumbered by a cast moved and touched him—quite suddenly she was awake. Kirk let her fingers go.

"Hello, Kirk," she smiled feebly.

"Hello."

There was silence for a bit. "I don't know what day it is."

"You haven't even been here for twenty-four hours yet."

Hesitatingly she began the questioning that inevitably had to come. "When will I know?"

Kirk slowly explained to her the stretch of time ahead, the good indications he already had seen.

She spoke softly, "You know, all the times I had to struggle just to get myself to sit at the piano, wishing I had never seen the instrument. I felt so tied to it and on occasion feeling it was in possession of me. And now—now—I don't know what I'll do without the piano. It was my salvation . . ."

"Don't jump to conclusions. I've told you I expect you to be able to play again. Start wiggling your fingers."

"But my arm is stiff—I can't move them."

"That's the cast and the bruise. Come on, start!"

"No, I don't want to think about it. Pierre suggested I breathe a little first—give myself time—relax and rest. He's right, and he also suggested it might be time to possibly reevaluate a change in direction."

"He's wrong!" His cutting response stung her.

He realized instantly his reaction was too sharp and too direct, unfair for her at this vulnerable time, but he had to follow through, gentling his tone. "I think his judgment is incorrect for you. You've struggled too long with your music. If you are going to throw it aside, do not use your arm as an excuse. Do it because in your heart you don't want it any more."

She stared at him, suddenly angry—he wasn't making sense. She probably didn't even have a choice. Turning her head from him, she wished Pierre would come back to comfort her again. He had been so helpful in making her try to accept the possibility of a life without music, planning the days ahead for her, relieving her of the responsibility of doing it herself.

"Vanessa, I know what it is to struggle, too. We've both worked so hard for what we wanted. Now you'll have to work a bit harder, you'll have to go back over territory already gained and relearn things, but you must not give up. Don't take the easy way out. It's not you."

"You think you know me so well," she shot back, glaring at him.

"You know I do," he responded angrily.

"I never wanted music, not as a career, in the first place."

"Maybe in the beginning, but what about now?"

They looked at each other hard, her bitterness and pique flaring up then receding, Kirk fighting his own rage brought on when she quoted Pierre.

"Come, Vanessa, it's not good for you to get so excited. Relax—you have time for all of this."

He lifted the wrist of her uninjured arm and wrapped his big hand around it to check her pulse, sitting on her bed as he did so—she could feel his warm leg against hers. Vanessa leaned back on the pillow, not wanting to look at his virile, rugged face any more. It was too disturbing to her. She couldn't believe how disturbed she became just looking at him. She heard the divider being drawn over, he was leaving.

"I'll be back to see you soon. Now you start wriggling your fingers." She was furious with him and at herself. Again he riled her, like so many times in the past, like the first meeting they had ever had on the plantation—the day she had lost her way in the fog.

Through the window Vanessa watched the gloomy day turn to night. There were sounds of heavy breathing and restlessness from the other patients in the ward room, and now and again a moan from pain or perhaps despair. She edged her way over on the bed and pushed back the divider, opening up the room to her view—nine beds, a few empty. She watched for a long time—now and then a nurse or doctor would pass by in the gaslit corridor. JoJo had come and gone. Vanessa appreciated her own bed clothing, but made her return to the house in Chelsea to rest, assuring her she was in very capable hands. Hours passed—the quiet was eerie, and she wished she could fall asleep to help pass the time. As Big Ben sounded eleven P.M., she saw a figure approach the room and lean on the doorjamb for support. It was Josiah, and although she was anxious to see for herself that he was all right, she didn't look forward to knowing about the sad young woman and her horrid man who had done this to them. He slowly edged his way down the ward, checking the occupied beds along the way to find her. Quietly she called to him, "Here Josiah. I'm in the end bed."

"Vanessa. I couldn't sleep." He swayed on his feet and grabbed quickly for the bedpost.

"Josiah, here, sit down."

"I guess I'm not as well as I thought—this is my first time getting around on my own. I'm still nauseous and see funny things in front of my eyes."

"We're a fine pair."

Now that all of the easy conversation was over, an awkward silence fell.

"Josiah, I was so worried—are you really all right?"

He sat down heavily on her bed and then fell forward across her legs, "Oh, Nessa, I've ruined your life—what can I do to fix things? What will I tell mother and father? They will hate me forever. I just shouldn't go on living."

"It will be all right, Josiah. I will help you—you'll see. They love us all so much—they'll help see us through."

"But I can't tell them, Nessa. I just can't—it would break their hearts."

She thought for a moment, wondering if she should force her brother to do what was right and honest.

He approached the next thought slowly, still forming the presentation in his head. "Nessa, I thought we could say we were attacked, set upon. You know how terrible the streets of London are. They would believe that. We could say we were coming home from the theater when two men jumped out of an alley and stole our money. Kirk says the police were here, asked some questions and were satisfied that we were not to blame for that awful man's death."

"Oh, Josiah," she started to tell him to admit the truth and he would feel better, but she couldn't—his face was so pitiful. "All right, Josiah, I don't want to add to your anguish, but at some point I think you must speak with father about what happened. But when you're ready, my brother."

The house at Portman Square had been silent—almost like a sealed tomb, when life in the form of a little boy cried out, "I want my mommie. Why won't you let me go to my mommie? Mommie!" he screeched hysterically.

The nanny tugged at him, trying to distract the overwrought child. "Your mother's resting, Kenneth. You'll see her soon."

"No. I want to see her now—please, Nanny." The tousled curls hung down his face, and his little hands clenched into balls to rub his tear-filled eyes. "Is she going to die?" he sobbed.

The thought had been there since the previous evening when he ran into his playroom to find his cherished canary dead at the bottom of the gilded cage.

"Master Kenneth. You mustn't think such things."

The child broke loose from her grasp and ran down the narrow stairs to the floor below to his mother's bedroom. Nanny caught him just as he was about to burst into Sillar's room.

"You must let her rest. Your mother's very tired. Perhaps you can see her later—at tea time."

She had a tight hold on him, but he rested his head on the door. "Mommie, mommie," he begged. "Tell her to let me in. Don't you want to see me? Je t'adore."

When there was no answer, he turned to his nanny, pitifully, the small face was crunched into wrinkles, the tears now overflowing into rivulets, ran down the creases of the small face into his nose and mouth. His upset had been building. Sillar had not come out of her room in several days—not seeing anyone except Clara, who brought her a tray and took it away an hour later untouched. When he saw the lifeless form in the cage and death was explained simply by Nanny—the reality took hold that his pretty yellow bird would never have life again to chirp and fly around the cage. Little Kenneth's big round eyes expressed shock and his tiny body stiffened and remained tense.

Sillar heard her son and her heart pained, but she was so inert, she could not lift her head or call out to him— her son—a child she loved with all her being. Never before had she lost her spirit so—her fight. Energy seemed sapped from her forever. The decline had been so swift, like a sharp ax splintering soft wood.

Although high noon, the room was in darkness, the shades drawn, the wine-velvet draperies pulled. The only spot of light was the dying embers in the grate of the fireplace, but she knew the room by heart—the silken walls with matching canopy above her head, the loose side panels of the same fine material overdraped with wine velvet. If only she could raise her hand, she could touch the cool, silk material for reassurance. In a curio cabinet

on the far wall there were Chinese figurines of jade and
ivory and coral—hung between the tall windows was a
Ming Dynasty painting on gold silk depicting a garden,
and in the corner of the picture tiny creatures busy with
household activities; she knew every figure in the work. A
Chia Ch'ing coromandel black and gold lacquered screen
which stood over nine feet high separated her dressing
room from the sleep area—a treasure given to her by
Blamford only last spring. The whole room gave her
immense pleasure. How could she go back to something
else? A frightening thought took hold: Do you possess
possessions or do they possess you?—then a blankness overtook her again. She had been in and out of awareness
since that day.

His threat kept ringing in her ears: she must never see
Kenneth again. If she did, he would expose her for what
she really was, and she and her son would be removed
from this house.

She had given the note to JoJo when she was here the
first day when she hadn't been quite so weak—her only
contact with anyone from back home except Kenneth in
all these years. Little JoJo—she had sat next to her bed
for hours, saying very little—asking few questions. She
had not come back, so Sillar didn't know if the letter
had been delivered to Kenneth, and thought it strange
JoJo didn't return to inquire about her health—not that
she wanted her to come back to see her in this state.

Remembering now that JoJo had told her that Kenneth
had left for the country for a while, she became frightened
again—her heart fluttering and her breath short. What if
JoJo couldn't get the letter to him and Kenneth came
here? She was certain the house was being watched. Why
couldn't she help herself? She tried to rise but the action
was only in her mind, her body didn't move at all.

The wheels of a carriage clattered on the cobblestones
then stopped at the front of the shop. There were doors
opening and closing quietly—footsteps on the stairs—tiny
feet and grown-up feet—doors opening and shutting again.
The carriage pulled away and the house became silent.
She slept—or she moved into such a deep depression,
time had no meaning.

Her eyes fluttered—her consciousness was being pricked
by a sound. There it was again—a tapping on her door.

Then it opened. Sillar managed to turn her eyes, Clara was there holding a tray.

"Madame?" she called softly. "Are you awake? I've brought you something to eat."

"No. Nothing," she managed to whisper. The thought of food nauseated her.

Clara placed the tray on the marble-topped table near her bed.

"You have got to have something to build your strength. I went to the butcher's special for marrow bones and made you beef broth—it's good and strong, and I added some sherry, not the cooking sherry but your good brand. I took the liberty."

The concerned young woman went to the fireplace and poked up the embers. When it blazed, she put on another log which caught immediately, the flare brightened the room somewhat. She came back to the bed flustered, but trying to help.

"Begging your pardon, ma'am, can't I put on a light or open the draperies? It's so dark and depressing in here for you. You'd feel better with some light."

"It's all right—leave it."

"But, ma'am."

Sillar closed her eyes, and Clara didn't know what to do.

"Don't you want me to send for a doctor? There is one down the street."

"No. Just leave me be . . ."

Clara had to bend close to hear what she was saying.

"I just want to be alone."

"Yes, ma'am."

Church bells rang in the distance. Clara went to the tray anyway, lit a candle on the table and brought the bowl of steaming soup and a starched white napkin to the bed. As she approached, Sillar again declined, but the woman persisted soberly.

"You've got to take something, ma'am. You'll lose all your vigor. Nanny and I are so worried—especially Master Kenneth."

"My son?"

"Yes, ma'am."

"Where is he?" Her head was deep in the pillow, the voice dry and raspy.

The maid brightened. "Master Kenneth is with Lord Blamford. He came and took him away."

A low plaintive wail came from Sillar. The poor woman became frightened and hastened to explain.

"It's the usual day for Lord Blamford to take Master Kenneth to the ships."

"Kenneth," she screeched. "My son."

Clara put the bowl down on the night table, not remembering the heat from the bowl would leave a ring.

"Madame? Are you all right?"

Large tears spilled out of the sunken black eyes. The church bells continued to ring in the background.

Winds whipped in from the North Sea, stinging Kenneth's face and making his eyes water. He reined in the highly bred horse, skittish and all eager to go with the wind, and looked out at the turbulent water, churning fiercely, forming stiff white caps on the mountainous waves. A strange feeling was starting to take hold of him as the sound of church bells reached his ears. He reasoned it had to come from the old church in the village several miles away. The peals were uneven and quivered as they were transported on the strong winds reminding him of an urgent cry for help. As if drawn, he turned his horse in the direction of the sound.

Suddenly snowflakes whirled around his head as he rode along the rim of the ridge trying to find a path leading directly inland—further along, the flurries stopped just as suddenly as they had begun. The air was heavy and bitter cold, but it did not stop the thrushes from singing their sweet song on the bare boughs. His thoughts were of Sillar and his recently discovered son. A beautiful delightful child born of tenderness and desire. At that moment he decided he must see him again and soon. He had been starved these past years for affection and wanted to hold onto this precious boy. The child had his mother's capacity for love—he felt it instinctively and vowed he was not going to lose him.

He passed the gamekeeper's house and waved. Birds swarmed about waiting for the bread crumbs the man and his wife were casting out, making sure the food was evenly distributed. Politely, they directed him to the village church, and he tipped his hat as he rode on. They were friendly enough people, not like the guests arriving at the house for the nuptials—those he found to be involved in games and social behavior, the rules of which he didn't understand or wish to. Jamie, he felt, was from a different cut of cloth, but he worried how Amanda, a naive girl really, would survive among this set.

She seemed so excited and taken with it all, he couldn't get her to sit still and discuss her forthcoming marriage. But he would try to have a serious discussion with her on the subject before going back to America. She had to have some preparation and Georgina was acting just as bemused. Kenneth was pulled in two directions—so much of what he loved was to remain in England, but he had to return to his land, his work. He wondered if there was any possible chance of getting Sillar to return, but she had so much here—what could he offer her there. He was, after all, a married man. He knew how he felt about her but it was a love he had buried in the past, and he hoped he would be successful in burying it in the future if necessary. But his son, Kenneth, Jr., that was another matter. No. He had no intention of losing the youngster. He shivered with the cold, and the flurries were starting again, soon the snow would be coming down in earnest, covering the ground.

On reaching the outskirts of Ashby village, he saw the church, an old building built of rough-hewn stone and heavy oak beams. The bells had stopped tolling, but he could hear the organ being played—wedding music—and saw Hatfield's pony cart parked outside the entrance. He thought it odd that Jamie never rode horseback but took the pony cart or a tricycle when surveying his land. There was a fine stable with prize riding horses, and Kenneth wondered not only now but on previous occasions why Hatfield didn't ride. It was hard to imagine an English country gentleman who was not an expert horseman. Then, there were the jumping trophies in the game room with Hatfield's name on them and a painting with him astride a magnificent jumper. It struck him that something was amiss.

29

Except for Emma sitting at the organ, playing laboriously, the church was empty. He walked down the aisle and went to her. The full-breasted girl was surprised to see him and her plump face lit up in a dimpled smile. She was practicing for the wedding, she told him happily.

"I am really quite good," she told him openly, "but some of the music Amanda and Lord Hatfield selected is not too familiar to me, so I have to practice and practice until I get it right—the music must be perfect."

Hatfield had arrived a few minutes before and was visiting her father in the vicarage, discussing the town school of which her father was also headmaster. Kenneth informed her he wasn't seeking him, just out for a ride and looking around. The young girl gushed on—she was excited about the coming event and the fair the village was holding on Saturday for the bridal couple. She was to run a booth for a ring toss, and had carved out a replica of a big ugly bird for the game—one would have to ring its neck with all the three hoops to win a prize. The villagers and tenants for miles around were looking forward to the reception at the manor house after the wedding, she declared. Everyone was so pleased that the house would be the center of activity again—it had been so gloomy for all of them. Kenneth was glad that his daughter would have this guileless young woman near her, and he hoped their friendship would continue to grow.

When he got outside, the pony cart was gone. He headed back to the house. It was approaching tea time, and he had made up his mind to return to London after the fair on Saturday to see Sillar and his new-found son and also visit with Vanessa and Josiah. He was uncomfortable here and anyway, his heart was in London. He would discuss it with Georgina and be hanged with it if she disapproved of his leaving.

He cantered through the woods on the hard ground fast becoming slippery as the wet flakes fell. He thought he spied a dapple-gray horse running parallel with him twenty or so feet away in the thicket. The rider looked dark, dressed in a bright jacket and fur hat—possibly a gypsy he thought. Why would he be trying to race with him in this strange way? He slowed his horse to a fast walk, the man did the same, the sky was darkening and heavy shadows surrounded him. He hit the flank of his horse with his crop and they took off, so did the other horseman, outdistancing him by a narrow margin. He was fast approaching the grounds of Ashby Manor, but he was still being raced—chased—or followed. He brought his horse up short, and the rider was taken by surprise but did likewise.

Kenneth stood up in the stirrups. "You there. Who are you and what do you want?"

There was no answer. Slowly, Kenneth trotted toward the other horseman, who made no effort to flee. They came face-to-face. The snow whirled around them, and dusk was settling upon them. Kenneth spoke civilly with undertones of annoyance.

"My name is Kenneth McIver."

The man was quick to reply—or more accurately—to defy.

"And I am Rupa."

"Might I ask why you are following me?"

"I do not follow you. I am riding my animal in the forest for exercise."

At this point Kenneth was nonplussed and didn't know what further to say. The man was an arrogant cuss with wild dark hair curling in ringlets around his face and down his muscular neck—a gold earring ringed one ear.

"Then I will wish you good day."

"That is your privilege," he responded.

As Kenneth rode the rest of the way, anxious now to get back to Ashby Manor, he couldn't shake the feeling that he was still being followed.

He approached the front of the house from the side and

saw Amanda gaily playing with Peony on the front lawn.
The little dog was trying to catch the falling flakes, and
Amanda was happily chasing with him. When she saw her
father she ran to him just as he was dismounting. A groom
appeared from the stable yard and took the horse.

"Oh, Daddy, isn't it beautiful—the snow is so wonderful. I think we are going to have a white Christmas.
Won't that be glorious for the wedding?"

"Yes, my darling. Glorious."

She looked so like a child in her gray bonnet trimmed
with white fur and the sapphire-blue-velvet fitted coat.
Small white-kid boots covered her tiny feet. Hatfield's tricycle stood at the drive.

"Amanda, why doesn't Jamie ride a horse around the
grounds?"

She was all smiles and sweetness. "I don't know, Daddy."
Amanda was never interested in horses like Vanessa.
"There are other ways to get about."

"Yes. But I am just puzzled why he has such splendid
horses but doesn't ride them."

"I suppose he keeps them for his guests. Does he have
to ride like everyone else?"

"No. I suppose not. Is your mother in the house?"

"She's in her room, resting before tea time. She's exhausted just thinking about all the festivities taking place
in the next week."

He met Miss Shields on the stairway, holding a large
ring of keys. The woman rarely spoke to him, but he
stopped her and asked if she knew the train schedule to
London. She coldly informed him that there was one in the
evening and one early in the morning. The morning train
being the better because it arrived midday whereas the
evening train pulled into London late at night. He thanked
her for the information, deciding to take the early train
the following Sunday.

Amanda ran down the road a way, playing with Peony
—the little animal was barking and leaping—happy to be
running and frolicking with her mistress. She was not
aware she was being watched by Rupa on his horse from
behind a giant oak at the edge of the clearing on the parklike grounds. Behind him was a thick forest. She ran to a
holly bush, broke off a tiny branch and tried to teach

Peony to fetch, but the dog just kept rolling over or dancing around her in circles. Then the little animal took it into
its head to run toward the forest, with Amanda after him
trying to catch him, fearful he would get lost in the woods.
Suddenly, she heard the thunder of horse's hooves and saw
Rupa coming—he charged at her and swooped her up with
his strong arm and held her at his chest as he rode off with
her into the forest, the little dog scampering after them
barking frantically.

When Amanda comprehended what had happened, she
was terrified and screamed at him, "Let me down, you
ugly beast!"

He laughed at her, flashing his strong white teeth. Her
small fists beat at his chest, which made him laugh all the
harder. Just as suddenly, he kissed her roughly, hurting
her lips, then dropped her to the ground and rode off into
the snowy twilight. Peony reached her, and started to lick
her face. She was petrified as she picked herself up and
ran to the house going directly to her room, locking the
door, too numb to comprehend what had just happened.
She knew she would not tell anyone for fear it would de-
file her in some way.

30

Blamford pushed open the door and strode into the dark room. Clara was behind him, frightened.

"Draw those curtains and light the lights," he commanded. As it was being done, he walked over to the big four-poster and stared down at Sillar.

"Madame, it is time you rose from your bed." He was shocked to see the deep hollows under her eyes—eyes usually bright and shining now dim and lusterless, and how thin she had become in the last few days. The long, thin finger pointed to the tray. "What's that?"

"Food, sir. I brought Madame some broth earlier in the day."

"Did she eat any?"

Clara nervously pulled back the napkin, although she already knew the answer. "No, sir. She didn't touch it."

"Take it back downstairs and reheat it. Is that spirits I smell in the broth?"

"Yes, sir. Sherry."

"Add more. Make it good and strong. But before you go, prop her higher with pillows."

Clara went over to Sillar and lifted her gently, raising her. Then eager to leave the room, she took the large silver tray and hastened to do his bidding, afraid of the man, however, feeling what he was doing was for her mistress' benefit.

All this time Sillar just lay there like a puppet on a string, her gaze never leaving Blamford. She was relieved he had brought her son home, having had a crazy fear that he had taken him away, but she was still powerless to move.

He looked down at her, again he reminded her of a high court judge about to pass sentence.

"We will get some broth in you—and then we will talk."

"No," she managed to murmur.

Placing his pince-nez on his high-bridged nose, he studied her more closely.

"Is that no, you do not wish broth or no, you do not wish to talk?"

She continued to stare at him as if seeing him for the first time.

"Come, come, you must have an answer."

She tried to raise her dry voice. "Get out of here."

"And leave you to waste away? You seem to have a sense of death about you, my girl—rather unlike the Sillar I knew in the past."

She made no response. In a swift movement, he threw back her covers and swung her legs over the side of the bed—surprised at the soiled nightdress and the odor of perspiration—she appeared not to have been changed in several days. Wobbling at the edge of the bed, he held her firmly so she would not fall back.

"You are a mess. How can you stand yourself?"

Her head hung, she slipped out of his grasp onto the oriental rug. He left her there—a totally humiliated human being. Past scenes of slaves being sold on the auction block lit up in her mind—joking men making women show their teeth—feeling their bodies—buying and owning them. Her hand slowly reached for one of the posts, weakly she tried to grab hold of it, then tried to get leverage with both her hands to pull herself back onto her bed.

Blamford snapped at her. "Get up, woman. Can't you help yourself?"

Beads of spittle drooled from her mouth as she tried to raise her body—she was grunting, trying to get her knees under her.

Finally, the man dragged her limp body to the fireplace and managed to push her into the French Bergere chair. Sitting so upright made her dizzy, but he was determined and got her to hold her head up. He placed the small marble-topped table in front of her as a prop and went to the bellpull. Clara was there in a few minutes looking anxious.

"Bring some hot water and soap and wash your mistress. Then find her a clean nightdress."

"The broth is almost ready, sir. Shouldn't she be fed first?"

"She will be clean and freshly dressed before she eats."

The woman ran from the room, and Blamford took a side chair, placing it near Sillar, and straddled it. Neither one talked—Sillar stared at the marble top of the table—lost in her haze, slumping further down, until her head almost reached the table. He came over and lifted her head back.

"Sit up. Force yourself to do so."

Clara was back with the water, which she poured in a basin on the washstand. Coming to Sillar, she was embarrassed as to how to start, she had never done such a thing before.

"Remove the gown and wash her down." When he saw her hesitate, he went to Sillar and removed the soiled nightdress from her body. Clara was appalled, but said nothing. She started to wash the listless woman's body, putting a towel under her to do her lower parts. At the end, she washed her face gently and smiled at Sillar. Finally going to the armoire to get a fresh gown, which she pulled carefully over her mistress' head.

"Now go and bring the broth."

"Yes, sir."

When she left the room, Blamford went to Sillar's dressing table and got a silver brush he had given her. Then he came to her and tenderly started to brush the long black Indian hair. When her head started to droop forward again, he pulled it back.

The steaming broth was brought in, and he ordered Clara to spoon-feed her, holding Sillar's head to make sure she would cooperate. When he was satisfied with the amount that was fed her, he commanded Clara to put fresh linen on the bed. A few minutes later, they lifted Sillar to her feet and forced her to walk around the room several times—finally placing her on the bed, propping her up once more with pillows. There was a hint of color in Sillar's face, and her eyes looked a little brighter, but he could also see an expression of total defeat on her face.

Blamford sat in a chair by the fireplace and took out a

long, thin cigar, rolling it in his bony fingers in appreciation of the fine tobacco.

"Clara," this was the first time he had addressed the maid by her name, "bring down little Kenneth so he can visit with his mother."

The little boy, all scrubbed and combed, couldn't contain himself on seeing his mother. He pounced on the bed and covered her face with kisses. She raised her arms and held him tenderly, cooing sweet words of love back into his ear.

He settled down in the crook of her arm, satisfied his mother was fine and wanted him.

"Mommie, I met a dirty little boy today—by the ships. He was standing in the mud looking for things—pieces of nails, anything so he can sell it for money. Can I do that, Mommie? Can I look for things on the river banks? Uncle called him a mudlark."

A child of poverty she thought—her precious son, for the first time, met a street urchin, one scrounging for junk to earn a piece of bread. Is that what the future holds in store for us if I don't comply?

"You are forgetting the present for your mother, Kenneth."

The child looked at Blamford, round-eyed, then remembered.

"It's in my pocket, sir. I didn't lose it."

"I didn't think you did. But give it to your mother now."

He fished in his small pocket and brought out a gift box. "This is for you, Mommie, a present."

He placed it in her hand, but she didn't open it, the loving look leaving the face of her son to gaze wretchedly at Blamford, who smiled back at her benevolently.

"Open it, Mommie, you are going to be so pleased."

Little Kenneth untied the ribbon and lifted the cover for her. Inside was a polished pink shell—the childish fingers lifted it out. "Isn't it beautiful—Uncle says it comes from the South Seas. Where is the South Seas, Mommie?"

"Far away, my beloved, way out of our reach."

Her son managed to snap open the shell, and sitting inside was a large, glowing black pearl.

Blamford rose and went to the bed to view more closely mother and son.

Sillar raised her eyes to him. "It must have cost a great deal of money."

"Money is no object when it is something I want."

As if afraid he would be taken from his mother, little Kenneth clung to her neck as the man hovered over them.

"I will leave you to enjoy the company of your son. He needs his mother as do others. I will return on Sunday— we can have our talk then."

He strode out of the room in lordly fashion. After all thought Sillar, he is the Duke of Blamford, luck of birth had given him the right.

Sleepily, the little boy in her arms looked up lovingly at his mother. "Can I stay here with you, Mommie? Je t'aime."

"I love you, too, my son. So much."

"Are you better? My mother is not going to die?"

"No."

His body relaxed—he sighed contentedly.

"Tell me a story. Will you? Please, Mommie."

Shadows from the candle on the night table danced across her face. "I will tell you one—about a little slave girl in Charleston."

"Why was she a slave?"

"Who knows—such things do happen."

"Was she a slave because she was bad?"

"No. It was because her skin was black."

"Does the story have a happy ending?"

"I won't know until it is finished."

"My canary died."

"I know. That's the way of life, my son."

"Ugh!" He settled deeper in her arms. "Tell me about the little slave girl."

She looked out the window seeing time fade back—a way of life—a story? A little slave girl. . . .

The old buckboard rumbled down the cobble streets of Charleston in the early morning. Peering through the slats of the cart were two giant black eyes—completely awed by the sights. She had never seen such beauty, fairyland gardens behind tall iron fences, rich houses painted pretty colors, churches with tall spires. It was spring, and the city was ablaze with brightly colored flowers. She asked her mother sitting on the box up front with the driver what they were.

"I don't know what they are called, Sillar," said her mother, "and you hush now. We are almost there."

When they got to a corner the wagon stopped and she spotted a street vendor carrying baskets of these colorful blooms.

"Mister, what are those flowers you have in the baskets?"

The toothless man with an old straw hat on his white woolly head came to the wagon and looked down at the child huddled against the slats.

"Ain't you never seen camellias and lillies and hyacinths before, child?"

"No, sir. I never have."

"Where you from that you ain't seen no flowers?"

"Oh, I seen flowers, but not like those. I come from the Blue Ridge Mountains in the pine country."

Her mother watched her but said nothing. They had been traveling for three days through the back country to get here, and she was frightened about what the end of the journey would bring.

The driver of the wagon, once a strong slave driver, now in advanced age was weary and anxious to deliver his cargo, human and otherwise. He inquired of the vendor, "Can you tell me if we are on the right street to reach South Battery?"

"Yes—you is on the right street—just keep going till you can go no more."

"We are looking for the McIver Furniture Factory."

"It's there—you can't miss it."

The driver, Izard, raised his whip but was stopped by the street vendor.

"Jes' a minute. I want to give this child some flowers."

He pulled out a bunch and handed them to Sillar.

"But I ain't got no money," she exclaimed.

"I don't want your money, child. I want you to enjoy these beautiful Charleston flowers."

"I thank you," and she held the flowers in her dirty hands as if they were fragile pieces of glass.

They pulled into the yard of the factory, which smelled of wood shavings, glue, and varnish. Old Izard got down, and after inquiring about Mr. McIver, disappeared into the building.

Sillar's mother, in her twenties, sat up straight, looking as if she had a pole strapped to her back to keep her spine rigid.

Sillar looked at the bundles of which she was a part—dusty canvases covering pieces of furniture and scant possessions belonging to her and her mother tied in ragged parcels. She tried to rub off some of the dirt and grime on her face, when suddenly a second-story window flew open and an angular man with a shock of white hair leaned out the window to study the wagon and its contents.

"You," he shouted to Sillar's mother, "come on up here. Where's the young one?"

She raised her head a little higher and stood until her skinny figure was a little above the slats of the buckboard.

"Oh," said the voice with a strange burring accent, "I thought you were another dirty bundle. Follow your mother up here." The window closed with a bang. There was a stiff breeze off the water, and Sillar shivered as she followed her mother into the building.

"Momma? You think he is gonna sell us to someone else?"

"I don't know, child. We will find out soon enough."

They stood in front of Angus McIver, who held the just-delivered letter in his hand.

Sillar stood as close as possible to her mother, proudly looking up at her. She loved her straight blue-black hair, oiled and coiled around her head forming a topknot. The tresses framed the high-cheeked, olive-skinned face and enhanced the smouldering dark eyes specked with glints of yellow and amber. The long straight nose with flaring nostrils was alluring in a wild way. She knew her mother possessed great beauty and hoped she would grow up to look just like her.

Angus McIver was staring at her mother, "What are you, part Indian?"

Old Izard answered for the silent woman. "Yes, sir, that's what she is—her mammy was full Creek Injun, married one of Mr. Lassiter's drivers; Rain here is their daughter, and the little one, Rain's daughter, is called Sillar."

"Why is she called Rain? Was it pouring when she was born?"

"Cats and dogs," laughed Izard.

Sillar watched him as he continued to study her mother. She was wearing a long skirt of a dark calico print, cinched tight at the waist and a low-necked cotton blouse of a brighter print—the mixture of yellows and reds complimented her light olive skin. Sillar, barefoot, was dressed in a gray sack dress, which had been clean when they left but was now caked with dirt from the arduous journey out of the mountain country of South Carolina to the semi-tropical region of Charleston.

"Can the woman talk?"

"Sir, she can talk. Ask her a question."

"She is acting so quiet. I thought maybe she had something wrong with her."

"No. Nothing wrong. She's jes' a quiet woman."

Angus McIver waved the letter at them. "Do you know what it says in this?"

Rain nodded her head. Sillar clung closer to her mother's skirt.

"It says I have inherited you in payment for a bad debt."

Old Izard was quick to defend his master. "Mr. Lassiter, suh, is dying, and he wants to make sho his trusted slaves are taken care of—families not to be separated and to find kind masters."

"How does the old devil know I'm a kind master? Some think of me as the meanest man in town."

Sillar started to shake, and her big eyes were blinking uncontrollably. Angus McIver, a virile man in his fifties, started to laugh—his light-blue eyes twinkling. A tall man of slight frame, he had a paunch which hung over his belt slightly that now shook with his laughter.

"I can't believe that old devil is paying me off with two women slaves and some old furniture I probably made for him a long time ago. The money I lent him last year was two thousand dollars, and what do I get in return? A woman with hands that look like they don't know the meaning of work and a child who makes a scrawny chicken look healthy. Then he has the nerve to say in this here letter that his debt is paid in full."

"There's some fine furniture in the wagon, Mr. McIver.

Some brought over from the old country by Mr. Lassiter's family a long time ago."

"Oh!" There was a look of interest in the tall Scotsman's face. "What do you call fine furniture? Furniture is my business."

"Well, suh, I think you is gonna be surprised."

"How long you been with Lassiter?"

The black man looked sad as he answered Angus McIver. "All my life—I was born on the Lassiter land, so was my pappy. I don't know what I is gonna do when he dies. He's the last except for relations in other sections of the pine country—so I don't know. I'ze too old to be sold to another. But Rain and her child, they is young and strong. They will serve you good—jest you wait and see. Rain is fine with the needle, and she is teaching the young 'un."

"So that's why you have such soft hands." He looked Rain up and down with appreciative eyes.

The woman returned his gaze. Sillar felt compelled to say something. "My ma makes beautiful things . . ."

"Not that abomination you're wearing."

"No, sir. I made that."

"Don't your ma talk? It's depressing to have someone around who has no tongue."

"Oh, she talks," said Izard quickly. "More an' likely she has nothing to say."

Her eyes pleaded with her mother, who had been very withdrawn since they left the Lassiter plantation—their home.

Old Izard explained to Angus McIver, "Rain's husband was killed in the lumber mill—a stack of fresh-cut boards shifted and crushed him."

"I'm sorry to hear that." The remark was genuine, and he referred once again to the piece of paper in his hand. "It says if I agree to take you in payment, I can't resell you or separate you from each other, but to tell the truth, in this case I'd rather have the money—all I could really use are some strong field hands for my plantation on St. Helena Island. And then again, I don't have to accept all the terms written on this piece of paper."

Due to her nervousness, Sillar scratched her head.

"You got lice, child?"

Izard was quick to defend, "That child is clean. She

and Rain lived off the kitchen behind the big house. They didn't live in the slave quarters."

"How come? She have trouble getting along with the others?"

Sillar became stiff in her fear—that was exactly why she and her mother had to live near the big house—sleeping on the floor of the storage room off the kitchen. The other slaves never treated them like they were one of them and the children rarely played with her, yet they were blacks—it was something hard for her to understand. Mr. Lassiter had told Sillar in his hoarse whisper as he lay on the great bed near death, that he would try to get her and her mother somewhere so they wouldn't be sold on the auction block. For the last weeks they were there, Sillar, her thin body straining under the weight, carried warm water up to him because the only thing he enjoyed now was spongings several times a day. Most of the other house slaves had been sold off slowly during the last year to help keep him going financially.

Angus McIver rubbed his paunch. Sillar could hear it growling. "Tell me—Sillar, is it?"

"Yes, sir. It be Sillar."

"Can your mother cook? My manservant does the cooking when I am in Charleston, and he is giving me the bellyaches."

She lit up, proud to announce, "My ma cooks good—real good."

"That's fine, but what am I going to do with you? Can you earn your keep or am I going to have to feed you till you grow and then maybe you will be fit for some kind of honest work?"

"I'ze ten years old—I can do a good day's work. Clean, run errands, help in the kitchen . . ."

The man smiled, and Sillar wasn't sure if he was laughing at her or pleased at what she had said.

"If I sign this agreement as written, which Izard will take back to Lassiter, I will become your master and be bound never to sell you or separate you except under the most dire circumstances. How do you feel about my becoming your master? remembering what I just told you: I'm the meanest man in town."

Rain's head sank to her chest, and Sillar was confused—then desperate—"We will try to be good. Please don't send us back—we don't want to be sold at no auction."

"What do you know about auctions?"

"I heard talk—I know. I want to be with my ma."

"All right, child. I'll sign this." Which he did with a great flourish. "Now let's go down to the wagon and see what junk the old devil sent along with you two."

Angus was surprised when he unwrapped some of the canvases. One piece, an Empire card table, was made of mahogany and rosewood with satinwood inlay. He whistled out loud displaying his admiration for the workmanship—carved harp designs supported the sides, another was an exquisite antique Penbroke tea table. Sillar was pleased at his regard for the pieces of furniture.

They were sent to the house on Meeting Street. Once again Sillar was enthralled with the beautiful gardens she espied through the ironwork fences and tall gates, many overhung with Spanish moss and flowering vines—the lush greenery was everywhere, a delight to her childlike vision.

The slave quarters behind the house were in sad neglect from disuse. Conrad, who was Angus McIver's body servant, slept in the house, and only an elderly black who functioned as gardener and stableman lived in the quarters. Until recently there had been a house servant who cooked for the master when he was there, but she had been sent back to the big house on the plantation. Conrad was doing all the chores including the cooking, so Rain would be useful in Charleston, although for a frugal Scotsman, a luxury.

Sillar and her mother immediately set about clearing out a place for themselves in the quarters—a small room over the carriage house—so they would be high enough to enjoy the view of the garden from the small window. When Angus came home that evening, a simple good meal was served him, and Sillar, hiding behind the dining room door, saw he was pleased.

She had learned he didn't live in the beautiful house on Meeting Street very much, only when he came to inspect and make sure the work was going well at the furniture factory. His main interest was his beloved plantation. Distressing now, was overhearing the complaint that she and her mother couldn't, unfortunately, be moved very easily to the plantation, where he would get more out of them,

especially her. He stressed they would have a difficult time
fitting in with the other servants and hands, perhaps causing friction because of their mixed blood. The same as before she whimpered to herself. Again, she didn't know
where she belonged. Her grandmother, now dead, filled
her with Indian stories of bravery, spirit, and pride, while
her pappy, always a humble man who acquiesced when
need be due to his upbringing, always said, "You're a
black, baby—that's yo people." But they didn't take to her
and on occasion made fun of her and her looks. She
listened further to her new master as he continued confiding in Conrad.

The woman, he said, didn't have the brightest of per-
sonalities that would attract friendships at McIver Hall,
but noted with interest, Rain's good looks. "Well, we'll
see," he said.

Later, Sillar perched in the branch of an olive tree,
watched Angus McIver as he sat on a cushioned bench
in the garden enjoying the soft balmy twilight, puffing on
his after dinner cigar. A figure appeared from the kitchen
house and Sillar was surprised to see it was her mother,
freshly dressed, with a red bandana tied around her head,
large hoop earrings adorned her ears. She regally carried
a small silver tray holding only a coffee cup and a single
red rose. Carefully, she placed the fluted tray, just polished
to a high gloss, on a wrought iron table next to their new
master—then waited. Surprised, he sipped the coffee while
his appreciating eyes slowly surveyed the woman in front
of him. The lonely man smiled—his bony fingers reached
out to rub the fabric of her skirt—finally speaking, so
quietly, Sillar didn't hear. After a few moments, Rain
nodded her head affirmatively. The business finished, she
started back toward the kitchen. Sillar stared after her
mother until she disappeared.

Snowflakes hit the window and melted instantly, running down the pane like dirty raindrops. The candle next
to the big four-poster bed was nearing its demise and
sputtered, giving off very little light. In her arms her son
was half asleep. She took off his little jacket and loosened
the starched shirt. Like a small animal reacting to stimulus, he burrowed closer.

Slavery—she allowed herself to think about it. Conveniently, she had obliterated the very idea from her mind. No more. Women being bought and sold in so many ways. Her mother using her body to secure their future the only way she knew.

The black pearl shimmered in the iridescent shell, catching the last light of the candle. She admired the jewel—itself entrapped in the mother-of-pearl bed—a very expensive gift—more of a bribe?—payment for services received? Yes, the price was high—the only difference from the plight of her mother, but maybe the price had even been higher for Rain. How far had she really come as a human being?

Kenneth's soft snore made her smile—she hugged him, reassuring herself of what she did have in life.

Thomas McIver. The trouble started for her mother when the young man arrived unexpectedly from military school in Virginia—sent home on probation.

Before that, they had thought their lives were settling a bit. The first spring had passed quickly, and they entered into the heat of summer. Sillar never tired of the garden even when the semitropical sun was intense—she breathed the fragrant air in gulps, so many different varieties of flowers squashed together, making it all look like a giant bouquet. The roses were full-blown like small cabbages—the orange blossoms felt lovely and cool—the waxy petals crunched pleasantly between her fingers. She and her mother spent many happy evenings there, the gardener patiently teaching them the names of the blooms, their peculiarities and how to care for them.

During most days, after their chores of tending the McIver house, she and her mother were hired out to a dressmaker who had a fashionable shop on King Street—the Scotsman had found an extra way for them to earn their keep when he was not there. The wages were paid to him, and he in turn gave them a very small percentage of the money received. Sillar dreamed of buying their freedom from the meager savings, but her mother just nodded weakly at her foolish expectations.

Thomas McIver was at the house one hot evening on their return from the shop—quarrelsome and frightening

—his booming voice bouncing through the house. Sillar learned from the gardener that she should stay out of his way. He was out of sorts with everyone, the gnarled man remarked. Angus McIver was due to arrive any day, the fever season had long started in the swampy sea islands, and he always spent the summer in the city to escape infection. Sillar prayed he would come soon.

One morning when she was dusting the upper hall, she saw her mother come out of Thomas' bedroom limping and adjusting her long skirts—a grim look on her face. He had sent for her to bring his breakfast as he did every morning. Suddenly, he appeared at the doorway to his room, he stood naked, his hair disheveled, with a mean look on his young face, and told her mother to come back, he wasn't through with her yet. Besides, he smirked, she had forgotten his breakfast tray. The door shut again and she went downstairs to wait—it was getting on to the time when they should leave for the dress shop. Waiting outside on the street, her small body shook, and she was very afraid.

Usually she took such pleasure sitting on the steps in front of the townhouse, always amazed that the beautiful doorway leading from the street did not open into the house but opened to a long porch she learned was called a piazza. In the center of the piazza, which faced the garden, was the main entrance that led into the center hall. There was a second-story gallery also, where she and her mother would sit in the evening when it got too hot in the garden to catch the sea breezes. But her mind would not be diverted—something terrible was going to happen if Angus McIver did not get there soon. Her child's heart stopped racing when he did arrive later in the week and the house settled down again to being a regular household. She and her mother had to give up the outside work during his stay as their duties were many, especially with the two McIvers there. But toward the end of that summer, the most horrible thing happened for her.

Angus was away in the northwest of South Carolina buying lumber for his factory, and Rain ran away. She was caught, and Thomas McIver sent her to the Charleston workhouse to be whipped by the keeper. Sillar tended her when she came back to the slave quarters, her back covered with deep cuts and bruises. Sillar was heartbroken

because her mother had run away, not only from the
McIvers, but from her. She had been abandoned. For days
Rain did not look her daughter in the face and then finally, one night, she took her in her arms and said how sorry
she was, but she felt there was no hope. The men of the
family were using her, and Thomas was ripping her apart
—there was nothing else she could do. She begged Sillar
not to hate her for running away.

The fall came and Angus went back to the plantation
for the picking season and Thomas McIver returned to the
military institute. However, he was back several weeks
later, the gardener telling Sillar he had been expelled
again due to some devilment. Angus McIver made him go
to work in the factory, but he still wore his military
jacket unbuttoned as he swaggered about and kept his
firearms and sabers in his room in good repair. Toward
winter, her mother ran away again and this time they did
not find her. Sillar was sent to the plantation on St. Helena
Island to work in the big house, mainly in the sewing
room as she, like her mother, had become very good with
needle and thread.

There was excitement throughout McIver Hall when
Kenneth, the elder son, came home for the Christmas
holidays. Sillar would never forget her first view of him.
It was love at first sight—the handsome face, lean and
angular behind light stylish sidewhiskers. This was his first
visit home in a year—his recent vacations from school
had been spent on visits to the West—places she never
heard of before—Chicago, Kansas, Wyoming. She learned,
as she sat on the drafty staircase the first night he was
there, staring at him, he would be graduating from Yale,
the school was called, that summer, and his father was giving him a grand tour of Europe as a present before settling
down on the McIver plantation. He liked farming, he had
said. She sat all attention—ready to be at his service quickly in case he wanted a glass of water from the sideboard or
needed her to go on some kind of errand. The living room
was filled with neighbors and relatives welcoming him
back. She hated the girls who circled around him like
moths to a flame. Of course, he absolutely took no notice
of her—why should he, she was just an overgrown skinny
black kid.

She remembered her extreme upset when the news

came on the day she turned twelve that he was to be married to a young lady from Memphis—he had met her while on the Grand Tour. They arrived in a great flurry, and a flighty, demanding, but extremely pretty young woman became the mistress of McIver Hall, and Georgina disliked her instantly—probably she was suspect of her light skin, a color that had also made her an outcast on the plantation—she was still a loner. But Siller, undeniably Rain's child, was also her father's daughter (a gregarious man when not intimidated by authority), made friends easily, and slowly, over the years at McIver Hall, the house servants came to accept her and honestly enjoyed her company. However, she never became a trusted or faithful servant to Georgina McIver, a very possessive and obsessive person—in many ways controlled by material things. On her stays in the Charleston house, she acquired silver services, bolts of fine fabrics for draperies and bedspreads, imported laces for tablecloths, china from England and France, and spent a great deal of time involved with their care. The house on Meeting Street as beautiful as it was before, became ornate and fussy under her dominance.

The years passed, and as Sillar matured, she felt that all was not right with Kenneth's relationship with his wife. More and more he would be off on trips, often saying he had a meeting at the Agricultural Society on St. Helena. When she was eighteen, he came home one night too drunk to navigate the stairs to his room. Sillar, who had been waiting for his return, something she practiced quite frequently, aided him to his study in the back of the house, helping him undress. He was completely oblivious to who she was. Finally, she got him on the couch, loosened his clothing and was covering him with a blanket when he unbuttoned his trousers and pulled her to him fervently. She stared at his strong hard erection as he started to murmur, "Love me, love me." She managed to free her wrists from his strong hands and gently, tentatively, because she had never done it before, stroked him, the organ becoming more rigid as he bucked his hips—she brought him to a climax, then watched him move into a deep sleep.

She knew he didn't remember the happening, but he took to looking at her, somewhat puzzled, as if trying to recall something. Eventually she became his bedwench—

the first love she had known since her mother had abandoned her.

The candle was spitting as Sillar released her precious little son, sound asleep next to her. She placed his curly head on the pillow and blew out the final gasps of flame. Tomorrow she would force herself to go to the park with him, and she would figure out their future—in no way would she abandon her son. Sometime soon he would have to be told—and to be made proud of his heritage.

31

The hospital was still relatively quiet—Kirk was just finishing his early-morning rounds when he decided to check again on Vanessa. He was surprised to see the divider pulled and JoJo standing just outside the frame, her arms filled with fresh clothing. Stepping inside the cubicle, he was amazed to see a distinguished looking man, with a full beard and monacle bending over Vanessa, listening to her chest. Pierre stood on the other side of the bed full of concern.

She looked startled when she saw him, not quite knowing how to act. "Kirk, I didn't think you'd be here so early."

"I see," he answered quietly.

The man straightened and addressed himself to Kirk, who recognized him immediately—a fashionable doctor from Harley Street. No doubt Pierre had sent for him.

"Good morning, sir. I am Dr. Gregson Hall, I shall be taking over the case—no need for you to attend to the patient any longer."

"Vanessa," he said coolly, "did you consent to have this man take over?"

"Now, now, Doctor. Let's not burden the patient—she's been through quite a time. I am moving her to a private clinic I have where she shall be watched carefully. The possibility of an infection following this kind of operation is high."

"There won't be any—I used the Lister method. She will be perfectly fine."

"Oh, you are one of those doctors. Are you saying you positively guarantee there will be no infection or fever?"

"No, there are cases . . ."

"Precisely. Get the patient dressed and we will get her to more private surroundings."

JoJo came in and took in all the faces. Pierre ordered her to do Dr. Hall's bidding.

Kirk raised his voice. "The patient does not have to be moved to another hospital—she's being well cared for here."

The doctor from Harley Street was getting annoyed. "My good doctor, I don't know if you are aware who I am. Besides, Lord Hatfield and I belong to the same club. Now, if you don't mind. I am a very busy man. I intend to have around the clock nurses for Miss McIver."

In vain Kirk looked at Vanessa. Her expression told him she was caught in a predicament—completely at sea —not knowing what to do.

She tried to explain to him. "Pierre thought it was best —Dr. Hall is very experienced in these matters."

"But did you consent to his bringing in another doctor without telling me?" His voice rose in volume. "Did you, Vanessa?"

Pierre put his hand possessively on her shoulder. "I think you've said enough, Kirk."

The bearded gentleman raised himself to his full height and imperiously adjusted his monocle. "If you can't control yourself, Doctor, I will have to speak to your superiors. Please take your leave."

The devastated young woman shook her head, "My arm, Kirk—I have to try."

He was so enraged, he stormed down the ward, hearing from Dr. Hall.

"My, my. A man that emotional should not be tending patients."

In the corridor he came upon Nurse Piercely—she obviously was aware of the situation.

"Do you think my voice is too loud for a doctor?"

She studied him sadly, "It is difficult when one is in love with the patient."

He was a bit taken back by her remark.

"You still have to sign her out—if you wish."

"Did you check her temperature this morning?"

"Yes. Completely normal."

"Well, she could go home at this point. But my guess is someone finds it advantageous keeping her an invalid."

He took the clipboard from her hand and signed Vanessa's release.

"And Josiah McIver?" She handed him another form.

"Him, too?"

"Yes."

"Come along. I'll check him first before I release him to that puffed-up dandy."

They walked along hurriedly.

"Will she be able to use her arm fully to play the piano?"

"You mean in concert performance?"

"Yes."

"That remains to be seen."

In the apothecary shop on the ground floor, the telegraph used to summon ambulances was clicking away unattended, and the old man who tended the horses was the only soul in the courtyard. Kirk had come out to take a walk, to get away from the hospital, wanting to forget about the scene he just had with the Harley Street doctor. He was upset, extremely so.

The old man spoke to him as he passed. "You're lucky to be goin' off duty, Doctor—they was all called out. Seems like there'll be a heavy load this morning."

He walked along St. Thomas Street, forcing himself to take deep breaths of the winter air, and started toward London Bridge. Suddenly, he heard the first explosion coming from the wharves. Black funnels of smoke pushed violently into the air. There was another explosion.

He raced back to the hospital and into the ambulance yard.

"When an ambulance returns, rush it to the south of London Bridge. There's trouble there."

"I thought I heard something. Sounded like gunpowder blowing up," the man yelled as he watched Kirk take off again.

The acid smell of smoke and fire stung his nose and eyes as sprays of fire shot up from the stern of a cargo ship. Another explosion rocked the area, and Kirk was almost knocked off his feet. Men, their clothes aflame, were hurling themselves from the deck into the filthy waters of the Thames.

He climbed aboard and saw deckhands desperately rolling barrels of flammable oil off the deck.

"Get off," he yelled at them. "Get off. Run!"

The prow of the ship was a blanket of fire as he tried to free bodies trapped by rolling cargo. A few crewmen were frantically pushing kegs of brandy toward the prow of the ship, hoping to stem the fury of the flames, but the hold was sending out billows of black smoke and the sound of the raging fire from below signaled the hull would soon be consumed from under them. Again he screamed, "Get off—it's about to blow!" Suddenly the main mast, its shaft weakened by the fire, crashed to the deck, pinning two men. Kirk rushed to them and tried to raise the shattered column, but it was wedged into the hold.

"Quick, get axes—it has to be cut." He yelled to men running around him, then knelt between the two men trying to keep them calm. Kirk tore a bit of sail cloth to press against the profusely bleeding head of one of them. He used his jacket to beat out the small fires started around them by falling clumps of burning rigging.

"Just hang on—we'll have you out of here as soon as possible."

One of the fallen weakly said, "No, mate. You go—no need for you to die with us. We're trapped here."

"Hang on," he cried. "You'll see," he comforted, "you'll be freed in time to get to the pub for a pint of bitters before noon."

Three men with axes made quick work of cutting the mast, and they draped the freed men over their shoulders and climbed down from the ship as an ambulance pulled up to the wharf. Now showers of fire rained onto the roof of the warehouses, and small clusters of fire sprang up all over. Even though the fire brigades had arrived and were at work a second ship at the wharf was now being rapidly consumed by flames.

Fortunately, there was no wind blowing and the wet weather of the past weeks had moistened the old timber of the wharves and warehouses. The fire raged for several hours and Kirk fought along with the fire fighters trying to save men who were trapped or too injured to move, then getting them into the ambulances that rushed back and forth from the hospital. Finally, past noon, the fire dwindled and spewed its last gusts of flame, then smoldered.

He accompanied the last of the wounded to the hospital. His own arms and hands were burned, his hair singed.

Late in the day he went to the ward where Vanessa had been, hoping against hope that she would still be there. But the bed was empty and all traces of her gone.

32

Emma and her father, Reverend Jenkins, awoke to the sound of hammers putting the finishing touches on the kiosks for the fair, which would take place around the grounds of the town hall adjacent to the church. They dressed quickly, then stood together in front of the kitchen stove, sipping their tea, holding their cups tightly with both hands to bring warmth to their fingers. There was no desire to sit and have a proper breakfast, not with the feast they would have later. Emma knew by heart the abundant variety of dishes that would be served, since she and their housekeeper had been in charge of organizing the menu and relegating the various dishes to those expert in their preparation.

The vicar helped Emma wrap her heavy plaid shawl around her shoulders and together they walked across the grounds to the hall, their feet crunching the crystal frost where the sun hadn't yet reached. They passed a small group of young men in front of a cooking fire, hand-turning a spit with pigs that had been roasting through the night. They had been warming their insides with shots of whiskey and bitters. Soon their wives and mothers would arrive and send them home to sleep off their vigil, but for now they continued basting the meat, exchanging ribald stories and smoking cigars. Since the *Illustrated London News* had published a sketch of his royal highness, the Prince of Wales, cantering across Newmarket Heath with a cigar in his mouth, almost every young man throughout the country took to his "smart" new habit.

In the townhall meeting room, a handful of the older women from the village were busy hanging bunting of rough muslin, decorations of green boughs, and winter corn around the hall.

As they stood back to admire their handiwork another group of volunteers arrived—men carrying large cauldrons of stews and soups smelling deliciously of leeks, beef, and mutton. They were directed to the side yard, where the vats were hung on large steel hooks over the mounds of wood fires.

Tables in the hall were being filled with an abundant supply of herring caught by the farmers who, during this time of year, turned to fishing once the harvest was in. No pheasants or quail were included on the menu, as everyone knew, including Jamie, that the prized plump ones were on his land and poaching was strictly forbidden. It mattered not though, since they expected to have their fill of the tasty birds at the wedding reception the following week.

Toward ten o'clock a steady stream of villagers arrived: young couples with babies wrapped in heavy blankets, sedated by a full morning meal at their mother's breast and now turned over to the grandmothers and maiden aunts or widows who were delighted to spoil them for the day— the young parents grateful for the time free from responsibility for a short while.

The gypsies arrived bringing along only one of their caravans, a performance wagon, whose side was lowered and formed a stage on which they would entertain, sing, dance, and at times give a short play. Following behind were several of their finest horses to compete in the main event—a race. The bridles and saddles of their animals were adorned with braid and scarves.

As high noon approached, a long line of Hatfield carriages could be seen at a distance, winding their way down the hill from the manor. On seeing their approach, the villagers lined up to welcome the guests of honor. Jamie, the McIvers, and their house guests piled out of the carriages, high spirited and ready for another in a long line of festivities that would follow this week. Their attire was simpler and less formal than their usual wear, but it was in marked contrast with the drab cotton and woolen tweed outfits worn by the villagers, whose only ostentation was a bright shawl, a gay scarf, or plaid caps worn by the men. The gypsies were at the other end of the spec-

trum, outshining the honored guests. They were bedecked
in bright multicolored clothing, hair flowing wildly, both
the men and women wearing showy jewelry and head
scarves, and the faces of the women striking due to the
bold stroke of makeup.

A proud villager, an aging woman, knowing of Jamie's
sweet tooth, led him to the dessert table off to one side
and removed the large cloth that covered it. She glowed
under his praise as his eyes surveyed the treats of baked
apples, batter and apple pudding, breads with marmalades,
cakes of every kind, and gooseberry pie made from the
last berries of the season and promised to save him a
piece for after his meal. When the eating began shortly
after noon, the married women congregated among the
food tables staying close to the dish they prepared, waiting anxiously for the first compliments to be heard.

Tankards of cider and bitter ale were being drunk in
quantity, and as the sun dropped toward the west, the
competitions of the day now began: foot races, hurdle
leaping, horseshoe pitching, and a sack race—the men,
sewed up to their shoulders in sacks, jumping forty yards
out around a flag and then forty yards back. Some of the
young men had brought along dice, and their hard-earned
pence were being gambled away in very short order behind the hall, away from the watchful eyes of Lord Hatfield.

Amanda strolled about the hall on Jamie's arm, enjoying
the deferential treatment extended her. She felt royal and
played the role to the hilt. The young children curtsied to
her and when she approached a game booth everyone
would step aside immediately so she could try her luck,
and they applauded excitely when she hooked the three
hoops on the goose's neck that Emma had made.

Amanda had great fun trying her luck at other games
of chance, pleased with the small favors she won. Only
when they passed the drapery hung as a partition by the
gypsy queen for privacy as she read fortunes, did her
happiness falter slightly. There was a young gypsy boy
standing by the drapery playing strains of a melodic air
for the line of people waiting to have the Bibi tell them
what their future held. Thoughts of Rupa began to wend
their way back into her mind, and she reached back to
hold onto Jamie's arm. Only then did she realize that he

had gone off. Her eyes quickly scanned the hall, and through a window she caught sight of him having a hearty exchange with some of the local men. She was grateful at that moment that a group of local musicians started playing dance music drowning out the fiddler.

Amanda stood by watching the young people dancing, tapping her foot to the rhythms wishing so that she could join in. She saw a young man inviting Emma to join him, and she searched out her father, finding him standing with a small group from the house. Ardell was at the center regaling the crowd with stories of the chic set. The duchess was holding onto Kenneth's arm, and Georgina eyed the bold display of seeming intimacy with great annoyance but was too intimidated by this powerful personality to show her displeasure.

Amanda approached him, "Daddy, join me in a reel."

"My dear daughter, you are trying to embarrass your father. You know I don't dance well. Your Uncle Thomas or Jamie would be delighted I'm sure."

"Jamie is off talking with the locals about farming and other silly business matters and none of the young men will ask me to dance because I'm betrothed to the Lord of the Manor." She cast a jealous glance at Emma and the other young women of town tripping gaily about the floor, thinking it so unfair, since she felt it was her day and if anyone should be the center of attention, it was she.

Georgina, never able to stand Amanda's pouting and startled by her behavior in front of Ardell, nervously blurted out, "Amanda darling, I have a much better idea. Why don't you have the gypsy read your fortune?"

"Oh, Mama, don't be ridiculous—they can't tell the future. It's all a fabrication."

Georgina was flustered—all was not going well for her. Since they arrived in the country, she noticed a change in her relationship with Amanda—at first it was minor things, but yesterday Amanda went ahead with Miss Shields on the seating arrangements for the formal dinner without consulting her—the thoughtless act hurt to the quick; and this morning before leaving for the fair, Amanda consulted Miss Shields on the packing of her things for her honeymoon—the kind of organizational planning she never would have attempted without her mother. No, there were too many things, too many quick dismissals of her suggestions, to excuse her behavior as merely bridal nerves.

Ardell, amazed by Amanda's sullenness and demands, handed her a coin. "Come, Amanda, your mother is right. It's such a lark. You're being much too serious for such a young child."

Amanda bristled at her future sister-in-law's calling her a child. She was certain she did it to vex her—like so many little digs—the honeyed manner of addressing her, then a smile, sometimes a false laugh, and always a reference to her being so young, not accepting her as a mature person —an equal. "Since it will please all of you so much, I shall have my silly fortune told."

The old Bibi sat in the dimly lit area at a table heavily covered with Persian throws. In the center was a crystal ball resting on a square of black velvet. Her eyes were closed, the lids heavily painted with kohl, her hands laid out flat on either side of the ball.

At first Amanda was afraid to speak—it seemed as though the gypsy was in a deep trance. "Madame," she said tentatively with a slight tremor, "I would like to have my future told."

For a time the gypsy didn't move or speak, then without opening her eyes responded, "Sit down in the chair across from me. Please remain as still as possible during the reading. You may ask questions, but do so in a low voice. Now put your hands on the glass for a moment and let us concentrate using as little effort as possible. Whatever comes must be natural."

Amanda laid the coin from Ardell on the table and touched the ball, feeling a surprising warm sensation.

The gypsy drew in several deep breaths and then started her reading—gazing fixedly into the crystal ball.

"There are visions appearing, shapes of clouds." Then she was silent—Amanda asked impatiently, "What do they mean?"

"Patience—that is essential or you will disturb the magnetisms."

Although she was frightened by anything mystical, she still doubted anyone could see images in a plain glass ball. She resigned herself to wait out the gypsy.

"The visions remain in the distance, which means what they will now tell us happened a long time ago or will happen in the future—they are turning slightly crimson in hue, a sign of disappointment, great loss."

The last words shook Amanda's composure, and she started to regret she had allowed herself to be pushed into this situation. She never wanted to know too much about herself, feeling some things should be left uncovered and not delved into.

The Bibi gasped and sucked in her breath. "Now they are gone—there is a face, haggard, worried—it is on the left of the crystal so it is real, not symbolic. It is a woman, an older woman. The scene is playing itself out—the young woman with her is angry. She is turning from the older woman, who has tears in her eyes. She is fading—now gone from my sight."

The gypsy closed her eyes, then blinked her lids open and gazed again into the ball. Her right hand passed over it, "We are seeking strength from you, crystal," and then her left hand passed over, "and sensitivity."

Amanda shifted in her seat and cleared her throat, uncomfortable in the setting.

The gypsy became disturbed, almost fearful, "The clouds, they've reappeared, strong billowing clouds—they are milky—you are unsettled in your mind and there is a bed with an adult lying in it appearing on the right side of my glass. This signifies sickness.

"There is . . ." she hesitated and frowned, then started to speak again, but shook her head. "No—no."

"What do you see?"

"No, it is not important." Amanda knew she was lying. She saw something she didn't want to tell her. "What is it?" she asked, frightened.

"It is not clear enough to read—it is confusing. Let's go on. Try harder young one, your concentration keeps slipping."

Again the Bibi shook her head as though trying to chase away the images she saw, her hands continuously moving over the globe.

Amanda spoke quietly, a worried expression on her face, "Is it about my marriage? Do you see darkness around that?"

"The clouds ascend—I fear they say yes."

"But my marriage will take place, won't it?"

"The message is not clear. It comes and goes."

Her composure was beginning to slip because of all this discussion about her marriage, bringing to the surface all the fears she had been suppressing—Jamie's age, the strangeness of this land, the difficulty she had communicating with his friends, his sister—this is why she didn't want to know about the future—it was better to live it one day at a time.

"Will I be happy?"

"They are not moving, they are confused. Now they begin to move to the left. They are finished speaking to us. They have no more to say."

Both sat there quietly, exhausted, then the gypsy slowly covered the crystal with a piece of dark green velvet and went back into the same trance that Amanda found her in when she first entered. Amanda drew back the curtain and blinked her eyes, trying to adjust to the sudden rush of light. She approached the waiting group, "Well, it is as I guessed—happiness with a wonderful man—only good news. I wonder how she could know all that?" she finished sarcastically. Not wililng to discuss it any further, she drew her cloak tightly around her and left the hall.

She meandered about the edge of the crowd watching the contests, trying to shake the gloom that had descended on her from the reading. A horse brushed against her, scaring her, since it immediately brought to mind her last encounter with Rupa. Jumping away, she turned her ankle and fell to the ground. The young rider leaped from his horse and helped her up, "I'm so sorry, miss. I guess neither one of us was looking where we were going."

"It's all right." She flicked the dirt from her cloak and as she raised her head there he was just a few feet away, sitting in lordly fashion astride his horse watching her. The angle of the sun backlit him, blinding his features, making him seem all the more ominous.

Amanda was frightened—feeling as though a great magnet was pulling her into his sphere. Suddenly he turned, and his horse jogged to the starting line for the main race of the day, "The Hatfield Coin," so called because for centuries the lord of Ashby Manor awarded the winner, when a race was run, a gold coin of great value. As her eyes followed Rupa, still unsteady and feeling faint, Emma rushed up and grabbed her by the arm.

"Come, Amanda, quickly, the race is about to start.

We don't want to miss it. We can see it better from the starting line. Amanda, are you all right? You look so pale."

"Oh it must be because you've been dancing so much and you're so flushed next to me."

The seven horsemen lined up as the rules were being read.

"All riders will round the flag on the distant hill, then head due north along the cliffs to the Watts place, around his barn and straight back here. There are markers showing the path and judges watching along the way, so no messing about."

They were off—jackets flapping, bodies bent forward low on the necks of their mounts, encouraging their steeds. The riders could be followed the long distance to the hill —the terrain having only slight rises and low shrubs. They rounded the pole still all in a tight bunch, headed north along the sea then soon disappeared behind a grove of pine trees and were lost from sight. Everyone immediately turned fifty degrees to their left even though it would take the riders a good ten minutes to be seen coming over the far hill at the edge of Watt's farm.

Last bets were quickly being placed and shouts of early bravado were heard, "No way anyone can beat my horse. You could tell Jake was holding him back waitin' for the others to tire then he'll let him out in the finish." Twice a shout went up, "I can see them." Then laughter, "Drunk already and such a young man."

Finally the cry proved true, and Amanda strained her eyes with the rest, but there was no guessing to be made. Only the dapple gray, Rupa's horse, was in front, with no other horses in sight, his rider's jewelry and adornment catching the sunlight.

33

With the excitement of the race over, the sun slipped behind the trees and no longer warmed the day. The cold air chilled their tired bodies. Everyone gratefully collected in the hall for the final events of the day.

Jamie took Amanda's arm and led her onto the small platform at the front of the hall. From his jacket Jamie took the box holding the gold coin and presented it to Rupa, the winner of the race. The gypsy took the coin, fondled it in his hand and then to Amanda's horror, he approached her, his eyes holding hers. She thought what in God's name was he going to do, wishing she could run and hide somewhere. He took her hand and kissed it. "For the beautiful lady who will soon belong to all of us." Amanda was offended by his remark, an oblique comment, nevertheless, to her, a clear reference to his pursuit of her and his desire to have her. She couldn't bear his mocking tone, and worst of all, her continuing fascination by the audacity of this rogue to mock her and her fiancé, and all that they stood for.

She looked to Jamie who was smiling, obviously delighted with his gesture, having totally missed Rupa's impropriety. The coin burned in her hand, and as the group collected in the hall applauding the act, she murmured a low thank you and turned her body toward Jamie, trying to break off any further contact with Rupa.

"Jamie, please put it back in the box and hold it for me."

Next the Reverend Jenkins climbed on the raised platform and the townspeople pressed forward, obviously anticipating what they knew was coming next. "Your Lordship, Miss McIver, the future Lady Hatfield, as you have

327

witnessed today, the residents of the town of Ashby are very happy about your coming marriage. We commissioned our own blacksmith, George Martin, standing over there, to craft a gift especially for you that would in small measure convey our deep and continuing affection for the Hatfield family."

Two men carried a large package up to the platform. Jamie deferred to Amanda, and she hastily unwrapped the gift from the villagers. She couldn't disguise her disappointment at what faced her: a pair of andirons in the shape of lions like those on the Hatfield crest, but more grotesque and forbidding. Horrid were the eyes set with stones, which would glow a beastly amber when firelight blazed behind them.

Amanda was reeling from the day—it was all too much. While Jamie was giving their thanks and everyone was climbing back into the carriages, her mother came up to her. "Oh Amanda, I've never been so happy—isn't all of this wonderful!"

As she stepped into the carriage, she looked back at her impatiently. "Yes, Mother," she retorted in a surly tone.

But Georgina persevered, "Now, you must remember to thank all of the people—write them charming notes. And tomorrow I'll figure out where to put all of the wedding presents, and we'll set the andirons in the large entrance fireplace, or better yet, your master bedroom, yours and Jamie's."

"Mother, please, no more—I have a wicked headache and I don't want one more thing said about what plans you are making."

Georgina was devastated—this was the second time today Amanda had talked to her in this way—almost shutting her out.

Despite the fact that the residents and guests of Ashby Manor had a full day Saturday at the fair, followed by a formal dinner at the house, most everyone was up early Sunday and consumed a hearty breakfast, in preparation for a hunt. Jamie gathered them in the courtyard, and the grooms brought in the horses they would ride into the park lands in search of grouse and partridge.

Amanda was there too, but Ardell, with several other ladies, were ready to take a more leisurely morning ride. Georgina, however, remained in bed. She was a late riser and didn't believe in exercise. Besides, she was determined to avoid bidding Kenneth and Thomas farewell. She had protested as loudly and vehemently as she could, with no success, on their leaving for London. She felt Kenneth was deserting her. She needed him for support. This visit wasn't as easy nor as much fun as she had anticipated. Jamie, who was so receptive in the city, was off in nine different directions here, so she barely had a chance to talk with him, and Ardell was impossible—she could hardly communicate with the lady. But most distressing was her relationship with Amanda. A mother knows when a daughter gets married she expects to loose her to her husband in some ways, but it was happening so suddenly that she wasn't prepared. She didn't feel this way when Vanessa was married. Of course that was at home, where she was surrounded by family and friends. But this was a strange country, and it felt more alien now than it ever had before, and that awful Miss Shields seemed to be getting very close to Amanda—actually trying to usurp her mother's place.

Amanda bid her uncle and father goodbye and then watched their carriage pass through the archway and down the long driveway. Jamie came up, kissed her on the cheek and helped her onto the mounting block. "I shall see you with the ladies for lunch." It was the custom for the ladies to ride out on the lovely days and join the men on the hunt for lunch. The footmen would ride along with the ladies in a carriage piled high with wicker baskets filled with food and refreshments.

Amanda looked curiously at Jamie getting into the small carriage with the gillie. It occurred to her that what her father mentioned was true—Jamie never rode a horse. She put her hand to her face covering the area just touched by his lips. It was strange, Jamie's kiss felt no more exciting than her father's had. She was convinced that it was love she felt for him, but had always imagined she would feel tingly around the man she would marry. She decided the reason she was questioning her feelings was because her new position was so overwhelming, it was a bit awesome. Then too, Rupa was on her mind. She felt ashamed waking with thoughts of him, his body, his sensuality in her mind.

It wasn't proper, but she didn't seem to have control over his image popping into her head. To her he was vulgar, with crude manners, acting more like an animal—yet there was an excitement about him that no other man had ever prompted in her before. She shook her head angrily—it wasn't right to be thinking of a man other than her fiancé.

"Amanda, come along, you're holding us up—we're all ready to go." Ardell barely waited for her to mount her horse before she whipped hers into a fast trot.

The ride was exhilarating—each day they took a new route through the park lands, and Amanda had to admit that Ardell was a wonderful guide, having spent her childhood roaming this land. One thing she was learning more and more to enjoy was riding. When she returned to London for the season, she would try to ride each morning in Hyde Park along Rotten Row, with the fine ladies of society. Finally, they stopped for a rest, in the distance sounds of gunshots could be heard.

Ardell danced her fine horse in a small circle near Amanda as she remarked, "The men must be having a good hunt—there should be many birds on the table tonight. My husband must be like a child at Christmas now. I just wish he would put some of his verve for hunting into other activities."

Amanda was taken aback at Ardell's open criticism of her husband and the laughter of her friends at the comment. But she also thought of it as a good moment to ask her something that was troubling her, and leaned to Ardell, asking in a private tone, "Ardell, why doesn't Jamie ride horses?"

The eyes of the Duchess of Leighton narrowed, "Have you talked with him about it?"

"No, there's never really been an appropriate time to do so since I've noticed it. He's so virile and active, it just doesn't seem consistent."

Ardell had a tight look about her face as she stared at her, rather meanly she thought. "He had an accident when he was in his twenties—he fell from a horse and hit his head on a rock."

"So he's frightened by it then? Why didn't he tell me?"

"Unlike many people, he's not a complainer. I would just

let it pass if I were you. Besides, do you think this is the proper place to discuss this issue. You are about to marry one of the most important men in England—a brilliant politician—and to become a countess—if the nuptials take place, and your behavior in public, my dear, should have more decorum. Come let's get on with the ride."

"You go on without me. I'm going to ride down to see Emma—about the wedding music. I'll join all of you for lunch with the men."

They took off without her, never looking back.

Lost in her thoughts, she didn't realize that there was a horse and rider off to her left behind a giant oak. The gypsy followed her discreetly as possible as she headed toward the village. As she neared the church, she had the sensation she was being followed and her heart started to pound. Frightened but anxious to know if her fears were well founded, she turned to look behind and saw him. The fearful man, as he increasingly seemed to her, raised his hand in a mock salute then turned back into the woods.

Emma was not in the church or the parish house, but on the town hall grounds, helping with the last of the cleaning up from the fair.

"Amanda, are you all right? You look as though a ghost was chasing you."

"No. I've been out riding, and I guess I wasn't quite up to it with all the excitement of yesterday."

"Oh, Amanda, your wedding has caused such excitement, especially among the women of the village. They are all sewing beautiful dresses for the affair and everyone is eating sparingly, saving room for the great feast, but most talked about are the new lavatories," she covered her mouth and barely got the words out, diffused by giggles. "None of them have ever seen one, much less used one— or the luxurious soaps. I've told them that each guest will be given his own hand towel embroidered with the Hatfield crest and that there's hot and cold running water in the basins. Oh, it's such fun."

Amanda suddenly missed her old friends back home, especially Carolyn. She missed her most of all at this time —they grew up together in Charleston, and when they were twelve, made a solemn promise not to be married unless the other could be present. Emma picked up her spirits somewhat and in some ways filled in the empty space left by Carolyn. Too often she felt inadequate when she was with Ardell and all the upper-class ladies, but she felt at ease with Emma and it was nice to hear from her that she was the center of attention in the village.

34

The church bells rang in the distance as JoJo passed Marble Arch heading for Portman Street—that was where she had to turn to get to Sillar's house off the Square. She listened to the melodious bells chiming a Christmas carol and also signifying services on that Sunday morning were about to begin. She would have liked to attend church, especially at this time, to give thanks—Vanessa was on the road to recovery—and pray she would eventually have complete use of her arm, but she did not want to be away from the house in Chelsea too long. So, she said her prayers with the bells ringing in the background as she hurried on her way, feeling God would understand. Sillar had also been a concern, and she said a prayer that she was fully recovered from her illness, feeling amiss not to have called on her earlier. Christmas was only a week away—they were leaving in a few days for the country and the wedding—this was the only time, really, to see her friend from back home.

Presents wrapped in colored tissue paper were under her arm—one, an old metronome of Vanessa's, for the child. Sillar had told her she had a son, she did not see him the last time she was there—the boy had been out with his nanny, but learned he liked to play the piano. The pendulum had been polished until it gleamed—she hoped the little boy would like it—some children were disappointed when they received useful gifts.

JoJo had wanted to question her about the boy but felt it impolite. If Sillar wanted to tell her all about it, she would.

The shop still had a sign in the window saying CLOSED.

333

Going around to the service entrance, she discovered a small backyard. Pieces of stone and marble sculpture decorated the area, and instead of grass there was crushed gravel under her feet. She spied the door and pulled the bell. Clara, the housemaid, recognizing her from having been there before, let her into a warm cheery kitchen. JoJo smelled the porridge and the cookies baking in the oven. It was a large room, with oak beams and great wooden cupboards—herbs grew in the window boxes, and bunches of thyme and basil were hanging to dry. The smells were delicious and inviting. In the center of the room was a large round table, and she saw the boy sitting there toying with his bowl of food.

"Madame Sillar—is she better?"

"Yes, miss."

"I'm so pleased to hear that—I've brought her a gift—can you tell her I'm here?"

"I don't know—she is resting."

The boy chimed in—interested. "Did you bring me a present?"

She loved the way the curly head tilted to get a better view of her. She went to him.

"Are you Sillar's little boy?"

The child gave her a mischievous, winning look, "No."

"You're not?"

Clara looked at him disapprovingly. "Master Kenneth, you must tell the truth."

The name had a quick effect on JoJo—a frown creased her brow.

"I'm telling the truth," he said. "She asked if I were a little boy—I'm a big boy—uncle told me."

JoJo laughed, "Your uncle sure is right—you are a big boy."

Kenneth was pleased. "Did you bring me a present? You have something under your arm."

"I certainly did—one for you and one for your mama —yours is for when you play the piano."

The little face showed puzzlement. "Isn't it a toy?"

She sat next to him and placed the gifts on the table. "Yes and no. But it's fun—makes noise."

The small fingers touched the stiff paper. "Can I open it now? I don't have anything to do."

"I don't know. Don't you put your presents under the Christmas tree and open them on Christmas morn?"

"No. Those are the presents left on the night before Christmas. These gifts you can open anytime."

"I see," she said—her big black eyes twinkling in pleasure from the exchange with Sillar's child. "But I still think you should ask your mama."

Disappointment crossed his face, but in an instant he perked up with another idea, "Can I see the present you brought my mama? I won't tell."

"Well—I don't think so. That's her special present for her to open—I'll tell you about it if you like because I made it myself."

"You did?"

"Yes."

"Can I make one?"

"I don't think so unless you can sew. It's a tea cozy."

"I know what that is—it keeps the teapot hot."

Clara spoke from near the stove, where she was busy putting food into the warming oven. "Eat your porridge, Master Kenneth—it is getting cold."

The name again struck JoJo as peculiar and she was suspended in thought when suddenly Sillar was there, standing in the doorway, dressed in a long, gold-quilted velvet robe trimmed in satin. Signs of gray were evident in her black hair. JoJo had not seen them before, and she also gave the appearance of having lost quite a bit of weight. Kenneth immediately ran to his mother, who took him into her arms.

"Look, Mama, a black lady. Is she a slave?"

A shocked giggle escaped JoJo's lips—Sillar caught her breath—then hastily tried to explain. "It was just a story I was telling him the other night—about a slave girl in Charleston."

A moment of understanding passed between Sillar and JoJo. Clara took the sugar cookies from the oven—Kenneth ran to watch. "Can I have one, Clara—they look so good."

"Clara, I'll finish that. Why don't you leave—it's your afternoon off—Nanny has already gone."

"I'd be glad to stay, ma'am, if you need me."

"No, no. It is only right you should have your time off."

The maid left the room, and Sillar carried the sheet of cookies to the table and invited JoJo to sit—the kettle was boiling she said, and they could all have refreshments and the freshly made goodies. Kenneth wolfed down the sweets, his mother not having the heart to limit the number he ate. Both women watched him adoringly.

The news of Vanessa was very distressing to Sillar.

JoJo explained to Sillar that she hadn't had a chance as yet to give Mr. McIver her letter, but would on seeing him when they went to the country.

"You're sure he won't be in the city before that?"

"Of course not." Then JoJo had a sudden thought. "Why don't you and little Kenneth come home with me for the afternoon. Seeing you both would so cheer Vanessa."

A guest was coming for tea later in the day, Sillar explained, but Kenneth begged to go—he had never seen a broken arm and would like to go with the black lady— he so liked her he said as he ran to hug her tight. JoJo felt a gush of love pour forth—no one had ever grabbed her in that way before.

The eyes were all excitement. "Tell mommie I have to go."

"Can he, Sillar? I'd like to have him with me."

The boy jumped up and down, "Please, Mommie, please."

Sillar had to laugh at his exuberance. "All right." Then with quiet significance, "I do think you should meet more of the McIvers." And in her head she thought, after all, my son, you are one of them.

They climbed the steps together to the nursery floor to dress the child for his day's outing. He elected to wear his sailor suit, and Sillar scrubbed him from top to bottom in the copper tub before she dressed him.

"JoJo," he shouted as his mother rubbed him hard with the towel, drying him thoroughly before he went out into the damp, cold day, "Can we go to the wax museum? They have fake people who are all dressed up and look real."

"He's talking about Madame Tussauds, a favorite place of his."

"I've never been there—is it far? I can't be away from home too long—my mistress might need me."

"What's a mistress?"

Sillar was embarrassed by the turn in the conversation but decided he had better hear what JoJo had to say.

"That's the lady I work for—Vanessa."

"The one with the broken arm? Are you a maid?"

"Yes, that's what I am."

"Is that because your face is black?"

Sillar stopped the toweling. "Clara is a maid and she's white."

"Clara is Clara," he pouted.

"She is also our maid—she works for us—helps with the house."

"Oh, Mommie, I want JoJo to work for us. Can't we have two Claras?"

They all laughed—Sillar throwing up her hands. "He is at the stage where it is one question after another."

"Well, it's good you are so smart, you can answer him proper. I never seen a youngster so bright."

The complimentary talk delighted the child, and he ran around the room hooting and hollering, with the two women chasing after him, trying to get him dressed.

"Not only is he smart," shrieked Sillar, "he's part injun." She stopped, for she realized what she had said.

35

Tears ran down her face as the icy wind blowing from the Thames stung her face and cut through her heavy clothing as if they were made of the thinnest cotton. In spite of the discomfort, she urged herself to move at a good pace along Cheyne Walk on the river embankment. The confinement of the past days and the trauma of her broken arm had caused the unleashing of so many disturbing thoughts and memories, buried no longer—a constant part of her again. The sleeping tiger at the gate had awakened in full fury, and her protective shell had been cracked open. She breathed deeply, trying to clear her head and calm her nerves. Needing a diversion, she stopped to watch the swift current carrying ships and barges up and down the river—someone is always going away and someone is always coming home and some were left to sail the seas, rudderless—forever. The two bridges within her view were heavy with traffic—and the masses of gulls flying overhead hawked harsh cries, seemingly in protest to what they saw around them.

The river was at its widest here, but it did not stop her from seeing Battersea Park on the other side. Josiah, so devastated since the accident, following her around like a puppy dog lamenting her plight, wanted to take her there for an outing on the first good day, but there hadn't been a good day since the accident—only dreary, gray days.

There was a sharp pain—the good arm went immediately to the injured one—it was so stiff—the sling heavy on her neck. Dr. Hall had told her to stay indoors, to keep warm, but she was feeling so crushed and had to get out— to feel openness around her, breathe the salt air.

Now it felt numb, like a piece of useless wood. Massaging the sausagelike fingers through the woolen gloves helped, but not much. Three months she would have to wear the cast—three months. For God's sake, she couldn't even dress herself or lace her shoes. She felt so completely alone—more tears welled up in her eyes to mix with the ones caused by the wind. Pierre had been so sweet these last few days: the private hospital, being there most of the day and night, bringing her books and special foods.

The failed marriage—had the problem been with her? Her immaturity, not knowing how to really deal with a complex man like Pierre Bonneau. Things said to her by him at her bedside could lead her to believe he wanted to be with her again, but he never actually made a positive statement or declaration. She wiped away tears that were chapping her face. This was not the time, anyway, to make decisions of that sort. She felt a tie with the river—caught within constricting boundaries until nature forced an overflow. She was trapped within herself and her own personality. Would she remain contained or overflow and leap her boundaries? The river—churning now, choppy—always witnessing some form of life and death. Life, she wanted to shout—she wanted life! The realization had been rising these past few days that in a way she had been functioning but hardly living.

Sasha—he would be home right after Christmas—this will be a shock to him as well. She felt little hope for her arm, it felt so useless. Now what was she going to do with her life? Aram had been an experience—a brief encounter, yet so revealing—an awakening. He had taught her in that one vivid night a great deal about herself—a sensuality she never suspected she possessed. Would she know that excitement again? What bliss when that excitement and pleasure produced a child through love. She moved on— thoroughly chilled, sniffling from the cold, her face feeling chapped and raw—positive her nose was red as a beet, but the air did feel good—bracing.

Still trying to divert herself from her troublesome thoughts, she forced herself to look around. It seemed so quiet for Chelsea—not many people about—the walk along the river uncrowded. Of course it was Sunday, so no shouts came from the barges as they unloaded their heavy cargoes. When they first moved here, she and Amanda had witnessed the drowning of a cart horse—one of the animals cruelly used to pull granite blocks, paving stone, and bricks up a slippery ramp—it had lost its footing and tumbled back into the water—drowning before it could be rescued. She learned there was special rigging kept nearby to recover the heavy corpses. There was also equipment in a nearby pub to drag out human bodies when they floated down the muddy waters of the Thames —not an uncommon occurrence.

A brave Italian organ grinder appeared from a side street—he tipped his hat, and she desperately searched her pocket for a copper or two. He should be rewarded she thought, out in this weather trying to make a living. After looking at the contribution rather sadly, he sighed and went toward an old pub down the road, giving up on the frigid day. It was all she had, she wanted to explain, having left the house without her purse, but it was useless. What good would it do—certainly the sentiment would not fill his cup.

She continued on, more slowly than before, thinking she really liked Chelsea, feeling more at home here than any other section of London, not understanding her mother's dislike of the neighborhood that had a feeling of a self-contained village with all sorts of houses and shops. Of course it did attract the people of the arts. Tudor House stood across the street from her—the home of the famous painter-poet, Dante Gabriel Rossetti, one of the founders of the Pre-Raphaelite Brotherhood. She had so admired the thinking of the brotherhood, but unfortunately, the idealistic years of the group had ended several years before. Rossetti was a friend of Sir Robert's, and although she had never met him, she did hear from Robert's enthusiastic lips all about how they revolted against the mechanization and eclecticism of the arts in these Victorian times and how they abhorred the deterioration in craftsmanship. How marvelous, she pondered, to do something that would change an existing reality—to go against convention, brave enough to open oneself to criticism and ridicule. This handful of men, said Sir Robert, started a movement back to the Italian primitives, looking also to nature for inspiration and to hand production again in the crafts, hating the use of machines turning out cheap copies.

He was always so full of news and gossip about the group and their colorful escapades.

She passed Tudor House; it was beautiful, very old, with wrought iron work and a tall gateway giving the impression of an entrance to a fine estate, but right in the heart of Chelsea.

A man appeared at the gate, wearing a wide hat and long cloak flapping about in the strong wind, making him look more like a giant bat than a human being. He called to her.

"Did you by any chance see a raccoon? He seems to have escaped."

She was just about to reply she hadn't when another man approached from the rear of the house holding a furry creature by the scruff of the neck. After a few words, they disappeared around the other side of the house, no doubt to put the escapee back into its cage. She knew there were charming balconies at the rear, overlooking a large garden, where she had been told Rossetti kept all sorts of wild animals and birds. Many a night she heard the hoots of his two owls. Their names, she heard from Robert, were Jessie and Bobbie.

The man who spoke to her must have been Rossetti himself. His wife had died from an overdose of drugs, possibly, it was rumored, self-inflicted. Robert took great pleasure in describing his housekeeper, a plump, decorative woman who had been his model at one time.

The cold was too much; she could take it no longer, but she felt better for it and was looking forward to sitting by the fire with a good strong cup of hot tea. JoJo was off visiting Sillar. Josiah had been in his room all morning studying, so eager now to do what he thought was expected of him. With his help she would start a nice Sunday dinner for them. There was beef to be stewed, carrots, potatoes—a well-aged piece of cheese to be savored along with fresh crusty bread, and a pumpkin pie bought yesterday from the bake shop.

As she neared the street where she lived, a harsh clanging of a bell ripped across the neighborhood sending a shock through her—so reminiscent of the sound on that dreadful nightmarish night a little over a week ago.

Hurrying the rest of the way, she was further horrified

to actually see an ambulance pulling up to the front of her house. She stopped, not able to move any further, her good hand going to her mouth to stifle a scream, fearful that something unexpectedly might have happened to Josiah. She was amazed to see a familiar figure hop off and wave to the driver who sped off again as if being chased by the devil, ringing that horrible bell. Too stunned to be happy to see him, she slowly started down the street as Kirk turned.

"Vanessa," he shouted and ran to meet her.

She noticed his extreme thinness for the first time. The dark blue seaman's jacket hung loosely on his lank frame, probably purchased when he was a much heavier man. The checkered wool cap was set on his curly blond head at a jaunty angle, giving him a rakish appearance. She felt his strong hands on her shoulders and looked up to the rugged face, red as a flame from the sharp wind.

"Hello, there," he said gaily as he studied her with an expert eye. "You've got color, or is it the cold?"

"It is no doubt the frigid air."

"But you're feeling well."

She was happy to see him now—it was the vehicle that brought him that had thrown her. As if reading her thoughts, "I'm sorry about arriving the way I did. It was the only way I could get here quickly. I don't have much time—almost none."

"But it's Sunday."

"That's right—a work day."

"I see. Well, no matter. It got you here."

"Yes." The broad smile was winning, the deep-blue eyes crinkled at the corners. On an impulse, he kissed her cheek, not caring they were in the middle of a street in Chelsea.

Vanessa was astonished.

He tweaked her nose. "Been thinking about you—wondering about your arm and how you were doing."

"All right, I think—getting along."

As he talked, his hand went to her sling as he felt for her fingers.

He seemed to be concentrating on her eyes. "Any pain?"

"Not too much—it comes and goes. Is this a professional call?"

"You could say that—you taking laudanum?"

"Why, yes. How can you tell?"

"It shows in your eyes. Don't take too much—only when necessary. It's a very depressing drug."

"Shall we go inside—this is the first time I've ever been examined on the street."

He laughed, "I can't say this is the first time I've examined a patient on the street."

Her face wore a bewildered expression.

"There are accident cases—people hurt on the road."

"Of course, how foolish of me."

They walked to the small house in silence, and she opened the door, entering. Kirk followed her and once inside, he took her in his strong arms and kissed her soundly on the lips. In a stunned voice she asked, "Why did you do that?".

Devilishly he answered her—his lips close to her ear. "A great urge came over me. I had it out there but controlled myself by just kissing you on the cheek. Did you mind?"

"I don't know—I haven't had time to think about it."

"Oh, oh. That's bad."

"Why?" she questioned in a puzzled voice.

"When you have to think about it—why that's not good, not good at all. You have to feel not think about it."

"Oh. Thanks for the lesson. It just took me by surprise."

Suddenly, Vanessa felt the unseen presence of the nurse between them. The nurse who had tended her in the operating room, and she became jealous. "You're a terribly physical person, aren't you?"

"I hope so . . ." He moved in again as if to kiss her—she moved away—it was too quick—she wasn't ready for this kind of contact with Kirk. It might confuse her thinking.

"Are you afraid?"

"I was, Kirk. I still am. I'll put on water to boil for tea. You must be chilled through from riding atop that ambulance."

He finished helping her with her coat and watched intently as she pulled her glove from her injured arm.

In the cozy kitchen she lit the kerosene lamp rather clumsily—he put fresh coal in the stove to build the fire and filled the kettle with water. Vanessa busied herself getting cups and biscuits from a tin in the cupboard.

Straddling a chair, he tilted his head to talk to her. "That girl came back. Daphne."

"Oh." A shadow of horror crossed the lovely face. "Did she want to start further trouble?"

"No. Nothing like that. She needed a doctor and didn't know where to turn."

"What for?"

Surprised that she didn't know of Daphne's condition, "Why, pregnant—almost six months."

Vanessa clutched her chest. "Josiah?"

"No. The man who died."

The relief was evident. "What did she want then?"

"She was experiencing a great deal of pain—the child was starting to abort."

"I'm sorry . . ."

"Daphne wasn't when I told her what was happening—she was actually pleased."

"Did the woman lose the child?"

"No. I put her in the hospital and assured her, with care and rest, we might be able to save the baby. But I don't know if I really am doing her a favor. She listened after I gave it to her very plain—miscarrying this late in pregnancy could endanger her life as well."

"I'm glad you're trying to save the baby—life is a very precious thing."

A long pause stretched before them. Then rising from the chair deliberately, he stood over her—the strong face etched in concern.

"Vanessa, your fingers, they're stiff and swollen."

She slowly curled them under to form the comfortable ball now becoming natural to her.

"How long have they been that way?"

"Since the beginning."

"No. I had them moving freely at Guy's right after the operation. Have you been exercising them?"

"Dr. Hall said not to move them."

His temper flared immediately. "Dr. Hall! Goddamn! Didn't I tell you that you must keep wiggling them . . ."

"Yes, but—"

"No *but*'s" he interrupted vehemently. "Why didn't you do it? The circulation has to reach your fingers. If it doesn't . . ."

"But Dr. Hall . . ."

"Good God. You want to use your fingers normally again, don't you?"

"Of course. This has robbed my whole life."

"That's ridiculous."

"It is not ridiculous. It's easy for you—you have two perfectly good arms. Why do you flare so, it's upsetting."

He came to her and touched the milky-white puffed fingers. "I'm sorry, Vanessa. That was foolish of me. I was concerned about the stiffness I see and feel."

"You have an odd way of showing concern."

The long sinewy fingers rubbed her hand, "Wiggle them . . . come on. Move them."

"I don't want to." Hurt by his manner, she was very close to tears. "Let me go—the water is boiling."

"No." He did not let go of her. "I want you to move those fingers. Wiggle them!"

She tried but the agility was not there. Imploringly she searched his frowning face, but instead of sympathy, she got gruffness.

"If you don't get them working early, there will always be stiffness. Now try—hard."

"Dr. Hall said the time for therapy will be after the cast is removed and the bone is thoroughly healed."

The exasperation covered his face. "That's too late in my opinion. You've got to exercise the fingers now—they're not broken and your arm needs blood pumping through for healing and to keep limber."

Indignation spread through her. "Do you profess to know more than Dr. Hall?"

His deep voice was tinged with smoldering fury. "Maybe. Good God, I sure as hell don't want to see those fingers suffer atrophy." He dragged her roughly toward the piano he saw in a room off the parlor. Sitting her down, he placed the cast on the wooden case framing the keys. Unfurling the stiff fingers, he put them in position. "Press down, Vanessa—push."

"No."

"Why not? Don't you trust me?"

"I'm afraid," she cried out.

"Don't be! Do as I say, put pressure on your fingers and play."

"No. It might separate the break . . ."

"It can't, I tell you. The cast is holding it firmly in place. Press down on the keys."

Waves of remembrance came over her—another time and place when he was also frantically pleading with her at Wind Flower. The troops were surrounding the house —gunshots tearing at the air. *Get upstairs, quickly. Damn it, girl. Get upstairs.* He had screamed at her, trying to protect her from harm.

Turning her eyes from his steady gaze she whimpered: "It hurts."

His tone became gentler but still commanding. "Let it hurt. Your arm is sore—that's all."

"Do you really and truly think it's all right?"

He sank to his knee and looked into her lovely face, all creased with fear and worry. "Oh, my dear. Please have faith in me. I may not be a Harley Street doctor, but I think I am a good one—I believe in what I am telling you to do because I've seen it work before. Vanessa, the cure is up to you."

There was the same clanging sound and rattling of wheels on the cobblestone that brought him.

"Damn, he's back for me."

Her eyes widened, "So soon?"

"Yes. Officially I am not off duty. I grabbed a ride—the driver was bringing home a patient, nearby. Now you stay there and use those fingers and when you are not pressing on the keys, keep wiggling them until you feel they will fall off."

Josiah came down the narrow stairs just as Kirk had reached the front door.

"Dr. Yoors."

"Josiah. How are you? Feeling all right?"

"Yes, fine."

"Good. Keep that way!" He was gone—the sound of the bell rang in their ears as the ambulance raced toward the hospital.

The swollen hand was still on the keyboard. Josiah moved sympathetically to her. "What are you going to do, Vanessa?"

"What do you mean?"

"I heard everything from upstairs. Are you going to listen to Yoors or Dr. Hall?"

"If it were your problem, what would you do?"

"I don't know. Kirk is from home. We've known him a long time."

"Yes. He seems to always be there when I need him."

He was right, her cure was up to her—bodily and spiritually. She had to start filling the blank spaces of her life. The sound that came from the piano was weak—with effort and pain, she lifted her hand and brought it down again. This time the sound was stronger. Her good hand ran over the keys—it was the first time she had been near the instrument since the accident.

"Vanessa, do you ever think of home?"

"Lately, quite often."

"Me too. I think I'll go with Father when he returns. He's very eager for me to go with him."

"I know. And he needs you. I think it's a wise decision."

"Why don't you come back with us?"

"I just might. I'll give it some thought."

"Do come." He lovingly placed his young hand on her shoulder. "Vanessa, wiggle your fingers—keep them moving. That's an order."

36

Kenneth and Thomas parted at the train station. The trip in from the country had been uneventful, with very little conversation between them. Thomas felt his brother was unusually subdued—he was not a great conversationalist, but today he seemed especially nonplussed. He tried to discuss the meeting he had planned with Harriet later that day, hoping Kenneth would agree to go along, but there was barely a response, so Thomas dropped the subject, resigned to go through the painful experience of begging for additional money once more, on his own. There was no way to put it off—their time left in England was short—only a few days here in London, then they would travel back to Ashby Manor for the wedding and then a boat home to Charleston and St. Helena. He had tried to find another way to obtain the money they desperately needed but had run into dead ends at every turn—Harriet was the only course.

He had decided to see his old friend, Judah Benjamin, first—he would help clear his mind and gather the toughness to approach Harriet. On the boat over, she spent the entire trip in her cabin, not seeing anyone, tended by her personal maids. Since they arrived in London, he had tried several times to broach the subject with her, but she was evasive and immediately would change the topic, frequently turning to a discussion of Pierre and Vanessa. Sometimes she cursed Vanessa, then other times talked about a reconciliation. He would have to be very careful—feel the temperature of the situation before cautiously going forward, not antagonizing her in any way.

Judah's office was at 4 Lambs Bldg., Middle Temple.

His office was warm and filled with richly tooled law books. A prominently displayed book on the shelf was his own volume on the sale of personal property, which had come out a little over a year before and was a great success. Judah's home was the antithesis of his office—simple and sparsely furnished—the abode of a man living on his own and interested only in his work. That's why he spent a good part of Sunday in his office as well—it was much more comfortable.

Thomas took great pleasure in spending time with Judah. Of all the leaders of the Confederacy, he was recognized by most as the wisest. Jefferson Davis had great humanity, but Judah was shrewd. Jefferson had sought his opinion on every major issue and considered him his closest confidant. When the end of the Confederacy was at hand, it was Judah who stayed calm—so many of them talked of fighting on, but he saw their destiny and told them. Then he started his flight south to Florida, moving on to St. Thomas and London. He never looked back nor bemoaned his fate.

Judah rose from his chair to greet him, "Dear friend, what brings you here?" He was an unattractive man, short and very pudgy—the more weight he gained the shorter he seemed. His hands and feet were much too large for his frame, and the full face was swarthy, surrounded by short kinky black hair. The dark heavy beard mixed with gray made him look more like a shopkeeper than a distinguished barrister. What saved his odd looks were his deep-black eyes, which always sparkled and showed a keen interest in everything. They disarmed anyone who met him and were one of his strongest assets in the courtroom.

"I need courage, Judah. We are struggling so hard, and today I find it hard to summon up the reserve to continue on."

"Ah, but you have to, Thomas, the future is all there is. Look at this fifty-eight-year-old friend of yours. A few years ago I had to start over as an apprentice in a law firm— me, the supposed great Southern statesman. I have built a new life—rising like the phoenix."

They sat for a bit, that lovely silence that two friends can share not having to say anything, and for Thomas the silence was most unusual, but their minds working together, their emotions and feelings for one another permeated the room.

"Judah, have you thought of returning home?"

"This really is my home now. My parents were natural born British subjects—I feel comfortable here—I've been accepted to the Bar and the English have been marvelous to me. They are quiet and agreeable." He smiled mirthlessly, "And you know there are a few Northern radicals who would like to have a piece of my hide. They never forgave Breckinridge and me for being the only members of the Cabinet to escape scot-free. No, I'll stay here and be close enough to Paris so that I can see my wife who has chosen to continue living with our daughter."

"I miss you back home—we could use your acumen to help defeat those damned Republicans. Can you imagine, a government of Negroes deciding the future of South Carolina. They are squeezing every cent out of us for taxes: on income, sales, telegraph, gas, even a dollar a head per dog and a dollar on every one hundred dollars of cotton on hand. The taxes are excessive and oppressive. The Negro politicians want to raise taxes to the point of confiscation."

"Thomas, you have given me one more reason to stay exactly where I am. You know that Jefferson and Varina have gone home. He finally became tired of all the schemes, the desperate get-rich-quick ideas—tin mines, gold mines. He is to become president of the Carolina Life Insurance Company. Poor Jefferson, when he first came here he was treated like royalty, a welcome relief from his years in jail, but when he needed their backing, their financial support, no one knew his name. He allowed himself to be buffeted about by self-pitying Southerners. I wish I could have helped him and also could help you. I know there were rumors of my absconding with Confederate money, but it's just not so. I too have had hard times. The money I made from my cotton stored in the West Indies was carried away with the demise of the illustrious banking firm of Overend, Gurney. But I know what I want, and I've got a firm start—I won't quit and you can't either."

"I am almost more willing to work side by side with a Negro in a cotton field than to face Harriet Bonneau this day. She's a dried-up lady, old before her time, who loves to see me grovel. The only thing that really makes her happy is to see me beg for the money—pocket money to her—to keep us afloat. I already know the scene that will be played out. I shall have to hear about the fact that she is a poor woman alone in the world and she has to guard every cent for her old age when she won't be able to keep her plantation running, and because of my niece Vanessa, her son has turned against her, et cetera, et cetera. Oh God, how I hate what I have to do."

Judah smiled, "She is an old crow, isn't she. I don't envy you. But have patience—who knows, in time she along with the new politicians and the carpetbaggers may be gone from your life."

"I suspect, of them all, Harriet Bonneau will tenaciously hang on to the last."

Thomas stood before the large fireplace in the Claridges Hotel lobby warming his hands, while waiting for the desk clerk to ring Harriet. In the sitting room off the lobby, guests were seated about on comfortable groupings of chairs and sofas, being served tea by men in black satin knickers, red velvet jackets encrusted with gold braid. Their hair was powdered, and they wore fine white stockings, and black shoes with grosgrain bows. Their uniforms never changed, held over from a much earlier period, and would probably remain that way for some time into the future.

He ran over in his mind how he would start the conversation, but he dismissed each sentence as it was formed —nothing seemed right.

Upstairs, the Negro servant showed him to her sitting room. "Mistress Bonneau will be with you shortly—she says to make yourself comfortable."

He couldn't stay seated—he felt all jumpy and anxious. Pacing the room, he did not realize Harriet had entered and was watching him.

"Thomas, you'll wear a hole in the carpet."

"Oh, I'm sorry, Harriet, I didn't see you come in. May I take this occasion to wish you a happy holiday season."

She moved to a large Queen Anne wing chair and motioned for him to sit in the love seat across from her.

"So, Thomas, you've come for money. I knew we would get around to sorting this out before you left. I just wondered why it has taken you so long."

At least she brought up the subject, so had spared him the embarrassment, but he prepared for a biting confrontation.

"Do you have your fingers worked out? Let me see."

He had struggled long hours putting together the information. She always scrutinized them carefully. He watched her, her fingers tapping the arm of the chair, as she studied his sheets of facts and figures. She had the annoying habit of coughing and clearing her throat constantly when she was concentrating. He was prepared for the haggling to begin.

"Well, you seem to have done your usual fine job of putting together the required information."

"Harriet, I've cut everything close to the bone. There's little if any room for movement. I . . ."

"I agree, Thomas, you may have the money . . . all of it . . . exactly as you outlined."

He was ready to press his case further when after a few moments, what she said sunk in. He felt confused—at a loss. "But I—"

"Thomas, you may have what you need and in addition I am willing to loan you the start-up money for the furniture factory. It's the right time to get that producing again. The McIver name is well known in South Carolina, and all my instincts tell me people will soon start putting their homes in order. It's a good investment for me. I'll contact my lawyer and you and he can work out the details."

He was still flabbergasted—never did he expect anything like this. What was going on?

"Well, I guess that settles all, unless you have something else on your mind."

"No, I'm very grateful. All we McIvers are."

She waved her hand dismissing him, but when he reached the door, she stopped him. He turned, looking at her face, afraid she had changed her mind, a dark morose expression colored her aging face.

"I'm sorry about Vanessa. You know that I have had my moments of being less than fond of her, but they were because I was mainly confused by my feelings about my son. But I was so sorry to hear the news from Pierre."

"News? What news?"

"You don't know? Why she broke her arm. Pierre said she shall never be able to use it properly again."

"Oh my God. I didn't know—I haven't been to the house in Chelsea yet."

"It's because of her that I have agreed to the money. Pierre is going to persuade her to be married again and to return home. I felt it only right that I make things easier for all of you and thereby relax her mind."

He was terribly surprised. "But you have been telling me all along of your disapproval and I conveyed that to the family."

"Circumstances change."

He should have known that something dramatic had happened to make her so generous suddenly. "I must be going—Kenneth will need my help."

37

Early Monday morning a courier came dressed in the livery of the queen, which caused great excitement in the household. Victoria was at Sandringham, her son's country estate not too far away, spending the holiday. The note said Jamie was needed on urgent business and must arrange to join her immediately. He was certain that there was some business to discuss, but doubted that it was that urgent. It was more likely the queen was also curious about what was going on with his wedding. She couldn't stop meddling, and he was certain since she did not accept their invitation to the ceremony, she nevertheless wanted a first-hand report to date. He would arrange to take a boat from Great Yarmouth around the northern point of Norfolk and down to King's Lynn and Sandringham, the trip being quicker than overland.

Jamie returned late the next day after everyone had finished tea. The pressure of the trip and the week's events plus the thought of those to come were showing their effect—he was tired, with large dark circles rimming his eyes. He went immediately to his study. "Martin, tell Miss McIver I've returned and would like to see her when she has a moment."

"Yes, m'lord—she is ice skating—I'll send word."

"Isn't it too dark to skate?"

"Torches have been placed around the pond, m'lord."

Martin took Jamie's coat, placed his leather case next to his desk, then brought him the crystal decanter of whiskey, with matching glass. As he was pouring Jamie's drink the door opened.

"Give me a bit too, Martin." Ardell kissed Jamie, "Welcome back. Was the trip tedious?"

"Yes, tiring. She is a demanding woman."

"And on what pretext, what affair of state did she call you to Sandringham?"

"No pretext really, just more of the same, her constant concerns: relations between France and Prussia, then Gladstone is proposing bills which are distasteful to her, especially the Land Act, and of course, top on the list is finding suitable husbands for her unmarried daughters."

"And does she talk about supporting you for prime minister—it seems to me she uses you to discuss the affairs of her country and her household more than anyone else in government. It's about time she repaid you."

"It is not such a bad thing to be the close confidant of the queen."

"Not unless it causes jealousy among your peers and makes them think you have too much already. And besides you know the public is beginning to grumble openly about their 'unseen' monarch. Did you persuade her to open Parliament this year? It is the least she can do."

"She refused adamantly. Her excuse is that the low-cut dress will bring on a severe cold."

They laughed together. "On a more serious note, she discussed the Lady Mordaunt divorce case—that I believe was her main concern at the moment. The news will break shortly; it is believed the Prince of Wales will be subpoenaed to appear, and his letters to Lady Mordaunt, though innocuous, will be read in court. Quite damaging to the Crown, the queen feels."

"But he never had anything to do with her romantically. They've been friends for years, but not that way, and everyone knows she is quite mad and confined to an asylum. Surely the queen can use her influence to help out her son."

"She wanted me to try, but I reminded her that before the law all men are equal, including the Prince of Wales. The great sadness is Alexandra—she is a young woman with two small children and this has caused a schism between her and her husband. You know how Victoria feels about marriage and faithfulness. She carried on endlessly about the fast set and the lack of morals in society—feeling it will eventually effect all classes. It has consumed her."

"Well, in some ways it pleases me no end. She lectures everyone at court on their behavior. She insinuates her morals into everyone's boudoir and now the evil lust has come home to roost. She's a recluse hiding from the world, not even willing to perform the most minor of majestic duties like opening Parliament, and now she will have to publicly accept the real world whether she likes it or not."

"You are too hard, Ardell. She has suffered from the painful loss of her husband, who made her life have relevancy, and because you elected to drop out of her favor, doesn't allow you to gloat at her misfortune."

"And what does Bertie, the spoiled Prince of Wales, have to say?"

"Nothing much—he is rather pathetic, a twenty-eight-year-old man with no occupation. No wonder he gets into all these extraneous affairs." His eyes wandered about the room, slightly disoriented, as he sat down heavily in his chair.

"Are you feeling out of sorts? There is too much pressure on you now."

"I just felt a bit heady—don't worry."

Ardell, her eyes betraying the concentrated thinking going on in her head, broached the next subject cautiously, "Did she discuss your marriage?"

"Yes, we touched on it briefly, and she gave her promise to consider accepting Amanda at court. She seems to be open to the idea now."

"You promised yourself to reconsider this marriage?"

His tiredness caused him to react sharply, "That is enough, Ardell. I know what you think and what so many of our friends think. But the decision has been made and it's too late to change my plans."

"You may raise your voice to me, dear brother, as much as you like, but I will be heard. I must speak my mind. You are ruining your career by marrying her. She won't make you a proper partner either in your career or your bed. She is a twit—a tease."

"Ardell, don't demean my choice by such foul remarks. She is exciting to me—a fresh face. You almost sound jealous."

"God forbid that you get tired of her fresh face; she's

not like us. We have arranged our priorities correctly. Take note of her mother. It's obvious she doesn't enjoy a real relationship with her husband—a cold fish, unable to fulfill the true role of a wife. That daughter, your future wife, is an unhatched version of the mother."

"She is sensual and warm—we will be perfect together. And in any case, I don't think you're in a position to discuss the role of a proper wife."

"Take care that it is not just an outer shell. I am always wary of one who takes to wealth and its trappings as quickly as she and her mother have—it's a sure sign of an inner weakness."

There was a light knock, barely a brushing of the knuckles on the door, and Amanda came bounding in, her cheeks red from the cold.

"Hello, my love. Oh whiskey, what a good idea."

"Don't you think tea would be better, Amanda?" Jamie was taken by surprise at her request.

"No, no, Ardell has the right idea—I'm beginning to like the warmth of this liquid when coming in from the cold. Oh, Jamie, you should join us, we're having such fun. Most everyone is there."

"I can't, Amanda—I have a great deal of catching up to do."

"But I haven't seen you. You're not being fair. You don't seem to have any time for me lately."

Ardell drained her glass quickly and rose, "Well, I think I'll leave you two to discuss your wedding. See you at dinner."

"Yes, dinner. Amanda, I just wanted to let you know I was back—now I have pressing business."

She didn't take the hint, but pressed on as Ardell quietly closed the door, "But this is supposed to be our time. We should be together enjoying our prewedding parties."

"Amanda, this is my life and you have to accept my work as it is—it will never change."

She watched as he turned back to the stack of papers on his desk. "Well, I'm not so pleased with your queen giving you all these problems at this time, and you can tell her that when you see her again."

"You may be able to tell her yourself, Amanda. There is a chance she will receive you at Windsor when we return from our honeymoon."

He stood up from his desk and reached out to take her in his arms, but suddenly shouted out as though he had been struck a great blow from behind, "Oh no, Martin . . ." His body went stiff and fell forward landing against her body. She stepped back horrified and let him fall to the carpet. His arms and legs began to twitch, and he started to thrash about wildly, his body jerking, a bloody foam collecting in the corners of his mouth.

"Mother, Mother!" she screamed becoming rigid in her fright.

Martin came rushing in followed by Ardell and her mother. Ardell quickly stopped the entrance of a few of the guests who came running to help at the sound of Amanda's screams.

"It's all right everyone—a minor accident. Go back and enjoy yourselves. We'll all be there in a moment." She grabbed Amanda by the shoulders. She was watching Martin wiping Jamie's mouth, a large wet spot by his groin suddenly appeared and increased, spurting its way down his leg—he had wet himself.

"Oh, God, it's so awful, he's disgusting."

Ardell slapped her face. "Be quiet, Amanda, the company will become alarmed. No one is to know about this. He is having one of his fits."

With that Amanda ran from the room frantically, wiping her sleeve of the spittle that had dropped on her. Georgina tried to catch up with her, "Amanda, come back, it will be all right."

"No, let me be. I hate him—it's nauseating."

She ran through the courtyard and toward the stable, climbing on a horse loosely tethered to a post being groomed. She hiked up her dress to throw her leg over the saddle.

"Here, miss, if you like it will only take a minute to put a sidesaddle on."

She never answered but headed out with no destination in mind. The rising moon was hidden by clouds, and the night turned very dark. Fires in the distance drew her in their direction, and before she knew it she was at the edge of the gypsy camp.

"There is an illness . . ." the gypsy's prediction ran through her mind. Did she mean Jamie? What else had she

seen? There was something—she must know what is going to happen. Amanda was driven to find out. She dis-
mounted and approached the wagon Emma had told her
was the Bibi's. A short distance away she saw a group of
gypsies, some standing, some sitting around a large fire,
with a fiddler in the group bowing a plaintive song.

As she approached the wagon she heard the jingling
of jewelry and recalled the sound the Bibi's hands made as
they moved over the crystal ball. A tiny rim of light outlined the drapery inside the open door in the rear of the
wagon, casting a strange light on the gremlin and wild
animals painted all over the wooden frame. She heard
the low murmur of a woman's voice speaking in the strange
Romany tongue.

Amanda called softly, "Gypsy queen, are you in there?"
There was no reply, only the continuing sound of the voice,
melodically chanting, as though soothing a child. She
cautiously climbed the ladder stairs and pushed open
the door further. A transparent magenta curtain hung
across the width of the wagon, blocking from view most of
the interior, but she could see a figure on the other side and
the chanting voice was louder. Carefully, she drew aside
the curtain—the eyes—Rupa's eyes held her, stopping her
dead in her tracks. He was lying on a mountain of pillows
and oriental throws, and sitting on him was a gypsy woman, her back to Amanda—she was swaying and touching
Rupa, pulling open his shirt, rubbing his chest, his stomach,
his hips as she continued her sexual, singsong intonation.

Rupa watched Amanda—a bogus smile broke on his
face—his tongue circled his lips seductively—then his big
hands found the woman's skirt and raised it above her
hips, baring the lower part of her body totally and revealing his own nakedness. Amanda at last realized they
were making love, her eyes darted from the woman's bare
skin to Rupa's muscular legs and watched his hands firmly
holding the woman's buttocks, moving them faster and faster, heightening his own pleasure. He kept watching Amanda, his look and movements taunting her. Then he lifted
the gypsy woman high in the air off him and Amanda
had a full view of their nakedness. His mate screamed for
him and he spoke in Romany, a sound of lust, then lowered the woman slightly but suddenly pushed her high

again teasing her. Amanda was riveted to the sight, her lips curling at the edges, her eyes becoming slits. Finally he let her drop hard on his penis, and as it found its way into her again, she screamed with satisfaction. They rolled over and back and forth enjoying every bit of the orgasm. When it was over, Rupa rose, wearing only a satin vest, leaving the woman totally exposed. Amanda turned to run, but was caught in the filmy curtain. She groped about trying to free herself but fell to the floor in her desperation and then felt Rupa next to her.

"Why are you shuddering so—does it excite you?"

"Don't touch me—don't come near me."

She felt as though she were trapped in a cocoon, all wrapped up, pressed against a man's body that radiated more warmth than she ever dreamed possible.

"I knew you would submit to me. I am ready to take you—there has been enough teasing over the past few days."

She started to cry, "You are an animal, an insufferable animal—a pig."

He became angry, smarting from her words. "You are a stupid child. Get out of here you pretender. I only make love with women."

Roughly, he helped her to her feet and freed her from the fabric.

"Enjoy your wedding night. Try not to think of Rupa." He laughed as she stumbled from the wagon.

The church was lighted by a few kerosene lamps. She had no idea how long she had been sitting in the pew trying to collect herself—she had such doubts. Close to midnight, still distraught, she rode back to Ashby Manor in a slow cadence.

The next day Jamie knocked on her door twice, and Georgina spent almost an hour using every emotional appeal she could think of, from shouting at her, to weeping miserably, but Amanda refused to speak with anyone. She opened her door only to hand Peony out for a walk or to accept her meals brought personally by Miss Shields. Their only solace was that the food trays brought to her were returned completely clean of their contents. She was not so upset she couldn't eat.

Thursday morning Jamie resolved to have a showdown with Amanda. Her father and the rest of the family were due back from London, and the punishment was enough, making him feel enough guilt and shame to last a year, and he found himself wondering what he really wanted—was she right for him? Was she too young? Too naive when it came to the facts of life? But damn it—these were the very traits that made her so attractive, giving his dull life vitality, but was there a place for these hysterics in his life? Why not do as Ardell suggested and just arrange for a lovely woman to be ready and waiting when desire called? He held the envelope with the royal seal in his hand and decided he did love her, needed her as much trouble as she was, but now was the time to get the upper hand in their relationship or he would go through life being subservient and wrapped around the finger of a woman twenty years his junior.

He knocked at the bedroom door. "Amanda, it is Jamie, and I want you to open the door immediately." There was no response. "Amanda, you and I have a great deal to discuss. Open the door."

"Go away, Jamie—I don't feel like talking."

He refused to stand in the hallway of his own house begging, so went into the room next door—a small sitting room connected by a door to Amanda's. He tried the handle, but it was locked. He stepped back a few feet and then gave one great kick at the fragile lock, and the door swung open.

Amanda was sitting on the love seat near the fireplace, dressed in a red velvet robe, devouring a box of chocolates, with Peony beside her sniffing the contents. She gasped as he came hurtling through the door, but then assumed a pout.

The sight of her moved Jamie—he knew she was mostly playacting. Yes, she was childlike and it appealed to him, and yes, he was willing to be manipulated to a point, because it made him feel young and joyful. His first two wives were smart, sophisticated, but they were competitive, to a point of exhaustion at times.

"Amanda, we must patch things up. We are to be married in just four days."

"I don't want to—I can't deal with all of this. I'm frightened."

He tried to take her hand, but she pulled back.

"Well you must decide now what you want. The house is filled with wedding guests, the townspeople are readying for the celebration, gifts are arriving and the bride-to-be is nowhere to be seen. Tell me what you have decided."

"Why didn't you ever tell me?"

"After I told your mother, I assumed she would discuss it with you. As a matter of fact, she said she would. It would be better coming from her."

"My mother knew—she knew?"

"Yes, from the very beginning she's known. She saw me having one of my attacks."

"And she never told me. I can't believe that." She started sniveling again.

"Amanda, stop, we must decide."

"You never had children. Is it—is it your illness?"

"No. I can have children—it just never happened before, and the children will be perfectly normal. What I have is epilepsy. The attacks will never be worse than what you saw the other night and most of the time they will be so mild you won't even know I have them. The medicine I take helps prevent them. This is not hereditary because my illness came from a blow on the head."

"When you fell from the horse. Ardell told me."

"When we get to London I shall take you to see Sir Samuel Wilks. He's my doctor and the greatest expert on this illness—he will reassure you that life will be relatively normal."

She wiped her eyes and was beginning to look cheerier by the second. "I don't know."

Jamie drew the envelope from his pocket, "Lady Manley arrived last night for the wedding and brought this with her."

Her eyes lit up as she recognized the royal stationery and seal—quickly taking the envelope from his hands and breaking the wax.

"Oh, Jamie, it's from the queen for me."

Her eyes scanned the lines hurriedly and then started to read them a second time more slowly, thoroughly digesting their content. "She's invited me to the palace for tea to meet her and to be presented at court. Oh Jamie, how wonderful. Imagine me at the Court of St. James.

Quickly, I must get dressed—everyone should know. Oh, we will be happy—won't we?" She rushed to him, hesitated, then shyly, like a little girl who had misbehaved, put her arms around his waist.

It was late on the eve of Amanda's wedding when Georgina on the way to her room, stopped and knocked on Amanda's bedroom door.

"It's your mother. I've come to say good night."

"Come in, Mama." Amanda was already in bed.

"Wasn't it a wonderful party—it was what I needed to get over the shock of Vanessa."

She started tucking in the blankets under her legs and about her waist as she did when Amanda was a little girl. She felt so close to her—this was the child who would never desert her, who would take care of her in her old age. When all else fell apart, Amanda would be there for her, even if she had behaved a bit peculiarly these last few days.

"I can't believe it—my baby girl going to be married tomorrow, and to an earl. Imagine. Are you excited, angel?"

"Yes, I am. At times it's been difficult. My life will be so different, and there are so many responsibilities."

"Well, you know you don't have to worry, I'll be here with you. All the social graces you will need are second nature to me." Then she added grandly, "Lady Hatfield, the Countess of Raleigh." She giggled in her delight. "I just had to hear how it sounded out loud." She began puffing herself up with pride, not seeing Amanda's grimace.

"Daddy's really been so sweet, so concerned. I can tell he is moved by my marriage. And he has been lovely with Vanessa. I feel very grateful that I have such a helpful parent."

Georgina smarted with jealousy. "Well, the burden of Vanessa's injury will fall on me as always. He'll go back home, and I'll be left having to care for her. I've decided we'll stay with you and Jamie in London. It will be easier on me having the proper help and then I can be with you, to help you adjust. Miss Shields is difficult, but I've come to admire her—she has too much to keep track of, no wonder she's short at times."

"Have you thought about going home with Father? He seems to want that."

She looked up at Amanda tying her hair back with a ribbon, completely misreading the tone of her voice and the message.

"Oh, my dear girl, don't worry, your mother won't desert you."

"Mama, what I mean is I think you should go home with Daddy. That's your place."

"You can't be serious?"

"I am. I want to run my own house, make my own decisions. I don't need you to do that for me."

"But you're just a child . . ."

"I am twenty-two and refuse to be told I'm a child any more."

"Amanda, you're being very naughty. I know it's normal to have wedding jitters, but you haven't talked to me civilly for days and now at last when you do, you're rude. A mother knows when she is being shunned by her child."

Amanda didn't answer her, just stared off into the room. "I'll tell you a secret, Amanda, you would be a very sorry person without me."

"A secret? At last you're telling me your secrets. What other secrets are you hiding that I should know about?"

"Now, there's no reason to get so worked up."

"Why didn't you tell me about Jamie's illness? Why did you keep that secret from me?"

"I didn't want you to worry unnecessarily. He said his attacks would be few and Martin takes care of them, and you might never know."

"How ridiculous, and I did find out in the worst possible way. I don't need the kind of protection you want to impose on me."

Georgina's voice began to take on a note of hysteria, "I won't go—I won't leave you."

"I can't force you to leave London, but you will not live with Jamie and me. Now I think you should leave me alone. Tomorrow is my wedding day and I want to look radiant and untroubled." She turned in her bed, her back to her mother.

"Amanda! I'm your mother!"

There was no reply—she pulled the covers over her head.

Georgina clenched her fists in frustration and rapidly shook them in the air. She had lost—all this time she was able to sidestep around Kenneth, but Amanda, her precious likeness, had finished with her in one short conversation.

38

There was a hush in the private chapel at Ashby Manor. As the final words of the ceremony were spoken, the Reverend Jenkins pronouncing them man and wife, there was a visible sigh of relief on Jamie and Amanda's faces. In her satin dress with the long train caught by bouquets of pale pink silk flowers, the bride was like a confection. The headpiece was a mass of the Brussels lace Vanessa brought her, flounced about her head in a soft cloud. Ropes of pearls formed a collar at her throat, and a large diamond on a long thin chain settled low on her bosom. She had barely made it through the ceremony, leaning heavily for support, first on Kenneth to walk up the aisle and then on Jamie as they exchanged vows—her dress shaking along with her body. She raised herself now on her tiny feet to accept Jamie's polite kiss, but his hands dug into her arms as he held her possessively.

The small group of guests and family left the chapel and walked behind the couple into the Great Ballroom, shimmering with light from the four large crystal chandeliers, all set for the reception this Christmas evening. There they were greeted by a line of footmen dressed in the formal livery of Ashby Manor: royal blue quaker coats worn with purple knee breeches, the color scheme made popular by Victoria.

The townspeople, waiting anxiously, applauded as the couple stood and waved from the top of the marble staircase leading down to the ballroom. Jamie's previous two wedding ceremonies had taken place in London, with only minor celebrations being held at the great house, so the townspeople were especially jubilant. He was thoroughly enjoying this moment—truly amazed at the transformation in the people who always looked so ruddy and plain, now looking splendid in their fancy attire.

The immediate family formed a reception line, Georgina standing between Amanda and Kenneth. She enjoyed hearing the effusive compliments about her daughter, especially, "She looks just like you madame—an American beauty." She buried her own concerns for the moment, thinking that somehow before Amanda left on her honeymoon they would all be straightened out.

Amanda was feeling wonderful—she hadn't anticipated such an instantaneous change in her essence—she truly felt like a different person, and she could feel herself standing in a different way, holding her body more regally.

Martin came by, "I am so pleased your Ladyship, and at your service." After him stood Miss Shields, dressed in a lovely floral frock, almost unrecognizable because of the softness it brought to her personality. The servants in the room went about their duties, but their attention was very much keyed to whether or not Sara Shields would finally let go of her devotion to the second Lady Hatfield. She was a hard woman to work under and if she didn't accept the new mistress, their life would be even more impossible. They would be in the middle—unable to please their new mistress for fear of offending Miss Shields and vice versa. She took Jamie's hand, "God's blessing on you Lord Hatfield . . . ," at last she faced Amanda, "and on you too, Lady Hatfield." Though there was a grimace on her face when she said it, the servants and the bridal couple knew there would be relative harmony in their household.

When Miss Shields moved on to the McIvers, she turned cold again and the felicitations she extended were issued through a tightly clenched jaw.

After the toasts and the feast, everyone was grateful when the dancing started, led off by Jamie and Amanda, anxious to relieve the uncomfortable feeling of their full stomachs. Vanessa stood to one side watching, happy for her sister and for her family, which was finally coming out of a long period of bad fortune. Kenneth sidled up to her, "Are you looking for a fine beau to dance with?"

"Are you asking me, sir?"

"I thought, with your bad arm and my bad rhythm, we

would make a fine couple. Here, we can dance in the shadow of these palms."

They laughed aloud at the awkwardness of her sling, not immediately noticeable since she had it made in the same rust brocade fabric to match her dress. A Strauss waltz was playing and they swayed together, Vanessa humming along. When the waltz ended a mazurka started, and the townspeople were freer (the faster dances more appealing to them), giving them a chance to kick up their heels and release any inhibitions they felt by being in Ashby Manor.

"I won't even attempt this, Vanessa," as he guided her off the floor. "Let's go to the dining room for a refresher."

Amanda watched Rupa leave the ballroom and decided to follow him. She had been aware of his presence—whenever she looked up he was there, hovering nearby, silent but staring at her. He was making her angry. She found him standing midway down the length of the long gallery by the french doors that opened onto the terrace. She walked on her toes toward him, trying to avoid the drama of hearing the heel of her shoes hit the marble floor. When she came near him, his back to her, she waited for him to turn, knowing he was aware of her presence, but he held still. "I want to speak with you." He turned slightly, showing his profile—handsome and exotic, the one gold earring catching the light from the wall sconce.

"You are to leave me alone—I don't want you to come anywhere near me. When you see me, step out of my path."

"Yes, Lady Hatfield."

"And stop mocking me. I have a new life, and I want to be left alone."

"No need to worry—we gypsies will be gone in the morning—not a trace of us will be found."

"Good—I'm delighted. That's all I wanted to hear." As she started to go, feeling surprisingly deflated, he spoke.

"Lady Hatfield, your relief is temporary—we return each year at the same time for one month, so you and I shall have an opportunity to renew our interests."

"I've just told you, I want nothing to do with you. Make no more advances to me—stay away from Ashby Manor or I shall have to ask Lord Hatfield to deal with you."

"You won't do that, and next year when I come, who knows? You shall be a woman then, a lady with a year of love behind her. You know desire grows and keeps reaching out, especially when not fully satisfied."

"You are shameless." She stormed off, but was still in earshot when he called after her, "Have a good wedding night, Lady Hatfield."

She hastened back into the dining room, bumping into Vanessa. "Careful, Amanda, I need this other arm."

"I'm sorry, Nessa, Father. I was just rushing back to Jamie. It must be getting on to the time we are to leave for our honeymoon. Would you find Mother and come say farewell."

As she continued on, her veil billowing out behind her, Vanessa, confused, turned to her father, "Is she all right, Daddy?"

"I hope so—I hope all this is what she really wants and that it will make her happy. I've tried to talk to her, but I have as much trouble reaching Amanda as I do your mother. All I could extract from Georgina last night was that the two of them had a mighty tiff. She was beside herself, not being able to come to grips with the fact that through this marriage she was not about to find a new glorious life but was being tossed back into the old one, complicated by the loss of a daughter who she had been living through and who suddenly turned from her. I wish I could relive so much of my life. All the mistakes I have made. However, that's easily said from hindsight. May there be happiness for all of us." He fingered Sillar's letter in his inside breast pocket.

"You will have me back in your hands for a bit if you don't mind. I've decided to return with you and the family to South Carolina."

"Well I'm delighted, but does this mean you're going to give up your career? I would hate to see that happen, if only because I love bragging about your accomplishments."

"No, it's a positive move. I need to be home, to rest someplace where I can quietly collect myself."

"Well nothing would make me happier, but please don't be disappointed when you see the place. It is very, very different from what it was. I don't know what your mother will do when she sees it."

She touched his face tenderly, "What would have happened if there had been no war? Do you think we still would be just a great big noisy family like before?"

"Possibly, honey, but the tides of life take us in so many directions—and we poor men just can't seem to stop creating havoc and destroying."

"I've seen Matthew Brady's photographs of back home —such devastation. When we left, things were in sorry shape, but not like that. At least there won't be the bombardments and the fear of marauders striking our own land and home. Now it will be rebuilding for the McIvers, not tearing down, especially with the loans of Harriet Bonneau."

"Does that bother you, Vanessa?"

"Not at all—we are neighbors, after all."

"Don't let it influence you in any way."

"It won't, Father. I promise."

They reached the bottom of the steps just as Amanda threw her bouquet—it was caught by a young villager who squealed in delight—her awkward beau nearby flushing in embarrassment. When Vanessa raised her eyes again to the bridal couple, they had disappeared—off to start their new life.

39

The women sat in the small sitting room strewn with
boxes, tissue paper, and old suitcases, drinking tea out of
cracked china cups—Kenneth excused himself, tired of listening to their chatter, content he had put in a proper appearance for Georgina's sake. For the most part they were
down at the heels Southerners, martyrs all, licking old
wounds, come to say goodbye to Georgina who was holding court, regally, bragging about her connections now with
English society. Envy and jealousy showed in most of their
faces and that pleased Georgina no end. Only an hour
before she was applying layers of powder to cover her puffy, red-rimmed eyes from all the crying she had done since
her rejection by her darling Amanda and the fact she was
practically on the boat going home to God knows what
—her life was over. But she certainly would not let these
women, supposed friends, see her in defeat, her excess of
pride would not allow the exposure.

Pansy, the wife of the schoolmaster, whose school
Amanda and Josiah attended when they first arrived,
seemed genuinely thrilled in her enthusiasm regarding the
wedding. The deaf woman sitting next to her was her
mother, brought along for the special occasion and an-
noyingly interjected her thoughts whenever one came upon
her. The frizzy gray head bobbed incessantly as if in
agreement with all that was said—in truth it was due to a
nervous tic—the old woman was antagonistic toward everything—being onerous and bitter over her family's lost position and lack of money.

Pansy gushed, "The French Riviera? Why Georgina,

how positively divine. Such a romantic place to spend a honeymoon."

"Well, Jamie, my son-in-law—Lord Hatfield that is—only knows the best. A Count DeGrasse has lent him his villa overlooking the Mediterranean."

The voice was loud—unfortunately, the old woman in her deafness had no sense of volume. "What did she say? Lord what's his name and Amanda are at sea?"

So used to her mother's affliction, Pansy leaned over to clarify for her in a loud voice, too. "No, Mother dear, Lord Hatfield has taken Amanda to the French Riviera."

"I heard that."

"It overlooks the Mediterranean Sea."

"Oh, that's nice," she acknowledged with a sarcastic smirk. "Probably rainy and cold this time of year. You tell me he is an old man?"

Pansy patted her mother's hand as she corrected her through gritted teeth, vowing never to tell her mother anything more in the future that she could repeat. "No, Mommie, dear—you've got it all wrong. I told you Lord Hatfield was a very fine gentleman."

"That's not the way I heard it . . ."

"Well, you must admit you have a tiny bit of a hearing problem."

"My hearing is perfectly fine—you ladies just don't talk loud enough—always whispering."

A snippy Southerner, Sara May, from an old family living for years now with the pain of failure—her daughter never having made it to the periphery of London society, and her son, the apple of her eye, had run off with a Chelsea barmaid, couldn't wait to knock down Georgina. The McIvers were Johnny come latelys in Charleston—really nobodies. "Funny he should choose the French Riviera—I hear the best people are going to the Italian Riviera—not the South of France."

Pansy's mother wrinkled her already withered face, clutching her shawl around her turkeylike neck: "Is there more tea? It's cold in here." Then turning to her daughter, "Tell her to stoke the fire. Her daughter's married to a rich lord—she can afford a little more coal."

Georgina jumped up immediately to cover her anger.

"My, my. What kind of a hostess am I being? There's

just no more tea in the pot. One moment, my dears, I'll get us some fresh hot tea, and I'll have Kenneth come in and fix the fire. I was so excited about everything, and I knew, as my dear friends, you would want to hear all the news; I just forgot my hostess duties."

She left the room, wondering what they would gossip about her as soon as her back was turned.

At the door to the kitchen before leaving the dining room, she paused as dear friend Pansy started, "Georgina doesn't look well. Did you notice the red eyes?"

Sara May was delighted that Pansy also noticed. "She's done a lot of crying if you ask me. I wonder why she's going home? Seems to me from what she says of his affection for her, the great Lord Hatfield would set her up in a house on Belgrave Square."

Pansy's mother, whose sharp instincts made her move in to hear more clearly as soon as Georgina was out of earshot, smacked her lips, projecting her own fears. "Probably wants to get rid of the old bat."

"I can't believe it—going home," said Pansy, shaking her head. "Why Charleston is still a mess—black troops patrol the city, and I'd like to know what she's going to do on that old broken-down plantation. I don't think the house has an entire roof—after all, she's gotten used to London life."

Immediately on seeing Kenneth in the kitchen, her façade broke, hysterical once more. "Did you hear them— did you? They profess to be my friends. They know Amanda kicked her mother out."

"Georgina, don't start again."

"I didn't start it—my loving child did. Now I am the laughingstock of all my friends."

"Don't be silly—they know only what you have told them."

She blubbered as she tried to pour the boiling water into the teapot, spilling it on the coal stove, which hissed steam from the splatters.

"Let me do that for you—you'll burn yourself."

Falling into the nearest chair, she dabbed her eyes with a dish towel. "For sure they know—why else would I be going back?"

"You are going home with your husband. They are

making remarks because your bragging about Lord Hatfield and mixing with English society set their teeth on
edge."

"Did you see how Amanda cried when she left on her
honeymoon. I know she was crying because she's scared
without me. She'll see—thinking she can run that house in
the country and the townhouse all by herself . . ."

"She'll not be doing it alone—she'll have expert help
from a staff who knows how to do it. She was crying because she will not be seeing her mother for a while—
very natural for a young girl."

"You don't understand these things, Kenneth—she's going to be very sorry—kicking me out after all I have done
for her."

"Stop saying that for God's sake—be happy for her. Let's
hope the marriage is a good one. Now take the tea into
your friends and be personable—they're a sad lot and
so are we."

Her bottom lip protruded and started to quiver—the
pretty babylike face wrinkled in preparation of the fresh
tears to be shed.

"And no more crying. We have other children, a daughter coming back with us who needs confidence and affection, the will to get out and try again, and a son who
needs all the help we can give him."

She grabbed the pot from him and left the room.

Alone again, he thought. More lonely than usual. He
forced himself to continue packing the kitchenware—putting the worn articles into crates to go on board with them.
Hatfield had offered to keep the house for them for their
extended London visits, he had said. Clearly, he also
wanted his wife to stand on her own feet, not to be smothered by her mother. A small piece of red metal by the
sink caught his attention—knowing what it was immediately, he picked it up—a toy soldier—his heart went
out to his other son, so young, delightful, happy—no
cares—the harshness of life not having touched him as
yet. When he had come to this house that Sunday afternoon and found him here visiting Vanessa and JoJo, he had
to grab him and hug him, run his fingers through his curly
hair.

"Why are you squeezing me?" the boy had asked.

"I don't know," he confessed.

"Is it because you like me?"

"Yes, I like you a lot."

"You're funny. How can you like me?"

"I just do. You seem like a very nice young boy." The child struggled to get out of his embrace—laughing.

"You want to see me stand on my head?" He did so without further ado, then ran to the piano. "I can play the piano, too. Do you want to hear me?"

His life was suddenly filled with freshness and enjoyment. Only to be taken away a few moments later when JoJo, listening with him as little Kenneth played the piano, handed him the letter Sillar had given her several days prior, begging him not to start anything that would destroy what she and her son had built, explaining what the little boy believed of his background and father. When Sillar came later to pick the child up, they didn't speak, his silence, he hoped, assuring her there would be no tampering with their lives. He had heard later she had reopened her shop and resumed the life she was living before their reunion in London. He had lost the little boy just after finding him—his lovely son. Well, he had another son who needed him desperately and he would tend to that, and a daughter, Vanessa, who needed to find happiness and contentment. Then he had his own personal life to straighten out—an impossibility? Probably. However, he would learn to live with it as comfortably as he could. He loved his children and the land he was trying to rebuild—it would take years to bring the property back to its glory, but he was going to strive to achieve its past excellence. And he took heart that maybe in time Josiah would join him in his dream, then father and son could work side by side. The war had split them apart but he was going to do his damnedest to bring them back together again, albeit they might live in distant lands.

He finished boxing the odds and ends in the kitchen but didn't want to leave the room until Georgina's friends, expatriates now, in his opinion, had left. Vanessa had gone to Pierre's, and Josiah was on the top floor packing, while JoJo was saying farewell to Sillar. Damn, he wanted to talk to Josiah—why should he sit and hide in the kitchen or mix with the ladies in the sitting room, pre-

tending. He pushed open the door, heard Georgina call
to him as he sprinted up the narrow staircase, saying he
was busy, he had something to discuss with his son.

Josiah, he felt, was pleased he was there and side by side
they packed the contents of the room.

40

Champagne was being cooled on the sideboard, and the crystal glasses standing next to the silver bucket gleamed festively in the light of the baroque candlesticks. Sir Robert was gay and amusing, telling one bit of juicy gossip after another involving high society. Vanessa enjoyed hearing his stories, but Pierre wore a dark expression, his face more lined than usual as he functioned graciously but perfunctorily as host at the midday meal. There was just the three of them talking in an intimate atmosphere. Sir Robert had been so pivotal to their lives.

Vanessa wished, as she thought of Sir Robert on this day, he had received something in return for all the care and help he had given them—her especially. Not that in their friendship she and Pierre had only been takers—users in a way.

Feeling at last mature for the first time in the presence of these two men, she explained to Sir Robert how much he had done for them. Sir Robert, his hawklike face beaming, told her how much he admired her new growth. Vanessa furthered her new womanly image by patting his hand warmly after his complimentary remark.

"You could say, in these last few weeks I have become a woman of the world." Facetiousness was the intent, but to Vanessa, behind the statement was an emerging truth.

Pierre raised his head abruptly, giving her a quizzical, disapproving glance. Suddenly another bit of awareness came to her: the look he gave her was reminiscent of the way his mother used to react to his remarks indicating wariness, and at the core, the need to control and suppress.

377

Robert grasped the hand that had patted his and held on to the strong fingers—his large round eyes twinkling and curious under bushy eyebrows.

"Tell me more, my dear. This is very intriguing. To what do you attribute this abrupt switch from wonderful girl to woman of the world?"

"This is ridiculous," interjected Pierre. "Vanessa is Vanessa."

"True," she acknowledged, "but with a difference." Pierre, she saw with increasing clarity, despite his sophistication, was a morose man, always creating an aura of oppression all around him. Again, she reflected, just like his mother. She shook off the heavy mantle that started to creep upon her again. Pierre had a power to reach her. "In Antwerp and Brussels, I met someone who said, 'Enjoy life—it can be glorious.' "

"A simple true statement—was this an old friend who told you this?"

"No, Robert, a stranger. A wise stranger who reached out and," she paused, blushing at the recall, "touched me."

The remark would be taken philosophically, of course, but it had spilled out of her like the Vanessa of old, before Pierre: impulsive, expressing her feelings, not burying them, eager to run, to be free, and anxious to be part of what was happening. The encounter with Aram had been instrumental in opening vistas for her, making possible a liberation from the woman she had become—full of fears: fear to feel, fear to enjoy, fear to expect and hope—in sum total—frightened of life.

"Don't tell the queen—'Enjoy life—it can be glorious.' The reclusive woman only sees *wermuth*."

"What's that?"

"Wermuth—Melancholy." He looked at Pierre sadly. "There is the urge in all of us to withdraw into ourselves, sometimes taking loved ones with us. We must fight that when there are adversities or when we can't quite deal with our own natures, indulgently making us hide in cocoons or glass bubbles to protect us from the cruel, harsh world. But in most cases protection actually is from ourselves. After all, we don't want to belong to what I call the living dead or filled with Victoria's favorite mood —wermuth."

"That's surprising you should mention Victoria. The man I met said that he was not a Victorian."

"He?" Robert's brows arched. "No matter—well, the queen's imprint is on the middle class only. The lower classes and the upper crust don't let her get away with that oppressing shroud. Nor should we allow anyone to sink us into a sad, narrow atmosphere." He raised his wine glass. "Enjoy life! Live!—glorious it can be."

Pierre did not like the turn in conversation. His single purpose for the gathering had been to try at the last moment to change Vanessa's mind regarding her return to South Carolina, thinking Robert would help in the persuading. Hoping it would end the direction of the talk, he said rather testily to his old friend, "You sound as if you want to compete with the great Buddhist Siddharta—spouting all this wisdom and philosophy."

"Compete with the enlightened one? No. My remarks, I would say, come from experience with eyes wide open."

The Indian servant entered, carrying a large silver salver with the main course. Geeta, his childlike daughter, dressed in flowing sari, a red dot on her forehead indicating her caste, was by his side. She silently removed the white china serving plates (rimmed with narrow bands of gold) and replaced them with pale blue translucent dinner dishes patterned with intertwining leaves in light greens. Pierre's taste in every detail of his home was always exquisite.

A pink jellied mound was placed on her plate—she looked up and saw the two men watching for her reaction.

"Salmon mousse."

"Yes, my darling." Pierre spoke quietly, "It was served at our first dinner together."

"I was also there," interrupted Robert, "and I imagine you've had a good many Salmon mousses since then."

"No, I really can't recall another time. How sweet of you, Pierre, to serve it today."

When the servants withdrew, he turned to Vanessa and intoned seriously for her ears only, but overheard by Robert, who was very alert to everything being said, "The biggest mistake of my life was getting a divorce."

It was out, uttered. An amazed look appeared on both

their faces—by not verbalizing the fait accompli—it some-how didn't exist as a reality. It was there in limbo. The word had opposing effects on both of them An aston-ishing release came over Vanessa. Oh, she had heard her mother talk of it in hushed tones, but this was some-thing else—a fact hitting home. She was really a free person with a right to her own choices and had had these options since her exodus from Charleston.

To Pierre, pure instinct warned him that he had prob-ably lost the one person he held most dear. He just couldn't accept that. All the Eastern religious training had not washed away the real man—his personality too deeply etched—inbred.

Robert, friend to both, seeing the effect of the mo-ment, desired to help free both or at least one of them from the strong existing ties, almost umbilical, connect-ing a vital and free spirit to an overpowering still-life ex-istence. She had been held down, smothered by Pierre's personality even though they had been living apart. The hold he had over her, it was so clear now on this gray winter's day, had not diminished. The legal procedure of divorce had not released her guilt or emotions until pos-sibly this very moment. He asked gently, wanting to know, "Why did you get a divorce, my friend? It certainly is a stigma to a woman."

Pierre's olive skin was ashen. "I thought at the time it would be best for Vanessa."

"Your instinct was and is probably correct. Perhaps it is time for both of you to let go—get on with your lives."

It was time to go. Pierre helped her with her coat. "Please Vanessa, let me go with you. The afternoon is turning dark."

Sir Robert stood behind his host and saluted her with his glass of champagne. He knew she was suddenly strong enough to be free—free of being pressured by people forcing her to conform to a mold of convention.

"I will not feel at ease until I know you are home safe. This is a silly idea of yours, my love." The anxiety he felt for her safety lined his fine, elegant features—a lock of silver-tinged hair had fallen across his forehead.

He is such a beautiful man, she thought. "Don't worry. I'll be fine."

"Let me come at least part of the way."

"No, Pierre, and that's final.

"Goodbye Robert."

Raising his glass higher in a toast to her, "Conquer the world, my girl. Save me a ticket for the next concert."

"I will, my friend."

"Vanessa, I'll come by in the morning to say bon voyage properly, and I have some rose cuttings I wish you to take back to be planted in the gardens at McIver Hall. My mother is also taking some back."

He was still trying to hold on, to retie the cord. She knew which ones he was referring to—Vanessa's Music, a beautiful pink tea rose. He loved her—she knew that with a certainty now, and she loved him and always would. They had shared a great deal together, but it was not a love you could live with daily. He was a mesmerizing man with a dual personality, one which shut her out completely at times and one terribly involved with his feelings for her, but always with such a tenseness in whatever he did.

Stepping back into the entrance foyer, she kissed him on the cheek. He grabbed her in desperation, holding her for a long moment, then lifted her face to his. She saw in his eyes deep wells of loneliness and confusion—the cool, aloof exterior so belying his internal complexities. His lips, warm and soft, met hers in a lingering kiss. She could hear the heavy intake of air through his nostrils. She experienced no arousal, but a strong endearment, a tenderness, but his hold over her was broken. Her feeling of inadequacy suddenly lessened.

"Tomorrow—I'll see you tomorrow."

"Yes, Pierre. We'll say goodbye then."

"Not goodbye, Vanessa, only au revoir."

She hurried along, her tall elegant body moved freely, buoyantly, happy in her new-found independence. Shouting from the billyboys filled the air—what an odd, marvelous name, she thought, for the river barges—billyboys. She wondered how it came about. Leaning over the railing she listened to the argument going on between the men on two barges vying for the same mooring. There was life—life being lived.

A cart rattled down the cobblestones, and the man pulling the fruit and vegetable wagon tossed her an apple. She caught it in her good hand and tossed back a coin.

"Bless you, miss, and top of the day to you."

"Thank you—have a good day yourself."

She took in a whole volume of air, voraciously bit into the apple, and then suddenly changed her direction,
heading for King's Road. It was time for action. There
she hailed a hansom carriage and directed the red-
faced cabby driver to take her to Guy's Hospital on the
other side of town.

The ride seemed endless—finally coming to London
Bridge where they crossed to High Street and she saw
Guy's Hospital in the gathering twilight.

All she could find out was that Dr. Yoors was off
duty, and they were adamant about not giving out his
home address. She would just have to return later that
evening when he would be there. No matter how urgent
she made her plea, there was the cold refusal. Frantically she tried to remember the name of the nurse who had
tended her who she had seen with Kirk. Finally, after
describing her, the attendant came up with it, "That could
be Nurse Piercely. I believe she works with Dr. Yoors."

"Piercely. Yes, I believe that's her name. Is she at the
hospital now—she possibly could help me."

The uncooperative attendant at the desk reluctantly
leafed through some sheets of paper. In her impatience,
Vanessa twisted and turned, spying a figure leaving
through a side exit down the corridor. It could be—it was
—the woman she had seen with Kirk. Nurse Piercely.
She moved quickly trying to catch up with her. When she
got to the exit, the woman was waiting for some carriages
to pass before crossing the street. Vanessa called, but with
the din of early evening traffic, was not heard. Waiting to
cross, she jumped up and down to keep the woman in
sight. Moving down the street the woman turned the
corner—Vanessa made a dash across just as Nurse Piercely was lost to her view. She couldn't leave London without seeing Kirk she told herself—and if she came back
later to the hospital when he was on duty, their meeting
would be so public.

She was distraught when she reached the side street in
the darkening light and the nurse was nowhere in sight.
Then fleetingly she saw a woman disappear into one of the
buildings, and she ran in that direction. It had to be her.
When she got there, a terrible thought possessed her and,
knowing it to be true, she stopped midway up the stoop

transfixed. Nurse Piercely was visiting Kirk. The purpose of that visit was too distressing to think about. She backed down the steps and did an odd thing for her—she did not go away, but crossed the street to wait—not able to bring herself to leave as she would have at another time in her life.

Passersby scrutinized her with curiosity, but she didn't care. The lamplighter came around and lit the gaslamps. Seemingly an eternity passed, when actually it was only about ten minutes before Nurse Piercely came out again, catapulting Vanessa into action.

"Nurse Piercely," she shouted from across the street.

The woman turned, not able to fathom who would be calling her. Dodging carriages, she made her way to the nurse, who was not pleased when she saw who it was. "You," she exclaimed.

They were abreast now—two women wanting the same man.

"My name is Vanessa McIver."

She interrupted, "I know who you are." The cheery, friendly personality was no longer.

"I am looking for Dr. Yoors, and he isn't at the hospital."

"Correct."

"Would you mind telling me where he lives? It is important that I see him." Disturbing to Vanessa was the comely appearance of the woman—on the short side but pleasing and voluptuous, pleasant for a man to cuddle.

"Can't do that—it's against the rules." She started to move down the street.

"But I leave tomorrow for the United States."

The news stopped Barbara Piercely. "Does Kirk, Dr. Yoors, know that?"

"No. That's what I want to tell him."

"That you are going?"

"Yes."

"Still, we are not supposed to give patients home addresses of the doctors."

"But Kirk and I are old friends from back home. I think you know that."

"Perhaps." She walked away. "Have a good trip, miss," she tossed over her shoulder.

Vanessa raised her voice, demandingly. "Is it the house

you came out of or is it someplace else?" She couldn't assume it was the house down the street—suppose she had been wrong?

The nurse spun on her heels and came back to her. Vanessa knew immediately—a woman scorned.

"Why did you have to come back into his life? Everything was going along so well. Well, maybe it will again after you leave."

"His address, please—you have no right to make the decision you are making."

The woman knew Vanessa was right and she raised her eyebrow archly. "Number 12, down the street—the house I came out of. Second floor—rear."

"Thank you."

They glared at each other for a moment then both turned on their heels to go in opposite directions.

She rang the bell at number twelve, her heart triphammering. A thick-waisted woman with small squinting eyes opened the door to the dilapidated building. Once inside, however, she noticed the place was spotless though threadbare.

"Dr. Yoors!"

The landlady's face was immobile. "Upstairs—rear room." Then she padded to the back of the house.

The stairway and hall were dark, the flame in the gas fixtures burning very low. Pausing in front of his door, she said a little prayer, "Please make this turn out right . . ." The knock was loud, she startled herself.

The deep voice from the other side of the door was full of sleep, "Go away, Piercely, I told you before, I just want to sleep."

Excitement raced through her. "It's me. Vanessa McIver."

The door was opened in an instant—a look of stunned surprise on his strong face. Wearing only pajama bottoms, the bones of his broad shoulders and rib cage showed plainly through his lankiness; however, his long arms were muscular and bulging. She started to lack courage in the further explanation of her impulsive plan.

"Vanessa, it is you. Something wrong?"

"No. I wanted to speak with you—ask you something."

"Give me a moment and I'll put on some clothes, and we can go down to the parlor."

"Can't I come in—the parlor would be a bit awkward."

His eyes widened as he tilted his head to see her more clearly in the dimly lit hall.

"It is just a room—a bed, a dresser, a chair."

"Sounds just right. For a bachelor, that is."

"Well, it has its drawbacks."

Vanessa boldly stepped forward, and he gave way to let her pass. She saw the rumpled bed and his clothing thrown across a chair. There was a good fire in the grate —books were everywhere, in stacks on the floor, on the dresser and a bookcase over a small desk near the single window.

"I could have the landlady bring us some tea if you like."

He seemed uneasy—not knowing what to expect or how to act. She enjoyed that. "No thanks. I've had my fill of tea." She turned and faced him—he was still standing at the open doorway.

"Aren't you going to shut the door?"

"I don't know—it doesn't seem proper somehow."

"Shut the door—Dr. Yoors."

He smiled a sly smile. "Yes, ma'm." The closing sound was quiet but powerful. He leaned against the closed door—his slender hips thrust forward, the curly blond hair mussed from sleeping, poked up in different directions and fringing his forehead. He crossed his arms. "Your arm giving you any trouble?"

She wiggled the fingers for him. "No. The pain comes and goes but is bearable." She started to unbutton her coat with her one hand—he didn't move to help her—just watching her actions—fascinated.

"Are you serious about taking that coat off?"

Frustrated a bit, she answered, "Very."

With the grace and ease of a jungle animal, he crossed the short space and, starting at the neck, slowly unbuttoned her coat, the deep-blue eyes studying her.

In a swift change, her voice became girlish, small, "I am going home tomorrow."

He eased the outer garment over her shoulders, then placed it over his own clothing on the only chair.

She could not see the expression on his face, only the broad back narrowing down to the small hips, his muscular legs pushing against the thin material of his pale beige pajamas. As she removed her hat, she released her hair from the pins—the long tresses hung down to her waist. Deliberately, she placed the hat on the dresser and turned to him as she flung her hair back. There was a deep frown on his face.

"Do you mean going home to South Carolina?"

"Yes. I am going back with my mother and father."

She thought she saw a flicker of relief cross his face. Moving backward a few steps, leaning against the wall for support, she asked him sweetly, "I want you to make love to me." His eyes never left her face—she noticed his breathing got heavier.

His long, slender fingers rubbed his chin as he pondered what she had just said. "That wouldn't be possible."

She was shaking, "Why not?"

Throwing up his arms in the air he asked, "Are you crazy?"

"Maybe. But I want you to make love to me."

"Why? Because you are going home."

"Why not. You make love to other women."

"Not love, Vanessa. I have sexual intercourse with other women."

"Then do it with me."

"No." Then after a pause, "You're special."

She knew she had really come home, "Please—don't you want to have sexual intercourse with me?"

"Lady, I've wanted to make love to you since the first day I saw you." He crossed to the window to draw the shade—they were almost in total darkness except for the fire in the grate.

"Are you sure?"

"Positive."

The sling was removed gently—he rested her arm in the cast on the nearby dresser as he unbuttoned the top of her dress to expose her breasts. "You're beautiful." Then he held her in his arms—his bare chest was warm against her as his lips crushed against hers, hungry and almost brutal.

There was a steady flow of moisture and quick little spasms between her legs. The strong fingers pushed back all the strands of hair from her face. "Oh my darling, darling, Vanessa. How long I've waited."

She raised her face again to his and this time they were lost in the kiss—a perfect communion. She ran her fingers down his spine.

"You feel so good—my sweet, my beloved. Oh God, Vanessa."

He started to pull at her skirt, raising it until his hand was underneath—then lifting the front of it until the thin material of her underclothes was against the thin material of his pajamas. Her whole body was experiencing such a sense of well being and extreme ecstasy she thought she would scream and she did, Kirk suppressed further cries of desire by covering her mouth with his own. She pulled her head away in her excitement.

"Please enter me." His fingers were in and out of her vagina trying to bring her to a climax.

"I can't, my darling—I'm too close—I don't want to explode inside you."

"Kirk, Kirk, that's what I want. I want to feel you inside me—filling me with your love."

After, he raised himself on his elbows and looked down at the beautiful woman he loved, kissing her eyelids, her nose, and finally tonguing her lips.

"I love you," he said.

"I love you—so much," she answered. Then after a moment, "Was I all right?"

He threw his head back and laughed, "Vanessa, you are one hell of a woman."

41

The concert hall in Berlin was packed. The maestro was energetically leading the symphony orchestra in the first part of the program. He finished to thunderous applause. Vanessa stood in the wings impressed with his artistry. After a number of bows, the applause died down, and he looked toward where she was standing. She could see Sasha standing on the other side of the stage—waiting. JoJo was no longer with her and she missed her—but so pleased she was back home going to normal school to become a teacher—her travels and living abroad had opened new vistas for her. The maestro was beckoning for her —she walked on stage—proud—head held high—the applause grew and she smiled radiantly, an accomplished woman. He left her and went to the podium. She sat at the piano, erect, waiting. The music began—the tempo was perfect. Her eyes went toward the front row where her husband was sitting. She was so happy she had made him come. A little respite from his work at the hospital was what he needed. Soon they would be moving to New York where he was going to work on the staff of Bellevue Hospital. Husband and lover—all in one—how lucky she felt.

The baton pointed to her, and she played, enrapturing the audience and herself, her music so much more fulfilled. She could see the conductor nodding his approval. Before she knew it, it came to an end. There were shouts of bravo. The aged man came to her and kissed her hand as he raised her to her feet to lead her downstage toward the audience. They were rising to their feet as the

388

shouts of bravo swelled—she faced them to accept their acknowledgement.

Kirk was on his feet, shouting approval for his wife—pride puffed within him, and he had to laugh when Vanessa turned profile, the protrusion of her stomach quite evident—their love child making his presence known.

A Special Preview of
the powerful opening section of
the phenomenal bestseller

THE RIGHT STUFF

by

Tom Wolfe

Although this is the story of America's heroes—
the first flyguys in space—it is also the story of
their wives. While the hero was aloft, his wife
faced harrowing uncertainties and still had to be
a performer with the whole world watching.

Within five minutes, or ten minutes, no more than that, three of the others had called her on the telephone to ask her if she had heard that something had happened out there.

"Jane, this is Alice. Listen, I just got a call from Betty, and she said she heard something's happened out there. Have you heard anything?" That was the way they phrased it, call after call. She picked up the telephone and began relaying this same message to some of the others.

"Connie, this is Jane Conrad. Alice just called me, and she says something's happened . . ."

Something was part of the official Wife Lingo for tiptoeing blindfolded around the subject. Being barely twenty-one years old and new around here, Jane Conrad knew very little about this particular subject, since nobody ever talked about it. But the day was young! And what a setting she had for her imminent enlightenment! And what a picture she herself presented! Jane was tall and slender and had rich brown hair and high cheekbones and wide brown eyes. She looked a little like the actress Jean Simmons. Her father was a rancher in southwestern Texas. She had gone East to college, to Bryn Mawr, and had met her husband, Pete, at a debutante's party at the Gulph Mills Club in Philadelphia, when he was a senior at Princeton. Pete was a short, wiry, blond boy who joked around a lot. At any moment his face was likely to break into a wild grin revealing the gap between his front teeth. The Hickory Kid sort, he was; a Hickory Kid on the deb circuit, however. He had an air of energy, self-confidence, ambition, *joie de vivre*. Jane and Pete were married two days after he graduated from Princeton. Last year Jane gave birth to their first child, Peter. And today, here in Florida, in Jacksonville, in the peaceful year 1955, the sun shines through the pines outside, and the very air takes on the sparkle of the ocean. The ocean and a great mica-white beach are less than a mile away. Anyone driving by will see Jane's little house gleaming like a dream house in the pines. It is a brick house, but Jane and Pete painted the bricks white, so that it gleams in the sun against a great green screen of pine trees with a thousand little places where the sun peeks through. They painted the shutters black, which makes the white walls look even more brilliant. The house has only eleven hundred square feet of floor space, but Jane and Pete designed it themselves and that more than makes up for the size. A friend of theirs was the builder and gave them every possible break, so that it cost only eleven thousand dollars. Outside, the sun shines, and inside, the fever rises by the minute as five, ten, fifteen, and, finally, nearly all twenty of the wives join the circuit, trying to find out what has happened, which, in fact, means: to whose husband.

After thirty minutes on such a circuit—this is not an unusual morning around here—a wife begins to feel that the telephone is no longer located on a table or on the kitchen wall. It is exploding in her solar plexus. Yet it would be far worse right now to hear the front doorbell. The protocol is strict on that point, although written down nowhere. No woman is supposed to deliver the final news, and certainly not on the telephone. The matter mustn't be bungled!—that's the idea. No, a man should bring the news when the time comes, a man with some official or moral authority, a clergyman or a comrade of the newly deceased. Furthermore, he should bring the bad news in person. He should turn up at the front door and ring the bell and be standing there like a pillar of coolness and competence, bearing the bad news on ice, like a fish. Therefore, all the telephone calls from the wives were the frantic and portentous beating of the wings of the death angels, as it were. When the final news came, there would be a ring at the front door—a wife in this situation finds herself staring at the front door as if she no longer owns it or controls it—and outside the door would be a man . . . come to inform her that unfortunately something has happened out there, and her husband's body now lies incinerated in the swamps or the pines or the palmetto grass, "burned beyond recognition, . . ."

My own husband—how could this be what they were talking about? Jane had heard the young men, Pete among them, talk about other young men who had "bought it" or "augered in" or "crunched," but it had never been anyone they knew, no one in the squadron. And in any event, the way they talked about it, with such breezy, slangy terminology, was the same way they talked about sports. It was as if they were saying, "He was thrown out stealing second base." And that was all! Not one word, not in print, not in conversation —not in this amputated language!—about an incinerated corpse from which a young man's spirit has vanished in an instant, from which all smiles, gestures, moods, worries, laughter, wiles, shrugs, tenderness, and loving looks—*you, my love!*—have disappeared like a sigh, while the terror consumes a cottage in the woods, and a young woman, sizzling with the fever, awaits her confirmation as the new widow of the day.

The next series of calls greatly increased the possibility that it was Pete to whom something had happened. There were only twenty men in the squadron, and soon nine or ten had been accounted for . . . by the fluttering reports of the death angels. Knowing that the word was out that an accident had occurred, husbands who could get to a telephone were calling home to say *it didn't happen to me*. This news, of course, was immediately fed to the fever. Jane's telephone would ring once more, and one of the wives would be saying:

"Nancy just got a call from Jack. He's at the squadron and he says something's happened, but he doesn't know what. He said he saw Frank D—— take off about ten minutes ago with Greg in back, so they're all right. What have you heard?"

But Jane has heard nothing except that other husbands, and not hers, are safe and accounted for. And thus, on a sunny day in Florida, outside of the Jacksonville Naval Air Station, in a little white cottage, a veritable dream house, another beautiful young woman was about to be apprised of the *quid pro quo* of her husband's line of work, of the trade-off, as one might say, the subparagraphs of a contract written in no visible form. Just as surely as if she had the entire roster in front of her, Jane now realized that only two men in the squadron were unaccounted for. One was a pilot named Bud Jennings; the other was Pete. She picked up the telephone and did something that was much frowned on in a time of emergency. She called the squadron office. The duty officer answered.

"I want to speak to Lieutenant Conrad," said Jane. "This is Mrs. Conrad."

"I'm sorry," the duty officer said—and then his voice cracked. "I'm sorry ... I ..." He couldn't find the words! He was about to cry! "I'm—that's—I mean ... he can't come to the phone!"

He can't come to the phone!

"It's very important!" said Jane.

"I'm sorry—it's impossible—" The duty officer could hardly get the words out because he was so busy gulping back sobs. *Sobs!* "He can't come to the phone."

"Why not? Where is he?"

"I'm sorry—" More sighs, wheezes, snuffling gasps. "I can't tell you that. I—I have to hang up now!"

And the duty officer's voice disappeared in a great surf of emotion and he hung up.

The duty officer! *The very sound of her voice was more than he could take!*

The world froze, congealed, in that moment. Jane could no longer calculate the interval before the front doorbell would ring and some competent long-faced figure would appear, some Friend of Widows and Orphans, who would inform her, officially, that Pete was dead.

Even out in the middle of the swamp, in this rot-bog of pine trunks, scum slicks, dead dodder vines, and mosquito eggs, even out in this great overripe sump, the smell of "burned beyond recognition" obliterated everything else. When airplane fuel exploded, it created a heat so intense that everything but the hardest metals not only *burned*—everything of rubber, plastic, celluloid, wood, leather, cloth, flesh, gristle, calcium, horn, hair, blood, and protoplasm—it not only burned, it gave up the ghost in the form of every stricken putrid gas known to chemistry. One could smell the horror. It came in through the nostrils and burned the rhinal cavities raw and penetrated the liver and permeated the bowels like a black gas until there was nothing in the universe, inside or out, except the stench of the char. As the helicopter came down between the pine trees and settled onto the bogs, the smell hit Pete Conrad even before the hatch was completely open, and they were not even close enough to see the wreckage yet. The rest of the way Conrad and the crewmen had to travel on foot. After a few steps the water was up to their knees, and then it was up to their armpits, and they kept wading through the water and the scum and the vines and the pine trunks, but it was nothing compared to the smell. Conrad, a twenty-five-year-old lieutenant junior grade, happened to be on duty as squadron safety officer that day and was supposed to make the on-site investigation of the crash. The fact was, however, that this squadron was the first duty assignment of his career, and he had never been at a crash site before and had never smelled any such revolting stench or seen anything like what awaited him.

When Conrad finally reached the plane, which was an SNJ, he found the fuselage burned and blistered and dug into the swamp with one wing sheared off and the cockpit canopy smashed. In the front seat was all that was left of his friend Bud Jennings. Bud Jennings, an amiable fellow, a promising young fighter pilot, was now a horrible roasted hulk—with no head. His head was completely gone, apparently torn off the spinal column like a pineapple off a stalk, except that it was nowhere to be found . . .

In keeping with the protocol, the squadron commander was not going to release Bud Jennings's name until his widow, Loretta, had been located and a competent male death messenger had been dispatched to tell her. But Loretta Jennings was not at home and could not be found. Hence, a delay—and more than enough time for the other wives, the death angels, to burn with panic over the telephone lines. All the pilots were accounted for except the two who were in the woods, Bud Jennings and Pete Conrad. One chance in two, acey-deucey, one finger–two finger, and this was not an unusual day around here.

Loretta Jennings had been out at a shopping center. When she returned home, a certain figure was waiting outside, a man, a solemn Friend of Widows and Orphans, and it was Loretta Jennings who lost the game of odd and even, acey-deucey, and it was Loretta whose child (she was pregnant with a second) would have no father. It was this young woman who went through all the final horrors that Jane Conrad had imagined—*assumed!*—would be hers to endure forever. Yet this grim stroke of fortune brought Jane little relief.

On the day of Bud Jennings's funeral, Pete went into the back of the closet and brought out his bridge coat, per regulations. This was the most stylish item in the Navy officer's wardrobe. Pete had never had occasion to wear his before. It was a double-breasted coat made of navy-blue melton cloth and came down almost to the ankles. It must have weighed ten pounds. It had a double row of gold buttons down the front and loops for shoulder boards, big beautiful belly-cut collar and lapels, deep turnbacks on the sleeves, a tailored waist, and a center vent in back that ran from the waistline to the bottom of the coat. Never would Pete, or for that matter many other American males in the mid-twentieth century, have an article of clothing quite so impressive and aristocratic as that bridge coat. At the funeral the nineteen little Indians who were left—Navy boys!—lined up manfully in their bridge coats. They looked so young. Their pink, lineless faces with their absolutely clear, lean jawlines popped up bravely, correctly, out of the enormous belly-cut collars of the bridge coats. They sang an old Navy hymn, which slipped into a strange and lugubrious minor key here and there, and included a stanza added especially for aviators. It ended with: "O hear us when we lift our prayer for those in peril in the air."

Three months later another member of the squadron crashed and was burned beyond recognition and Pete hauled out the bridge coat again and Jane saw eighteen little Indians bravely going through the motions at the funeral. Not long after that, Pete was transferred from Jacksonville to the Patuxent River Naval Air Station in Maryland. Pete and Jane had barely settled in there when they got word that another member of the Jacksonville squadron, a close friend of theirs, someone they had had over to dinner many times, had died trying to take off from the deck of a carrier in a routine practice session a few miles out in the Atlantic. The catapult that propelled aircraft off the deck lost pressure, and his ship just dribbled off the end of the deck, with its engine roaring vainly, and fell sixty feet into the ocean and sank like a brick, and he vanished, *just like that*.

Pete had been transferred to Patuxent River, which was known in Navy vernacular as Pax River, to enter the Navy's new test-pilot school. This was considered a major step up in the career of a young Navy aviator. Now that the Korean War was over and there was no combat flying, all the hot young pilots aimed for flight test. In the military they always said "flight test" and not "test flying." Jet aircraft had been in use for barely ten years at the time, and the Navy was testing new jet fighters continually. Pax River was the Navy's prime test center.

Jane liked the house they bought at Pax River. She didn't like it as much as the little house in Jacksonville, but then she and Pete hadn't designed this one. They lived in a community called North Town Creek, six miles from the base. North Town Creek, like the base, was on a scrub-pine peninsula that stuck out into Chesapeake Bay. They were tucked in amid the pine trees. (Once more!) All around were rhododendron bushes. Pete's classwork and his flying duties were very demanding. Everyone in his flight test class, Group 20, talked about how difficult it was—and obviously loved it, because in Navy flying this was the big league. The young men in Group 20 and their wives were Pete's and Jane's entire social world. The associated with no one else. They constantly invited each other to dinner during the week; there was a Group party at someone's house practically every weekend; and they would go off on outings to fish or waterski in Chesapeake Bay. In a way they could not have associated with anyone else, at least not easily, because the boys could talk only about one thing: their flying. One of the phrases that kept running through the conversation was "pushing the outside of the envelope." The "envelope" was a flight-test term referring to the limits of a particular aircraft's performance, how tight a turn it could make at such-and-such a speed, and so on. "Pushing the outside," probing the outer limits, of the envelope seemed to be the great challenge and satisfaction of flight test. At first "pushing the outside of the envelope" was not a particularly terrifying phrase to hear. It sounded once more as if the boys were just talking about sports.

Then one sunny day a member of the Group, one of the happy lads they always had dinner with and drank with and went waterskiing with, was coming in for a landing at the base in an A3J fighter plane. He came in too low before lowering his flaps, and the ship stalled out, and he crashed and was burned beyond recognition. And they brought out the bridge coats and sang about those in peril in the air and put the bridge coats away, and the Indians who were left talked about the accident after dinner one night. They shook their heads and said it was a damned shame, but he should have known better than to wait so long before lowering the flaps.

Barely a week had gone by before another member of the Group was coming in for a landing in the same type of aircraft, the A3J, trying to make a ninety-degree landing, which involves a sharp turn, and something went wrong with the controls, and he ended up with one rear stabilizer wing up and the other one down, and his ship rolled in like a corkscrew from 800 feet up and crashed, and he was burned beyond recognition. And the bridge coats came out and they sang about those in peril in the air and then they put the bridge coats away and after dinner one night they mentioned that the departed had been a good man but was inexperienced, and when the malfunction in the controls put him in that bad corner, he didn't know how to get out of it.

Every wife wanted to cry out: "Well, my God! The *machine* broke! What makes *any* of you think you would have come out of it any better!" Yet intuitively Jane and the rest of them knew it wasn't right even to suggest that. Pete never indicated for a moment that he thought any such thing could possibly happen to him. It seemed not only wrong but dangerous to challenge a young pilot's confidence by posing the question. And that, too, was part of the unofficial protocol for the Officer's Wife. From now on every time Pete was late coming in from the flight line, she would worry. She began to wonder if—no! *assume!*—he had found his way into one of those corners they all talked about so spiritedly, one of those little dead ends that so enlivened conversation around here.

Not long after that, another good friend of theirs went up in an F–4, the Navy's newest and hottest fighter plane, known as the Phantom. He reached twenty thousand feet and then nosed over and dove straight into Chesapeake Bay. It turned out that a hose connection was missing in his oxygen system and he had suffered hypoxia and passed out at the high altitude. And the bridge coats came out and they lifted a prayer about those in peril in the air and the bridge coats were put away and the little Indians were incredulous. How could anybody fail to check his hose connections? And how could anybody be in such poor condition as to pass out *that quickly* from hypoxia?

A couple of days later Jane was standing at the window of her house in North Town Creek. She saw some smoke rise above the pines from over in the direction of the flight line. Just that, a column of smoke; no explosion or sirens or any other sound. She went to another room, so as not to have to think about it but there was no explanation for the smoke. She went back to the window. In the yard of a house across the street she saw a group of people . . . standing there and looking at her house, as if trying to decide what to do. Jane looked away—but she couldn't keep from looking out again. She caught a glimpse of *a certain figure* coming up the walkway toward her front door. She knew exactly who it was. She had had nightmares like this. And yet this was no dream. She was wide awake and alert. Never more alert in her entire life! Frozen, completely defeated by the sight, she simply waited for the bell to ring. She waited, but there was not a sound. Finally she could stand it no more. In real life, unlike her dream life, Jane was both too self-possessed and too polite to scream through the door: "Go away!" So she opened it. There was no one there, no one at all. There was no group of people on the lawn across the way and no one to be seen for a hundred yards in any direction along the lawns and leafy rhododendron roads of North Town Creek.

Then began a cycle in which she had both the nightmares and the hallucinations, continually. Anything could touch off an hallucination: a ball of smoke, a telephone ring that stopped before she could answer it, the sound of a siren, even the sound of trucks starting up (crash trucks!). Then she would glance out the window, and a certain figure would be coming up the walk, and she would wait for the bell. The only difference between the dreams and the hallucinations was that the scene of the dreams was always the little white house in Jacksonville. In both cases, the feeling that *this time it has happened* was quite real.

The star pilot in the class behind Pete's, a young man who was the main rival of their good friend Al Bean, went up in a fighter to do some power-dive tests. One of the most demanding disciplines in flight test was to accustom yourself to making precise readings from the control panel in the same moment that you were pushing the outside of the envelope. This young man put his ship into the test dive and was still reading out the figures, with diligence and precision and great discipline, when he augered straight into the oyster flats and was burned beyond recognition. And the bridge coats came out and they sang about those in peril in the air and the bridge coats were put away, and the little Indians remarked that the departed was a swell guy and a brilliant student of flying; a little too *much* of a student, in fact; he hadn't bothered to look out the window at the real world soon enough. Beano—Al Bean—wasn't quite so brilliant; on the other hand, he was still here.

Like many other wives in Group 20 Jane wanted to talk about the whole situation, the incredible series of fatal accidents, with her husband and the other members of the Group, to find out how they were taking it. But somehow the unwritten protocol forbade discussions of this subject, which was the fear of death. Nor could Jane or any of the rest of them talk, really *have a talk,* with anyone around the base. You could talk to another wife about being worried. But what good did it do? Who *wasn't* worried? You were likely to get a look that said: *"Why dwell on it?"* Jane might have gotten away with divulging the matter of the nightmares. But *hallucinations?* There was no room in Navy life for any such anomalous tendency as that.

By now the bad string had reached ten in all, and almost all of the dead had been close friends of Pete and Jane, young men who had been in their house many times, young men who had sat across from Jane and chattered like the rest of them about the grand adventure of military flying. And the survivors still sat around *as before*—with the same inexplicable exhilaration! Jane kept watching Pete for some sign that his spirit was cracking, but she saw none. He talked a mile a minute, kidded and joked, laughed with his Hickory Kid cackle. He always had. He still enjoyed the company of members of the group like Wally Schirra and Jim Lovell. Many young pilots were taciturn and cut loose with the strange fervor of this business only in the air. But Pete and Wally and Jim were not reticent; not in any situation. They loved to kid around. Pete called Jim Lovell "Shaky," because it was the last thing a pilot would want to be called. Wally Schirra was outgoing to the point of hearty; he loved practical jokes and dreadful puns, and so on. The three of them —*even in the midst of this bad string!*—would love to get on a subject such as accident-prone Mitch Johnson. Accident-prone Mitch Johnson, it seemed, was a Navy pilot whose life was in the hands of two angels, one of them bad and the other one good. The bad angel would put him into accidents that would have annihilated any ordinary pilot, and the good angel would bring him out of them without a scratch. Just the other day —this was the sort of story Jane would hear them tell—Mitch Johnson was coming in to land on a carrier. But he came in short, missed the flight deck, and crashed into the fantail, below the deck. There was a tremendous explosion, and the rear half of the plane fell into the water in flames. Everyone on the flight deck said, "Poor Johnson. The good angel was off duty." They were still debating how to remove the debris and his mortal remains when a phone rang on the bridge. A somewhat dopey voice said, "This is Johnson. Say, listen, I'm down here in the supply hold and the hatch is locked and I can't find the lights and I can't see a goddamned thing and I tripped over a cable and I think I hurt my leg." The officer on the bridge slammed the phone down, then vowed to find out what morbid sonofabitch could pull a phone prank at a time like this. Then the phone rang again, and the man with the dopey voice managed to establish the fact that he was, indeed, Mitch Johnson. The good angel had not left his side. When he smashed into the fantail, he hit some empty ammunition drums, and they cushioned the impact, leaving him groggy but not seriously hurt. The fuselage had blown to pieces; so he just stepped out onto the fantail and opened a hatch that led into the supply hold. It was pitch black in there, and there were cables all across the floor, holding down spare aircraft engines. Accident-prone Mitch Johnson kept tripping over these cables until he found a telephone. Sure enough, the one injury he had was a bruised shin from tripping over a cable. The man was accident-prone! Pete and Wally and Jim absolutely cracked up over stories like this. It was amazing. Great sports yarns! Nothing more than that.

A few days later Jane was out shopping at the Pax River commissary on Saunders Road, near the main gate to the base. She heard the sirens go off at the field, and then she heard the engines of the crash trucks start up. This time Jane was determined to keep calm. Every instinct made her want to rush home, but she forced herself to stay in the commissary and continue shopping. For thirty minutes she went through the motions of completing her shopping list. Then she drove home to North Town Creek. As she reached the house, she saw a figure going up the sidewalk. It was a man. Even from the back there was no question as to who he was. He had on a black suit, and there was a white band around his neck. It was her minister, from the Episcopal Church. She stared, and this vision did not come and go. The figure kept on walking up the front walk. She was not asleep now, and she was not inside her house glancing out the front window. She was outside in her car in front of her house. She was not dreaming, and she was not hallucinating, and the figure kept walking up toward her front door.

That the preacher had not, in fact, come to her front door as the Solemn Friend of Widows and Orphans, but merely for a church call . . . had not brought peace and relief. That Pete still didn't show the slightest indication of thinking that any unkind fate awaited him no longer lent her even a moment's courage. The next dream and the next hallucination, and the next and the next, merely seemed more real. For she now *knew*. She now knew the subject and the essence of this enterprise, even though not a word of it had passed anybody's lips. She even knew why Pete—the Princeton boy she met at a deb party at the Gulph Mills Club!—would never quit, never withdraw from this grim business, unless in a coffin. And God knew, and she knew, there was a coffin waiting for each little Indian.

Seven years later, when a reporter and a photographer from *Life* magazine actually stood near her in her living room and watched her face, while outside, on the lawn, a crowd of television crewmen and newspaper reporters waited for a word, an indication, anything—perhaps a glimpse through a part in a curtain!—waited for some sign of what she felt—when one and all asked with their ravenous eyes and, occasionally, in so many words: "How do you feel?" and "Are you scared?"—America wants to know!—it made Jane want to laugh, but in fact she couldn't even manage a smile.

"Why ask *now?*" she wanted to say. But they wouldn't have had the faintest notion of what she was talking about.

Anne, as well as the other wives of the potential astronauts, were thrust into the spotlight. They were forced to take their own risks as their husbands embarked on adventures more thrilling and dangerous than anything previously attempted.

Read the complete Bantam Book, available October 22, 1980 wherever paperbacks are sold.

THE LATEST BOOKS IN THE BANTAM BESTSELLING TRADITION

Bantam Book Catalog

Here's your up-to-the-minute listing of ove
1,400 titles by your favorite authors.

This illustrated, large format catalog gives
description of each title. For your convenience
it is divided into categories in fiction and noi
fiction—gothics, science fiction, westerns, mys
teries, cookbooks, mysticism and occult, biogra
phies, history, family living, health, psychology
art.

So don't delay—take advantage of this speci:
opportunity to increase your reading pleasure

Just send us your name and address and 50
(to help defray postage and handling costs).

BANTAM BOOKS, INC.
Dept. FC, 414 East Golf Road, Des Plaines, Ill. 60016

Mr./Mrs./Miss_____
(please print)

Address_____

City_____State_____Zip_____

Do you know someone who enjoys books? Just give us their names
and addresses and we'll send them a catalog too!

_____

Mr./Mrs./Miss_____

Address_____

City_____State_____Zip_____

_____

Mr./Mrs./Miss_____

Address_____

City_____State_____Zip_____

FC—9/78